BILL SMITH
3RD
KU-072-195

Last Dance At The Wrecker's Ball

By Robert Douglas and available from Hachette Scotland

Night Song of the Last Tram
Somewhere to Lay My Head
At Her Majesty's Pleasure
Whose Turn for the Stairs?
Staying on Past the Terminus
Last Dance at the Wrecker's Ball

Last Dance At The Wrecker's Ball

ROBERT DOUGLAS

First published in 2012 by
HEADLINE PUBLISHING GROUP

1

Cataloguing in Publication Data is available from the British Library

ISBN 978 0 7553 8030 5

Typeset in New Baskerville by Palimpsest Book Production Limited, Falkirk, Stirlingshire

Printed and bound by
CPI Group (UK) Ltd, Croydon, CR0 4YY

Headline's policy is to use papers that are natural, renewable and recyclable products and made from wood grown in sustainable forests. The logging and manufacturing processes are expected to conform to the environmental regulations of the country of origin.

HEADLINE PUBLISHING GROUP
An Hachette UK Company
338 Euston Road
London NW1 3BH

www.headline.co.uk
www.hachette.co.uk

ACKNOWLEDGMENTS

With many thanks to my friends at Headline . . . my editor, Martin Fletcher, his assistant, Lucy Foley, Veronique Norton and Joanna Kaliszewska.

Then there is Myra Jones who copyedits *and* proofreads me! Mike Melvin who has, yet again, designed a spot on dust jacket. Special thanks to Bob McDevitt who started as my publisher, became my agent – and is always my pal!

Extra special thanks to my wife, Pat. With each book her input becomes more incisive *and* valuable!

Finally, we come to the guys who, even before I started to write, have never failed to inspire me, entertain me, and kick-start me into another day . . .

The lyrics and voice of Johnny Mercer, the class of the Artie Shaw Orchestra and the unadulterated pleasure when the Jackie Gleason Orchestra got together with the trumpeter Bobby Hackett, plus a large swing section. Gleason, a man who couldn't read a note of music – yet knew what he wanted to hear! They do it for me. Every time.

A SHORT GLOSSARY

For those thinking of taking an 'A' level in Glaswegian

Ah: dialect pronunciation of I

From aw' airts and pairts: from everywhere

An ashet: a plate or dish, usually for steak pie

The Bells: the moment on 31st December when one year changes to the next

Dander/daunder/donner: walk or stroll

To dicht: to wipe/clean

Dreich: wet, miserable weather

Eejit: idiot

To flit: to move house

Gallus: someone over-confident, full of themself

Hirple: to limp, walk badly

Lug: an ear

Maist: most

Ming/mingin: a person, or house, which smells badly, is unclean

Talk pan loaf: to affect a posh accent

Wally close: a beautifully tiled close or entrance

THE RESIDENTS OF 18 DALBEATTIE STREET IN THE YEAR 1971

'The Top Landing'

Archie CAMERON, age 54.
Ella CAMERON, age 52.
Archie jnr. age 31.
Katherine, age 25.
Archie is an ex-para. Captured at Arnhem, 1944. He is a metal turner at Howden's Works.
Ella is a confectioner at the Lux Tearooms in the city.
Archie jnr is finishing a prison sentence at the moment.
Katherine works in a lawyer's office in Hope Street in the city.

Eve FORSYTH, age 59.
Lexie FORSYTH, age 26.
Eve, a widow, moved in in 1965. She has a part-time job as a cleaner at the City Bakeries on the Maryhill Road.
Lexie recently split with her long-term partner. She is a florist at Kinnaird's on the Maryhill Road.

Agnes DALRYMPLE, age 63.
Unmarried. Serves behind counter at same branch of City Bakeries as Eve, next door.
Served in the Land Army during the War.

'The Second Landing' or 'Two-Up'

Frank GALLOWAY, age 58.
Wilma GALLOWAY, age 44.
Frank is a bus driver, Wilma his conductress, at Maryhill Depot.
Frank was a widower (wife Josie) when he met Wilma.
Formerly lived in single-end on the top landing.
Frank served 4 years in Royal Navy during war.

Flat Vacant.
Not to be re-let.

Alec STUART, age 71.
Irene STUART, age 73.
Alec is retired. Former manager at Andrew Cochrane's grocers on Maryhill Road
Irene is a housewife.

'The First Landing' or 'One-Up'

Dennis O'MALLEY, age 70.
Teresa O'MALLEY, age 68.
Dennis is retired. For many years a brickie's labourer.
Teresa has a part-time job cleaning offices for two hours every morning.
Both southern Irish. Emigrated to Glasgow in 1920s.
Two daughters. Siobhan lives in Airdrie. Rhea lives on the landing.

Flat Vacant.
Not to be re-let.
('Granny' Thomson used to live here.)

Robert STEWART, age 43.
Rhea STEWART, age 43.
Sammy, age 20.
Louise, age 19.
Robert is a foreman at Rossleigh's garage on Maryhill Road.
Rhea works in office at Macready & Son, Solicitors, in Wellington Street.
Sammy is a student at Glasgow University.
Louise is an assistant at West End Modes on the Byres Road.

'The Close'

Bert (Albert) ARMSTRONG, age 51.
Irma ARMSTRONG, age 44.
Bert is a long-distance lorry driver. Newcastle born.
German-born Irma works at Campbell-Duffs ironmongers on Maryhill Road.
Son, Arthur, age 20. Apprentice.
The family are about to move to the Molendinar Housing Scheme (Estate).

Billy McCLAREN, age 57.
Drena McCLAREN, age 51.
Charles McCLAREN, age 20.
Billy is a self-employed painter and decorator. Drena only works now and again.
Son, Charles, is apprentice motor mechanic and works with 'Uncle' Robert (upstairs) at Rossleigh's.
Oldest son, Billy junior (age 31) is a police sergeant. He lives in Milngavie.
Billy senior was a P.O.W. during Second World War.

Mary STEWART, age 71.
Widow. Mother of Robert on landing above.
Her husband, Samuel, died in 1965.

CHAPTER ONE

Spring Has Nearly Sprung

Thursday, 8th April 1971. Archie Cameron junior lies on his side in bed, reading Ian Fleming's *Thunderball*. He sometimes wonders what took him so long to make a start on the Bond novels. Still, better late than never. He's totally absorbed in this one; far removed from his bed as he traipses around Europe with 007. A sudden metallic noise startles him as the cover on the door's spyhole is flicked open, then repeated as it swings shut. As Archie turns down the corner of a page to mark his place, there comes the expected 'click' from outside and the cell is plunged into darkness. He listens to the screw's slippered feet scuff along the landing to the next door. Bastards! Always put that light oot when you're in the middle of a good bit. He reaches out into the dark, accurately places the paperback in the middle of the cell's only chair. The sigh he gives could be mistaken for someone breathing their last. Thank Christ Ah've only a few more months tae put up wi' this. He lies with eyes wide open, though there's nothing to see but blackness. You would'nae have tae put up wi' it if ye stopped thieving. Well, stopped getting caught. Face up tae it, Archie, you're no' exactly Raffles. You're thirty-wan years auld and you've spent mair time *in* the pokey than oot of it, this last ten years. You wasted your twenties. Are ye gonny dae the same tae your thirties? He turns onto his back, stares at the unseen ceiling. And what aboot Ma? You've caused that poor soul nothing but grief. Yet she still trails oot on the bus every month fae Glesga tae Stirling. Then pays for a taxi up tae Craigmill Prison. Brings me fags tae smoke on the visit. Sweeties. Books. He feels his eyes grow moist. And Ah take it aw' for fuckin' granted so Ah dae. My sister huz the right idea. Katherine often comes along wi' her tae keep her company, but never comes in tae see me. Jist waits at the gate lodge. Cannae be bothered wi' her loser brother. Huh! Ah don't blame her. Then there's ma faither. Did'nae half dae his bit during the war. Right wee tough nut when he wants tae be. He gave up on me years ago. Threw me oot the hoose. Ye don't get many chances from ma faither. He yawns. Ah suppose if Ah wiz him – Ah would'nae let me through the door either!

Archie lies still for a while, deep in thought, far removed from sleep . . . 'Ach!' He throws back the bedcovers, sits up. Finding his prison-issue jacket, he puts it on over the pyjama top. Slips his feet into the felt slippers. Lastly, he reaches for his towel, wraps it round his neck like a scarf, tucks it inside the jacket. Climbing out of bed, he finds the Bond novel in the dark, lays it on his pillow. He now quietly moves his chair against the wall, directly underneath the high cell window.

Once up on the chair, he slides the small ventilation pane to the right and is immediately skelped on the face by a draught of ice-cold air. Eyes narrowed, he looks through the four-inch square opening. Barely a mile away, in a dip, the lights of Stirling sparkle in the clear night. It must be about half ten. Cars occasionally criss-cross the few roads he can see. As each one passes he wonders who is inside. Young? Old? Married? Where are they going? Where huv they been? Whoever they are, he envies them. Now and then, near the edge of town, he can make out people on foot. Couples, groups. Singletons. He somehow has a feeling that the good folk of Stirling are happy with their lives. Content. It's probably not true, but it pleases him to think they are. He especially enjoys his sightseeing on clear, moonless nights. Like tonight. From his vantage point, high up in Craigmill top security prison, he drinks in this beautiful panorama. The brightly-lit town, isolated midst dark hills. Above it, a vast black canopy embedded with stars. More than he ever saw during his Glasgow childhood. Although he never tires of this view, he's always aware he's not a part of it. Never will be. He's an outcast. A prisoner looking out of a cell window. Recently, this has started to depress him. It won't be long until that insistent bloody voice will start putting its neb in . . .

Why aren't you a part of it, Archie?

Because Ah'm in jail, daeing time.

So why don't you pack it in? Give it up. You know you're a crap thief.

He slides the small pane shut. Climbs down. 'Gonny shut the fuck up!'

It's next morning. In Dalbeattie Street.

Agnes Dalrymple wipes the wooden draining board surrounding her sink. Rinses the dishcloth, wrings it out, drapes it over the brass tap. She raises the lower sash of one of the double windows. A lively breeze drifts through the gap, makes the curtain wave. She looks out into the back courts from her top-storey flat. Whit a lovely day. Ah've mibbe picked a good week tae be off. She can see along the length of Cheviot Street's back courts. Facing her, at the far end of this stretch, are the rear windows of a recently emptied tenement block in Rothesay Street. One or two folk left their curtains hanging when they flitted oot. Agnes has nothing to do but look at the drab, empty building. It's lifeless windows stare back.

A movement catches her eye. Above the roof of this forlorn tenement she can see the top few feet of a crane. It has begun to sway back and forth. She knows that lower down, out of her sight, it's swinging a huge steel ball hanging from a chain. The wrecking ball. Although the building she can see from her window was emptied weeks ago it is, as yet, untouched. The crane stands on the other side of it, four-square in the middle of the abandoned Rothesay Street, demolishing the tenement block on the far side. All she can see of it is its roof. Well, half of its roof. The rest has already gone, along with a large part of the building. She watches the top of the crane move in what seems to be a leisurely manner. Listens as a wall is hit. Though she can only hear it, she can picture it in her mind's eye. It's jist like listening tae the wireless. The crane appears to curtsey to the tenement. This is followed by a dull thud, then the sound of debris clattering into the street. Most times it doesn't seem to be too much, but now and again a big section of outer wall gives up the ghost – and takes inner walls and floors with it. Then it's different. She'll hear a thunderous crash, the top of a crescendo, then a diminuendo which often ends with a counterpoint of broken glass. My God! It's the blitz all ower again. Jist like the night Kilmun Street got it. Sometimes she'll feel the vibration through her feet as ton upon ton of large stone blocks give up – after a century – and collapse into the street. From her window she cannot see a single workman. It's as though it just seems to happen. And because of this she finds it all the more frightening. As she looks at the top of the crane, a stretch of the tenement's roof catches her eye. It suddenly drops like a lift. Large slates, wooden joists, brick chimney stacks complete with terracotta pots, simply plummet out of sight. Seconds later, gouts of black soot which have successfully evaded sweeps' brushes since Victoria was Queen, billow upwards in the breeze for a moment, then drift off, newly homeless.

CHAPTER TWO

Flitting Oot

Easter Sunday, 11th April 1971. 'Zat it, Bert?' As he speaks, Billy McClaren footers about, pushing items of furniture closer together in the back of the open lorry. Hopefully stop them sliding around on their journey to the new Molendinar Housing Scheme.

'Aye. That's it, marra.' Bert Armstrong tightens the rope round them.

'Yah. That is all our wordly goods.' His wife, Irma, looks at their few belongings. 'It does not take long to empty a single-end.' She sounds, and looks, sad.

Archie Cameron produces a twenty packet of Players. Before he can open them, Bert reaches out, grips his wrist. 'Naw, naw, hinny. If yees are ahll good enough t' give us a bit hand, the very least Ah can dae is t' crash the ash.' He continues to restrain Archie until he's able to counter with a packet of Gold Flake.

* * *

It's a few minutes later. The smokers smoke. Some lean against the side of the lorry. Ella Cameron and Drena McClaren join the group. Moments later, so do Robert and Rhea Stewart from 'one-up'. A warm April sun shines onto them from just above the tenement opposite.

'It's nice in the sun, in't it?' says Drena. No one has given voice to it, but they are all aware the moment is fast approaching when Bert, Irma and twenty-year-old son, Arthur, will climb into the lorry and leave Dalbeattie Street. For good.

Irma looks at the double windows directly above the close. 'Have you noticed, someone has broken one of Granny's windows?'

Ella laughs. Shakes her head. 'Irma! Granny huz been deid nearly ten years. There's been at *least* three different tenants in that hoose since she went.'

'Och! But I know, Ella.' She looks up once more. 'For me, these are always the Granny's windows.' The men smile. Drena leans forward. 'Ah'm wi' you, hen. Ah never think o' them as anything else but Granny's windaes.' She draws herself up. 'And Ah'll tell youse another thing.' She points dramatically upwards. 'Ower the years, whenever that hoose huz been empty, Bella Thomson moves back intae it until it's re-let!' She looks round the assembled company.

'Sure an' she's right! She's not tellin' ye the word o' a lie.' All heads turn as Teresa O'Malley, as though on cue, steps out of the lengthening shadows in the close. She turns to her daughter. 'How many times have Oi said that t' you, Rhea?'

Ella looks at Drena, then Teresa. Shakes her head. 'Ah'll bet ye we're the only close in Glesga that's got *two* Gypsy Petulengros living up it!'

Rhea offers herself as witness for the defence. 'She diz, mind. Every time that hoose has been vacant, Ma often comes back fae her wee morning job, pops her head roon' ma door and says, "Ah just caught a wee glimpse of white hair at Bella's windae, as Ah came along the street!"'

Drena stabs her husband's upper arm with a finger. '*See*! Billy McClaren. How many times huv Ah telt you Ah've seen the auld soul?'

'She's still looking after us so she is. Just loike always,' says Teresa.

Ella draws on her cigarette. 'She's gonny huv her work cut oot by the end o' the year, mind, when we're aw' scattered tae the four winds.'

Robert Stewart contributes. 'Rhea! Tell them about the time Granny made contact wi' you.' He tries hard to keep his face straight.

'Ah'll gie ye "contact", Robert Stewart. Ah could huv drapped deid at your feet so Ah could.'

'What happened, Robert?' asks Archie.

'It was the last time the flat was empty. Teresa had been telling Rhea that she'd seen Bella at her windows again. Just a few days earlier I'd happened to come across a spare key Granny had given us for her door. Oh, years ago. Back in the fifties sometime. When I found it, I thought, och, might as well hang on to it. Just as a wee remembrance, a keepsake . . .'

Rhea interrupts. 'Keepsake? Very near the death o' me.' She tries to pretend she's huffed.

'As I was saying. I'd come across her key,' Robert smiles, 'and it gave me an idea. I looked out our window, waited until I saw Rhea coming home from work. Then I nipped out onto the landing and let myself into the empty flat. It was a winter's night, early dark. So I wait 'til I hear Rhea coming up the stairs. Just as she steps onto the landing, I start rattling the letterbox from the inside and going, "Rheaaa! Rheaaa!" in a high-pitched screech . . .' He stops for a moment to parry a right hook from his wife, then continues . . . 'She lets oot such a scream and I hear her footsteps as she makes a dive for oor house. I open Granny's door – and Rhea's gone! Her message bag is lying on the landing where she dropped it, and I can hear her in oor lobby, shouting, "Robert! Robert! Come quick! Where are ye?"'

Rhea bristles. 'That wiz stupid! Ah hud half a dozen eggs in that bag. Two of them got broke!'

Drena looks at her. 'Eeee! Ah think Ah'd huv drapped in a deid faint, Rhea.'

'Ah know. Can ye imagine? Ah'm aboot tae step ontae the landing. Granny's hoose huz been empty for months. And suddenly her letterbox starts going mad – and she's shouting oan me through the door!'

It's thirty minutes later. The spring sun continues to shine. But . . .

Archie Cameron is first to grasp the nettle. 'Well, this is

very pleasant, folks. But it'll no' be sae nice if we're still here at nine o'clock the night. It's forecast tae turn chilly.'

'Yah. You are right, Archie.' Irma looks up again. 'Oh! I do wish the kids had not smashed a window of Granny. I remember, like yesterday, when Bert and I arrive from Newcastle.' They hear a catch in her voice. 'I can still hear the sound of her window going up. And she tells us to come in for . . .' Irma stops. Looks at everybody. 'Remember? "A dish of tay" when we have emptied the van.' Bert Armstrong reaches out, strokes his wife's back. 'Noo divn't get tha'sen upset, pet.' Their friends and neighbours smile.

Teresa O'Malley sighs. 'Aye. For about sixty years, every newcomer t' this close had to go in to her house and sit round yon table for a drink o' tay – on the day they arrived.'

'Aye, everybody.' Ella leans forward. 'Except Ruby Baxter!'

'Eeee, God! You're right,' says Drena.

Ella continues. 'Yet,' she looks around, 'it wiz Ruby Baxter paid for the auld sowel's funeral!'

'Aye. She did. Well, it wiz Ruby's man – Fred,' says Billy McClaren.

'Sure, and 'tis the same thing,' declares Teresa.

Another ten minutes have passed. Bert Armstrong looks at his watch. 'We'll have t' be gannin', Irma.'

'Yah, I know, *liebchen*.' She turns to Billy and Archie. Tries hard to think of something to say. Anything, as long as it will hold back the moment of departure. 'And I *zoh* remember when you two speak to me in German and tell me you are *Kriegsgefangener* during the war . . .'

'Aye,' says Ella, 'and they've never bloody stoaped since. Especially oan a Setterday night when they've hud a few pints.' She shrugs, 'Ah'll tell ye. If Hitler hud managed tae get oot yon bunker and flitted intae a single-end up this close – he'd huv fitted right in!'

'Oh, michty me, Ella! But always, we have so much laughs when you get onto the boys!'

Rhea changes the subject. 'Ah wonder how long it'll take ye tae get used tae no' sleeping in a recess bed any more, Irma? Ah'll bet you'll miss no' having walls on three sides of ye. It's gonny be really strange, lying in a bed in the middle of a room.'

At this, Irma's hand goes to her mouth. She and Bert turn, look at one another. 'Oh, *Mein Gott*! The *bett*! We forget to tell the shop it is time to bring it to the new house.'

Archie looks at Billy. He nods toward the Armstrongs, then points to the ground. '*Die mussen auf dem boden schlafen. Die hat kein bett*!'

Drena turns. 'Huz the new bed no' been delivered?'

'Naw,' says Billy.

'Oh, my God!' Drena looks at Irma. 'And the morra's Easter Monday. Goldberg's will be shut. It's gonny be Tuesday night at the earliest, afore ye get tae sleep in a bed, Irma.'

'Ah! Help *mein* Boab! Two nights we must sleep on the floor, Bert.'

Her man shakes his head. 'Ah said to yee years ago, Irma, we should have got the metal frame and springs taken oot o' the recess – and got a proper double bed pushed into the space like most folk have. Then that bed would be on the back o' the lorry.' He sighs. 'Haway, let's go, pet. It'll be dark soon.'

Irma looks at her neighbours. Tears well in her eyes.

Archie Cameron steps forward, puts his arms round her. '*Liebe* Irma . . .'

Ella interrupts, purses her lips, nods her head – and even manages to tap a foot. 'Dae ye think we could mibbe huv it in English, so's the rest o' us can underfuckin'staun' whit yer sayin'!'

When the laughing dies down, Archie gives her a pained looked. 'As it so happens, Ah wiz *gonny* go intae English. Because nooadays ma German's rusty. It's no' good enough tae say the things Ah want tae say . . .'

Ella cuts him off. 'Huh! Yer German wiz *never* good enough, pal. In fact, there is some doot as tae whether or no' your *English* is up tae it . . .' She has to stop as she and the entire company break up at the sight of her beleaguered husband.

Archie's eyes seek out his fellow Kriegie, who is also convulsed. 'Humph! You tae Brutus! Ah thought for auld times sake. For *kameradschaft*! You'd huv stuck by me, Billy McClaren.'

Billy manages to control himself. Shrugs. 'Ah cannae help it. *Komisch ist komisch*, Erchie!'

Archie turns back to Irma. 'Whit Ah wiz gonny say, hen, wiz that you and Bert are the first yins tae move up tae Stobcross Avenue in the Molendinar. But before the end o' the year, once they finish the rest o' the avenue, Drena, Ella and Teresa are aw' moving tae within a couple of doors of ye. You're no' going abroad ye know. We're still gonny be neebours.'

'Yah, but not everybody goes to the Molendinar. Robert and Rhea are wanting to move to Wilton Street, and they also will take the mother of Robert to live with them . . .' She stops as they hear footsteps pattering along the close. Agnes Dalrymple emerges from the ever deepening shadows. The close lights haven't come on yet. 'Oh, Irma! Ah meant tae come doon earlier.' She blushes. 'Ah wiz watching that auld fillum on the telly. That wan wi' Robert Doughnut.' She thinks hard. '*Goodbye Mister Chips*. Eee! Ah fell sound asleep. Auld black and white pictur's are the best cure for insomnia ever invented.'

'Oh, I'm glad you waken in time. We are ready to go, Agnes.'

'Aye, so am Ah. Ah'd huv been kicking maself if Ah'd missed you. We've been too long the 'gither in Dalbeattie Street.'

'Ma! C'mon.' Arthur Armstrong decides to intervene.

Once more, Irma looks around, again on the brink of tears. She looks at the close, then all the way up the frontage of the building. 'The first day I come into this street, it was 1949, only four years after the war. Because I am German, well, I think maybe folk will not be . . .'

Billy McClaren cuts in. 'We weren'y worried aboot *you*, hen. You were welcome. It wiz the thought o' huving a big

Geordie fae Newcastle moving in. That's whit hud us oan edge!'

'Hey! Now mind, lad.' Bert laughs with the rest. He turns, looks up at the roof and chimney pots of the tenement across the street. Only the thinnest sliver of sun can be seen, about to slip out of sight for the night. 'Arthur! Take a haud of yer mother on that side.' Bert takes her gently by the other arm. 'It'll be late by the time we get t' the Molendinar. Ah'll have a job finding Stobcross Avenue in the dark, pet.'

Once more Irma's hand goes to her mouth. '*Dark*!' She turns to look up at her husband. 'Did you get the electric switched on, *liebchen*?'

'Oh, Gawd!' Bert Armstrong buries his face in his hands. He eventually emerges. Looks at his friends. 'Does any of yee have a bit candle gannin' spare?'

CHAPTER THREE

As Long As You've Got Your Mammy

The dark-haired young woman, struggling with two suitcases, makes it to the top landing at 18 Dalbeattie Street. 'Pheww!' She steps over to the middle of the three doors. The cases are gratefully laid down. She takes a moment to look at the combined letterbox and nameplate. K. Forsyth is engraved into the brass. Kenneth. A wave of sadness washes over her. She reaches out, runs her fingertips along her daddy's name. Aw' the years this was on oor door in Knightswood. Thought it would be there for ever. Not finish up on a single-end in Maryhill. And ma mammy a widow. She twists the butterfly bell in the middle of the door. Like every one she's ever came across, it grinds more than rings. She hears movement – behind the door on the right. It opens. Agnes Dalrymple squints out onto the shadowy landing. 'Can Ah help . . . Oh! It's Eve's daughter, in't it? Ahhh, Alexandra if Ah mind right . . .'

'Lexie! Ah prefer, Lexie.' She smiles. 'Always think ma full title's too highfalutin'.' She points to the door. 'Is ma mammy no' in?'

'She is. Well, she's doon the sterrs at the minute. At least Ah think she is. Ah heard her door shut a wee while ago. Ah'm sure she went doon tae the second storey. She's pally wi' Wilma Galloway. Oh, her and me are pally as well. But Ah think she went doon tae Wilma's.'

'Right. Will my cases be aw'right if Ah leave them here?'

'Of course they will.' Agnes pauses. Opens her door wider. 'Mibbe best tae put them in ma lobby. Wilma will probably ask ye in fur a cuppa.'

'Thanks.' Lexie Forsyth lifts her two cases. After placing them in the lobby she turns towards Agnes. 'Was it you that got ma mammy that wee job in the City Bakeries?'

'Aye. It was.'

'That was good of you. It's ideal for her.'

'Och, it's jist a wee cleaning job. Four hours a day, Monday tae Setterday. But it's handy. Ah work in the same branch. Further doon the Maryhill Road, near St George's Cross.'

'Aye, I know. She enjoys it. And it supplements her widow's pension, tae.' Lexie steps back onto the landing. 'Right. It should huv Galloway on the door. Ah'll away doon and see if she's there.' She turns. 'Is that the couple that work on the buses?'

'Aye, that's them.'

* * *

Wilma Galloway opens her door.

'Hi! Ah'm Lexie Forsyth. Eve's daughter. Eh, Agnes up the stairs thinks she might be in visiting you?'

Wilma smiles. 'She is indeed. In ye come for a minute.' She stands to the side. Turns her head. 'It's your daughter looking for ye, Evie.'

'Oor Lexie? Goodness!'

The two women walk into the kitchen. Eve Forsyth sits at the table, looking expectantly towards the door.

'Six o'clock in the evening? Bit early for a visit, hen. Is everything aw'right?'

Her daughter shrugs. 'Aye – and naw!'

Wilma pulls a chair out from the table. 'Ah've jist made two cups o' milky Nescafe for your ma and me. Ye wantin' wan?'

'That'll be nice. No sugar for me, thanks. Ah could dae wi' a bit caffeine efter lugging ma two cases up them stairs.'

'*Two* cases!' Eve looks at her daughter, turns toward Wilma. 'Awww my God! Sounds as if Ah'm aboot tae get a ludger.' It's not said with any vehemence.

''Fraid so, Ma. Malcolm and me huv split up.' She opens her arms wide. 'Have'nae had a big row or anything. Quite amicable Ah suppose. We've baith realised it's no' working, so it's time tae call it a day.' She looks at Wilma. 'Been living the 'gither a couple o' years. Never got round tae getting married – which now turns oot tae be a blessing!. We've nae kids either.' She gives another shrug. 'So that's another problem less.'

'*Huh*! It's a problem for me, pal.' Eve sips her coffee.

'Ah've got used tae sleeping in the recess bed on ma own. Noo Ah'll huv tae share it again!' She gives an unconvincing, 'Humph!'

Lexie winks at Wilma. 'Don't let her kid ye on. She'll enjoy having one of her lassies back in the hoose.'

'Sez who?' asks Eve.

'If Ah mind right,' says Wilma, 'you work somewhere doon the Maryhill Road, dain't ye?'

'Aye. Ah'm at Kinnaird's fruit shop, on the corner o' Wilton Street. Ah do the flowers for them. Been there nearly three years.'

Eve cuts in, 'She's self-taught, ye know. Got a natural talent for it.'

'Good for you, hen,' says Wilma. She's about to say more, but they hear the handle turn on the outside door, footsteps in the lobby. Wilma nods in the direction of the door. 'This'll be the Lord and Master. He's been away for the messages. Frank diz maist o' the cooking.'

'Lucky you!' says Lexie. 'Malcolm could jist aboot go for a takeaway.'

Frank Galloway enters. He carries a shopping bag and a plastic carrier. A Senior Service dangles from his lips, he has one eye closed against the smoke. 'Well! No' many guys come hame wi' the rations and find three film stars sitting in their kitchen!'

Wilma looks heavenward. 'Auld silver tongue strikes again, eh? Don't pay any attention. His patter's alwiz mocket!' She puts on a serious face. 'Could Ah remind you, Frank Galloway, it's aboot eighteen years since rationing finished. You've been fur the messages – no' the rations!'

'Ach! It's force o' habit,' says Frank. Wilma introduces her husband to Lexie. She finishes with . . . 'She's moving back in wi' her ma.'

'Are ye, hen.' He takes the cigarette out of his mouth. Nods in an upward direction. 'That used to be oor flat ye know. Wilma and me lived in that single-end for aboot eighteen months afore we got this room and kitchen.' He glances furtively around, as though concerned he'll be overheard. He leans towards Lexie, lowers his voice. 'For a year o' that time we wur'nae married ye know!'

'Big deal!' says Wilma.

Frank has been emptying the shopping bag while he speaks. He pauses, a Milanda sliced loaf held aloft. 'Hey, Ah'm a good Catholic boy Ah'll have ye know. Taught by the Christian Brothers.' He nods in Wilma's direction. 'And that wee skelf sitting therr, led me intae mortal sin so she did!' He looks at his visitors. 'Remember Bette Davis in the fillum, *Jezabel*? That yin makes her look like Mary Poppins! Need Ah say any mair?' He stops unpacking, looks up at the ceiling. A beatific smile spreads over his face. 'Mind, Ah fair enjoyed every minute o' it!'

Wilma blushes. 'Will you stoap telling everybody oor private business, Frank Galloway!'

'Wellllll! Lexie's needing something tae cheer her up. Aren't ye, hen?'

Eve rises to her feet. 'Ah think on that note, Wilma, it's

time we were away up the sterrs. Jist in case he comes oot wi' any mair revelations.'

Lexie looks at her mother. 'Ah can see why ye like coming doon here.' She pauses. 'Tae save ye cooking, Ma. Will Ah just go and get two fish suppers?'

Eve halts at the door. Looks at Frank and Wilma. 'Mmmm! Huving her back might no' be as bad as Ah think.' She points a finger at Lexie. 'But mind, let's get wan thing straight. You're sleeping at the *back* o' the recess bed, next tae the wall.'

Lexie Forsyth smiles. 'It's a deal!'

CHAPTER FOUR

Semantics Versus The Samba!!

Rhea Stewart rises from the table, starts to clear it. As she walks to and from the sink, carrying dishes, she looks at 'her gang'. Robert has moved to a fireside chair with Saturday's *Evening Times* – The Pink – and what's left of his mug of tea.

Twenty-year-old Sammy and his sister Louise, a year younger, remain at the table. A student at Glasgow University, Sammy is always up for an argument. Preferably political. Louise, an assistant at the upmarket West End Modes on the Byres Road, couldn't care less. But now and again . . .

'We're having a demonstration in George Square on Sunday morning, Sis. Protesting about America being in Vietnam and Cambodia. Would you like to come? Give us a bit of support?'

'Naw!' She's filing her nails. Doesn't look up.

'Why not?'

'You lost ma support when ye said "*morning*". Sunday's the only day Ah get a long-lie.'

Her brother tuts. 'You've got no soul, you.'

'Aye, Ah huv. But it likes a long-lie tae.' She continues with her manicure. Hasn't looked up.

Her mother turns on the Ascot heater, filling the basin with hot water for the dishes. She looks at her daughter. 'Why are you reverting tae broad Glesga, Louise Stewart? Ah hope you don't talk like that tae your customers ower in Hillhead.'

'Of course Ah don't. Ah talk pan loaf tae them.' Her father smiles behind his paper.

'So why are ye talking tae your brother like that?' enquires Rhea.

''Cause it gets up his nose. The longer he's at that Uni the posher he's getting. If this is him efter three years, God help us by the time he graduates. It'll sound as if Malcolm Muggeridge huz moved in!' Robert Stewart raises the paper higher. The other three hear it rustle as he stifles a laugh. He knows 'the game's afoot'.

Sammy's cheeks flush. He's determined to keep his cool. His sister can get under his skin faster than the most articulate member of the Debating Society. He takes a couple of slow, deep breaths. Sits back. 'I'm afraid I can't figure that out, Louise.' He furrows his brow as if to show how hard he's thinking. Samuel does a good 'furrow'. 'Why should your use of Glasgow dialect bother me?'

Louise stretches out the fingers of her left hand. After a brief inspection she resumes filing.

'Because, brother. You are supposed tae be so left wing. A man o' the people and aw' the rest of it. No' only dae ye claim tae be a socialist, but you're also studying Sociology – the favourite subject for all do-gooders and bleeding hearts!' She stops filing. 'So if you're wanting tae show solidarity wi' working folk and aw' the rest of it – why huv ye abandoned *your* Glesga dialect?' She leans forward. 'That is something that wid show you come fae the streets. Boost your "street cred". The way you talk nooadays is aw' put oan. An affected accent. Dead phoney!'

Robert lowers The Pink. 'Mind, you've got a case tae answer there, Sammy. You try to make out you're this revolutionary socialist, somewhere tae the left of Karl Marx . . .'

'Mair like Groucho!' murmurs Louise.

Robert has to stop and laugh before he finishes his sentence . . . 'so why adopt this frightfully posh way of talking?'

'After three years at Uni, Dad, it's simply that I've fallen into a more polite, proper way of speaking. Plus, if I were to speak the way I did a few years ago, the tutors – and my fellows – would continually be saying, "Pardon?" "Say again?" It would be hopeless.'

Louise jumps in. 'Efter three *years* at Uni? Huh! You began tae talk like that the day efter ye got your letter telling ye you had a place!'

'I did NOT!'

'You did SOT! Ah remember coming hame fae work in the middle of your second week, stepping intae the loabby – and fur jist a minute Ah thought, Ah did'nae know ma mammy knew Noel Coward! It wiz you through the kitchen talkin' tae her.' From behind the paper there comes a choking sound. Rhea is forced to turn her face to the sink and, shoulders shaking, start rubbing hard with the scourer at an imaginary dried-in bit.

'You're just making that up, Louise Stewart!' Sammy's face flushes. He racks his brain for a clever piece of repartee. Preferably a one-liner. Nothing comes.

Louise fills the silence. 'Ah'll bet ye Rabbie Burns did'nae talk pan loaf, nae matter how grand the company he wiz in. Ye should alwiz remember, "To thine own self be true!"' Louise is now hitting her stride . . . 'Oh, and can Ah also point oot, Rabbie Burns is wan o' the most popular poets amongst your communist friends ower in Moscow!'

'Well said, hen,' says her dad. They look at Sammy.

He rises. 'Ach, the perr of you can go and bile your heids! Ah'm sure youse will understand THAT aw'right!' He storms out of the kitchen.

'Ah think that's "game, set and match" tae you, hen!' says her Dad.

Rhea turns to her daughter. 'You can be a right wee minx at times, Louise Stewart.'

It's a couple of hours later. Sammy has departed for a place where he'll be more appreciated – the Students' Bar at the Uni. Louise has left to meet up with a fellow vendeuse from

West End Modes, Chantelle (aka Jessie Brown). After a glass or two of Beaujolais – Beau-jolly in 'Chantelle-speak' – they will be taking themselves off to the Locarno Ballroom in Sauchiehall Street. Both are devotees of 'the dancin'.' Rhea looks up at the mantelpiece. 'Just gone eight o'clock. Ah think Ah'll start getting ready. Ah like taking ma time on a Setterday night.' Robert yawns, stretches out his arms and legs. The newspaper slips onto the floor. 'Huv ye had a nice wee snooze, darling?' enquires Rhea.

'Lovely!'

'We're meeting Frank and Wilma at the Bar Rendezvous, aren't we? They're gaun for a meal tae that restaurant o' theirs. Tombola.'

'Stromboli!' Robert watches as Rhea begins to undress; slips out of her skirt. She has never taken to tights, wears stockings and suspender belt every day. They never fail. He clears his throat. 'Seeing as we've got the house tae ourselves, Rhea . . . There's plenty of time for a wee bit hunky-dory in the recess bed before we go oot. Do ye fancy?'

She tuts loudly. 'See you, Robert Stewart!'

'Now you know you never really enjoy it at night. You're always worried in case one o' them two is awake through the room.'

'C'mon then.' She walks over to the bed, climbs onto it.

'Ah'll just go and put the snib on the door.' As he makes for the lobby he sees her reach down to her suspenders. 'Aww! Keep the stockings on, hen.' He looks at her. 'Ooh, mammy-daddy!'

She laughs. 'You'd better no' ladder them, mind.'

'If Ah dae, Ah'll buy you another perr. In fact *two* perr!'

It's ten past ten when Frank and Wilma Galloway stroll into Le Bar Rendezvous on the Woodlands Road. They immediately glance over to the left. Ruth Lockerbie, *proprietrix extraordinaire*, sits on her high stool at the end of the small, curved bar. She raises her left arm straight up in the air, waves with her fingers. As could have been forecast, the long tortoiseshell cigarette holder is in her right hand. Rich blue smoke rises languorously from a Black Sobranie, mingles with that from the more mundane Players, Capstans and Gold Flakes. Frank Galloway will soon be adding a Senior Service to the mix.

'I see Rhea and Robert are already in,' he says to Wilma. They skirt the edge of the bijou dance floor, make for the select group which has Ruth at its centre. 'It's jist nice at the minute, Wilma. No' too many in. Plenty of room tae dance.'

'Ah like when it's like this, Frank. Then you can swing me oot and pull me back in when we're daeing a quickstep.' They join their friends. Kisses are exchanged. Broad smiles. They all love a Saturday night together at Le Bar Rendezvous. Especially Rhea. Everyone knows she adores it. She turns towards the newcomers. 'Did youse huv a nice meal at . . . what's its name?'

'Stromboli.' says Frank. 'Aye, we did. Always do. You two should come with us some night.'

'What is "Stromboli"? Is it an Italian dish?' asks Rhea.

'It's a volcano.' Frank thinks for a moment. 'Ah can't remember if it's on Sicily, or on the mainland.'

'Yeah. I'm like you,' says Robert. 'I'm almost certain it's Sicily.'

'Ah weesh Ah hud'nae asked,' mutters Rhea. 'It's turning intae *University Challenge*!'

It's minutes later. Multi-layered conversations are going on. Ruth suddenly sits up straight on her stool so as to see over the heads of the dancers. 'WONDERFUL! Look who's just come in. Vicky Shaw.' They all look, wave.

'Eeeh, she's with somebody.' Rhea is having a good look.

'I'm glad,' says Ruth. 'I thought the poor darling was never going to get over losing Johnny McKinnon.' They watch, smile, as Vicky and her escort approach. Ruth climbs down from her stool, opens her arms. 'Vicky, darling. You don't know how glad we all are to see you. It's been far too long. Welcome back!'

Vicky looks at Ruth then at her other friends. Her eyes moisten, but not because of the warmth of the welcome. It's seeing her girlfriends with their men. Just the way it's always been. But not for me. Not any more. Johnny's not here. She wants to cry . . . 'Oh! Let me introduce you to Steve Anderson.' There is much shaking of hands and exchanging of names.

'Where's my George?' Ruth stands on one of the struts of the stool to gain extra height. She spots her husband, attracts his attention, beckons for him to come over.

'Look who's here, darling.'

The entire company smile as George Lockerbie's face lights up. Vicky Shaw is kissed, then hugged so tight she can hardly breathe. '*Far* too long, Victoria. Depriving your friends of your company.' He is introduced to Steve Anderson . . . 'So, what line are you in, Steve?'

'Ah, second-hand cars. I've got three showrooms in the city.'

'Good man yourself! Right. What would you and Vicky like to drink?' George looks at his friends. 'What would everyone like? Then we can all drink a toast to celebrate having Vicky back with us.' He turns to Steve, 'And hopefully a new recruit to our ranks.'

It's twenty minutes later. 'I must try this dance floor, Vicky.' Steve offers his partner a hand and they make their way onto the floor. The resident five-piece combo is making a good job of 'Summertime'. Frank and Wilma are already dancing. Robert Stewart decides to get a round in while most of the clientele are dancing and the bar is not so busy. Rhea sidles along the bar as Ruth raises her Campari and soda, with ice, and starts to drink . . .

'Ah'm no' struck on him!'

There's a cough, Ruth leans forward, puts her open palm under her chin to catch any drips as she chokes. She pats herself just below the throat, looks at Rhea. 'Me neither.'

'Soon as Ah clapped eyes oan him,' says Rhea, 'Ah thought, Ah'm no' gonny like you.' The two of them watch as Vicky and her new friend glide by. 'He's at least ten years younger than her.' Rhea purses her lips. 'He's a full heid shorter than her,' she sniffs, 'and he cannae look ye in the eye when he talks tae ye.' She bristles. 'There's more than that, but Ah cannae put ma finger oan it at the minute!'

Ruth contributes. 'Yes. As soon as he came over, I thought, I'll bet this is a nasty piece of work.' She sighs. 'Poor Vicky. She's lost since Johnny died.' They watch the pair dance past once more. Ruth continues. 'Do you know the first thing that came into my head when I looked at the two of them?' She doesn't wait for an answer. 'Remember that case a few years back – the film star Lana Turner and her gangster boyfriend, Johnny Stompanato? It was in all . . .'

'*Hah*!' Rhea's hand goes to her mouth. 'That's it! You're right. He wiz younger than her and he wiz knockin' her aboot. And he got stabbed tae death!'

'I don't know why Vicky can't see it.' says Ruth. 'He is NOT right for her.'

Rhea watches the couple dance by. 'Huh! He's no' right for anybody!'

CHAPTER FIVE

Visits

Alec and Irene Stuart, each carrying a message bag, approach the close at 18 Dalbeattie Street. 'Whit time is it, Alec?'

He pulls a gold half-hunter pocket watch from his top pocket, holds it in the palm of his hand. The chain of its silver Albert snakes elegantly up to the buttonhole in his lapel. He flicks the lid open. 'Twenty to one, dear.'

'I think I'll away in and see Mary for ten minutes. It's six years this week since she lost Samuel, you know. She's a wee bit down. Can you manage both bags up the stairs, dear?'

'No bother at all. I'll start lunch. Don't be too long, dear, I know you and your "ten minutes".'

Since she's lived alone, Mary Stewart has always kept the door of her downstairs flat locked. She answers Irene's knock. 'Oh! Hello, hen. Whit a nice surpise. Ah hope you've time for a wee blether?'

'That's why Ah've called in, Mary.'

Ten minutes later finds them sitting opposite one another, waiting for their tea to cool. 'Are ye managing any better wi' them new decimal coins, Mary? Got the hang o' them yet?'

'Oh! Don't mention it. I am *never* gonny get away wi' yon carry-on. Robert and Rhea and the grandkids keep saying, "It's dead easy, Granny." *Huh*! No' when you're intae your seventies it's not. The government should have waited 'til all the auld folk died, before they brought that in.'

Irene tries not to laugh. She knows Mary is serious. As old friends do, they fall silent for a moment or two. An extra loud crash of stone, wood and rubble makes itself heard. They look at one another.

Mary Stewart sighs, shakes her head. 'Have ye ever heard such a depressing sound? With me being in the house by maself, I've got nothing to do but listen tae it. Every time Ah hear another crash, it makes me think of aw' the families that lived in that bit ower the years. Folk jist like oorselves . . .' Her voice fades as myriad pictures, like a kaleidoscope, run through her mind. They are all of glimpses she has taken, when out shopping, of the slowly disappearing Blairatholl, Rothesay and Cheviot Streets. Half-demolished tenements giving up their secrets. The wallpaper of bedrooms and kitchens exposed for all to see. Mary feels it's as if she's surprised someone in their pyjamas. 'Ah find looking at these buildings when they're half knocked doon, makes me sad, Irene. If Ah stand for a while Ah can get quite melancholy. In every house you can see how the tenants decorated them for the last time. And that always leads me on tae thinking what stories they could tell – if walls could only talk.'

'Aye, Ah know whit ye mean. It's a whole way of life coming tae an end, Mary. Anyway, at least you're no' going oot tae yin o' these housing schemes. Once Robert finds a big enough flat tae rent in Wilton Street or Crescent, you'll be moving intae a red-sandstone building. Imagine, Mary. Bay windows and a wally close. Eee! We've always thought o' them as toffs' hooses, haven't we? And you'll soon be living in yin. No more huving tae go oot tae the lavvy in the close wi' a candle in your hand.'

Mary manages a smile. 'Aye. Though mind, all of you folk who lived up the stairs, oot o' the draught, were always better off. The wind used tae howl straight through this close from street tae back court. It always blew the candle oot. Every time.' She starts to laugh. 'Ah've seen me sheltering the flame wi' one hand and getting as far as the lavvy door. But, Ah'm holding the key with the hand that's protecting the candle . . .' They both start laughing in anticipation. 'So Ah'd go tae put the key in the lock – whoooosh! – the wind blaws the flame oot. The only way tae do it on a night like that, was tae go oot wi' the candle unlit, open the lavvy door in the dark and step intae the shelter of the pitch black toilet. When Robert was wee, he was convinced there were ghosts and ghoulies lurking in the lavvy. Trouble was, if I'd been listening tae a scarey play on the wireless – so was I!'

'Oh, but you'll like living along that end of Wilton Street. Trees everywhere. Front gardens either side of the closes. Yet you're near enough tae be able tae donner roon' tae the Maryhill Road for the shops. Ah'd imagine the rent will be quite dear?'

'It will. But Robert's foreman at Rossleigh's Garage, and Rhea's got a good job doon at Macready's. They can easily afford it. Ah've offered tae contribute, but they'll no' hear tell of it.'

'Aye, they're good kids. A credit tae you and Sam. And Teresa and Dennis.'

'What are you and Alec gonny do, Irene. Are ye going oot tae the Molendinar scheme?'

'We're gonny try it. But really, it's just tae see what it will be like tae live in a brand new hoose, with its ain bathroom. But if we find we miss the city, well, we'll jist try and get an "exchange" back intae the toon again. Or rent something. But Ah'll tell ye, it would have tae be self-contained. Red-sandstone.' She snorts, 'Nae mair shared lavvies on the stairs. Not at oor age.'

It's just gone two o'clock on that same May afternoon. Another resident of Number 18, Ella Cameron, is rising from her seat in the double-decker bus which has brought her from Glasgow to Stirling. She lets out a grunt as she pulls herself up. Jeez-oh! Ah'm as stiff as a board. You'd think ye were bloody sixty-two instead o' fifty-two. She looks out the window. Four taxi cabs sit on a nearby rank.

Twenty minutes later finds her dipping into her leather purse to pay the cabbie; plus a two-shilling tip. She exits the vehicle, looks up at the stark, castle-like gate lodge of Craigmill top security prison. Instantly feels depressed. The wind is blowing a young gale. It always bloody is. As she approaches the large, metal-studded gates, the small wicket gate is opened. The officer on duty smiles. 'C'mon, hen. Come in oot the wind.'

She knows his face from previous visits. 'Aye. Winter or summer, the wind alwiz seems tae be blawing up here.'

'Ah think that's why we've never had anybody escape.' He takes the visiting order from her. 'It's too tempting for them tae jist stay put in their nice warm cells.' They both laugh.

She's sitting in the waiting room, occasionally glancing at those there with her. This place alwiz bloody gets me doon. Wid'nae be so bad if Ah could find somebody tae have a decent blether wi'. She looks around. The majority are youngish women, trailing kids. Undisciplined kids. Plenty of them. Jeez! Their men might hardly ever be oot o' the nick, but they alwiz seem tae be oot long enough tae put their wives up the bun. An officer leans in the door, looks at her. 'Right, Mrs Cameron.'

She recognises him, too. Seen him often over the last few years. Christ! It'll no' be long until Ah'll be gettin' an invite tae the Staff Christmas Party!

They leave the waiting room, walk side by side towards the visiting block. 'Your Archie hasn't got long to do now, has he?'

'Naw. Aboot six weeks or so.'

'I'm one o' the officers on his landing. I must say, he's not a bad lad. Keeps himself well away from the trouble-makers. And he's a good grafter in his workshop. The laundry.'

'Aye. Ah wish the bugger would work as well ootside as he seems tae do inside. Might keep himself oot o' bother if he could haud doon a job.'

The officer laughs. 'You have no idea how often that's the case. It's hard to figure out. When they're outside, even if they've got a job, it never seems to last.' The conversation peters out as they enter the visiting room.

Archie Cameron junior sits at a Formica-covered table, leaning on his elbows. He's trying not to make it too obvious he's observing the carry-on between Big Bernie Bankes and his visitor – a female who is most certainly *not* Mrs Bankes. He watches as they make another attempt to break their record on who can get their tongue furthest down the other's throat. Jeez! It's a good job Bernie has his back tae me. Cannae see me looking. As the young woman leans forward to re-engage with Bernie, yet again, her legs part under the table and Archie gets a free view all the way up the minuscule skirt she's wearing. Oh, man! Can very near see whit she had for breakfast. My cock is fucking throbbing. The screws are all turning a blind eye.

They're no' gonny mess wi' Big Bernie, the human tank. Well, only if they have to, *and* when they are 'team-handed' – with truncheons already drawn. Not for the first time, Archie gives thanks that the big man's bailiwick is on the south side of the city: Gorbals, Govan, wherever. Ah hope tae Christ he stays on that side o' the Clyde. There would'nae half be some trouble if he tried tae spread his operations as far north as Maryhill. He thinks about it. Though mind, Nathan Brodie would huv something tae say – or more accurately – something tae *do* about that. Archie smiles to himself as he recalls the novel, *The Godfather*. It would take a Don Corleone tae topple Nathan. Big Bernie relies solely on muscle. Nae finesse whatsoever. In Glesga, nine times oot o' ten violence, or the threat of it, is usually enough. It's been tried a time or two against Nathan. So far he's always been able to think up some tactic to see them off. Only once did it look like war was gonny break oot. And Nathan hud difficulty recruiting enough muscle tae deal wi' it. Archie smiles. So he sub-contracted. Calls were made tae connections in Edinburgh, London and Manchester. Favours were called in and heavies supplied 'on loan' until the crisis was over.

A movement by the door catches Archie's eye. His ma has jist come in, escorted by Mr Younger. He feels his heart lift. She doesn't spot him at first in the busy visiting room. God! The poor soul looks tired, worn-oot. He feels a pang of sadness. And guilt. You've caused a lot o' that. Maist of it, yah useless git! You've got the best ma in . . . She sees him. He watches her face light up. She straightens her shoulders, immediately looks years younger. All this just for him. A great surge of affection for her floods over him. You huv got tae make it up tae this wumman. She'd walk ower broken glass for you if she had to. And you? What have *you* done for her? Well, there wiz the time you stole money oot her purse a few years back, shoved her against the table when she told you off! As she walks over to him and he sees the genuine 'pleased tae see ye' smile on her face, he feels deep shame. Quickly blinks tears away before she gets to the table.

'Hello, Ma!' He kisses her. Gives her a hug. He's only started to do that lately. It's the influence of the weekly film show in the prison chapel. Especially if it's an American film. They always give their ma a kiss and a hug. And their brothers and sisters. And if it's an Italian-American, or New York Jewish picture, Jeez! Aw' their close friends, male *and* female, get hugs as well! Every bugger gets hugged. Be honest, Archie. It's quite a nice thing tae do. After Ma gets her monthly kiss and hug they sit down facing one another. 'Was your journey aw'right?'

'Aye, fine, son.' Ella never enjoys the first minute or two of a visit. It's as if they are strangers. Conversation is always stilted. 'Eh, that officer wiz saying he knows you quite well.'

Archie looks. 'Aye, Mr Younger. He's wan o' the screws on ma landing. He's not a bad guy as screws go. Always fair.'

'He wiz saying, you're no' a bad lad.' She looks at him. 'Ah nearly said – if he's no' a bad lad, how come he's alwiz in and oot the buggerin' jail?' As it's too close to the truth, he makes no reply. Avoids eye contact. She reaches into her bag, places an already opened twenty packet of Players on the table. 'Therr ye are. Jist dig in whenever you want wan.'

'Thanks, Ma.'

It's halfway through the visit. There are thirty or so cons at other tables with family and friends. As usual, those with small children are finding it difficult to keep them quiet. The ones around school age are the noisiest: totally undisciplined as they become bored. Ella is also being distracted, and annoyed, by the actions of Big Bernie Bankes and his paramour. She stares at them with a clear look of disapproval on her face. Turns to Archie, says, *sotto voce*, 'Ah'm surprised them officers urr letting these two carry on like that. Look at the way the older kids are staring at them. Should throw a bucket o' watter ower the perr o' them!'

Archie blanches, bends his head closer to his mother's ear – the one not facing the romantics. He speaks through gritted teeth, his lips barely moving. 'Ma! That's Gig Gernie Gankes. He's the toughest gastard in the jail. Leave it alane, will ye. If he hears ye, he's liable tae gatter ma grains oot!'

Ella draws back, looks at him askance, shakes her head. 'If Ah wiz you, Ah'd pack in the ventriloquist classes, son. They might let ye huv a refund oan the dummy!'

Ella judges it must be getting near the end of the visit. She doesn't look at her watch, in case she hurts his feelings. 'You're awfy quiet, son. Whit's the matter?' She looks closely at him.

He returns her gaze. 'Got something Ah want tae say tae ye, Ma.' He lays a hand on top of hers. For a moment Ella wonders if it's her birthday – and she's forgot. 'On ye go, son.'

She hears him take a deep breath. 'Aw' the years Ah've been getting intae trouble wi' the polis, in and oot the prison, you've never, ever, heard me say, "Ah'm gonny try and go straight when Ah get oot." Have ye?'

'Naw. Ah've hoped Ah would hear ye say it. But naw. Ye never have.'

He gives an embarrassed laugh. 'Well, Ah've found this sentence hard going. There wiz a time when Ah could have done it standing oan ma heid. But not any more.' He shifts in his chair. 'Ah'm dying tae get oot. And when Ah dae – Ah intend tae *stay* oot!'

She places a hand on each of his. 'Oh, Archie! You know there's nothin' would please me better.'

He looks at her. 'Dae ye know what's brought it on? It's me turning thirty while Ah've been in. Ah'm now thirty-one. It was the realisation that Ah spent more than *six* years of ma twenties in the bloody jail. It keeps coming intae ma mind. They years are lost. Ah cannae get them back. Six o' the prime years o' ma life jist thrown away. Locked up in a cell every night. Kidding maself on that being in the jail means Ah'm a tough guy. It diz'nae. It means Ah'm a fuckin' mug! 'Scuse the language, Ma. Being in prison gies ye tons o' time tae think. Especially when you're in a single-cell like me. You only get wan life. Imagine spending maist of it in the jail.' He shakes his head, gives a laugh that is anything but. 'When Ah think of it, Ah *should* be locked up – for being bloody stupid!' He looks at his ma. Her eyes are full.

'But do ye *really* mean it, Archie? And dae ye realise, that when ye get oot, you cannae go running aboot wi' the crowd you've always palled up wi'. They'll jist drag ye doon again.'

'Aye, Ah know. Ah've gave it lots o' thought. Got it all worked oot, Ma. Ah'll be getting a steady job, so as Ah'll have money in ma pocket. That's the main reason why Ah get intae bother. Ah don't work. Ah've nae money. So Ah go thieving.' He shrugs his shoulders. 'And Ah alwiz get caught. Ah'm a useless thief!'

'Well, if you dae start work and keep oot the jail, your da will eventually come roon'. Once he sees you really mean it.'

'Ah! Well that's what Ah want ye tae do for me. A couple of years before Ah got sent doon he'd already put me oot the hoose.' Archie holds his hands up. 'Oh! Ah don't blame him. Ma faither is'nae the type o' man tae put up wi' a thief in the hoose. Even if it is his son.' He reaches for another cigarette. Lights it. 'Ma probation officer, Mr Carson, is gonny get me fixed up wi' a job. Driving a van.' He sniffs. 'Be a change from a getaway car. But Ah'd really like tae huv a sit-doon wi' ma da. Tell him whit Ah've told you. Ah'm gonny ask him tae let me back into the hoose. Ah'll find it easier tae go straight if Ah'm back hame again. And Ah'll tell him:

if Ah blot ma copybook, even once, he'll no' need tae throw me oot – Ah'll leave under ma ain steam. Ah really think Ah can make it work if Ah'm not in one o' them probation hostels. They are too depressing, Ma. Lonely. In fact, they're enough tae drive ye tae crime – jist for something to do! If Ah'm tae make it work, Ah need to be back hame.'

'Right, son. Ah think Ah'll be able tae get him tae meet ye. You've never asked for oor help in the past. If you tell him *exactly* whit you've jist told me. Ah know your da. Like ye say, you've never once said you were gonny try and go straight. This is the first . . .'

The officer, Mr Younger, appears at their side.

'Sorry. Time's up Ah'm afraid. Ah've given you an extra twenty minutes.'

'Aye. Ah noticed, Boss,' says Archie, 'thanks very much.' The screw walks back to his table.

Ella rises. They kiss. She gives him a smile. For a moment he catches a glimpse of the old ma. 'And there's another bonus if ye manage tae stay oot the jail, son. You have nae idea how heart sick I am of travelling tae Stirling oan that fuckin' bus every twenty-eight days!'

CHAPTER SIX

Whose Move Is It?

'Just keep the change.'

'Thanks very much, sir.'

George Lockerbie steps back, stands beside Ruth. They watch the Hackney cab easily complete a U-turn within the width of the street with room to spare. As it heads back towards the Maryhill Road, Ruth looks around. 'Oh, doesn't Dalbeattie Street look sad?'

'You've just beaten me to the punch, darling.'

They look at the empty tenement opposite. Rows of identical dark windows look down. The absence of almost all curtains and blinds shows it has been abandoned. Smashed panes of glass here and there give further evidence. George points down at the tarmac. 'The Corporation isn't bothering to sweep the road as often as they used to.' He looks up at the windows belonging to Number 18. 'I see what used to be Granny Thomson's hasn't escaped either. Och, well! I suppose that's life.' Ruth takes his arm and they enter the close. As they pass the downstairs door where he once lived, he does his sums. Jeez! Twenty years since I lived here. They begin the climb to the first storey.

'At least the residents still seem to be taking their turn for the close and stairs,' says Ruth.

'Yeah, I noticed. If you think about it, they have to. It could be months before this building is cleared. It would go downhill rapidly if the neighbours stopped keeping it clean.'

George raps Robert and Rhea's door, then opens it. 'Anybody in? Your visitors are here!' He smiles as he hears the expected response from Rhea.

'Aw, cummon! In youse come. Pleased tae see ye. You're late!'

'We are *not*!' says George.

'Ye are *sot*!' says Rhea. 'You wur supposed tae be here at seven. No' twenty-past!' She skips over to the kitchen door for a kiss and a hug. After he has supplied both, George holds her at arms-length. 'You're still keeping up the elocution lessons by the sound of it, hen.'

'Definitely am. Recently graduated magna cum Nikki Lauda!'

'Clear the way if ye don't mind. Can't wait any longer.' Robert Stewart pulls his wife and George into the kitchen. Ruth, lit from above by the lobby light, stands just inside the front door. He opens his arms wide. 'I'm ready for the highlight o' the week. No! I tell a lie. The month!'

He kisses her on both cheeks, then a peck on the lips, leads her by the hand into the kitchen. He turns to George. 'I'd imagine you must know how Frank Sinatra felt – when he was married tae Ava Gardner!' He points to Ruth. 'Knowing you can kiss a movie star whenever you feel like it.'

'Yeah. Now you mention it, Robert. You're right. Then there's also how I feel about our marriage certificate. I sort of look on it as, well – the gift that keeps on giving!'

Ruth looks heavenward. 'Gaaawd! Pass the sick bag, somebody.'

Rhea grimaces. 'Zat no' enough tae gie ye the boke?' She gives a sigh. 'And whit aboot me? Ah've had tae live for years, wi' the knowledge that ma man loves another.'

'Okay then, Ah'll stop.' says Robert. 'Anyway. Give me your coats and Ah'll hang them oan the lobby floor!'

They have just finished the main course. 'We'll huv a wee blaw fur ten minutes before Ah get the pudding,' says Rhea.

'Let me guess what's for dessert,' says George. 'Mmm, perchance profiteroles, darling?'

'Naw.'

'Mayhap *Schwarzwalder kirschtorte*?'

'WHIT?'

'Perhaps not. Okay, I give in.'

'Bread and butter puddin' – wi' DOUBLE cream!'

'You little temptress!'

'Ah know!' Rhea empties her glass. 'That's not a bad

drop o' scoosh, George.' She peers at the label. 'Merr-*lot.*' Smacks her lips loudly. 'Aye, not a bad drop at all, that.'

'Would you like a little more, cherie?'

'Naw thanks, Ah'm no' changing tae sherry. Ah'll stick wi' this Merr-*lot.*'

'Oh, God!' Three heads turn as strange noises begin to issue from Ruth. She puts her glass down, eventually manages to control herself. She hiccups. Looks at her watch. 'It's not yet ten and that's the first attack of the giggles. Rhea Stewart, will you stop it!'

'Stoap whit? Ah huv'nae done anything. You're gonny huv tae ration your wife wi' the drink, George.' Rhea looks around the table. 'Ah think Ah'd better make the coffee now – and bring it in wi' the pud.' She gives Ruth a knowing glance. 'Try and sober up, Ava!'

It's now gone eleven o'clock. Second cups of coffee have been poured. 'Where are the kids, tonight?' enquires Ruth.

'Sammy's ower at the Uni bar wi' his cronies,' says Robert. 'And Louise is off tae the dancing with her fellow assistant from West End Modes. La belle Chantelle.'

'Oh!' says Ruth. 'Now isn't that the perfect name for somebody working on the Byres Road? Couldn't be more suitable if she'd made it up.'

'She did!' Rhea sniffs. 'Her name's actually Jessie Broon!'

'And talking about going upmarket,' George looks at the hosts, 'I take it you haven't yet found anything along the North Kelvinside end of Wilton Street?'

'Not so far,' says Robert. 'We've got our name down with

a few factors who look after the red-sandstones along there. Some of them have their cars serviced with us at Rossleigh's. So I'm on "first refusal" with a couple of them.'

'Mmm. It's a pity Fred Dickinson doesn't own something along there,' says Ruth.

'Are you holding out exclusively for the far end of Wilton Street?' asks George.

'If it gets to eviction-time, we'll *have* to take one of the nearby streets. You know, Belmont Street or Gardens. They're all lovely flats. It's just that Wilton Street is handy for the Maryhill Road. Means my mother can toddle along to the shops every day. Keep in touch with her old friends.'

George looks at Ruth. 'Do you want to tell them our news, darling?' The Stewarts' heads turn as one. Ruth tries to look mysterious; reaches for the ever-present tin of Black Sobranie. All eyes are on her as the insertion of the black cigarette into the tortoiseshell holder becomes a production worthy of Samuel Goldwyn . . .

Rhea breaks the silence. 'Ah hope this news is gonny be worth the scunnering wait?' At last it's time. George supplies a light; the pungent smell of *Mittel Europa* drifts up and hangs round the unlikely destination of a pulley in a Glasgow tenement.

'See when we get up the morra morning,' says Rhea, 'you could swear blind the Turkish tram drivers union hud a meeting in oor kitchen last night – and they were aw' smoking Pasha!' Ruth chokes as a mouthful of smoke goes down the wrong way. The assembled company becomes helpless as they watch her laugh, cough and dab her watering eyes. It's more than a minute before she manages to say, 'Rhea Stewart! It was my intention to appear cool and sophisticated – à la Marlene Dietrich – as I laid an important titbit of news on you and Robert.' She pauses for another cough. 'Instead, thanks to you, I've finished up looking more like Lucille Ball!' She lays the cigarette holder down on the ashtray. 'I daren't take another draw.'

Robert comes in. 'Hah! I'd forgotten about Pasha cigarettes. I remember nights in the Blythswood, just after the war, when "good" fags were still on the ration. And it was easy to get Pasha – 'cause naebody wanted them. There was always some poor soul, dying for a smoke, who'd eventually light one and you'd *instantly* smell it. Within seconds a voice would come oot o' the dark, "Oh, God! Somebody's jist lit a Pasha!" And the hall would be in stitches.'

'Right, darlings.' Ruth seems to have got her second wind. She looks at Rhea and Robert. 'You aren't the only ones who will soon be on the move. *We* are leaving Agincourt Avenue!' She pauses for dramatic effect.

Rhea's hand flies to her mouth. 'Ye cannae! Oh, Ah could'nae bear the thought o' never again being in that gorgeous Art Deco flat. Especially when there are some first-time visitors with us. You know Ah jist *love* tae see the effect it huz on them.' She pauses, thinks hard for a moment. 'Oh, God! Ah weesh ye had'nae told me. Ah adore that flat o' yours.' She stops again. 'Some o' the best nights of ma life huv been spent up there.' She sighs. 'Ah feel like greeting!'

'Oh, my God!' Ruth slides her chair over beside her,

puts an arm round her shoulders. 'No, darling. You *will* be back up in it again. Because where we're moving to is even better. Truly!'

George leans across the table, takes both of Rhea's hands in his. 'The new flat will look exactly the same, Rhea. Just as you've always known it, but it will be even *more* Art Deco than before! That's a promise.'

Rhea, still saddened by the shock news, looks warily at the two of them. 'But how *could* it be? It's jist beautiful the wye it is.'

George continues to hold her hands. 'I'll tell you how, darling girl. At the moment, we live in an Art Deco flat – set into a late-Victorian building. But we are about to move everything. Just as it is, exactly as you've always known it, to where it was *meant* to be. We've bought a flat in an Art Deco building!' He sits back in his chair. 'You'll soon be able to see all our furniture, pictures, ornaments, lighting, in a setting which was made for them.'

'*Ah-hah*!' The other three turn to look at a smiling Robert Stewart. 'And I'll bet you I know where you're moving to.'

'Right,' says George, 'I'll give you *one* guess.' He points a finger at Robert. 'Though, being aware that you love Art Deco as much as we do, I'd think one guess is all you'll need.'

Ruth also looks at Robert. 'Yes. He'll know.'

'Well, Ah huv'nae got a clue.' Rhea still looks depressed.

Robert smiles at his wife. Lays a hand on top of hers. 'If they're moving to where I think they are, Rhea, you can believe what they're telling you. It *will* be even better than

Agincourt Avenue.' He turns to look at their guests. 'I'll bet you're moving to Kelvin Court?'

Ruth claps her hands. 'Got it in one, darling!'

'Are you renting – or buying?'

'We're buying,' says George. 'A two-bedroom flat.'

'Can I be nosey,' asks Robert, 'what *does* a flat cost there? It's a prestigious address.'

'We won't get much change back from ten thousand pounds,' says Ruth.

Rhea chokes on a mouthful of Merlot. 'TEN thoosand! There is'nae that much money in the world! And wid somebody mind telling me, where is Kelvin Court?'

Robert shakes his head. 'She's got a memory like a hen.' He turns to Rhea. 'You know when we're driving oot the Great Western Road, away from the city. And not long after we pass the boating loch. On the same side. We come to yon lovely big flats. And every time, I always say to you, "Aren't they *so* moderne." Ah always comment on them as we go past. Ah think I read somewhere, they were the last Art Deco buildings to be constructed in Glasgow. Built just before the war.' He looks at her. 'Remember? I point them out every time.'

The company watch as the realisation she *does* know them, spreads over Rhea's face. 'Oh, aye. Ah dae know the ones ye mean. They're oan the left. Set back fae the road a wee bit.' She looks at George, then Ruth. 'Aye, they are lovely, them. Ah'm beginning tae see whit ye mean.' She gives it some more thought. 'Ah think ye could be right. Ah'd imagine your stuff *will* look even better in there.' She thinks some more about it. 'It'll aw' go the gither so it will.'

'Oh, I am glad!' says Ruth.

'Ah hope when the time comes, you'll be huving a big hoose-warming once you've settled in?'

'We most certainly shall, darling.' says George. He leans forward. 'I'll tell you what, Rhea. On the night, *you* will be the guest of honour. How's that?'

Ruth claps her hands in delight. '*Ohhh*! What a good idea, George.'

Rhea manages a smile. 'Oh, noo that wid be nice.' She thinks some more about it. 'And, eh, dae you think you could mibbe lay in a few bottles of the Merr-*lot*? Ah'm getting partial tae yon.'

CHAPTER SEVEN

Time's A Drag

'SLOP OUT!' The shout from B Wing's Principal Officer is picked up and echoed by the screws on the four landings. The cons stand ready at their open cell doors, piss pots in one hand, aluminium jugs in the other. The response is immediate. All over the cathedral-like wing, the hum of murmured conversation is replaced by the pounding of three hundred pairs of feet as inmates step out, in a style reminiscent of Olympic walkers, as they jostle their way along the narrow walkways towards the recesses on either side of each landing. Running is not allowed. In less than a minute there are long queues at each of these small sluices. The air inside them, and their immediate vicinity, is fouled by the stench from the night soil of so many men. In spite of this, a screw stands outside each sluice to keep an eye on things. A crowded recess is a popular 'place of choice' for many assaults or chibbings (stabbing or slashing).

Archie Cameron junior's cell, B4-27, is about as far away from the recess on his side of the landing as it can be. He's long ago given up the race to get there early. Instead, he has tried to train himself to become inured to the smell, as he shuffles along in the queue. It's fifteen minutes before he gets his turn. Taking a deep breath of already fouled air, he holds it, and steps into the white-tiled room where the smell is at its worst. He makes for the large sink. Emptying his piss pot straight down the drain, he quickly rinses it under the cold water gushing from the large faucet. As ever, he determines he won't look closely into the sink. Without fail, it always draws his eyes. Aww, man! Some dirty bastard has emptied his pot well away from the drain. A large piece of shit lies trapped in a corner, the strong flow of water keeping it pinned there. Even with his face half-turned away he is still aware of the dark mass against the white china. It lies there. Unmoving. Malevolent.

As he turns, makes for the hot water tap, he knows he can't hold his breath much longer. The guy at the tap moves off. I might make it. He thrusts his jug under the tap. Knows that by now the water will be barely lukewarm. The early guys get the hot stuff. Man! I hate shaving in cauld watter. He steps out of the recess, exhaling as he does. He sucks in air which no longer reeks of shit and piss. It is now of unwashed bodies, sweat and disinfectant. The smell of prison.

Ten minutes later he's down on B2, in the breakfast queue. As he nears the hot plate he leans out, tries to see what's on offer. Porridge, of course. Mmm, a fried egg on a piece o' fried bread. Nice. Ah'll take three slices of ordinary bread as well. And the spoonful of jam. Not bother wi' the pat o' margarine. Got plenty butter left from the half pound Ah bought in the canteen.

'Hello, Erchie!'

The voice is familiar. He was conscious somebody had come along and slipped into the queue behind him. He turns. 'Fucking hell! Fancy meeting you here.' He pretends he's pleased to see Elky McCann, another Maryhill boy. He isn't. Can't stand the little weasel. 'Huv ye jist been sent doon, Elky?'

'Aye and naw. Been remanded in custody for sentence. Ah'm back up in court in a fortnight. They want tae dae aw' the usual shite. Probation report and aw' the rest o' it.'

'Oh, aye.' The conversation falters as they reach the hot plate, pick up an aluminium tray, have their breakfasts served onto them by the orderlies, their pint mugs filled with tea at the urns. All this under the watchful eyes of two screws. He reluctantly waits for Elky and they fall into step as they head for the metal stairway.

'Whit landing have they put ye on?'

'The threes. B3–17.'

Thank fuck for that, thinks Archie. If he was on the fours he'd never be away fae ma door, borrowing books, mooching a smoke. 'Ah'm up on the fours.'

They step onto the short bridge which spans B3 from side to side, about to part, Archie to climb the last flight of stairs to B4, Elky to walk along B3 to his cell. There is a sudden commotion. Shouting. They stop. All over the wing, cons stop. All over the jail. Being on the bridge, they have an uninterrupted view, looking down towards the circular 'centre' of the prison. Screws are shouting, their tackety boots clattering, their keys and key chains jangling as they sprint along the slate landings. The racket is coming from round the corner, in A Wing. This wing, just like B and C Wings, runs onto the circular centre like a spoke in a wheel. At the moment only the A Wing cons can see what's happening. Suddenly, like a startled rabbit, a con, grey-uniformed like all convicted men, darts out from the end of A4, climbs up onto the circular, balcony-like railing overlooking the centre, and forces his way sideways, through a gap in the wall of anti-suicide wire netting. He reaches up for the black-painted tubing which carries wiring to an isolated lamp, suspended fifty-feet above the centre. Seconds too late, three screws reach the hand rail. All those watching, officers and prisoners, are now hushed. The cons who are spread over stairways and landings, holding trays and mugs, seem frozen to the spot – as though taking part in a game of 'Statues'. Other screws arrive, but are shooed back, told to leave it to the three on the scene.

'Son, that won't take your weight if you go out any further.' Archie knows the screw who's speaking. Mr Black. Works in the censors' office. The young con makes no response. Hand over hand he edges further out of reach, legs dangling fifty feet above the centre. The thin metal pipe begins to sag.

'Fuck sake!' mutters Elky.

'Listen, son. Whitever your problem is, Ah promise ye

we'll get somebody tae talk tae ye. See whit can be done for . . .'

'Ah'm daeing a "nine". Naebody can dae anything fur me.' His voice quavers. Mibbe he'll change his mind, thinks Archie. 'Ah cannae face a "nine".' He edges out further. There's a sharp 'crack' and the length of tubing the con hangs from separates into two parts and comes away from the cable. The brightly coloured wiring twangs up in the air – out of his reach. There's a synchronised '*hah!*' from screws and cons alike as they take an involuntary breath. The young man seems to dwell in mid-air for a split second. Then he is left with just one section of tubing as the other half flutters away. Archie tenses, draws his head down into his shoulders, grips the tray so tight it hurts the joints of his fingers. Through narrowed eyes, which won't shut, he watches it all unfold. The first part – which seemed to have been in slow-motion – is over.

The young con falls silently. As he gathers speed, his body turns until he is horizontal, parallel to the floor. Archie will always wonder if this was deliberate. He still holds the piece of tubing. At just this moment, if someone dropped the proverbial pin, it would resonate loud and clear all over Stirling Prison.

The sound of him hitting the tiled centre, is something Archie will never forget. If he hadn't seen it, only heard it, he would have wondered why someone had thrown a side of beef – and a coconut – off the fours down to the centre fifty feet below. Unfortunately, he also sees it.

The loud, squelching 'splat' of the body hitting the tiles

is bad enough. But the bony sound as the con's head splits wide open, the instant shower of blood – and what can only be brains – spattering for yards in all directions is horrific. Even then it isn't fucking over. There is a short period when the body and its limbs twitch. Archie instantly recalls the almost forgotten time he had seen a dog hit by a lorry on the Maryhill Road. It did that terrible twitching tae.

People now find their voices. Archie turns to Elky. 'Awww, fur fucking fuck sake! Why did he dae that?' Further along B3 a con vomits. Elky looks green. He can only shake his head.

'Right, c'mon boys. Back tae your cells. Nae good hanging aboot looking at the poor soul.'

Archie climbs up to the fours. As he reaches his cell he looks at his tray. At the congealed egg on the piece of fried bread. Both now cold. A wave of nausea rolls over him. A screw hurries along his side of the landing, locking doors. Archie waits until he reaches him. 'Boss, five minutes ago a wiz really looking forward tae this breakfast. Ah could'nae face it noo. Ah'll jist huv the tea. Ah seen the whole fuckin' thing.' He lays the tray on the landing, outside his door.

The screw gives a rueful smile. 'As ye know, if a con refuses a meal, we're supposed tae make him keep it in his cell until the next mealtime. Huh! Ah don't think that rule will apply the day.'

Archie steps into his cell. The screw takes hold of the door handle. 'Ah'm jist aboot tae go for ma breakfast, tae. Mug o' tea and a fag is aboot all Ah'll manage this morning.'

He quietly shuts the door. As the footsteps fade, Archie looks around his cell. The everyday sounds of a prison wing begin to filter through the door. Things already getting back to normal. He reaches for his baccy tin. As he rolls a fag he looks at his few, familiar items of 'personal property'. Especially the cork board with the snapshots of Ma, Da and young Katherine pinned to it. He sits on his bed, takes a deep draw on the roll-up. And starts to cry.

It's quarter past ten before the centre is cleaned up and the wings begin to be unlocked. B Wing is sent out onto the big yard for an hour's exercise. The talking point is almost exclusively this morning's incident. Archie walks round on his own, deep in thought. Not for long.

'That wiz fuckin' something this morning, Erchie, wizn't it?' He has unwanted company.

'Aye.' He can tell Elky is trying to make it appear the suicide hasn't bothered him too much.

'You huv'nae got much longer tae dae, Erchie, huv ye?'

'Naw.'

'Eh, Erchie. Ah could'nae tap ye for a smoke, could Ah?'

He stifles a sigh. He'd wondered how long it would be. 'Aye, nae bother.' As they continue to walk he reaches into the top pocket of his battledress-type jacket, brings out his baccy tin, opens it. He's already prepared in advance for this moment. Next to a new half ounce of Old Holborn, is another wrapper, holding just under a quarter ounce. He takes it out. 'Here ye are.'

'Aww, thanks Erchie. You're a pal!'

He tries not to smile. He's well aware this little toerag will do the rounds of all the Maryhill boys today. By tonight he'll huv more baccy than me. By the end of the week the little fuckpig will be loan-sharking it – for double back!

Elky is quiet for a moment while he rolls a fag on the move. Then . . . 'Can ye gie's a light?'

Archie stops. 'Fuck me! Dae ye want me tae smoke it fur ye as well?' He reaches for his matches. Supplies a light. They walk on again, Elky takes a draw, indolently blows the smoke up in the air. 'Nathan Brodie called up tae the hoose tae see me a couple o' days ago. Said if Ah got sent doon, Ah wiz tae tell ye tae call intae the yard and see him when ye get oot.'

An icicle stabs Archie deep inside his stomach. 'Oh, did he. Well, Ah'm afraid Nathan's gonny be disappointed if he thinks Ah'm going back tae work for him. Ah'll call in tae see him. But it'll be tae tell him Ah'm taking early retirement. Ah'm finished wi' this fuckin' game. Getting too auld fur it.' He looks straight ahead as they stride round the yard. He's aware Elky's looking at him.

'Oh! Nathan's gonny be sorry tae hear that, Erchie.'

'Aye, nae doot.' Archie turns towards him. 'Huv ye ever gave it any thought, Elky? Nathan makes the biggest part of his living fae crime. The scrap yard, the Saltire Club and the couple o' garages are jist fronts. But huv ye ever noticed, he never diz any time? He plans aw' these jobs. Gets mugs like us tae dae them. He takes the biggest cut. And if we get lifted by the polis we alwiz obligingly say nuthin'. Take the rap oorselves.' Archie stops walking for a moment, restrains Elky by the arm. 'Every other fucker diz time, except Nathan. Dae ye no' think it's time we got wise tae oorselves?' He releases the arm. They resume walking. Archie continues to look at him. His gaze is making Elky uncomfortable.

'Well, Erchie . . . Ah mean, ye could'nae grass Nathan Brodie could ye? Fuck me! You'd be found floating in the Forth and Clyde Canal before the week wiz oot!'

'Ah'm no' oan aboot grassin' him. Ah would'nae dae that. Ah'm oan aboot telling him Ah'm giving up being a thief. Or tae be mair accurate – Ah'm giving up being a convict. This last few years Ah've spent maist of ma time *daeing* time! Ah'm fed up wi' Nathan and this Italian thing he's started. This Omerta!'

They walk on for another minute or so; Elky is deep in thought. He turns his head. 'Ah did'nae know Nathan hud took ower an Italian cafe. Never said a word tae me, Erchie. Where is it? Bearsden? Mulguy?'

Archie hasn't been listening, he catches the end of it. 'Whit the fuck are ye oan aboot?'

'Nathan's Italian cafe, restaurant, whitever it is. Did ye say it wiz called Omerta? Where is . . .'

Archie stops dead on the exercise yard. 'We were talking aboot no' grassing people. The Mafia huv this code, they call it Omerta! That's the Italian word fur silence. In other words, no' grassing yer pals.' He looks in bewilderment at Elky. 'Jeez! The next thing is, you'll be telling everybody Nathan's taking ower Jaconelli's!'

Elky blows his pinched cheeks out. 'Well, that's whit it

sounded like, Erchie. Ah heard ye saying something aboot "Nathan and this Italian business, Omerta". And Ah thought, imagine Nathan branching oot and no' letting oan tae me! Sorry, Erchie. Ah got the wrang end o' the stick.'

He goes back to the original subject. 'But mind, Erchie. Ah cannae remember anybody ever daeing whit you're thinking. Putting in yer notice. Ah've nae idea whit Nathan wid say tae that.'

'Well, it'll no' be long 'til Ah find oot. C'mon!' They resume walking round the yard.

CHAPTER EIGHT

Knowing When Tae Ask

Ella Cameron pushes the front door open. 'Are ye in?'

'In ye come, hen.' As her best pal enters the kitchen, Drena McClaren rises from her fireside chair. 'The kettle's no' long biled. Ah'll put it back oan the gas. No' be a minute. Tea as usual?'

'That'll be lovely.' Ella pulls a kitchen chair out, wearily sits down at the table. Drena now stands by the cooker, watching the kettle. 'Huv ye spoke tae Archie, yet?'

'Naw. Ah'm gonny have tae dae it the night. The boy's getting discharged on Thursday next week. Oh God! Ah don't know whit Ah'll dae if his faither says he's no' letting him back intae the hoose.'

Drena pours boiling water onto the teabags, stirs the brew, puts the lid back on the pot. 'Ah would think whit's gonny bother his faither, is the fact that Archie junior has'nae lived in the hoose wi' the rest of youse for, oh, how long?'

'It's roon' aboot five years since he put him oot.'

Thirty minutes later Ella steps onto the top-storey landing, finds her key, lets herself in to the quiet flat. She looks at the alarm clock on the mantelpiece. Nearly six. Better get the dinner started. As she hangs her coat up in the lobby she hears the familiar footsteps of her daughter, climbing the stairs. Ella opens the outside door.

Katherine smiles. 'Hi yah, Ma!'

'Hello, hen.' As Katherine takes her coat off, Ella steps back into the kitchen, starts laying out the ingredients for tonight's dinner. Her daughter calls through from the bedroom.

'Don't dae anything for me, Ma. Ah'm going oot early.'

'Huv you got a date, again?'

'Aye.'

'Same fella?'

'Aye.'

'Is that you and him going steady?'

'Sort of.'

'Diz he huv a name?'

There's a pause. 'Aye.'

'Is it a secret?'

'Naw. Of course it is'nae. He's, eh, called Dermot.'

'Huz he no' managed tae save up yet, and got himself a last name?'

There's another slight pause. 'Eh, Mulholland. Dermot Mulholland.'

'Mmm, sounds like a good Welsh lad!'

Katherine comes into the kitchen. She's put on a favourite dress. 'His faither's Irish. His mammy's Scottish. They're Catholic. Ah hope that's not a problem?'

Ella immediately bridles. 'Why the hell would Ah huv a problem wi' that? You're twenty-five years of age, Katherine. Huv you *ever* heard me, or your faither, run anybody doon because o' their religion. EH?' She clangs the aluminium pan she's holding onto the draining board. 'Whit a dumb thing tae say. Dae ye not know by now, yer faither and me urr'nae the least interested in aw' this sectarian shite. Never, ever huv been. Whit a stupid bloody lassie!'

Katherine tuts. 'Ah'm only asking, jist in case –'

'You should'nae huv tae. Ye know whit your da alwiz says if somebody asks him whit religion he is. "Ah'm Church o' Turkey!" he'll say. In other words – he's neither Catholic nor Protestant. He had so many good pals killed during the war, especially at Arnhem, that he lost whitever bit o' faith he mibbe had. You also know your da and me don't go tae church. Never huv. So if we don't bother aboot oor ain religion – why the hell wid we be interested in what somebody else is?' She gives her daughter another withering look.

Katherine goes into the lobby to fetch her coat, returns to the kitchen to put it on. Ella decides she might as well bring up another problem. 'Oh, and before ye go. Your brother is coming oot o' the jail next week. Thursday. He's determined that'll be his last time. He's made his mind up he's gonny go straight from now on.'

Katherine snorts. 'Aye. That'll be right!'

'He is. He really means it. And Ah'm gonny ask your faither if he'll let him back intae the hoose when he –'

'Aw, naw! Ah've got used tae him no' being here. Aw, Ma! Ah've had that room tae maself for years. It'll be awful having tae share it again.'

'Katherine, he's really determined tae stop getting intae trouble. The Probation Service have got him fixed up wi' a job. Jist you wait tae ye see the change in him. He's finally realised he's wasting his life, and it's time he did something aboot it. He's no' getting any younger, you know.'

Katherine gives a weak smile. 'It's your house. If Daddy lets him back in, and he behaves himself, well, we'll see how it goes. But if he falls back intae his auld ways, Ah hope you're no' gonny dae your usual covering-up for him.'

Ella shakes her head. 'If he gets intae bother, loses his job, anything like that – he'll be oot on his ear. Nae second chances. That's the deal. Well, Ah hope that's gonny be the deal.'

Katherine can hear the weariness in her mother's voice. Instantly regrets not being supportive. 'Does that mean you huv'nae asked Daddy yet?'

'Naw.' Tears come into Ella's eyes. 'Ah don't know whit Ah'll dae if he says "Naw". Ah don't think your brother will make it, unless he's back in the hoose.'

Katherine looks at her for a moment, then reaches

out, lays a hand on her forearm. 'You can tell Daddy, that Ah said Ah think he should let Archie back in. And Ma, as Ah'm going oot the night, there will jist be the two of you –'

Ella interrupts. 'Aye. Ah'd already intended tae talk tae him aboot it the night, hen.' She smiles. 'Why dae ye think he's getting steak, egg and chips fur his dinner – oan a Wednesday!'

'Right, Ah'm away, Ma. Ah'll see ye later on. Good luck.'

Two minutes later, Katherine Cameron is halfway down the stairs when she hears her father's tackety boots entering the close. They meet on the first of the half-landings.

'Hello, hen! You're oot early the night. Got a heavy date?'

'Aye.' She suddenly has an idea. Gives her father a kiss on the cheek.

'Oh! Whit huv Ah done tae deserve that, me darling?'

She looks straight at him. 'It's no' whit you've *done*, Daddy. It's whit you're *gonny* dae.'

'Eh?'

'Mammy's gonny ask ye something really important later on. Ah want ye tae know, that Ah agree wi' her. Okay? But also, Ah hope that you're gonny support her. That's aw' Ah can tell ye. Mammy will be laying the rest on ye. Cheerio.' He receives another kiss.

While he climbs the stairs Archie Cameron senior tries to work out what's going on. By the time he hits the top landing, he feels pretty certain he's figured it out.

* * *

As he enjoys his dinner, Archie is conscious of how nervous, on edge, Ella is.

'Dae ye want your tea topped up, Archie?'

'Please, hen.'

She places the teapot back on its cork mat. Sits down opposite him. Taking a sip of tea, she clears her throat. 'Eh, Archie, Ah want tae ask ye a big favour.'

'Mmmm, Ah thought ye might.'

She gives him a quizzical look. 'It's aboot oor Archie. He comes oot o' the jail next week . . .'

In a non-stop speech, lasting five minutes, Ella puts the case for allowing their son back into the house. Tries to impress on his father that Archie junior is genuine in his determination to 'go straight'. That he intends to leave his former ways – and friends – behind. And has the firm offer of a steady job, which he will be starting the day after his release. When she finishes her 'Case for the Defence' she lifts her mug and takes a deep draught of tea. With her heart in her mouth, she looks at her man. 'Whit dae ye think, Archie? Will ye let him back in the hoose? Please?'

'Aye. We'll gie him a chance.'

Ella is silent for a moment. 'You WILL! Oh, Archie . . .' She bursts into tears.

'Whit urr ye greeting fur? Ah've said "Aye" haven't Ah?'

'Ah expected ye tae say "Naw". That's jist wonderful.' She looks at her tough, no nonsense husband, feels love for him well up inside her. She rises to her feet, steps over to him, takes his face in both her hands and plants a lingering kiss on his lips. 'Thanks a million, Archie!'

'Aw, man! Ah've just hud ma dinner. And that wiz withoot the benefit o' anaesthetic!'

'Eee, yah cheeky bugger!'

Ella sits for a while, lost in thought, occasionally takes little looks at her husband. He's aware of this, but continues to sit at the table reading the *Evening Citizen*. He hears her draw a breath in, about to speak. Archie lets the broadsheet newspaper fall onto the table. 'Whit?'

'How come you gave in so easily, Archie?'

'Gawd! Can you no' take "Aye" for an answer?'

'You know whit Ah mean. It wiz you that put him oot o' the hoose in the first place. Ah did'nae expect you tae give him another chance so easily,' she shrugs, 'so Ah jist wondered – why?'

Archie looks at her. 'Well . . . He's not jist your son, ye know. He's ma son as well. So Ah don't mind giving him a last chance tae get a grip of himself. If it works oot, that'll be great. But if he falls back in wi' his auld crowd, gets intae trouble . . . It's Archie's turn to shrug. 'You'll no' be able tae put the blame on me, Ella. Ah'll have given him every chance. So if he finishes up back in the hands o' the polis, it'll be his own doing, hen. Not yours, not mine. Would you agree?'

Ella nods. 'Aye. That's being fair, Archie. But Ah think he's gonny surprise ye. In fact, Ah think he'll surprise himself. For this last year, every time Ah've visited him at the prison, that's aw' he's talked aboot. Getting oot, and making a go of it.'

Archie rises from the table. 'Right! That's enough aboot the boy. C'mon, Ella. We'll huv tae get a move on, get the table cleared and the dishes done. *Upstairs, Doonstairs* is coming oan shortly. Ye know Ah look forward tae ma weekly visit tae 165 Eaton Place.' He looks at her. 'Ah like a wee bit of drama in ma life noo and again.'

CHAPTER NINE

Great Minds Think Alike

It's just short of midnight on a Saturday. Ruby and Fred Dickinson are about to make a grand entrance into Le Bar Rendezvous. Well, Ruby is. Her timing is impeccable. She has persuaded Fred to linger between the inner and outer doors until the resident combo finishes the last of three foxtrots. She now sweet-talks him into waiting. 'Just another minute, darling, until the dance floor clears.'

Fred shakes his head. 'What a diva you are, Ruby Dickinson.'

She stands on tiptoe, kisses him on the lips while her Chanel No.5 stuns him. 'May I remind you, lovely husband, that it was the way I used to walk into Masonic dinners and Rotary Club dances that first made you want to steal me away from Bernard Baxter.'

He laughs. 'Ah! You are *so* right. But what if someone else fancies you – and tries to steal you away from me?'

He is kissed again. Her hand lingers on the back of his neck, just above his collar. 'They don't stand a chance. I didn't love Bernard. *You* I adore, Fred Dickinson.' She peeks through a gap in the doors. 'It's *just* clear. Right, darling. Every guy present is about to envy you. Avanti!'

Perfectly on cue, the double doors to the main room are thrust open and the Dickinsons – Ruby in the lead – take two steps into the club, halt, and let the Art Deco doors swish shut behind them. La Belle Ruby surveys tonight's audience. Knowing she has their attention, she keeps centre stage by striding diagonally across the empty dance floor. Fred, less theatrical, is content to walk round the perimeter.

Ruth Lockerbie, as ever, sits on her high stool at one end of the curved bar. She smiles as they approach, leans over towards Fred. 'Has she been watching *Casablanca* again?'

He casts his eyes heavenward. 'Got it in one! Ingrid Bergman and Paul Henreid entering Rick's Bar. I think we're safe enough in saying it's her all-time favourite scene, in any movie, in the history of the world – *ever*!' He kisses Ruth. 'Good evening, darling.'

'Ruby, how nice to see you!' The two women embrace, exchange greetings. Ruth leans back against the bar. 'In case you are thinking of going straight into scene two, darling, the piano player, on pain of death, has been instructed to refuse all requests for "As Time Goes By."'

Ruby shrugs. 'I don't want to worry you, darling, but

may I remind you that in the movie, Sam had also been told "Never to play that again!"' She smiles. 'He still finishes up playing it for Ilsa.'

'Touché!' says Ruth. 'Anyway, did you know that Vicky is in tonight?'

'Oh, good,' says Fred. 'Can't remember when we last seen her.'

'You're both looking very smart. Have you been at a function?' asks Ruth.

'We have indeed. A charity dinner at my Rotary Club was –' Fred stops speaking as Vicky Shaw returns to the bar. '*Vicky*! How wonderful! Ruth was just telling us you were in. Haven't seen you for an age.' He gives her a big hug and a kiss on each cheek. Ruby is also pleased to see her. 'Now I do hope this isn't just a rare night out. Tell me you're back socialising again?'

There's a pause in the conversation when Vicky's escort joins the group. She introduces him. 'Ruby and Fred. You haven't been at the club for a while, so you won't have, ah, met Steve.'

Ruth Lockerbie, from her viewpoint at the end of the bar, is well placed to observe Fred Dickinson's reaction to the newcomer. When Steve, unannounced, had walked over to join them, she'd seen Fred visibly stiffen. When Vicky introduced him as 'her friend' it was immediately clear to Ruth, that Fred was finding it difficult to be sociable. The smile on his face was so 'forced', she felt sure it must hurt. After seeing this reaction to Steve Anderson, Ruth has begun working out how to get Fred on his own. She wants to know why he doesn't like him. And she wants to know now – if not sooner!

Minutes later, George Lockerbie returns from a prolonged circuit of the room, socialising with regular customers while 'meeting and greeting' newcomers.

'Ah, George, darling. The next time Vicky is heading for the dance floor with Steve, will you immediately ask Ruby to dance? I want to be left alone with Fred for a few minutes. Haven't time to explain. Tell you all about it later.'

Less than ten minutes later conditions have been met. Vicky and Steve are dancing. George is leading Ruby onto the floor and Fred, ever the gentleman, proffers an arm to Ruth. 'We may as well join the others, dear heart. Trip the light what's-its-name –'

Ruth comes straight to the point. 'Not at the moment, Fred. There's something I want to ask you.' She nods in the direction of the dancers. 'We only have eight or nine minutes before they return.' She looks at him. 'It's six weeks or so since Vicky brought this Steve Anderson fellow into the club. Within *minutes* of meeting him, Rhea and I were in full agreement that he's a weasel. A nasty piece of work.' She gives him a questioning look.

'Hah! What good judges of character the pair of you are.' He gives a smile that is anything but. 'You can add me to your list, Ruth.'

'I thought so. Now, I'll tell you what I know of him, or I should say, what I've seen of him. I spotted him one evening getting on to her. She looked quite frightened. Cowed. Then,' she gives him a hard look, 'just a couple of weeks ago, in spite of attempts to cover it with makeup, Vicky came in with a bruise on her cheek.'

Fred's face tightens. 'Mmm, did she, now.'

'When he came over and joined the company tonight, it was easy to see you don't like him. I would like to know who I'm dealing with. And, more to the point, I want to know who Vicky has got herself entangled with.' She looks intently at Fred. 'I have no intention of letting my friend be used and abused by a jumped-up, second-hand car salesman. I'd like you to tell me what you know, Fred.'

'Ah! So, as we used to say in the RAF, you want "The Gen" on this Anderson fellow, do you? Well, he's not my type of chap at all. Tried to join my lodge a few months back. *Hah*! Feet never touched! Immediately blackballed. One of our members is also in the second-hand car trade. He let the committee know that Anderson is, mmm, to say the least, shady!' Fred takes a sip of beer. 'Okay, Ruth. What I'm about to tell you, darling, is what could probably be called, for want of a better word, *sub*-sub-judice! These are matters which have not yet been reported to the police. At the moment there are only two or three people in the car trade who know, or should I say strongly suspect, what Steve Anderson is up to.'

Ruth 'tunes in' to the band for a moment. 'We've got about two minutes 'til the dance ends.'

'Right! My friend, who is a dealer, recently took on a mechanic who used to work for Anderson. He told him that Anderson has been letting a certain gang, south of the river, borrow second-hand cars from his showrooms, put false plates on them, and use them for "one-off" robberies. *After* the job, they're driven straight back to the showroom, any scratches or bumps are repaired, and the cars are cleaned inside and out. Next morning, they're back on display with their original plates, in immaculate condition. Even if a witness has given the police a make of car and licence number, they are never going to find them. They don't exist. Anderson and the gang are convinced they're onto a good thing. At the moment, the few folk who do know what's going on aren't willing to go to the police – in case it's traced back to them. Anderson has been loaning these cars to a gangster on the south side, name of Bernie Bankes. He's in the papers now and again. They like to call him The Godfather. I think he's doing time at the moment. So there you are. You must keep schtum, darling.'

Ruth reaches behind the bar for the tin of Black Sobranie. Extracts one. 'How interesting, Fred. So, I now know that Vicky is not only mixed up with a nasty piece of work, but he's also a crook.' The Sobranie is fixed into the tortoiseshell holder. She reaches for her lighter, sparks it into life. The smoke curls out of her mouth and makes for the ceiling. 'He'll have to go, Fred. Johnny McKinnon would expect me to take care of Vicky.'

As the dancers return from the floor, Fred turns towards them, ready to greet Ruby. Ruth sits alone for a moment. Takes a contemplative draw on her cigarette. Watches Anderson as he escorts Vicky back to the group. You think you're a clever little chap, don't you? And I now know quite a bit about you – but you don't know about me. Mmm, what is that saying? It comes to her. Yes. Knowledge is Power!

CHAPTER TEN

Withdrawal Symptoms

An early morning in August 1971. Now and again a Corporation bus makes its way up, or down, the Maryhill Road. The reverberations from their engines roll along a quiet Dalbeattie Street when they pass its 'T' junction with the main road. There are fewer residents left to hear them nowadays. The small tenement block on the left, as you enter the street, has been empty of tenants for months. Lily's fruit shop is still open for business. The first tenement on the right has lost a quarter of its residents. Number 18, which is part of this block, is less badly affected. Two of its single-ends have been empty for more than a year. Irma and Bert Armstrong's single-end was vacated four months ago, when they flitted to the Molendinar. Because it was situated in the close, it has been boarded-up to stop kids gaining access and using it as a den. The other nine flats are still occupied. For the moment.

The sun eventually climbs above the rooftop of the evacuated tenement and shines across the street onto the front of the block containing Number 18. It blazes into the bedroom of Agnes Dalrymple's flat where, alas, it goes to waste. She lies on the shady side of the building, tucked up in the recess bed in her dark, north-facing kitchen. The heavy, bedside curtains are pulled, as are the blinds on the windows. As no sun ever falls on this side of the building, her kitchen is as dark as though it were dead of night.

It has gone six-thirty – her usual rising time – before Agnes stirs. Slipping a hand between the heavy drapes, she reaches for the alarm clock on the table, brings it into bed and holds it under the covers. Courtesy of its luminous hands she finds out what time it is. 'Awww! It's time tae get up for ma work.' She turns onto her back, soon begins to doze. She opens her eyes. 'Naw, it isn't. Ah'm on a week's holiday. Ohhh, lovely!' She turns round and coories in.

An hour later she's again dragged from a sound sleep, this time by a crash and some vibration. She ignores it. Next, it's by a small avalanche. 'Awww, that's them buggers started!' Minutes later, aided and abetted by the darkness of the recess bed, she dozes off yet again.

The bang of the irresistible wrecker's ball assaulting another wall, jars her awake. 'Jeez! That's awfy loud. Sounds like it's coming fae Cheviot Street!' She lies still, waits for the next one. Is reminded of the nights she used to lie and listen for the last tram. She looks at the curtains which shut her off from her kitchen. From the world. The bright morning is determined to intrude. Light is forcing its way in past the window blinds and filtering through chinks in her bedside curtains. She's now fully awake, but doesn't feel like getting up. You're on your hollybags, Agnes. Can huv a wee long-lie if ye want. She stares at a long sliver of light where the curtains don't meet. Her thoughts meander. This is another thing Ah'm gonny miss. Ye cannae beat a recess bed oan a winter's night. Cosiest place in the world. She sighs heavily. Especially oan the nights when Ah could listen tae the late-night trams going up and doon the Maryhill Road. Her eyes fill with tears. Oh! Yon wiz the loveliest sound. Wheels singing 'til they filled the night. She dabs her eyes on the edge of the sheet. That's nearly ten years ago. Memories of the last tram still intrude. She smiles. Though it wiz a rare event for me tae hear the last o' it. It would hardly get as far as Queen's Cross, before Ah'd be sound.

There is now enough light gaining forced entry past the bedside curtains for her to see the three walls which surround her and give this type of bed its name. Ah've slept in a recess bed maist o' my life. They don't build new hooses wi' recess beds. How will Ah ever get tae sleep, lying in a bed in an open room? Jeez! Where's the cosiness in that? On a winter's morn, when the fire's oot and the kitchen's cauld, these curtains make it ten degrees warmer in this wee nook. And think of aw' the kids who'll grow up, and never know a recess bed. She sighs for them. Poor sowels! Agnes leans up on her elbow, pulls one of the curtains to the side. Dearie me! Ten tae ten. Och! Ah might as well enjoy it. God knows where Ah'll be this time next year. Livin' oan the Molendinar Housing Scheme. Huh! Ah'd be happy tae bide here if they'd jist leave me alone. They could keep their new hoose!

On the landing below, Alec and Irene Stuart sit at their kitchen table, both in dressing gowns. Second cups of tea have been poured. The topic of conversation is also the encroaching noise of the wrecker's ball.

'That was definitely louder this morning, Irene. When I go for the paper, I'll have a wee look along Cheviot Street. They're maybe gonny leave the rest o' Rothesay Street for the time being. Make a start on Cheviot.'

'Aye. But they might start on Dalbeattie.' She pauses. 'That would mean it'll be sooner, rather than later, when we get oor eviction notice and have tae move. Dae ye think so?'

'Well, if we do, moving into a brand-new house will give us something tae look forward tae. The thing is, we've got an option, Irene. If we take tae living in a housing scheme, well, that'll be fine. But if we don't like it,' Alec opens his arms, 'we can afford to come back into the city and rent something. We might even be lucky enough to get an "exchange" with somebody in Maryhill, or maybe North Kelvinside. I've heard there are folk exchanging all the time.' He taps the table with a finger. 'But we will only be interested if it's a flat with its own toilet, Irene. That is a *must*! I do not fancy having to get used to sharing a toilet with new neighbours. Folks we don't know. Humph! Not at oor age!'

'Oh, Alec! Ah could'nae.' She tries to keep her face straight. 'Ah'm too auld tae huv tae get used tae new bums.' She giggles. 'Better the bums ye know than the bums ye don't know!'

He shakes his head, hides a smile. 'You are getting tae be so common lately. The day is not far removed, Irene Stuart, when I'll not be able to take you anywhere!'

'Oh! Well, as it so happens, Alec, Ah'll tell you where you *can* take me. Doon tae the Blythswood tonight.'

'What's on, dear?'

'Ah don't know.'

He shakes his head. 'So how do you know you want tae go?'

'Ah was talking to Frank Galloway. He was telling me, by next year it'll no longer be a cinema. It's going over tae full-time bingo! So Ah think we should go while we have the chance.'

'Oh, my God! The wee Blythsie. Is nothing sacred?'

Irene starts filling the kettle, about to wash the dishes. 'Once they stop showing films, that means our nearest cinema will be the Rio at Canniesburn Toll. Otherwise, we'll have tae start going doon the toon tae the pictures.' She begins clearing the table. 'My, but we've spent many a happy night at the Blythswood, haven't we?'

Alec has been lost in thought. 'Aye, it'll be a miss. I've always found it the cosiest wee hall. It's because it doesn't have a balcony. Makes it feel snug.'

'Dae ye remember the community singing during the war?'

'I do indeed.' He looks at Irene. Smiles.

'Ah wonder how many times you and I were in there, Alec, sitting quite near tae one another? Yet we never knew.'

'Ah! If I'd spotted you, you'd have known all right. Ah'd have sat beside ye and rubbed my leg up against yours. Played kneesy with ye.'

'So it wiz you, wiz it? Dirty devil! Ah very near sent for the polis that night!'

He shrugs. 'And now its days are numbered as a cinema. That's sad.'

Irene leans against the sink, a faraway look in her eyes. 'It is.' After a moment, she straightens up, inclines her head in the direction of their television set. 'Now, Ah know we enjoy oor telly, Alec, but when you think of aw' the picture hooses that have closed this last few years,' she points at it, 'that's got a lot tae answer for, hasn't it?'

He looks at their 21-inch, black and white television. Laughs. 'Hah! Funnily enough, I intended to say to you last night, but it slipped my mind, that I was looking in Curry's window, yesterday. They've got a sale on at the minute. The "Star Buy" is a 28-inch, 625 line *colour* set. Hey! The picture would knock your eyes out, Irene. Just over a hundred pounds. I don't half fancy changing to colour. This is a bigger screen, sharper picture – and colour! What do ye think?'

Her eyes light up. 'At the risk o' sounding like a

hypocrite – if we stick with our auld black and white Baird, will it stop the Blythsie, or any other cinema, from closing?'

'Not a one!'

'Mmm! If this is Curry's half-day, we'll have to hurry.'

He laughs. 'I'll give you a hand wi' the dishes, hen. We'll get down there all the quicker!'

CHAPTER ELEVEN

Great Day in the Morning!

The train slows as it nears the city centre. Archie Cameron junior feels certain he has left a trail of butterflies all the way back to the city boundary. After three years Ah'm back in Glesga! From elevated stretches of track, he now and again gets good views of various tenements. Most of them red-sandstone, some honey-coloured. Many still have the railings in their back courts intact. And swards of grass. Jeez! Proper back greens. Ah wonder what districts those were? But that was ten minutes ago. They are deeper into the city now. The tenements grimy and smoke-blackened. He's momentarily startled when the daylight suddenly vanishes. Then he realises they are running under the Central Station's vast canopy. He reaches into a pocket for his probation officer's letter. '. . . if you wait in front of WH Smith's kiosk, Archie, I'll be there around one-thirty. Best Regards. Everard Carson.' He smiles. Judges, barristers and probation officers alwiz seem tae huv names like that. He glances at his watch. Just efter one. Ah'll have a wee wander roon' the main hall thingmy . . . Concourse! Aye, that's it.

Carrying the plastic carrier bag he was given upon discharge this morning, he steps onto the platform, mingles with the flood of folk heading for the gate. He feels strange, isolated amongst them. Ah'm only used tae walking in twos, roon' and roon' an exercise yard. He feels certain he must have 'ex-con' written all over him – then tells himself that's bloody nonsense. He looks at those walking in front. Men, women, kids. All ages, different styles of dress. Probably no' even giving me a second-look. The feeling persists.

It's twenty past one when he walks over to WH Smith's. Starts looking at the magazines.

'Hello, Archie! I'm a wee bitty early.' As he turns, the probation officer's proffered hand is waiting for him.

'Oh! Hello, Mr Carson.' They shake.

'We'll go and have a tea or coffee in the refreshment rooms, shall we?'

'Aye. And Ah'll get maself something tae eat. Ah'm clamming.' Archie gives a sheepish grin. 'Ah was so excited this morning, Ah could'nae eat ma breakfast. Jist drank the tea. Ah've had nothing since supper last night.'

'Poor soul! Soon get you sorted out.'

They face each other across a Formica table. Everard Carson leans on his leather elbow patches, a cup of Earl Grey and an Empire biscuit in front of him. Minutes later, two egg and bacon rolls are placed in front of Archie.

'Oh, boy! Ah'm ready for these.'

'I was speaking with Mrs Kinnaird yesterday. Nice woman. Very helpful. Do you know her?'

'Ah used tae go into the greengrocer's wi' my ma, when Ah was a kid. Ah know her tae see. Don't think she'll remember me.'

'Mmmm. She knows about you, of course. There are two young women working in the shop. As far as they will be aware, you will simply be the new van driver. They don't know anything else about you.'

'Oh, that's good. Less embarrassing.'

The probation officer reaches into his briefcase, hands Archie a long brown envelope. That's the dates when I expect you to come down to the office to see me – and one or two other bits of information. I believe everything is arranged for you to live back at your parents'?'

'Aye, it is, thank goodness. My da says it's okay. Trouble is, I haven't seen him for years. Ma was the only one who ever visited me. My sister Katherine never came either.' He blushes. 'So, tonight might be a bit sticky when we aw' get the gither. Don't suppose anybody will know whit tae say. But it has tae be done.'

Carson looks him in the eye. 'You do realise, Archie, your mother and I do believe you when you tell us you're giving it up. Moving on with your life. If you let us down, fall back in with your old pals and your old ways . . .' He shrugs his shoulders. 'I can tell you now, you'll certainly break your mother's heart. She really has taken you at your word.'

'Ah know you hear it aw' the time, Mr Carson. And Ah used tae hear it on a daily basis when Ah wiz inside. But you don't know how heart-sick I am of daeing time. Wasting ma life. And Ah do know what it's daeing to my ma. The aulder she gets, the more it's gettin' her down. She's in her fifties now. Still a hard-working wumman. She deserves better than a toerag like me!' He sips his tea, swallows hard. 'It's, eh, a bit difficult for me to tell you this next bit, Mr Carson.' He clears his throat. 'Ah was lying in ma cell one night. About a year ago. When Ah suddenly thought – what if my ma wiz tae die while Ah'm daeing time. She'd die knowing her son is in the jail.' His probation officer can hear, almost feel, the emotion welling up in his voice. 'And it did'nae half hit me between the eyes. If that had happened while Ah was doing this sentence, Ah would never huv forgiven maself. Ah'm gonny go straight for my ma *and* for me!'

'Well said, Archie. The couple of times I've met her, I've always been impressed with your mother. She's a strong woman,' he leans forward, 'but you're her weak point. When you're in jail she worries about you all the time. It just wears her down!' Archie nods his head. 'Hah! Even when Ah'm oot, the poor soul worries aw' the time. What am Ah' doing? Who am Ah running aboot wi'? Will Ah get intae trouble wi' the polis again.'

It's ten minutes later. Carson sits back. 'Right, would you like a lift up to Dalbeattie Street?'

'Thanks aw' the same, but it would'nae dae any good. They're aw' at work. It'll be gone five before my ma comes hame. She's usually the first in.' They rise from the table. 'Ah'll tell ye what Ah fancy doing. Been dreaming about it for weeks. Ah'm gonny *walk* all the way up tae Maryhill. And when Ah pass Kinnaird's, Ah'm gonny wander intae the shop and introduce maself tae Mrs Kinnaird.'

'That'll be good. I imagine you'll enjoy that. Now don't forget, the two girls who work for her aren't aware you're newly out of prison. They'll probably find out in time. But at the moment, it might be best to let sleeping dogs lie.' He sticks his hand out. 'Good luck, Archie.'

'Thanks, Mr Carson. Oh! And thanks for the late breakfast. Ah fair enjoyed them rolls.'

Archie Cameron junior exits New City Road, safely crosses the large junction that is St George's Cross, and stops for a moment at the start of the Maryhill Road. The butterflies take off in formation, feel as if they've done a loop. He smiles. Ah'm hame!

Twenty minutes later he stands a few yards away from Kinnaird's, greengrocer's and florist. He looks at his watch; twenty past three. For the next few minutes he keeps an eye on the 'ins and outs' of customers, until he judges the shop should be empty. Except for staff. C'mon, Archie. Get it done! He enters the cool, shadowy shop. The smell of vegetables and fruit immediately takes him back . . . He's hanging onto Ma's hand as they enter the exotic shadowy premises . . .

Mrs Kinnaird is behind the counter on the right. She always is. He glances round the rest of the premises. No one to be seen. As if on cue he hears girls' raised voices, followed by laughter. Great! They're in the back shop. He turns back towards the counter. 'Eh, Mrs Kinnaird. I've just come in tae say, "Hello". Ah'm Archie Cameron. Ah'm starting tomorrow as your new driver.' As he speaks, he notices she still wears the same type of overall she wore all those years ago – a green, wrap-a-round one, like the dinner-ladies at the school.

'Oh, aye. Hello, son.' She looks him in the eye. 'Now, you're no' gonny be letting me down, are you?' He can't help smiling. 'Ah've nae intention of letting you doon, Mrs Kinnaird. Neither you or my ma. You can believe me.'

She continues to stand, four-square, looking into his face for a moment longer. 'That's whit Ah want tae hear, son. But time will tell, won't it?'

He nods. 'It certainly will.' Jeez! She could be my ma's aulder sister. Talk about two peas in a pod. He almost laughs out loud. Ah think my granda must have had a bike! Funny how Ah never noticed the likeness before. 'Eh, Mrs Kinnaird, Ah cannae get intae the hoose until ma ma and da come hame fae their work – jist after five. So would ye mind if Ah hang aboot, get the feel o' the place. Oh, and if there are any wee jobs tae do – bringing the stuff in fae the display ootside, sweeping up, Ah'll be quite happy tae muck in.'

She leans over the counter, keeps her voice low. 'Did ye just come oot this morning? It wiz Stirling ye were in, wizn't it?'

'That's an "Aye" tae both questions, Mrs Kinnaird.'

'Mmm! Well, you might as well meet the girls. They don't know aboot ye. Yet! LEXIE! JEAN! Come and meet oor new driver.'

There's a shriek of laughter which subsides before they make their entrance. The first one to appear looks to be in her mid-forties. She steps to the side, and, as though choreographed, a dark-headed girl is revealed. Archie, just in time, stops his mouth from falling open. Although he is newly-discharged from prison, and therefore every girl under thirty-five who has crossed his path today has been delectable, it is impossible for him to take his eyes off her. Even before Mrs Kinnaird does the introductions, he knows she will be Lexie. No way will she have an ordinary name. The Boss is brief . . . 'Lexie, Jean, meet Archie Cameron.' There are smiles and nods. A 'Hi-yah' from Lexie.

'Jean has been with me nearly fifteen years. Lexie does the flowers for me, and helps behind the counter when needed.'

Lexie Forsyth looks at him. 'Where have ye been working before ye came here?' She catches him on the hop.

'Eh, Ah wiz driving for the government. Sort of, eh, a civil servant.'

She narrows her eyes. 'Is that right. Anywye,' she turns to Jean, 'C'mon, we'll get finished up in the back.'

The next hour and a half passes quickly. At a couple of minutes to five the girls get their coats on, say their 'Cheerios' and depart. Archie has a few more words with Mrs Kinnaird before he leaves. As he walks up the Maryhill

Road, he starts thinking about the imminent meetings with his da and Katherine. It's years since Ah last seen them. It's gonny be really strange. Thoughts about the forthcoming meeting are put to the back of his mind when he notices that the girl, Lexie, is walking ahead of him. For a moment, he thinks about catching up with her – but decides against it. He contents himself by watching her stride up the road. Ah hope her and I get on well. Would'nae mind asking her out. She really is something, that yin. No wedding ring!

They aren't too far away from Dalbeattie Street when she pauses to look in a shop window – and catches sight of him. She looks hard at him, narrows her eyes, then sets off again. A moment later she turns left into Dalbeattie Street, then immediately crosses diagonally.

Archie is surprised when she turns into 'his' street. Even more so when she heads, unerringly, towards Number 18. She turns her head, sees he is still behind her. She halts on the pavement a few feet from the close, turns to face him, hands on hips. 'You huv got tae be joking, pal!'

Archie has been finding the situation amusing – until he realises how it must look to her. He feels his face flush. 'Believe it or not, Ah live up here.'

'Oh, ye do, do ye. So how come Ah've never seen ye coming in and oot?'

'Ah, because Ah've been working away.' As he says it, he knows it must sound so phoney.

'Whit landing dae ye live on?'

'The top storey.'

She actually snorts. 'Bad choice, sunshine. *Ah* live on the top storey – and Ah've never clapped eyes on you before today!'

'Dae ye know Ella and Archie Cameron?'

'Aye. Ah do.'

'Well, that's my ma and da. And Katherine's my sister. Ah'm Archie Cameron junior.' He watches as she assimilates this information. Then . . .

'Awww! Of course. You're the wan that's been in the jail aren't ye? *Huh*! You've been working away, aw'right.'

Archie feels himself flush with embarrassment, then break out in a cold sweat. He tries desperately to think of some clever reply. Spreads his arms wide, tries to speak. But nothing comes. He lets his hands fall dejectedly to his sides. Wonders if it's possible to die from embarrassment.

This act, so obviously a sign that he is lost for words, touches Lexie Forsyth. She looks at him. 'Aw'right, then. Ah'll believe ye. Cummon!' Side by side, in silence, they climb the six flights of stairs to the top storey. Archie, just out of jail, is dizzy from the smell and presence of her.

It's an hour later. Ella Cameron, her heart full, busies herself making her son's favourite dinner – a suet, steak and kidney pudding and home-made chips. He sits at the table. His ma has never stopped talking since he came through the door. Not that he's complaining. He just has to remind himself where he ate his dinner last night *and* who his dinner companions were. Now and again, when his ma has her back to him, he glances around the kitchen. It looks the same as always. How long is it since Ah was last in here? Three years in the jail. And two years before that when ma faither gave me ma marching orders. Five years. He looks at the time. No' be long 'til ma faither's coming through that door. There's another stab of nerves in his stomach. 'My da's definitely aw'right aboot letting me back in the hoose, is he?'

'Aye.' Ella half-turns from where she stands at the cooker. 'Ah telt ye. Ah thought he'd have gave me an argument. Not a bit of it. Said "Aye" right away. Nae hesitation.' She turns the gas down under the chip pan; too early to put them in. 'But mind, son. That's so as Ah cannae blame him for not giving ye a chance.'

He gives a rueful laugh. 'Oh, Ah know that . . .' He pauses as they both hear noise, movement from the outside landing. Ella looks at the clock. 'This'll be yer sister. She's alwiz in aboot this time.' The outside door opens, footsteps . . . 'It's jist me, Ma!'

Archie sits looking at the kitchen door, can hear her taking her coat off, other movements. At last the door opens. Katherine enters. Stops, looks at her brother, turns to her ma, smiles. 'Ah see Dillinger's hame!'

Archie laughs. 'Well, Ah'll tell ye what, Katherine. Since Ah last seen ye, you've no' half turned intae a bonnie lassie. And stylish with it.'

'Hasn't she?' says Ella. She feels a glow. For the first time in years her two kids are together in the same room.

'Ah'd like tae return the compliment,' says Katherine,

'but you are'nae looking very well at all, Archie. That three years in the clink have'nae done ye much good.'

'Oh, Katherine! Dae ye huv tae say things like tha –'

Archie interrupts his mother. 'You're dead right, Katherine. This sentence really got me doon. Ah sometimes used tae feel it wiz never gonny end. Which is why Ah'm going straight, like an arrow, from today onwards. Ah jist can't hack-it any mair. Don't mind admitting it.'

'Huh! Well that's no' a bad thing,' says Ella. She seems as if about to say more, but instead holds a hand up, cocks her head to one side. 'Here's yer faither!'

A treble spasm of nerves, maybe more, hooks Archie junior in the solar plexus.

As the Cantata for Tackety Boots approaches the landing, all three fall silent. The outside door opens, Archie junior hears, once more, the everyday noises from the lobby which always marked his father's return from work. He thought he'd forgotten them. As the kitchen door opens, a final stab of nerves – like a stiletto – pins him to the chair.

'Ah! So therr ye are!' Archie Cameron looks at his son, then at his wife and daughter. 'It's a while since we wur aw' in the wan room, in't it?'

'Ah think it's nice,' says Ella. 'Don't care whit anybody else says!' She draws herself up.

'Ah never said it wiz'nae, Ella.' He nods his head in the direction of Archie junior. 'Ah'm never ower happy when he's in the jail.' He shrugs. 'But every time he *has* landed in the clink, it's alwiz been his ain fault. Naebody else's.' He pulls a kitchen chair out from under the table. 'Anywye.

Let's get oor dinner.' He turns to Archie. 'And afterwards, Ah'll take ye up tae the Thistle fur a pint. Jist you and me.' He looks at Ella. 'So as we can huv a wee bit of a talk aboot, ohhh, whit should we call it? Rules and Regulations on being back in the hoose?'

His son smiles. 'Aye, that's fair enough, Da.'

Dinner has finished up being a fairly relaxed affair. Archie senior is now having, as he calls it, 'a good slunge in the sink'. Ella has gone down to Drena's – no doubt to give her a progress report. Brother and sister sit at the table. Archie junior leans forward. 'Hey, whit a laugh it wiz this efterninn, Katherine. Ah went intae Kinnaird's tae introduce maself. And Ah also met the two lassies that work in the shop –'

Katherine jumps in, points in the direction of the landing. 'Aw! Lexie works there, dizn't she?'

'Aye. That was the laugh. Ah was walkin' hame behind her. She thought Ah wiz following her. She turned roon' ready tae gie me a right sherrackin in the middle o' the street.'

'Oh! She wid soon dae that, Lexie.'

Archie drops his voice. 'Ah'll tell ye what, Katherine. Ah think she's a right knock-out. When Ah get tae know her a bit better Ah'm gonny ask her oot.'

Katherine chokes on a mouthful of tea. There's a splutter, followed by a bout of coughing. 'You huv *nae* chance, pal. Lexie Forsyth? She would'nae gie you a nod in the desert!'

Their father has been drying himself. He stops in the middle of towelling under an arm. Looks at his son. 'Ah've only spoke tae the lassie a few times, but Ah think you're raising your sights a bit high therr. Ah cannae see her being interested in somebody that's done time. No way!'

Archie junior recalls that first sight of her this afternoon. Looks up. 'There's nae harm in trying.'

CHAPTER TWELVE

Smoke Gets in Your Eyes

The Number 61 bus sits at its 'turn-around' point in Uddingston. Though the late September evening doesn't yet show any signs of dusk, the Leyland 'Titan' has all its lights ablaze. Now and again a breeze rearranges the pattern of brown and yellow leaves lying on road and pavement. Frank Galloway looks at his watch. 'Och, plenty time yet, Wilma.' He fetches a pack of Senior Service from inside his uniform jacket. She watches him go through his routine – vigorously tamping the cigarette against the box to firm up the tobacco at one end.

'Huv ye ever bent wan o' them?' She hides a smile.

'Never! It's an art, this.'

Wilma sniffs. She waits until the first curl of blue smoke rises into the air. 'Eh, 'scuse me. Thurr's nae smoking doonsterrs! Put that oot or you're aff!'

Her husband blows a perfect smoke ring. 'It's ma bus.

And can Ah also point oot, if ye put me aff – there's naebody tae drive.'

'Ah alwiz forget aboot that.' She lifts the large flask. 'There's still coffee in here. Ye want a refill?'

'Go on, hen.' They sit at either end of the three-seater bench seat, half-facing one another.

'This is oor weekend off coming up, Wilma. Do ye want tae dae the usual? Stromboli's for dinner then away for a wee jig at Le Rendezvous?'

She smiles. 'Might as well. We've never found anywhere better. Oh! Ah must remember tae call intae Rhea's. Find oot if her and Robert are going. She's alwiz a scream when she gets a wee drink doon her.'

Frank draws on his cigarette. 'Ah wish Vicky would pack in that Steve Anderson fella. Every time he comes intae the company he puts a damper oan it.'

'He diz'nae half. Huv ye noticed, Ruth never invites anybody back tae the flat on the nights he's in. She diz'nae want tae hurt Vicky's feelings by saying he's no' welcome. So naebody gets asked. Ruth cannae stand him.'

'Ah'll tell ye who else has nae time for him –'

She beats him to the punch. 'Fred Dickinson!'

'You've noticed have ye?'

'*Whit*! A blin' man could see it. Fred can hardly bring himself tae be civil tae the wee nyaff!'

'Sounds like you're no' ower fond of him yersel'.'

'Rhea says that Ruth is convinced he's no' treating Vicky right.'

'Aye, it's a pity she lost Johnny McKinnon.' He thinks

for a moment. 'Must be two years since he went.' He pauses again. 'Ah really liked Johnny. He was what Ah call a man's man.'

'Oh, he wiz wonderful,' says Wilma. 'Made you feel like a million dollars every time ye met him. Ruth took it very badly when he died. They had been friends for years, seemingly.'

'Ruth and him go way back tae the late forties. She used tae manage the Bar Deco on the Byres Road, near the subway. And as ye know, Johnny was further along, at the Hillhead Bar.'

She smiles. 'Dae ye know who he alwiz reminded me of?' She goes straight to the answer. 'Jack Carson, the American actor. Remember? He wiz in *Mildred Pierce* wi' Joan Crawford.'

Frank looks at her. 'Now you mention it. He wiz'nae half. He was exactly the stamp of him. Big stocky guy. Brylcreemed hair combed straight back, always in a double-breasted suit. You're right, hen. Even his manner was the same. Don't know why Ah never made the connection.' Frank sips his coffee, takes a contemplative draw on his cigarette. Wilma knows something is coming. 'If ye hud tae make a link between me and a star of the silver screen, hen, who wid it be?' She stares hard at him. Her face straight, lips pursed. Thinking.

Frank puts on his best 'matinee idol' persona. 'It should'nae be difficult, hen.' He rolls his shoulders, spreads his arms wide. 'Dare Ah suggest, eh, Rex Harrison?'

She snorts. 'Mair like Kathleen!'

'Whit a bad wee bitch you are! That's the thanks Ah get fur rescuing ye from your mother!'

Wilma nods towards the front of the bus. Frank turns just as an oncoming Number 61 flashes them. He rises. 'Time tae go, hen. Still, it's the last run o' the shift.' As Wilma refills the small ex-army pack with their piece-time stuff, Frank swings himself off the platform, taking a last draw on the cigarette. As he walks along the side of the bus towards the driver's cab, he flicks the fag end into the middle of the road, watches it throw off a shower of sparks as it lands. A minute later, comfortably seated in the cab, he presses the starter. As the engine fires with its usual healthy roar, Frank smiles, then engages gear. He glances into his mirror just before he pulls away, and the red glow of the cigarette end takes his eye in the lowering dusk.

A few days later. Late afternoon. Mary Stewart looks at the 'wag-at-the-wa' clock hanging to the right of the chimney breast; its little pendulum as busy as a fiddler's elbow. 'Mmmm?' Now, it's ten minutes fast. So it's really jist quarter past four. Should'nae be long 'til them devils stop for the day. She gets back to the story in the *People's Friend*. There's a distant thump – followed by a terrific crash. She feels the vibration through her feet. My God! Is there nae end tae it? They're getting nearer and nearer. Ah wish Robert and Rhea wid get the chance of a flat along Wilton Street. She sits back, gives herself up to daydreaming on how lovely it'll be living up a wally close. Soon, the pictures in her mind lull her to sleep.

The workmen round the corner in Cheviot Street finish for the day. When they switch off the heavy plant, a dusty peace falls over the area. In the silence, Mary Stewart drifts into a deeper sleep.

She doesn't hear the first two knocks. The third one does the trick. As she hurries to answer it she glances at the clock. 'Eeee! Ten past five.' She opens her front door.

'Ah wiz beginning tae think ye'd snuffed it!'

'Oh, in ye come, Agnes. Ah'll tell ye, Ah've just had the loveliest wee sleep. Best part of an hour. Once they demolisher fellas stop for the day, Ah'm oot like a light – wi' exhaustion! Ah'm so fed up wi' the noise o' them. Day efter day. Never stops.'

'Aye, thank goodness Ah'm at work six days a week. Hardly ever hear it.'

'And it's even worse, now they're at this end o' Cheviot Street. They make mair noise than the Germans ever did. Huv me demented soon, so they will. Anyway . . .' She points to what used to be her man's fireside chair, 'Sit yerself doon, Agnes. No' take long tae make a pot o' tea.'

'Ah'm jist ready for wan. Been run aff oor feet doon the City Bakeries the day. Nae let up.' Agnes gives a grunt as she reaches down for her message bag, lifts it onto her knees. 'Ah know you're partial tae a custard tart – not tae mention the occasional fern cake.' With the concentration, and dexterity, of a bomb disposal expert, Agnes Dalrymple withdraws two paper bags from her voluminous message bag. Lays them on the table.

Mary regards them. 'Eee, Agnes. Don't know what Ah'd

dae withoot ye. It's like living up the same close as Miss Cranston – high tea every night!'

'Ach, well. Diz ye good tae have a wee bit pleasure noo' and again.'

Freshly poured tea steams in the cups. Two cake stands have been produced and the newly revealed goodies placed on them. 'Jist a minute!' Mary opens a sideboard drawer and her hand emerges with two linen napkins. She lays one on each of their tea plates. 'Only the best, hen. We'll dae it in style.'

As Agnes raises her cup, she looks along the length of Mary's tiled fireplace. Her eyes widen. 'That match-striker. Wiz that what you took as your keepsake from Granny's?'

'It was.' Mary reaches for it, passes it to her visitor.

Agnes regards the small piece of yellow china. The rectangular section in the middle contains a few, now pale, red-tipped matches. On each of its sides it carries the four emblems found on a pack of playing cards. On its base is a ridged area for striking the matches. 'It's a nice wee thing, in't it?'

'Aye. These neat little ones were meant for card tables. Save people searching for a light when they were playing whist, or whatever.'

'Ah remember when pubs used tae have one or two match-strikers placed on the bar,' says Agnes, 'for the convenience o' their customers. Pub ones were big. Held lots o' matches.'

'Aye, Ah cannot remember the last time Ah seen one.

Folk either have their own lighter, or carry a box of matches.' Mary sighs. 'When ye think about it, it's no' that long ago since it was an everyday sight tae see somebody stopping somebody in the street, tapping them for a light. Remember? The wan who was smoking would hold the tip of his cigarette up, let the other yin take a light.'

'Eeee, God! You're right. Ah'd forgot aboot that. It jist shows how hard-up we were back then. Many folk could'nae afford tae buy fags *and* a box o' matches.' Agnes gives the subject some more thought. 'Dae ye also remember, Mary, for quite a few years efter the war – when tobacco wiz in short supply – some o' the newsagents and tobacconists would sell ye a single fag and two matches, if ye could'nae afford tae buy a five-packet!'

Mary shakes her head. 'Ah know. And that was after we'd jist *won* a war. Jesus-johnny! It's a bloody good job we never lost the bugger!' She bristles for a moment. 'Aye, when the war's on, they tell the men it's gonny be a "Land fit for heroes" when they come home. *Huh*!'

Agnes looks again at the match-striker. 'Them matches huv gone awfy pale, Mary.'

'They are the matches that were in it, the day Ah took it doon from Granny's mantelpiece. How long ago is that? Nine years?'

'Aye, it'll be that.' Agnes touches the heads of the matches with a finger. 'It's nice tae think that Granny put them in there, in't it?'

'It is. That's why Ah left them. It's a link wi' her. There's hardly a day goes by when it dis'nae catch ma eye. And jist for a wee second she comes intae ma mind.'

'Ah'm exactly the same,' says Agnes. 'Ah took her wally dugs if ye remember. And jist like ye say, whenever they take ma eye Ah gie her a wee thought.'

'But Ah'll tell you. If she's looking doon, she'll no' be ower pleased at the state o' Dalbeattie Street at the minute. Dust and muck aw' ower the place, and the Corporation no' bothered aboot sending the roadsweepers roon.'

Agnes is still lost in nostalgia. 'Whit wiz it Rhea took as a keepsake?'

'She took yon wee round tin that held tapers, for taking a light off the fire. Granny used them when she wanted tae light the gas. Save a match. And she also took the auld black kettle.'

'Aye, that's right.' Agnes thinks for a moment. 'And that's what we were talking aboot earlier. That's what tapers were for – tae save matches! And after you'd used it tae light the oven, or a gas mantle, you blew the taper oot. You could use them quite a few times until they eventually burnt doon and were too small.'

'You hardly see them now. Folk always have a box of matches nowadays.' Mary reaches for the teapot, begins to refill their cups. 'Ah suppose, in a way, it's a sign we're better off than we used tae be. You don't see men tapping yin another for a light in the street, and Ah cannae remember the last time Ah wiz in somebody's hoose and they had a box o' tapers lying in the hearth.'

Agnes sniffs. 'Aye, we're fair rolling in matches so we urr.' She tries to keep her face straight. 'Ah'm jist thinking, Mary. Ah wish Ah'd bought some shares in Bryant and May when Ah hud the chance!'

CHAPTER THIRTEEN

A Lack of Respect

Ella Cameron glances towards the mantelpiece. 'Twenty to eight. Time Ah wiz'nae here.' She takes a last mouthful of tea, turns the radio off, puts on her work-a-day coat, grabs her bag. Hurrying over to the sink she places the cup under the tap, fills it with cold water. As she turns away her eyes take in the cooker. Aye. It's switched off. Right. She opens the kitchen door. '*Oh*! My Christ! Urr you trying tae gie me a heart attack?' Archie junior stands in the shadowy lobby, behind the front door. 'Whit the buggering hell are ye loitering in here fur?'

He puts a finger to his lips. 'Shhhh! Lexie might hear ye. Ah'm waiting for her tae come oot her hoose.' He shifts from foot to foot. 'Then Ah hang aboot 'til Ah hear her hit the close before *Ah* come oot.' He blushes. 'And Ah catch up wi' her in the Maryhill Road,' he clears his throat, 'so as we can walk tae work the 'gither.'

Ella looks heavenward. 'Fuck me! Ye don't know the first thing aboot lassies, dae ye? Listen. Ye live on the same landing as Lexie. The two of ye work at Kinnaird's. And you're jist aboot tae, accidently oan purpose, leave fur work the same time she diz.' She shakes her head. 'And Ah suppose you'll jist happen tae be handy at five o'clock the night – when it's hame time?' She doesn't wait for an answer. 'Them lassies will be thinking Mrs Kinnaird huz hired the Boston Strangler tae dae the deliveries!'

'It's no' as bad as *that*! Ah don't see her that much. Ah spend a lot o' time oot in the van –'

Ella interrupts. 'Aye! But Ah'll take a bet, when ye *are* in the shop, she'll be sick o' tripping ower ye. Listen tae whit Ah'm gonny tell ye. Believe it or not, wance upon a time *Ah* wiz a lassie. So Ah know whit Ah'm talkin' aboot. This is only your second week in Kinnaird's. Lexie will rapidly go aff ye, if every time she turns – you're therr! *Don't* hang aroon' her aw' day long. *Don't* keep trying tae talk tae her. That lassie is the same stamp as your sister. She'll finish up telling ye you're getting tae be a nuisance. And that'll be it. You'll no' get a second chance from Lexie Forsyth, son. Take warning!'

The old Archie junior would have paid no attention. But the recently out of jail one is listening.

'Dae ye think so, Ma?'

'Ah *know* so!'

'Right. Ah'll take your advice.' He looks at his mother. 'Ah don't half fancy her, Ma.'

She glances at him. Sighs heavily. 'Come through here,

son. She might hear us talking when she comes oot her door.' They step into the kitchen. Ella pushes its door shut. 'Ah might as well tell ye whit else Ah think, Archie. Ah know you're attracted tae her. She's a very smart lassie. But Ah think you'll find Lexie Forsyth will not be interested in somebody that's jist come oot the jail.' She watches his face fall. 'Son, even if you were a hard-working lad, never been in trouble wi' the polis in your life, it would'nae make any difference. You're no' her type.' As she sees the disappointment in his face, tears come into her eyes. 'Listen, Ah'll be delighted if she goes oot wi' ye. But Ah jist don't think she will.' She picks up her bag once more. 'If ye don't believe me, it'll be easy tae put tae the test. Wait a few weeks until she gets tae know ye a bit better, then ask her if she'd like tae go tae the pictures or somewhere. But in the meantime, *don't* be hanging roon' her all the time. She'll think you're creepy. That's good advice, son.'

Archie has 'downcast' written all over him. He makes himself raise his head. 'Whoever said "the truth hurts" got it right, didn't they?'

'You cannae see it the way other folk dae, Archie. When ye told us last week that you fancied her,' she touches his forearm, 'your faither and Katherine said right away, you were out of your league.' She shrugs. 'And unfortunately, Ah huv tae agree. Ah'd think Lexie considers herself a cut above maist o' the folk in this close,' Ella pauses, 'because she is!'

'But that's probably one o' the reasons why Ah really fancy her. Ah also think she's special. Ah've never met anybody like her – and that's why Ah want tae go oot wi' her. Ah've never felt like this aboot a lassie in ma life.'

'That's probably 'cause you've never been oot the jail long enough tae get tae know wan!' Ella gives it some more thought. 'Look, we know *you* are really attracted tae her. But whit you have tae do, Archie. The hard bit! Is tae get her tae find *you* attractive. So for the minute, keep yer feelings tae yerself. Okay? The first step is tae get her tae *like* you. That's all. Like comes before love. Believe it or not that's half the battle.' She looks at the clock. 'Oh, my God! Ah'll be getting ma jotters. Ah'm gonny huv tae go, son. Ah'll see ye the night.' As she's about to exit, she stops. 'Like before love. It's in aw' the books!' He hears her clattering down the stairs.

'Ah will.' He steps towards the outside door. She's already on the second storey. 'Thanks, Ma!'

It's hame time. As Archie Cameron junior walks up the Maryhill Road, he keeps a hundred yards, or more, behind Lexie Forsyth. He's pleased with himself. It's no' often ye listen tae advice, but Ma will be chuffed wi' ye when ye tell her. Ah have'nae bothered Lexie or Jean at all the day. Did'nae hang aboot in the back shop talking tae them. He gets a glimpse of Lexie as the pedestrians between them thin out. Sighs as he watches the way she strides out. Ma might be right. Jist take it slowly. He catches sight of her again. But ohhh! What Ah would give tae take her oot. He contents himself with an occasional snatched look until . . .

'Erchie!' He looks around. Again . . . 'ERCHIE!' He

recognises the voice even though he hasn't heard it for years. The daydreams about Lexie melt away. He looks over to the other side of the road. His heart sinks. Big Joe Devaney has just stepped out of Johnny May's billiard hall. 'Want tae see you a minute, Erchie.' He waves his hand in a manner which is, most certainly, a summons for Archie to cross the road. Right now. Ah'd better go, otherwise it could be bother. Try and look as if you're pleased tae see the big shitbag. Huh. Ah could'nae be less pleased if Ah'd jist bumped intae Hitler! Ah've never liked this fuckpig.

Archie dodges a Corporation bus and makes it to the other side. He wonders if the forced smile on his face looks as phoney as it feels. God! Ma jaw's beginning tae ache.

Devaney looks at him. 'Ah wiz hoping Ah'd bump intae ye. Ah thought by now you'd huv been in for a game o' snooker wi' yer auld pals.'

Archie decides he's not going to lie. He looks at him. 'Ah'm trying tae go straight, Joe. So Ah wiz thinking it might be best if Ah stayed away from the auld stamping grounds. Avoid temptation. Know whit Ah mean?'

'Is that right. And Ah hear you're working, Erchie. Things must be really bad! Daeing deliveries fur Kinnaird's so they tell me. Ah hope she huz'nae still got yon auld message bike!'

He laughs at his own joke. Archie doesn't. 'Och well. As long as me coming oot the jail and getting a job, is giving youse aw' a laugh. Ah guess Ah huv'nae been wasting ma time!'

Devaney's jaw tightens. 'Aye. Well, Ah can tell ye wan

thing. Nathan is'nae ower pleased. He wiz jist saying tae me yesterday, "That's Erchie been oot nearly a fortnight – and never been ower ma door." Sounded a bit peeved.' He looks hard at Archie. 'And as ye know, Nathan Brodie is not a man tae upset. Likes people tae give him his place – a bit o' respect.' Devaney leans forward. 'And jist between you and me. He wiz wondering if you're daeing it deliberate!'

A stab of pure fear, ice-cold and sharp, hits Archie in the stomach. Fuck me! Ah'll be in deep shite if Nathan decides Ah'm trying tae be clever. He hopes his thoughts aren't showing on his face. Try and look relaxed in front o' this shitbag, Archie. He makes himself look Devaney in the eyes. 'Now that is wan thing Ah'd *never* think of daeing tae Nathan. He's been good tae me ower the years. It's jist that Ah've never hud a minute tae maself since Ah came oot o' Stirling. Anywye, Joe. Ah'll be oot in the van the morra daeing deliveries. Ah'll make time tae call in and see him. Diz he still use the scrapyard office as his main place o' business?'

'Aye. He's got managers running his other interests. But he still likes tae be where it aw' started for him. He's very sentimental, Nathan.'

As Archie listens to this crap, in spite of the predicament he seems to be in, he finds it difficult to keep from smiling.

Joe Devaney rubs his jaw, half-turns towards the entrance to the billiard hall. 'In fact, while it's in ma mind, Ah'll away in and use Billy's phone. Tell Nathan Ah've jist seen ye.'

Another shaft of fear hits Archie. he tries to sound casual. 'Oh, is Billy Webster still managing the hall?'

'Aye. He's in wi' the bricks, Billy.' As he's about to push the door open, Devaney stops, turns his head. 'If Ah mind right, wizn't it your faither that gave Billy that severe doing a few years back. Left him wi' the bad throat?'

'Aye, it wiz.'

'Mmmm. Billy wiz good back then.' He sniffs. 'Your faither must huv been a bit of a handful?'

'Still is. He's an ex-para.'

'Imagine that.' Devaney pauses. 'Is he still around?'

'Aye. Still going strong.'

'Zat right. Anywye, Ah'll gie Nathan a ring. He'll be pleased tae know Ah've bumped intae ye.'

Archie watches the door swing shut. Fuck! He turns, sets off up the road. You'll huv tae go and see that big bastard soon. Should huv went as soon as Ah came oot the jail. Got it ower and done wi'. You know his heid's full of aw' this 'Maryhill Godfather' shite. If ye don't go, he'll feel he has tae make an example of ye for no' showing respect. Ah remember Elky McCann telling me on the exercise yard, that since Nathan read *The Godfather*, that's aw' they get oot o' him. Respect! People huv tae show him Respect! Since he read aboot Vito Corleone, he's decided he's gonny be Vito Mulguy or something. Big daft cunt! Trouble is, it'll be nae joke if Ah piss him off. He's liable tae huv a couple o' guys jump me wan night when Ah'm coming oot the Garscube Arms. Or send roond some young fucker who's trying tae make a name fur himself – wi' instructions tae lay ma face wide open. Jeez! How stupid Ah wiz tae get mixed up wi' these toerags. How dumb wiz Ah back then? Ah used tae actually think that running aboot wi' them made me a big man. He gives a heavy sigh. Nae wonder ma faither used tae tell me, 'You huv'nae got the brains you were fuckin' born with!' He shakes his head. So noo Ah'm liable tae get intae trouble, for no' showing respect. Hah! Ah used tae be sick o' hearing that fucking word in the prison. And the best laugh wiz, the wans that hud latched on tae it, that were wanting this 'Respect' – wur the biggest shitbags in the jail. Like Big Bernie Banks and his hangers-on.

His mind spinning, all daydreams of Lexie gone for the moment, he turns the corner into Dalbeattie Street. If Ah wiz tae tell ma ma and da, they wid think Ah'm jist making it up. Ah'm liable tae be getting *intae* trouble because Ah'm trying tae keep *oot* o' trouble. Naebody wid believe it!

CHAPTER FOURTEEN

Taking Avoiding Action

It's a Saturday night. Ruth Lockerbie, the beating heart of Le Bar Rendezvous, sits where everyone expects to see her – on her high stool at one end of the bar. The resident combo are making a decent fist of 'Tuxedo Junction', the dance floor is busy. George Lockerbie is working the room, stopping at table or banquette to welcome patrons old and new . . . a brief conversation here, a joke there. Sometimes a sympathetic ear for a tale of woe. Glad-handing as he calls it. Ruth knows he especially enjoys it when there are football players or boxers in. She catches his eye for a moment and smiles. She looks at her watch. Twenty past eleven. Okay. I don't think Vicky will be in now. I'll collar the Dalbeattie Street bunch when this set finishes. With barely a pause, the sextet launches into its last selection for this round: 'That Old Black Magic'.

George looks over again as the first few bars of Cole Porter's masterpiece draw even more dancers to the floor. It's also one of their favourites. The boys are doing a pastiche of the famous Artie Shaw arrangement. Class piled upon class – the Ultimate! Ruth reaches for her tortoiseshell cigarette holder, then a nearby box of Black Sobranie. Resting an elbow on the bar, she enjoys the music for a moment as she looks around her kingdom – or should that be queendom? Blue smoke rises from most of the tables, hovers just below the ceiling. Now and again she catches the aroma of a good cigar.

As the dance finishes she looks for George, nods, mouths the word 'now'. He acknowledges. Frank and Wilma Galloway are the first to return. She takes both by their wrists. 'Just hang on a minute, darlings.' They are closely followed by Robert and Rhea Stewart. 'Will you all come down to the office for a moment? It's quiet in there. Something to tell you.'

Ruth opens the door at the end of the corridor. 'In you go.'

'Dae ye know what? Ah've never been in here before,' says Rhea.

'Nobody has, darling.'

Rhea looks at her friends. 'Ah hope she's no' about tae tell us we're aw' barred!'

Ruth shakes her head. Smiles. 'Try and make yourselves comfortable as best you can.'

Wilma and Rhea sit on two nearby chairs. Frank perches on the corner of Ruth's desk. Robert folds his arms and leans on the top of a metal filing cabinet. Ruth sits on the opposite corner of her desk from Frank.

Rhea is unsettled. 'Ah hope you huv'nae brought us in here tae gie us bad news, Ruth? Ah *hate* bad news – especially if Ah get telt it in the middle of enjoying maself!'

'If you let Ruth speak, you'd maybe find out!' Robert smiles, shakes his head.

Rhea persists. 'But Ruth seems awfy serious. Ah'm gettin' worried. Is it something terrible?'

'No, darling. I just wanted somewhere quiet, away from the music.'

Rhea puffs her cheeks out. 'Thank the Lord for that. Urr ye gonny tell us, then?'

'If she can get a word in!' says her husband.

'Who's interrupting noo?' she replies.

'If you start me laughing, Rhea Stewart, I won't be able to tell you anything.'

Wilma Galloway raises a hand, as though at school. She blushes. 'If you're no' gonny sit behind your desk, Ruth. Can Ah? Ah've alwiz fancied sitting at a big desk like they do in the fillums.'

It's Frank's turn to shake his head. He looks at Robert. 'We're gonny be in here aw' night.'

'Ah know.'

Ruth waits until Wilma changes seats. 'Right! Best of order, please. George and I became owners of a flat at Kelvin Court three weeks ago. As it was empty, we immediately arranged for electricians to come in and fit our lighting. The decorators then followed them, and at the moment it's the turn of the carpet-fitters. George and I are moving in this coming Monday and, all being well, within three days we expect to have the place as we want it.' From the corner of her eye she sees Rhea fidgeting. Ruth points at her. 'And as you should all know, because she is forever reminding you, Rhea will be guest of honour on the night of the housewarming.'

'Oh! Ah cannae wait!' says Rhea.

'However! There *is* a problem.' Ruth, suddenly serious, looks at each of them in turn. 'I do *not* want Steve Anderson to set foot in our new flat. I'm sure you must all be aware that Rhea, Fred Dickinson and I are all of one opinion. We cannot *stand* that man!'

'Nuthin' but a wee weasel!' Rhea draws herself up to her full height.

Frank Galloway raises a hand. 'I'd also like to join your club.'

'There are various reasons why he won't be welcome at Kelvin Court – some of which I can't go into at the moment. The main one, however, is the fact that he treats Vicky badly. And I *mean* badly –'

'I've noticed that!' All heads turn as Wilma Galloway interrupts. 'There huv been times, here in the club, when he thinks naebody's looking and Ah've had the feeling the wee nyaff is oan the verge of hittin' Vicky!'

'Well spotted, darling.' Ruth looks around. 'Unfortunately, that means I can't invite dear Vicky to the housewarming. At the moment, she and Anderson come as a pair. You may have noticed, whenever he and Vicky have been in on a Saturday evening, I *never* have anybody back to

Agincourt Avenue for a night-cap. I don't want him in my company, or in my house.'

'So how are ye gonny throw the housewarming party withoot Vicky finding oot?'

'We shall hold it on a Thursday night, Rhea.'

'Yeah! That should work,' says Robert.

'Ah don't get it?' Rhea furrows her brow.

'The club only opens three nights a week. The only night you folks come in, is a Saturday. And that's normally just once a month. Now and again, if you have something to celebrate, two of you might surprise George and me by coming in on a Friday.' She looks at her friends. 'But not once have any of you ever come in on a Thursday. And that includes Vicky.' She gives a sad smile. 'So next week, Thursday 26th August, I'll expect you all to gather here between eight and nine – just as though it *were* a Saturday night. And at the end of the evening we shall all repair to Kelvin Court –'

Rhea interrupts. 'Repair? Urr we expected to do some dae-it-yerself joabs for ye?'

The entire company hold their sides. 'The Brainess of Glasgow strikes again!' says Robert.

'No darling,' Ruth laughs. 'We shall all be dressed in our finery, and the only thing required of you will be some demolition work – on the canapés and champagne which will be waiting for us at the flat. Oh! And I hasten to add, Fred and Ruby will be with us of course. And then you will all, at last, get to see our Art Deco bits and pieces where they should be seen. Where they were *meant* to be seen

– in a newly decorated, purpose-built, Art Deco flat in Kelvin Court.' Ruth spreads her arms dramatically. 'Prepare to be ASTOUNDED, darlings!'

Robert Stewart jerks up from where he's been leaning on the filing cabinet, points at Ruth. 'Bugger me! It's Gloria Swanson. She's no' deid at all!'

CHAPTER FIFTEEN

Always the Unexpected

Archie Cameron junior turns off the Maryhill Road into Wilton Street, parks the Ford van a few yards along from the junction. He looks at his watch. Ten past four. Great! Time for a coffee, then give Lexie and Jean a wee hand tae tidy up . . . A knock on the nearside window startles him. He turns, and the sight of a policeman's uniform makes his heart jump. Ah huv'nae done anything – what's he want me for? As the polis bends to look in the window Archie catches sight of the sergeant's stripes, then the face of Billy McClaren. His childhood pal points to the door handle. Archie unlocks it.

Sergeant McClaren opens the door, takes his peaked-hat off, half-sits on the passenger seat with one foot still on the pavement.

Archie blows through puckered lips. 'You trying tae gie me a heart attack?'

'Aye, auld habits die hard. Anyway, how are ye doing? Ah hear you're making the big bid tae go straight.' He looks hard at Archie. 'But do you really mean it this time?'

'You can trust me. Ah mean it aw'right. Prison's a young man's game, Billy. It's like all of a sudden Ah cannae hack it any mair. The thought of –'

Billy talks over him. 'It'll be turning thirty that's done it. Ah've seen it happen a few times.'

'You're dead right. Ah turned thirty during ma last stretch and that's when it hit me. Right between the eyes! You're wasting yer life yah stupid bugger!'

'So ye finally got the message.' He turns in his seat. 'As ye know, your ma calls in every night that God sends and has a cuppa wi' mine. My ma was saying that's aw' she gets out of aunty Ella, lately. There's not a night goes by that she's not on aboot how well you're doing, and how much you like your job at Kinnaird's.' Billy McClaren looks at him. 'She'll take it badly if ye faw' by the wayside, Erchie.'

Archie swallows hard. 'Ah know. Don't worry. Ah've nae intention of letting her doon. Or maself.'

'Life's funny, in't it? When we were boys, there wiz'nae two better pals in the street.' He shrugs. 'Then you got mixed up wi' aw' them toerags doon at Johnny May's. Tell me something, Erchie. Has there ever been a recorded case of anybody going in therr *just* tae play snooker?'

'Hah! There's bound tae have been wan or two – but Ah never met them!'

'Once you got mixed up wi' Nathan Brodie's team, that wiz you fucked, Erchie. Anywye,' he smiles, 'whit's this your ma's been telling mine? Aboot you huving a big crush on that new lassie on your landing. Lexie something?'

Archie blushes. 'Jeez! Between Ella and Drena, ye cannae keep any secrets up that close.'

'Mind, Ah don't blame ye. Ah've passed her two or three times. She's a bit of a knock-out. Good job Ah'm an auld married man, or Ah would have been efter her maself!' He gives Archie a dig in the arm. 'Huv ye took her oot, yet?'

'No' so far. She's no' half playing hard tae get.'

'Well, good luck.' Billy looks at his watch. 'Time Ah wiz getting back tae the station. Ah'll tell ye what, how about us huvin' a pint the 'gither some time?' He laughs. 'Though it better not be in Maryhill . . .'

Archie snorts. 'Oh, naw! Christ! If they see us two the 'gither, half o' them will be thinking you're bent – and the other half will mark me doon as a grass.'

'Anywye, just keep going the way you're going, Erchie. It sounds like you're determined.'

As Billy turns, about to climb out of the van, Archie decides now is as good a time as any. Get it over with. He puts a restraining hand on his boyhood pal's arm. Tries to swallow the mixture of nerves and embarrassment in his throat. 'Eh, Billy, can Ah say Ah'm sorry for aw' yon times you used tae speak tae me if we bumped intae wan another and, eh, well, Ah used tae be such a fuckin' arsehole. Alwiz gave ye a hard time . . .' He looks at him. 'Ah don't suppose it'll be much consolation . . . but Ah alwiz used tae feel dead rotten efterwards. Ah'd think, why dae ye dae that? You used tae be best mates.'

'Och! Don't worry aboot it. Ah always knew it was just bravado. Tough guy shite.' Billy manages to keep his face straight. 'Ah jist used tae go back up tae Maryhill Polis Station, lock maself in an empty cell for ten minutes – and huv a wee cry.'

'Fuck off!'

Mrs Kinnaird looks up as Archie enters the shop. 'Did ye get aw' the deliveries done, son?'

'Aye, nae bother Mrs K. Most of the folk were in. The few that weren'y, Ah either got a neighbour tae take it in, or they'd left a note saying where tae leave it.'

'Good lad. Oh! While ye were oot, an order came in for a bouquet for somebody's birthday. Lexie's already made it up. It'll only take ye ten minutes. It's jist up the Maryhill Road, near the Star cinema. You know, the businesses that rent yon units that back ontae the canal embankment?'

'Aye. Them single-storey things. They're on the other side o'the Maryhill Road from where Lexie and me live.'

'Aye, of course they are. Jist a minute.' She sorts through the many pieces of paper scattered round the telephone . . . 'Got yah! Tommy's Tyres! Ye know it?'

'Aye. Ah've noticed the sign when Ah'm walking tae work in the mornings.' He looks at her. 'Have Ah time for a coffee before Ah go?'

'Och aye. He says they don't shut 'til half-five. Sometimes later if they're daeing a job.'

* * *

A freshly-brewed mug of Maxwell House in his hand, Archie saunters into the back shop. As usual, his heart gives an extra beat when his eyes fall on Lexie. She and Jean Dalglish sit at the work table, its surface littered with a dark greenery of cut stems and fallen leaves. This is highlighted here and there by confetti-like sprinklings of coloured petals.

'Hello, girls!'

He receives a smile. Jean speaks. 'It's awfy nice tae be classed as a girl when you'll no' see forty again, eh?' She nudges her workmate.

Lexie is in an indolent, end-of-a-working-day mood. 'Ah'm far too young tae know.' She stretches her long trousered legs out, then her arms. Yawns loudly. 'Jeez! Don't know why Ah'm so tired. Ah never go anywhere, do anything. Just go tae ma work.'

Archie is leaning against some shelves. Is this meant for him? 'That's why you're sae tired, Lexie. Boredom! If you'd let me take ye tae the pictures or the dancin', noo' and again, it would perk ye up. Ye know whit they say – all work and no play . . .'

Lexie looks at Jean. 'Gie him his due, he's a trier.' She turns back to Archie. 'Going oot wi' you wid probably be even *more* boring. Ah'd rather spend a night in wi' the toothache!'

'Zat no' terrible?' He turns to Jean. 'Good joab Ah'm thick-skinned.'

'Never mind, Erchie. If Ah wiz twenty years younger, and on the available list, Ah'd go oot tae the jigging wi' ye in a minute, son.'

'Och, but you've always been easily pleased,' says Lexie.

He smiles at Jean. 'Looks like the *two* of us are gonny get it, no' jist me.' He gulps down the last of his coffee. 'Anywye. Nae good hanging aroond here tae be insulted.'

'So where do ye usually go?' enquires Lexie.

'The auld yins are the best,' says Archie. 'Ah fell oot ma pram laughing at that yin.'

'Ohhh! And that's even *older*!' says Lexie. 'The first time Ah heard that – it wiz in Latin!'

Archie tries not to laugh. 'Anywye, Ah'm away tae dae ma delivery. See ye the morra, Jean.' He turns to Lexie. Bows. 'Good night, your royal nastiness!' Picking up the bouquet, he walks through to the front shop. Mrs Kinnaird stands behind the counter, silhouetted against the shop window as she watches folk pass by on the main road.

'Do ye think it would be a good idea, Mrs K, if Ah left the van where it's parked and just walked up the road and delivered this on ma way home?'

'Aye, good thinking. That's whit tae dae. Ah'll see ye the morra, son. Good night.'

'Good night.'

Fifteen minutes later he knocks, then opens the office door at Tommy's Tyres. Twenty feet away a tubular, Formica-topped desk dominates the small room. The chair behind it is swung round at the moment, its back facing him. The person sitting in it is leaning forward, riffling through files in the bottom drawer of a filing cabinet.

'Got a delivery of flowers for ye.' Archie ambles towards

the desk. He has only taken a few steps when he hears movement behind him. He turns. Big Joe Devaney is walking towards the office door. He feels a chill as he watches him stop, turn, then lean back against it. He folds his hands in front of him, then gives Archie the unfriendliest smile he's ever seen. Even as he turns round to face the desk, Archie knows who will be behind it. There's a loud metallic clatter as a filing cabinet drawer is kicked shut. The chair and Archie turn to face one another as though synchronised. Nathan Brodie glowers at him. All of a sudden it's as though someone has poured a jug of iced-water directly into his spine. His knees grow weak, his mouth instantly dries. With all his might he wishes he was back in prison. Safe. 'Oh! Eh, hello Nathan. Ah've been trying tae make time tae –'

'Don't talk fuckin' shite! Is that my flooers?' He holds his right hand out.

'Eh, aye.' Archie walks forward, hands him the bouquet. Brodie, without looking, swings his arm to the right, drops the fresh-cut flowers into a metal waste-bin at the side of the desk. He leans back in the chair, keeps his arms spread out, clenched fists resting on the desk top. 'Who the FUCK dae ye think you are, eh? Treating me like Ah wiz a naebody.'

You are a fucking naebody, thinks Archie. Wisely, his mouth contradicts him. 'You know Ah don't think that, Nathan. We go back a long wye. You know Ah would *never* disrespect you –'

Brodie interrupts. 'Zat right? So how come you've been oot the jail a couple o' months and not wance huv ye darkened ma door? Whit else can Ah call it?'

Archie's brain has never worked so hard for years. Possible answers come and go, are rejected at the speed of one o' them computer things. 'Nathan, it was jist that Ah could'nae face telling ye that Ah'm wanting tae pack the game in. That's the only reason. Ah thought you wid'nae like tae hear that. You *know* there is'nae another reason. You and me huv alwiz got on well. Ah jist did'nae know how tae tell ye Ah'm finished wi' the game. The truth is, Nathan, Ah don't want tae dae any mair time. That last stretch nearly killed me.' Archie is pleased with that. Already he can see the anger begin to leave Brodie's face.

'Ah'm fuckin' mair annoyed because ye did'nae think Ah'd appreciate whit you're saying.'

Archie decides to lay on the contrite. 'See! Ah knew that, Nathan. The longer it went on, the more it began tae dawn on me – Ah'll bet ye Nathan *would* understand.' That's enough, Archie! Don't overdo it. If he twigs on you're conning him he'll go mad. As he looks at Brodie he can feel cold sweat running down his sides from under his oxters. Is suddenly conscious that the hair at the back of his neck is wet, moisture from it trickling down the back of his shirt collar.

'Exactly! If you'd came and seen me when ye came oot o' Stirling, telt me aw' this, there wid'nae huv been a problem, son.'

It's the 'son' that does it. You're winning, Archie. You're gonny get oot o' here wi' your face intact. Don't fuck things up at the last minute. His thinking is clearer now. He looks at Brodie. Knows that Big Joe is blocking the door. Suddenly he feels angry. Who dae these bastards think they are? Another person. Another human being. And they think they can treat me like a . . . Whit wiz it ma da said the Nazis called everybody that wiz'nae German . . . Aye, *untermenschen*! Sub humans. He looks at Brodie. That's whit this fucking reptile thinks Ah am!

Brodie sits back once more. The heat is definitely going out of this. Archie says nothing more, averts his eyes, frightened in case he loses it all at the last minute. Brodie leans forward, rests his elbows on the desk. Archie can tell he's about to do his Godfather impersonation. All wise, benign, merciful – as well as being a stupid big prick! For fuck sake *don't* think things like that. If you take a giggling fit, they'll be pulling yer body oot o' that canal the morra morning! Ah . . . Brodie is about to speak. Archie puts on his best penitent look.

'Ah'll tell ye what Ah'm gonny do wi' ye, Archie. You're nae good tae me now, son. Every time you'd go oot on a job you would be that worried aboot gettin' caught, you'd be worse than useless.' He sits upright, spreads his arms wide, about to give benediction – then points dramatically towards the door. Jesus-johnny! He's gone from Brando straight intae Charlton Heston! 'You can go, son. This is the parting of the ways.' He wags a finger at Archie. 'But you'd better make fuckin' sure that you *do* go straight! If Ah get told you're daeing jobs for yerself. Or if you dae something that interferes wi' ma affairs – anything at all – you will be one sorry boy. *Ah* run

Merryhill. Don't you fuckin' forget it. Now go on, piss off!'

'You'll huv nae problems from me, Nathan. Ah'm retired. Permanently!'

Seconds later, the sweat on him turning cold in the early evening air, unable to believe his luck, Archie finds himself walking across the yard towards the Maryhill Road. Ah've done it! He resists the temptation to do a little jig. Nathan and Big Joe might be looking oot the windae.

CHAPTER SIXTEEN

Best Laid Plans . . .

'Oh, mammy-daddy!' Ella Cameron drops gratefully into one of Drena McClaren's fireside chairs, leans her shopping bag against a leg. Blows her cheeks out. 'Pheww!'

'Sounds like you've been busy doon the Lux Tearooms the day.'

'We huv'nae half.' She delves into her bag, pulls out a ten Woodbine. 'You wantin' wan?' She watches as Drena, little finger held at a supposed sophisticated angle, selects one. Ella purses her lips. 'Ah don't know why Ah waste ma time asking. Last time *you* refused a fag Atlee wiz prime minister!'

Her pal tuts. 'Well, it's fair enough, is it no'? Ah supply the tea.' Drena reaches down to the hearth, picks up a half-burnt yellow taper, sticks it between the bars of the gas fire. Seconds later, smoke from their cigarettes undulates up to the ceiling.

'At least the demolisher's men seem tae huv finished early the day. Noisy buggers! They're gettin' nearer and nearer, in't they?' says Ella.

Drena is about to pour the tea. She pauses. 'That's funny! Noo ye mention it, Ah've jist realised Ah have'nae heard them the day. The whole day.'

'Huv ye no'? That's unusual. Mibbe they're oan strike.'

It's some ten minutes later. Irma Armstrong, for the first time in months, enters the close at 18 Dalbeattie Street. A few paces in she stops at what was, for twenty-two years, the door to her and Bert's single-end. A heavy sheet of plywood has been nailed over it. '*Huh*!' Some *dumkopf junge* has scrawled Dally Boys Rule – OK! on it. She recalls how it once was . . . smart blue paint, the brasses gleaming. Her eyes glisten. How many times am I busy with the Brasso, or washing the close, and Archie Cameron or Billy McClaren come by? She smiles. Always with their POW German . . . 'Irma! *Wie eine gute Deutsche hausfrau – alles muss sauber sein*!' Everything must be clean! She gives a sigh, glances at the unswept close as she steps over to the McClarens' door.

'Halloooh! It's only me!'

Drena and Ella look at one another, smile. 'IRMA!' The inner door opens. Now wreathed in smiles, their former neighbour steps into the kitchen. The two women rise. 'Aw, Irma hen. It's lovely tae see ye.' Drena kisses her on the cheek.

'And that goes fur me tae, Irma. You're a miss, hen.' Ella kisses and hugs her, then holds her at arm's length. 'You're looking well, darling.'

Irma, instantly moist-eyed, looks at her two best pals from all the years at Number 18. 'Oh! It is *zoh* nice to be back here again. I cannot wait for the new houses to be finished in Stobcross Avenue, then you move up and we are all together. I hope they start building again soon.'

'Whit dae ye mean "start again"? Are they no' building at the minute?'

'No. They have been stopped for a few weeks, Ella. They run out of funds, or they need a new grant. Something.' She spreads her arms wide. 'I do not know.'

Ella frowns. 'The Corporation never tells us anything, dae they?'

Drena gives it some thought. 'That must be why they've stopped the demolition. They cannae knock this block doon until the new hooses are ready for us on the Molendinar Scheme. Or they would be making us homeless.'

'Mmm. But even so, the fly bastards huv'nae said a word tae us, huv they?'

'Oh! We'll be the *last* tae know, Ella. They'll be feart in case we kick up a stoor and it mibbe gets intae the papers. Probably the local elections are due, or some such.' Drena bristles.

'Ah'll tell ye who might know,' says Ella. 'Marjorie Marshall.'

'Aye. Ah'm forgetting Marjorie works at the City Chambers.'

'We'll leave it a few days. And if they don't start up the demolishing again, we might huv a wee walk alang Wilton Street and gie Marjorie and Jack a knock. Ah bump intae her noo and again oan the Maryhill Road. She's forever asking me when Ah'm gonny call roon' for a cup o' tea.'

Drena lifts the kettle, walks towards the sink. 'Anywye, noo that you've mentioned it. Important things first, girls. Tea?'

Thirty minutes have gone by. Third cups of tea have been newly poured. 'How dae ye like your new hoose, Irma?' Ella and Drena look intently at her.

'Wellll. I like the *house* very much. But oh, I wish it was just off the Maryhill Road.' She looks at her friends. 'The scheme can be so quiet. You look out the window sometimes – and it is deserted. Nothing to see but row after row of houses. No shops. Hardly any people. So little traffic. I am very glad I have my job at the ironmonger's. Monday to Saturday I am in the Maryhill Road. Then I go home at night,' she laughs, 'and I think maybe I am living in East Berlin!'

'Fuck me!' says Ella. 'Is it as bad as that?'

'During the day and early evening there are vans coming round . . . greengrocer's, butcher's and so on. Hah! Bert likes it because, about seven in the evening, the baker's van comes and he can get breakfast rolls – to have with his dinner! But I tell you, if I have forgot to buy the Oxo cubes or something. Oh! Help ma Boab! There is only one shop – a mile away at the other side of the scheme. What a trip!'

Drena looks at Ella. 'Mibbe we should hope they *huv*

ran oot o' funds. Then they might leave us in Dalbeattie Street for good!'

'Hah! Don't count oan it, pal.'

Irma looks at her watch. 'Michty me! It is five after six already. I have to go.' As if on cue, there comes the sound of tackety boots entering the close.

'Oh, oh!' says Drena. 'We've had it noo'. This is Billy.'

Ella turns to Irma. 'Whit a shame. If you'd jist left five minutes ago, hen, you might huv hud a clear run tae the Swiss border.' She holds a hand to her ear. 'But you've had it now. This is the *Kommandant* coming!' All three start laughing.

The kitchen door is pushed open. 'Ah'm hame Dree—' Billy McClaren's face lights up. 'IRMA! *Liebchen*! *So lange zeit*, hen.' He gives her a cuddle. Speaks to her in his rusty German.

Drena leans forward. Speaks out the side of her mouth. 'Ella, while he's distracted wi' Eva Braun,' she manages to keep her face straight, 'if *we* slip away right now – *we* might jist make it tae the Swiss border before *News At Ten*!'

It's a few days later, just after five o'clock. As usual, Drena and Ella sit drinking tea – and smoking Ella's fags. Footsteps enter Drena's lobby, then comes an indistinct voice 'Are ye in?'

'Fuck me! Ah think Irma's came back tae hand herself in,' says Ella.

'It is'nae, ya silly bugger! C'mon in, Rhea!'

The kitchen door is pushed open. Rhea Stewart, from two-up, appears. 'Hello, girls!'

'Zat you jist hame fae your work, Rhea?'

'Oh!' says Ella. 'It's a change tae hear ye ask somebody else that.' She turns to Rhea. 'Dae ye know whit it is? She huz asked me that question every night fur the last twenty years!'

Drena tuts. 'You're hard done tae so ye are.' She reaches for the teapot. 'Ye huving a cuppa?'

Rhea remains at the door. 'Naw thanks. Ah've jist popped in tae tell ye. At long, *long* last, we've managed tae find a four-bedroom flat tae rent alang Wilton Crescent.'

Ella claps her hands. 'Oh, that's smashing! We were beginning tae think ye were never gonny get wan. So when dae ye think you'll be flitting?'

'Sometime in the next fortnight. Probably the second week in September.'

'Robert's mother is moving tae live with ye, isn't she?'

'She is.'

'So that'll be another two flats boarded-up,' says Drena. 'How many empty hooses will that be up the close, once you've moved oot?'

Ella is first with the answer. 'That'll be five. Three single-ends and two room and kitchens. Five empty, seven still occupied.' The three women, all long-time residents at Number 18, fall silent for a moment. Each with her own thoughts.

Drena is first to speak. 'Och, it's sad really, in't it?'

'Aye,' says Rhea. It comes out as a whisper.

CHAPTER SEVENTEEN

Too Marvellous For Words

'Ah keep thinking this is a Setterday night. Ah'm no' used tae being at the Club Rendezvous on a Thursday.' Rhea looks at Ruth.

'Same here, darling.' Ruby Dickinson also looks at their hostess.

Ruth gives a half-smile, takes another languorous draw from the tortoiseshell holder, tilts her head back so as to blow the smoke upwards. 'Yes, you've all led such sheltered lives.'

Wilma Galloway has joined them halfway through this conversation. She smiles at Ruth. 'How is Rhea gonny launch the new flat? Smash a bottle o' champagne oan the door knocker?'

'Mmmm. Now you mention it, I suppose that would be as good a way as any. However, all will be revealed in a couple of hours. You'll just have to content yourselves.'

Rhea lets out a squeak. 'But ye know Ah'm nae good at contenting maself. Never huv been.' She does an excited little tap-dance on the spot, as though to prove it.

Ruby regards her. 'It looks more like you're needing to go pee-pee.'

'Oh, well of course, there's that as well!'

'Gawd!' Ruby casts her eyes heavenwards. 'Anyway, where have all the men sloped off to?'

'Need you ask?' Ruth inclines her head. 'They're all sitting over there in a banquette with Peter Keenan and his wife. They love talking to him. He's such fun.'

'Is he still boxing?' asks Wilma.

'Nooo! Been retired a few years now. He's a promoter nowadays, so he's still in the business.'

'Anywye! Important things first.' Rhea looks hopefully at Ruth. 'Ah hope ye don't close as late oan a Thursday as ye dae oan a Saturday. Ah'll never last oot tae one in the morning.'

'I'm planning on being at back at Kelvin Court for just gone midnight, darling.'

'Well mind,' Rhea purses her lips, 'if there's nae movement by ten tae twelve, Ah'm gonny set the fire alarm aff! Make *sure* the place is cleared fur midnight!'

It's quarter past twelve. The lift at Kelvin Court glides smoothly up to the first floor. It is its second trip in as many minutes. The door slides open and allows the last of the launch party to join the others. Reunited once more, three of the four couples stand quietly, not wishing to break the midnight hush. Rhea Stewart is undaunted. She looks around her. 'Ah'll tell ye whit. Ah'd be quite happy tae set up house oan this landing – never mind wan o' the flats!'

This is all that is needed to set them off laughing. Ruth presses a finger against her rich, red lips, urges them to 'Shush! Shush! Shushhhh!' The fact that they should be quiet, somehow makes them all the more giggly. They decide to try not looking at one another. This makes it worse. Ruth tries to be stern. 'Behave! I can see me being evicted before I've –' Unfortunately she has to break off and join in.

George Lockerbie finds the cure. He takes a Yale key from his pocket. 'Rhea. This is the door key. Open it just a few inches, reach in for the light switch, *then* open it wide so everybody gets to see inside at the same instant.'

Ruth and George stand either side of the door, beckon their guests forward until they are bunched-up behind Rhea. With growing anticipation, the giggling forgotten for the moment, they watch Rhea turn the handle, locate the light switch, then push the front door wide open and quickly step into the flat's entrance hall. Her fellow guests have started to giggle and laugh once more as they push and pummel one another, like children piling into a Saturday matinee, all determined to get a good place. After a few paces, they halt. There is a collective intake of breath. Ruth and George look at one another, smile as they listen to the comments . . .

'WOW! Isn't this something!' Ruby Dickinson takes a hold of Fred's sleeve.

'Jeez-oh! If this is the hall – Ah cannae wait tae see the living room!' says Wilma.

'OH! Yessss. I *knew* you two would get it right first time.' Robert Stewart nods in approval.

Rhea, says nothing. Slowly turns her head from side to side, tries to take it all in, absorb it. Facing her, and therefore the first thing to be seen by those invited to step through the Lockerbies' door, is a large painting in a dark silver frame. It is not only striking at first sight, but, as it is meant to do, it will continue to draw all eyes back to it. By Tamara de Lempicka – and therefore the essence of Art Deco – it is called 'Autoportrait' and shows a young woman in the cockpit of a green racing car. Though it appears to be an actual painting it is, in fact, an oleograph. A reproduction technique which gives an 'oil on canvas' effect – including brushstrokes. This striking work is further enhanced by being lit from above. The bold young woman looks down on them with such arrogance, a steely glint in her eyes, it would surprise no one to find, later in the night, she had climbed down and joined them.

Forcing themselves to look away from this enchantress, they take in the rest of the hall. The flooring is of wooden blocks in black, brown and the lightest beige, laid in a suitably moderne design. Except for the light shining down onto the painting, the rest of the lighting is subdued and shines upwards from alcoves. Running along the wall, underneath the painting, stands a long Art Deco table with three drawers. A telephone stands on it. If the company were asked for a first reaction to the entrance hall, 'Simple yet stunning' would be the consensus.

Fred Dickinson looks at his friends. 'Right! I would imagine we've just had our starter.' He turns to their hosts. 'Is it now time for the main course?'

'This way.' Ruth sweeps her right arm in the direction of the nearest door. Once again she moves the guest of honour into position. Rhea takes a last look at the painting. 'Ah'll bet ye she wiz a stranger tae the steamie!' The grand opening of the living room is delayed for a minute or two while Ruth leans on the Art Deco hall table, holding her side with her other hand as she takes a stitch. When she at last recovers, she looks at Rhea, shakes her head. 'Right. Same again, darling. Open the door about six inches, reach in for the light switch – then open it wide.'

'Eeee! Ah'm beginning tae know how the Queen feels when she's opening places.'

Seconds later it's done and they all hurry into the living room – and stop dead. Rhea's lips form a perfect circle. She turns to Ruth. 'Ohhhh! You were right when ye told me this would be even better than Agincourt Avenue. Noo Ah see whit ye mean. Ah get the message. This is your Art Deco furniture where it should be – in an Art Deco flat.'

Robert Stewart echoes his wife. 'It is absolutely brilliant, Ruth. Stunning!'

Ruby is next. 'Oh, darling! You really should get one of the leading magazines – *Vogue* or some such – to do a photo-shoot up here. I'm quite sure they'd jump at the chance. It's unique!'

The guests fall silent for a moment, try to take it all in. The extra-wide living-room window which curves outwards and stretches the width of the end wall, gives a panoramic view of the Great Western Road. The Art Deco armchairs and settee, which they knew from Hillhead, have been stylishly re-covered for their new setting, and look better than before.

'Come along everybody.' Ruth interrupts their absorption with the living room. 'I'll take you on a flying visit to the bedrooms. Then it'll be back here, coats off, drinks poured – and I made some sandwiches before George and I left for the club, tonight.'

'Ahhh!' Robert rubs his hands briskly together, then looks admiringly at Ruth. 'Tell me, does heaven know they're missing an angel?' He manages to keep a straight face.

Rhea screws *her* face up. 'Can Ah apologise oan his behalf, Ruth? When he's hud a few drinks, and he's in your company, as ye should know by noo – his brain turns tae mince!'

'What a succinct diagnosis, darling. Anyway,' she points dramatically, 'to the bedrooms!'

As they return to the stunning living room, it's to find their transition back to the thirties is complete. George has placed a Bunny Berigan record on the radiogram and the singer is lamenting that 'I Can't Get Started'. Wilma stops just inside the door, points to the large oval carpet which dominates the parquet floor. 'Before we had a look at the bedrooms, I had been about tae say, the pattern on this is absolutely perfect. Could'nae be any better if you'd had it made.'

'We did!' George and Ruth both laugh.

Frank Galloway whistles through his teeth. 'Bespoke was it! That would cost a pretty penny.'

'We had it woven to our own design.'

'Huh!' All heads turn towards Rhea. She tuts. 'Specially made!' She makes an involuntary bosom adjustment. 'Ah'm sure ye could huv found wan ready made at Goldberg's carpet department.'

CHAPTER EIGHTEEN

Remembrance of Things Past

'Shush a minute!' Rhea Stewart holds her head on one side. 'Ah think this is Agnes coming.' There's a momentary change of key as the climber steps onto the half-landing, then returns to her original beat, only louder, as she makes for the first storey. 'AGNES! Huv ye got a minute?'

The cha-cha for court heels stops outside the open door. 'Aye?'

'Jist come in.'

All four Stewarts stop eating as they listen to her footsteps enter the lobby, wait for her to push their kitchen door open. Agnes Dalrymple's familiar face appears. 'Hi-yah!'

'Sit doon for a minute. Got something tae ask ye. There's tea in the pot if you've got time,' says Robert.

'Naw, you're aw'right. Ah'll be making one when Ah get intae the hoose.' Agnes looks at the kids. 'So how's the world treating Sammy and Louise? Hardly ever see the pair o' ye nooadays.'

'Fine, aunty Agnes.' This is said in unison.

Robert takes a last mouthful of tea, chinks his mug down onto his cleared plate. 'Did you know the Blythswood is showing its last film this week, Agnes? It's going over tae full-time bingo from Monday.'

'Oh, my God! Is it? Ah cannae imagine the Blythsie no' being a picture hoose any mair.' She thinks about it. Tuts. 'It should'nae be allowed.' Sammy and Louise smile in sympathy.

'It's a sign of the times, aunty Agnes.' Sammy points towards the television. 'That's what's killing them off. It won't be long until there's not a cinema left in the suburbs. If you want to see a film, you'll have to go to one o' the big halls in the city centre.'

'Och! That'll be too much bother.' She turns back to Robert. 'So, is that what you've called me in for, Robert Stewart. Tae depress me?'

They all laugh. Rhea takes over. 'What we're thinking of daeing, Agnes, is getting a wee group of us the 'gether and going doon tae the Blythsie for a last visit.'

Their visitor is silent for a moment. 'That's a good idea, hen. That wid be nice. Sort of, ohhh, farewell tae the Blythswood kind of thing. Ah like that.' She looks at Robert and Rhea. 'Who else are ye thinking of asking?'

'Oh, quite a few,' says Rhea. 'My ma and da, Robert's ma, Drena and Billy, Ella and Archie. And Irene Stuart.'

'That's good, considering the close is half-empty.' She

pauses. 'Whit night were ye thinkin' of goin'?' Before her question can be answered, she speaks again. 'And whit's oan? Not that it'll make any difference.'

'We thought Thursday night would be best. It might get busy on its last Friday and Saturday. Ah would think we won't be the only folk who'll want tae make a last visit,' says Robert. 'And as it happens, it's quite a good picture that's on. It's called *The French Connection*. It's up for three or four Oscars. Sort of gangster thing. True story, seemingly.'

'Oh, that's yon drug thing, in't it? Ah read aboot it in a magazine. Right, ye can count me in.' She turns to Rhea. 'But Ah thought youse were flitting tae Wilton Crescent this week?'

'We're no' moving until the third of October. That's this coming Sunday. So we've plenty of time tae say cheerio tae the Blythsie.'

Agnes gives a mournful sigh. 'Eee, everything's changing so it is.' She shakes her head. 'And no' alwiz fur the best.'

The assistant manager shines the weak beam from his torch along the row. 'There you are. It's a good job you reserved your seats. We've been getting busier as the week's gone on.'

Rhea nudges him. 'By the end o' the night, John, you're gonny have tae strike a match – to see if your torch is oan. You could dae wi' some batteries.'

The man gives a rueful laugh. 'Trouble is, the boss says it'll be a waste o' money. Ah'll no' be needing a torch after Saturday!'

'Aye.' Robert looks around. 'If you had just been getting attendances like this over the last year or two, there would be nae need to change over tae bingo.'

'Well, not really, Robert.' The man shrugs. 'It would just have postponed the inevitable.'

The Dalbeattie Street group have entered during the interval. The shabby gold curtains, which they've known for years, cover the screen. The house lights are dimmed, but fail to hide that the hall badly needs decorating. Irene Stuart nudges Agnes. 'They are gonny have tae do this place up whether they like it or no'. Ye can get away wi' having the lights doon low in a cinema – but folk cannae play bingo in the dark!' They give each other 'knowing' looks.

Robert draws Rhea's attention to the small, stylised lights which stud the walls all round the auditorium. 'Those always used to remind me of the torch the Statue of Liberty carries. They've been there since we were kids, haven't they?'

'Aye, so they have.'

'If I ever hear they're going to shut this hall down, I'm gonny try to buy one as a souvenir.'

'Why? What wid ye dae wi' it?' Rhea leans to the side, gives him her best 'incredulous look'.

'Well, we haven't yet moved into our new flat, so I'm not quite sure where it would go.'

'Whit aboot the midden!' suggests Rhea.

He tuts. 'They are part of oor childhood. You cannae stand by and just let them be loast.'

'Zat a fact? So Ah take it, the day you retire fae Rossleigh's,' she keeps a straight face, 'you'll come stoating through oor front door, humping a petrol pump oan yer back fur a keepsake?'

'You've nae heart, you.'

Mercifully, just then the house lights dim further and the curtains struggle open. Showtime!

It's shortly after ten when they exit the Blythswood Cinema for the last time. They gather for a moment under the illuminated canopy on the Maryhill Road side; its rows of bulbs glare down on them – in spite of the dozen or more which are blown.

'Well, Ah'll tell ye what. Ah fair enjoyed that so Ah did.' Agnes stands looking at the 'stills' which advertise the film they've just seen. 'Nae wonder it's up for some Oscars. That's the best picture Ah've seen for many a year. Did you like it, Irene?'

'Ah did indeed.'

Archie Cameron and Billy McClaren stand together. Archie winks at his pal, then turns to speak to his neighbours. 'Hullo! Best of order, please! Best of order! Efter oor last ever visit tae the Blythsie, we cannae jist toddle aff hame tae oor beds. Wid'nae be right.' He points directly across the main road into Raeberry Street, to where the lights of the Shakespeare Bar glow enticingly in the dark. 'Ah think a wee night-cap, and a "Thanks for the Memory" toast, wid be appropriate under the circumstances.' He avoids Ella's eyes.

'Noo therr's a surprise!' says his beloved.

Robert Stewart comes to his rescue. 'Good thinking,

Erchie. This is, most definitely, the end of an era. We cannae walk away from the Blythswood withoot marking it.'

'Ah quite agree wi' ye.' Drena imperceptibly nudges Ella. 'And it jist so happens, Ah huv goat a big dawd o' chalk in ma bag. So ye can MARK IT tae your heart's content!' The assembled company watch in amusement as Drena, Ella and Rhea, have to hang on to one another.

Eventually order is restored. Ella eyes the menfolk. 'Now. Is it jist gonny be *one* night-cap?'

Dennis O'Malley speaks up. 'Ah, now Ella. T'ink about it. We've all spent many a happy night in there, especially during that last bit of unpleasantness wit' Germany. That wee hall was a Godsend, so it was. We *have* t' raise a glass to it. T'wouldn't be right to . . .' His voice fails him.

The landlord looks up in surprise from the *Evening Citizen* spread open on the bar. He does a quick head count of this late-night influx, breaks into a smile. 'Good evening, folks. What can I get you?' He folds the newspaper, rubs his palms together.

It's an hour later. Another round of 'final' night-caps has just been delivered to the tables. The conversation is flowing like brandy.

'If you had tae choose jist *wan* picture, from all of them you've seen at the Blythsie,' Mary Stewart lays her third glass of sherry on the table, looks at her wonderful friends and neighbours, 'whit would it be?'

'You start, Ma,' says Robert. 'Seeing as you suggested it.'

'Right!' Mary wags a finger for some reason. Rhea glances at Robert, mouths the word 'tipsy!'. Mary's finger stabs the smoke-filled air. '*Double Indemnity*! Ah loved that so Ah did. Fred McMurray and Edward G. Robinson.' She looks wistful. 'And Fred never looked handsomer!'

'Now that *is* a good choice, Ma.' Robert throws it open. 'Who's next?'

''Tis got t' be *The Bells o' St Mary's*,' says Teresa. 'Jayz! Oi wept buckets at that Oi did. Bing Crosby and Ingrid Bergman. Oh! Ingrid made a lovely nun so she did. Even himself had a tear in his eye,' she digs a sharp elbow into Dennis's ribs, 'didn't yer?'

Rhea shakes her head. 'Naebody wid ever guess ma mammy's a Catholic, wid they?'

'Are ye sure that wiz oan at the Blythsie?' says Drena. 'The reason Ah'm asking, is because Ah remember Ella and me hud tae take a tram doon tae the Grand tae see it. It wiz late oan in the war. Wizn't it, Ella?'

'Och, Ah cannae remember. That's as far back as ma first dinner. Anywye, Ah'll tell youse ma choice.' All heads swivel in Ella's direction. '*Mildred Pierce*!'

'Awww! Noo that *wiz* terrific,' says Irene Stuart. 'Joan Crawford. Do ye know whit. Ah went tae see that *twice* in the same week. Ah just loved it! And whenever Alec spots in the *Radio Times* that it's coming oan the telly,' she looks round the company, 'he'll say, "Your picture's on again this week, Irene." Anywye. Is it no' time we had a man giving us his selection?'

'Ah'd be quite happy tae gie ye ma choice.' Archie

Cameron tentatively picks up the gauntlet. 'But Ah cannae make ma mind up between *Casablanca* and *Sunset Boulevard*. Ah'm stuck!'

'Ah don't blame ye, Erchie.' Agnes Dalrymple leans across the table, lays a hand on his forearm. 'They are two stoating pictures so they are.'

'And what aboot you, Agnes? You like your pictures.' Robert looks at her.

'Wheww!' She blows her cheeks out. 'Ah'm like Erchie. Ah'm spoiled for choice.' She looks up towards the smoke-stained ceiling for inspiration. 'Ohhhh! *White Heat*! Cagney!'

'Ah, now mind, that's another good yin.' Billy McClaren nods his head. 'Ah'll tell ye. When you're put under pressure like this, and ye start thinking of aw' the great fillums you've seen . . .' Billy taps Archie's foot under the table. 'And could Ah also point oot, Ah'm at a wee bit of a disadvantage here. Could Ah remind you all, Ah wiz a guest o' the Third Reich from 1940 tae '45. So I, eh, have a bit of a gap in ma relationship wi' the Blythsie.'

'Fuck me!' says Drena. 'Ah wondered how long it wid be before "the war" goat a mention! It's a pity Irma's no here. We could let the pair of you huv a special dispensation tae get your heids the 'gither – and select your favourite *German* fillum fae them years!'

The film round-up has been exhausted, but Robert Stewart doesn't want to lose the mood. The momentum. He decides to open up another avenue of showbiz, throw it into the mix. He sips his lager, leans forward. 'Ah'll tell you what was another great loss when it closed.' He has their attention. 'Only this time it was for the whole city – not just Maryhill.' He looks at the expectant faces. 'When the Empire Theatre shut down.' He sits back.

'That wiz 1963. And that wiz most definitely a big loss. Ohhh, Ah loved a night at the Empire.' As Robert could have forecast, Agnes Dalrymple is first to pick up the baton and run with it. He encourages her. 'Ah remember back in the late forties, Agnes. You often used to come into our house, bursting wi' excitement because you'd just seen a great turn at the Empire.' He laughs. 'Then you'd sit down wi' a cup of tea and have us aw' enthralled.'

'Aye. Ah used tae be a regular back then. There wiz a new act oan every week.' Irene comes in. 'You must have seen some big stars. Because *everybody* appeared at the Empire back then. Television was in its infancy. Live theatre was still the king.'

'It was'nae half.' Robert decides to contribute. 'You'd see their new poster up on the hoardings. Most of the big cities in the country had an Empire Theatre back then. There was a chain of them. Their proper name was Moss's Empires. They used to book all the top-liners for a tour. A week in each city –'

Agnes interrupts. 'Aye, and Ah'll tell ye. You had tae be sharp doon at that box office. Me and ma pal, Ethel, we used tae start queuing aboot an hour and a half before the box office opened. If it was one of the big American acts, you *had* to. The tickets used tae go like hot cakes!'

'Ah'll bet you've seen some stars.' Rhea looks at Agnes with growing interest. 'Who have ye seen?'

Agnes sits back, concentrates for a moment. 'Ah started going regularly efter the war, when Ah came back fae the Land Army.' She holds her left hand up, spreads its fingers, starts ticking them off. 'Ohhh, Bing Crosby, Danny Kaye, Jack Benny, Bob Hope, Johnnie Ray,' she starts again at her thumb, 'Billy Daniels, Guy Mitchell, Frank Sinatra, Frankie Laine . . .'

'My God!' says Drena. 'You'd be quicker if ye listed who ye *have'nae* seen!'

'Aye. And back then, Drena, stars really were *stars*. Especially the American ones. You normally only ever got tae see them in films.'

'Ah'll bet ye Sinatra wiz great?' says Ella.

'He wiz. Yet, Ah'll tell you something you'll no' believe. All the week that he was on, you did'nae need tae book in advance! You could walk intae the foyer – *on the night* – and there wiz nae queue! Ye could buy a ticket for any part of the hall.' Agnes sits back. Looks around imperiously.

Ella looks at her. 'Get away with ye! Frank Sinatra? Jist walk straight in?'

Agnes is now in her element. All shyness gone. 'Ah'll tell you for why. This was either late '52 or early '53. If ye cast your mind back, Sinatra had left his wife, Nancy – and his kids – and wiz having this torrid affair wi' Ava Gardner –'

Dennis O'Malley interrupts. 'Jayz! And who could blame him?' This earns him another dig in the ribs from Teresa.

'You see, back in them days film stars did not do that.

Not in public!' Agnes prods the top of the table with her finger. 'His popularity absolutely zonked when it all came oot!'

'Aye, Ah'd forgot aboot that,' says Ella. 'It wiz all over the papers and magazines at the time.'

'The night that ma pal and I went, the hall wiz only quarter full.' Agnes looks around. 'But Ah'll tell you, what a performance he gave us.' She pauses for effect. 'Dae ye know whit he did? He told everybody in the back stalls tae move tae the front. Then he got all the folk in the balcony tae come doonstairs as well. At the finish up, he had this small audience sitting in the first thirty or so rows of seats in the stalls.' They watch her eyes grow moist, hear the catch in her voice. 'And then he sang his heart out. Ah'll tell ye, nowadays you'd be quite happy to pay £25 to see the concert we got that evening – and you'd still consider you'd had a bargain!'

'Was that the best turn you ever seen at the Empire?' Robert looks at her.

'Mmm, nearly – but not quite!' The mistress of all she surveys sits back, says no more.

'Jeez-oh!' says Drena. 'If it wiz somebody better than Sinatra, they must huv been *really* special. Come on! Don't keep us in suspenders any longer. Who wiz it?'

The enigma known as Agnes smiles at them as she milks it to the limit. She leans forward.

'Laurel and Hardy,' she says.

The laughter is spontaneous. 'You're kidding!' says someone. 'Get away wi' ye!' says another.

'It wiz the most magical evening I ever spent at the Empire – or anywhere!' says Agnes.

'So what did they do?' asks Irene.

'Not a thing!' She has their rapt attention. 'Didn't have to. They were Laurel and Hardy!'

'C'mon then, Agnes.' Ella looks closely at her. 'Tell us the *full* story.'

From the corner of his eye, Robert watches the publican sidle along to their end of the bar. Once there, he folds his arms, leans on the counter, turns his 'good' ear towards them . . .

'Ah'm certain it was 1954. They were both auld men by now. Their heyday long past. Had'nae made a picture for years. Anywye, somebody had persuaded them tae come oot o' retirement tae make this film. It wiz shot up in the Highlands wid ye believe –'

Ella cuts in, gives her a quizzical look. 'Are you making this up, Agnes Dalrymple?'

'Honest tae God, Ah'm no'.' Agnes laughs. 'For the life of me, Ah cannae remember its title. It wiz a black and white film. Cesar Romero wiz in it. Ah seen it later in the cinema. It wiz dire!'

Ella comes in again. 'She's making this up! Ah'm telling youse, she is making this up!'

Agnes laughs along with the company. 'Obviously, while they were over here tae make it, the Empire people must huv coaxed them intae daeing a short tour. So, they finished up daeing a week in Glasgow.' Agnes sips her orangeade, looks at her friends. 'Now, as you older ones will know, all through the thirties Laurel and Hardy were jist aboot the biggest thing in pictures. And as *everybody* should know, the thirties were hard times. The Depression, unemployment, and it wiz a regular thing tae go tae your bed hungry.' She shakes her head. 'It's funny when ye think of it. Things only got better when the buggering war came along!'

'Hah! Ye can say that again,' says Mary Stewart.

Agnes nods. 'Now all during the thirties, whether you were an adult or a kid, if you managed tae raise a couple o'coppers, one o' the great pleasures wiz tae go tae the local fleapit and see the latest Laurel and Hardy picture. Then ye could lose yerself. Forget aw' your troubles and laugh yourself silly. And when at last, reluctantly, you had tae come oot into the street, oh, you alwiz felt better. You were mibbe going hame tae a cauld hoose and a slice o' bread and jam – if you were lucky – but when you went tae bed, you'd lie in the dark and talk aboot the picture. "Remember that bit, remember this bit?" And laugh again at aw' your favourite scenes until you fell asleep.' She sighs.

'Oh, that is so true, Agnes.' Irene Stuart comes in. 'Oor James and me. If we had enough tae buy a sweetie, or go and see Laurel and Hardy, we'd dae withoot the sweeties. Every time!'

'Well, so here I am, sitting in the Empire that evening. Right from the start there was a strange atmosphere. The place was full. Yet there wiz'nae the same buzz of excitement you alwiz got when you were there to see a big star like Crosby or Sinatra. It was different. And somehow, you knew the rest of the audience felt the same.' She stops. Obviously trying to find the right words. 'It was normally popular big singers, or maybe comedy acts that came tae the Empire. You never, ever expected you would get tae see Laurel and Hardy. Their day was long past. You only ever seen them in the cinema – and *that* wiz back in the thirties. Yet, here they were in Glasgow. In a few minutes they were gonny be walking onto that stage! That same pair who, back in the thirties, were one of the few things you could depend on to give you a laugh. Then a voice said, "Ladies and Gentlemen. May we present, Laurel and Hardy!" And suddenly Oliver Hardy is walking out from the left side of the stage. He's taking those quick, fussy little steps that he always did.' Agnes pauses, swallows hard. 'But, oh, he wis'nae the big hefty man he used tae be. He'd lost a lot of weight. Did'nae look very well. Tired.' She sighs. Then smiles. 'And on comes Stan from the other wing. And he's taking them silly, big galumphing steps he used to take when he was trying to keep up wi' Ollie. He looked quite well. Older, but not too different from when he was in the films. And they both have their bowler hats on, and they're heading for centre stage.' She looks at her friends. 'Then, a wonderful thing happened. As soon as they'd been announced, the audience had begun to clap. But when Ollie actually appeared, well, the applause turned to cheers. Then when Stan walked on everybody, as if on command, simply stood up, cheering and roaring and clapping.' Agnes falters a second. 'It was as if we all realised at exactly the same moment – we are actually getting tae *see* Laurel and Hardy! This is oor chance tae thank them for aw' the fun and laughs they gave us. Let them see what they meant tae us. It's mibbe years ago, but we hav'nae forgot.' Agnes's voice quavers once more. 'You only have ma word for it, but it was quite simply love and thanks coming from that audience in waves and heading for those two old men up on that stage.' She looks around her. 'That's what it was. A standing ovation – for being Laurel and Hardy! It just went on and on and on. And the two of them stood in the middle o' the stage, bowler hats in their hands, waving them, continually bowing, and the tears streaming doon their faces. They hadn't said a single word since they'd came on.' Agnes sits back. 'So there ye are. That was the most wonderful evening I ever spent in the Glasgow Empire.'

'Dae ye see the time?' says Drena. 'Gone midnight! Urr we going hame tae oor beds?'

'Definitely!' Ella puts her fags and matches into her handbag. 'But listen!' She gently thumps the side of her clenched hand onto the table to get their attention. 'Now jist before we go, you'll have tae let me tell you *my* Empire story.' She reaches out to Agnes, lays a hand on one of hers. 'Now, Ah'm certainly no' trying tae steal your thunder, hen. Naebody could top what you've jist telt us. This is jist a quickie.' She looks at everybody. 'As Ah'm sure you all know, the second-house at the Glasgow Empire on a Saturday night, has *long* been known as "the graveyard of English comedians"! Most of the audience have come straight from the pub and they jist sit there, arms folded, and basically say, "Right. Make us laugh!"' Ella finishes her sherry . . .

'It would be, Ah think, around 1962. Mike and Bernie Winters were the biggest thing oan telly. So of course, they got signed up tae dae the Moss's Empires. Archie and me got tickets for the Saturday evening – second hoose.' She looks around knowingly. 'We'd got smashing seats in the stalls. At last, the time comes for the main act. The MC announces them, and Mike Winters – he's the "straight man" – comes walking oot ontae the stage to dae five minutes on his own. Jist topical patter. Anywye, he diz'nae get a single laugh. Not a titter. Ah felt sorry fur him. So, as he's about to finish his warm-up, his brother Bernie is supposed tae walk oot unannounced and join him. It's part of the act.' Ella struggles to keep from laughing, 'All of a sudden big Bernie appears from the wings. As ye know, he alwiz plays the daft yin. He's daeing a funny walk and chuntering away tae himself. He gets mibbe halfway towards his brother, when this broad Glesga voice comes from somewhere in the stalls – "Fuck me! There's two o' them!"'

It's well after midnight when the party vacate 'The Shakey'. 'Ah knew there would'nae be jist *wan* night-cap,' says Ella. Archie puts his arm round her. 'But you've enjoyed yerself, hen, haven't ye?'

As they reach the junction of Raeberry Street and the Maryhill Road, Robert Stewart stops for a moment, points across to the now dark, closed-for-the-night cinema. A blustery wind is making a couple of sheets of yesterday's *Daily Record* glide along the pavement in front of it. 'Just look at it, Rhea. We've been going in there since we were kids. And, when we were winching . . .' He breaks off, laughs. 'Ah'm just thinking. When I was a kid and used tae go tae the matinee, I always wanted tae be as near the front as possible.' He pulls Rhea in tight. 'Then a few years later, when we start going oot together, all of a sudden it's the *back* row I want to be in.'

'Aye,' says Irene. 'It will maybe look like it always has,' she sighs, 'but it won't be a cinema any more. What a shame.'

'It is.' Ella pulls the collar of her coat up, links her arm through Archie's. 'But it'll be an even bigger shame in the morning – when that alarm clock goes aff!' The group sets off up the Maryhill Road, chatting, laughing and reminiscing as if they had all the time in the world. Just before the road makes its gentle turn to the left at Queen's Cross, Robert glances back. If he narrows his eyes, he can just about make out the Blythswood's unlit canopy in the distance. Maybe.

CHAPTER NINETEEN

Grasping the Nettle

Ruth Lockerbie knows the confrontation has to happen. Sooner or later. She'd prefer sooner . . .

Vicky Shaw and Steve Anderson have just walked through the door into Le Bar Rendezvous. It's obvious they are in the middle of a spat. Ruth forces a smile, raises a hand in welcome. Vicky acknowledges, Anderson doesn't. They make straight for an unoccupied banquette. No walk over to say 'Hello'. No exchange of kisses. A sadness drapes itself over Ruth's shoulders – Vicky is wearing dark glasses again. She'll be bruised near her eyes. As the anger begins to rise in her, Ruth takes a calming draw on her cigarette. It doesn't work. Why does Vicky put up with this? Since Johnny McKinnon died she's been a lost soul. Look at her. Gets no enjoyment out of life any more. A medley of snapshot-like memories runs through her mind. The wonderful times we used to have together. Vicky and Johnny, George and Ruth. Days that were going to last for ever. '*Huh!*' These thoughts are interrupted when she becomes aware Anderson is crossing the floor, heading for the bar. He strides over to where she sits on her stool. 'Hiyah, Ruth.' He leans towards her. When she doesn't offer her cheek, he sways back.

'Hello.' She says it as coldly as she can muster, then proceeds to ignore him as the preparation of a Black Sobranie cigarette for smoking seems to become her main aim in life. He gives his drinks order to the barman and soon, as the silence lengthens, he begins to shift uncomfortably from foot to foot. This is followed by a session of finger-drumming on the bar. The unsettling silence gets to him. 'Ahhh, not a bad day considering we're now into October.'

'It is.'

Stefan sets up his drinks. Anderson takes one in each hand, turns away from the bar. 'See you later, Ruth.'

She makes no reply. As he walks slowly back to his seat, Ruth looks beyond him, at Vicky. She sits very still. Lost in thought. Lost in misery more like. Ruth sighs. As the dance floor clears she catches sight of George. He's doing his rounds. At the moment, sitting with a smartly-dressed couple. Probably in their late forties. Look as if they might be in business. Seconds later, he rises, heads for the banquette where Vicky and Anderson sit. She is kissed on both cheeks, he shakes hands with the weasel. *Huh*! Better you than me, George. After a brief conversation, he smiles, waves a hand, weaves his way back to the bar. 'All right, darling?' He touches her cheek.

'Yes.'

'Poor Vicky. She has a bruise on her cheekbone. Turned round in bed last night, didn't realise how close she was to the bedside cupboard. Caught her cheekbone on a corner –'

'Oh! For God's sake, George! Don't be so dim! It was a kitchen shelf last month!'

His mouth falls open. 'What was a kitchen shelf?'

'He's been knocking her about again!'

He glances over to the banquette, turns back to her. 'Steve?'

'*No*! Santa bloody Claus! Who do you think?'

'Jeez! Are you sure?'

'Certain! And so are Rhea *and* Ruby *and* Wilma. Why do you think she wears those sunglasses so regularly. She has marks to hide. That's why they haven't come over to stand with us. She knows I look closely at her. And in spite of the extra makeup I always spot the bruises. She's embarrassed, poor girl.'

George looks over at them again, then back to Ruth. 'That's awful! Ohhh, poor Vicky. But why doesn't she give him his marching orders? They're not married. Not even living together.'

'Oh, it's complicated, George. These last two years, since she lost Johnny,' he hears her voice catch, 'she's let herself go. Drinking too much. Allowing that reptile to dominate her –'

George cuts in. 'Can't *we* do something?'

'We will. Well, I will, darling. Leave it to me. It'll be better if it comes from me.'

'Mmmm, well.' He looks over at them, she's knows he's getting angry. 'Are you sure?'

Ruth looks up at him from where she sits on her stool. 'Trust me, darling!'

It's shortly after midnight. Ruth has spent most of the evening glancing over at the couple. Anderson has been drinking steadily. There has been very little conversation between them.

Mmmm. I wonder. Is there a possibility I might get a chance tonight? Ruth changes position, sits at an angle to the banquette so she'll appear to be watching the dancers. From the corner of her eye she sees Anderson start. He turns towards Vicky, leans to the side until his mouth is inches away from her ear. She is facing forward, rigid, frightened. He's obviously getting onto her. So intent is he with his bullying, he doesn't notice Ruth has turned her head, is now looking straight at them. She clearly sees him, twice, dig Vicky in the ribs. Short, nasty hooks which only travel a few inches. Vicky's mouth forms an 'Oh!' as they wind her. The blood rises to Ruth's head. It's taking all her willpower to stop herself running over to her friend's aid. But she's been reading the signs. Knows they will leave soon. He likes to get her on her own. It won't be long now. Ruth has rehearsed this scenario in her mind for a quite a while. Its time has come . . .

Minutes later, as forecast, Anderson rises. He waves his hand, thumb uppermost, in a peremptory manner, telling Vicky it's time to go. Ruth feels the gorge rise in her throat. C'mon, control yourself. She stares at Anderson. Oh! I am going to enjoy this. She forces a smile, raises a hand. 'VICKY! STEVE! A minute of your time . . .' She slides off the stool. Wants to be standing when they come over – take advantage of the fact she is inches taller than Anderson.

As they stop in front of her, Ruth, without a word, reaches out, takes hold of Vicky's forearms with both her hands, and gently swings her to the left until they stand side-by-side, their backs against the bar. 'Stay there a moment, darling.' By the time she turns back to Anderson, her face is firmly set. Looking down at him, she presses the forefinger of her right hand against his lapel. 'Don't you *ever* come back into this club. You are barred! And more important, do *not* speak to, contact, or in any way bother my friend Vicky in future. From this moment on, you are out of her life.' She moves her face closer to his, cocks her head to one side. 'Have you got that?'

'Who dae you fucking think you're talkin' tae? It's got fuck all tae dae wi' you. Tell her, Vicky.'

'Oh, really, Ruth. It's not as bad as it –'

Ruth half turns. 'Yes, I know it isn't. It's worse! Vicky, all your friends in the Saturday night gang are sick of seeing this weasel treat you like dirt –'

'You are pushing it yah snobby whore. Don't think being a woman will fuckin' save you –'

'Oh! Thinking of lifting your hand to me, are you? You're

such a tough guy with women. Well, you would be very wise to listen to what I'm about to say to you.' Again, Ruth presses her finger against his chest. Harder this time. 'If you attempt to bother Vicky, or me, in future, I'll immediately get in touch with the police to give them certain information that's come into my possession. I know they will be *very* interested to hear about the working arrangement you have,' she manages a smile, 'with a certain gang on the south side.'

Anderson's mouth opens, then shuts. The look on his face, and the pause before he speaks, confirms that what Fred Dickinson told her must have been spot-on. Anderson rolls his shoulders. 'Ah have'ny got a clue what you're on aboot. You're talking shite! C'mon, Vicky.' Ruth stretches her left arm out, presses Vicky's hand to restrain her. 'Oh well, if you tell me that's a load of rubbish. Fine! So it won't cause you any problems then, if I tell the police about that scheme of yours where you loan out used cars to criminals? What name does it trade under – Rent A Getaway Car?' She looks at him. His mouth opens, as if about to speak, then he thinks better of it. She decides to twist the knife a little further. 'When you've run a night club for the number of years I have, it's surprising the things folk tell you. Oh, and before you go. Purely as a matter of interest. What do you think will happen if the police raid Big Bernie, and he later finds out *you* were the root cause of all his trouble? I don't think he'll be best pleased.'

'You fucking evil bitch!' He steps towards her. She stands her ground. 'If you fucking think –' Just as he starts to speak, Ruth is aware of movement behind him. There's a sudden flurry, then a yelp from Anderson as he is gripped by his right arm, and simultaneously his left arm is forced up his back. From behind Anderson's shoulder, the face of Peter Keenan appears. 'Is he giving you a bit o' bother, Ruth?'

'He's thinking about it, Peter.'

The ex-champ turns his head, speaks into Anderson's ear. 'You bother ma friend and Ah'll fucking punch ye up and doon the length o' Woodlands Road. BELIEVE IT!' The final shout makes Anderson jump. Keenan looks at Ruth. 'Is he fur oot the door?'

She holds a hand up. 'In just a moment.' She leans closer to Anderson. 'And you should also believe what I've just told you. Cause trouble for Vicky, or anybody connected with me, and I'll start singing like a bird – and I *don't* mean the one on the Glasgow coat of arms – the bird that never sang!' She turns. 'Thank you, Peter. He's leaving now.' With his feet 'hardly touching' Anderson is frog-marched directly across the small dance floor and, to his embarrassment, ignominiously ejected into the night. A smiling Peter Keenan returns. 'Ah fair enjoyed that. From the very first minute Ah clapped eyes oan that yin, Ah took an instant scunner tae him.'

'Join the club! Thank you very much, Peter. That was wonderful. Will you take a drink?'

'Och, not at all. Ah'd better get away back ower tae the manageress. She'll be wondering what's been going on. Probably thinks Ah'm trying tae make a comeback! See yah!'

Ruth turns to Vicky. 'Pull another stool over, darling.'

As Vicky sits next to Ruth, she sees she is trying, unsuccessfully, to insert one of her cigarettes into the tortoiseshell holder. She looks at her trembling fingers. 'Here, let me do that for you.'

'You'll have to, darling. That must have taken more out of me than I thought. There was a moment when I thought the little rat was going to take a swing at me!'

As Vicky inserts the Black Sobranie into the holder, Ruth looks along the bar. 'STEFAN! A double cognac, please. Greek Metaxa. Same for Vicky.' She inhales deeply as her friend supplies a light, starts to calm herself as she watches the exhaled smoke catch up with that which lazily twists up from the end of the holder. Ruth reaches for her Metaxa and, ice chinking in the glass as she lifts it, lets half the measure slip down her throat. 'Oh, boy! Did I need that.' She looks at Vicky. 'Now, darling. Tell me I haven't put myself through all that for nothing? You won't let him back into your life, will you?'

'No.' Vicky gives a shuddering sigh. 'No, you're right. Don't know why I kept seeing him. I knew none of you liked him.' She looks at Ruth. '*Huh*! Even *I* didn't like him!' She holds a hand up as Ruth is about to speak. 'It's since Johnny's been gone. I've lost interest in myself. In life. Don't care about anything any more.' Tears, free at last, begin to run down her cheeks.

Ruth takes a sip of cognac, another languorous inhalation of Turkish tobacco. 'It was Johnny who made me do this tonight!' She lays a hand on top of Vicky's to stop her interrupting. 'This dislike of Anderson has really been getting to me. It's become a damned fixation. When the Dalbeattie Street irregulars are in, as soon as you appear with him in tow, it spoils the night for everybody. We can't stand him! As you know, you haven't yet been invited to Kelvin Court. All the rest have. I was determined that reptile would never step through my door. But tonight, darling, you *will* be setting foot in it. You're coming back with George and me, *and* you'll be staying for as long as it takes to get you sorted out.'

Vicky looks quizzically at her. 'What did you mean when you said, "Johnny made me do this"?'

'I've been so concerned about you and Anderson. Worried because you didn't seem able to break away from him. I kept telling myself, "Johnny would want you to do something about it." It must have been on my mind *so* much . . .' she pauses to finish her Metaxa, smiles, 'that on Tuesday night, I had such a lovely dream, Vicky. I was in the Hillhead Bar. Johnny and I sitting at his table.' She stops for a moment. 'Oh, it was so real. Just like old times.' As she listens, Vicky's eyes moisten again. 'And as I got up to leave, that was when he asked me. He took my hand, kissed the back of it like always, then said, "You'll have to split them up, darling. She can't do it on her own." And that was it. It was *so* vivid.' She laughs. 'Then I woke up – and when I realised it was a dream, I didn't want to waken up! I snuggled in under the covers and tried to get back to it. Oh, Vicky. I just wanted to be back in the Hillhead Bar with Johnny. Just for another wee while.' She turns to her friend, takes both her hands. 'You won't let Johnny and me down, will you?'

Vicky gives a sad smile. 'Not after what you've just told me.' She sits quite still for a moment. Then, 'How I wish I could dream about him, Ruth. Just now and again.' Tears, big tears, spill from her eyes once more and run all the way to her chin.

CHAPTER TWENTY

The First Day of the Rest of Your Life

It's late the next morning. A Sunday. Vicky Shaw wakes up in the guest bedroom at Kelvin Court. She looks around at first, not sure where she is, until the events of last night come back to her. 'Mmmm!' With a delicious feeling of indolence she turns round, coories in, and drifts back to sleep.

Just over a mile away, in Dalbeattie Street, there is no time for 'long-lies' this morning. Things have been stirring for the last two hours. A large van, bearing the legend Kelvindale Laundry, stands outside Number 18 with its rear doors open. It is three-quarters full of furniture and other sundry household essentials from two flats – Mary Stewart's and her son Robert's. In spite of the dwindling number of residents now living up the close, there are plenty of willing helpers.

Frank and Wilma Galloway, in their Glasgow Corporation

Transport uniforms, step out of their front door onto the second-storey landing. Wilma watches as Frank locks up, then waits for him to step to one side. Taking his place, she proceeds to turn the door handle rapidly from side to side, whilst pushing and pulling at the same time. Finally, to make *extra* sure it's locked, she shoulder-charges it.

'Noo, are ye sure that's locked, hen?' Having just taken a draw on a Senior Service, he accompanies his enquiry with rolling gouts of smoke spilling upwards from his mouth. He looks at his watch. 'We're early, Wilma. If ye want, there's time tae call in at the Maryhill fire station and huv a couple o' lads sent roon' tae put their shoulders tae it! Jist tae put yer mind at ease, hen.' He smiles benignly.

'That's jist stupit!' she says.

In a manner reminiscent of WC Fields, Frank recoils at this slight, as though cut to the bone. 'Ah'm trying tae be helpful, precious. Worried in case ye hurt yersel'. After aw', you're jist a wee skelf, dear. That door's too big fur ye.'

Wilma takes him by the arm, spins him round in the direction of the stairs. 'Aye, well you're no' too big fur me, Frank Galloway. C'mon, or we *will* finish up being late fur oor work.'

'Yes, beloved.'

As they step onto the first storey, Robert and Rhea Stewart's door lies wide open. Frank goes into the lobby, looks into their kitchen. It's cleared. The carpet has been lifted. Two pieces of broken linoleum lie on the dusty floorboards. On the wallpaper, clean rectangles framed in dust bear witness to where pictures and photographs hung until an hour ago. For the life of him, Frank can't remember a single one of them. He looks again at the abandoned kitchen. I suppose this will be us soon . . .

Wilma breaks his train of thought. 'Everybody must be doon at the lorry. We'll away and catch them ootside.'

'Aye,' he says. It sounds more like a sigh.

They emerge from the close. Archie Cameron and Billy McClaren stand at the rear of the vehicle, two tea chests in front of them. Voices, accompanied by muffled thumps and bangs, drift out of the van into the Sunday-morning street. Frank and Wilma walk over, stand beside Archie and Billy. 'Have you got enough hands tae manage?' asks Frank.

Work stops for a moment. Robert and Rhea and Drena McClaren, smile out at them. 'Och, aye,' says Rhea. 'More than enough tae flit oor room and kitchen – and Mary's.'

Wilma looks around. 'Where's Ella?'

'She's up the sterrs, in her ain hoose, making a stack o' bacon sannies and two pots o' tea. We cannae let them leave Dalbeattie Street wi' empty stomachs. Robert's ma is helping her.'

Frank looks at Rhea. 'Where's Teresa and Dennis? Ah thought Ah heard them earlier.'

Rhea looks up at her parents' first-floor window. Then drops her voice. 'Oh, God! Don't mention them. They are gettin' thurselves intae a right state! They started off giving us a hand. But wance we began moving *oor* stuff oot the hoose and intae the van . . .' She has to stop as her voice catches. 'That's when it hit them that we're no' gonny be living next door any mair. We'll be in Wilton Crescent – and they'll soon be miles away in the Molendinar Scheme. *Huh*! That's if they ever get the bugger finished!' Rhea blows her cheeks out. 'My ma kept huving tae stoap for a wee greet, and that wid set ma daddy away.' She lays a hand on Wilma's forearm. 'But wait 'til ye hear this. She eventually calmed herself doon, and we are aw' working away fine. Then suddenly she shouts, "IT'S BELLA!" She swore blind she had jist seen Granny, as clear as could be, looking doon at us from her auld window!'

Robert takes over from Rhea. 'So that was it. We sent the pair o' them up tae their hoose tae make a cuppa.' He coughs. 'Anyway, we'd better get on.'

'Eh, excuse me?' Rhea draws herself up. 'Are ye no' gonny tell them the rest? Don't be shy.'

Robert looks embarrassed. He pauses. 'Well, when I seen Teresa suddenly stop and look up at Granny's old windows. I glanced up as well . . .'

'Uh-huh! Aye, and whit did ye see?' demands Rhea. 'You've telt the rest o' us, so ye might as well tell Frank and Wilma.'

'Well. I definitely caught a glimpse of white hair. As if I'd caught somebody ducking away from the window, because they'd been spotted.' He shrugs. 'I'm just telling you what I saw.'

Frank looks at his watch. 'I'd much rather be here giving

you folks a hand. But Wilma and I are on at midday.' They give Rhea a kiss, then Frank turns to Robert. 'At least we know we'll be seeing you two regularly at the Bar Rendezvous.' At just this moment Sammy and Louise Stewart emerge from the close, each carrying a cardboard box. 'Goodness me!' says Frank. 'A Sunday morning, and these two are up before twelve!' He puts an arm round Sammy's shoulder. 'If the Students' Union find oot you were up before noon oan a Sunday, Samuel Stewart, they'll drum you oot!'

'Louise wiz jist as bad,' says Rhea. 'It wiz nearly ten before their faither chivvied the two o' them oot o' their beds. Ah hud visions of arriving in Wilton Crescent and oor new neebours keeking through their curtains, watching us carrying these two – still in their beds – oot o' the van and intae the hoose!' This accusation ends with a reflex bosom adjustment.

'Methinks, a slight exaggeration, mater,' comments Sammy.

'Whit did he jist say tae me?' enquires Rhea. 'Wiz that him being cheeky tae his mammy?'

Louise yawns. 'Ah never got back from the Locarno 'til efter two this morning. Ah huv'nae had ma full eight hours . . .'

The noise of a window being raised interrupts Louise's plea in mitigation. Ella Cameron's head appears from sixty feet up. 'There's a table groaning under the wecht o' bacon sannies and pots o' tea up here!'

Frank and Wilma step off in the direction of the

Maryhill Road. 'Right! We're away, folks. All the best!' says Frank.

'Cheerio!' says Wilma. 'See ye at the Bar Rendezvous.'

It's an hour later. The sandwiches have long gone, but the ever-appetising smell of fried bacon lingers in the air. The teapots lie cold and empty. The conversation, so bright and sparkling until twenty minutes ago, is faltering. The time is nigh for three generations of Stewarts to leave 18 Dalbeattie Street. For ever.

'Ah'm afraid we're gonny have tae bite the bullet,' says Robert.

'Oh, Jayz!' mutters Teresa.

The room is suddenly silent. Pin-droppingly so. The few stalwarts who can usually be relied on to think of something to say – Archie, Billy, Ella and Drena – find they are at a loss for words. Mercifully, this heavy silence is broken as hurrying footsteps enter the close. Their volume increases as they begin climbing the stairs, clickety-clacks echoing up the stairwell.

'Who is this?' says Drena. They listen in silence as, now and again, the feet take some flights two at a time. Every head turns in the direction of the open doors as they reach the top landing. There's the rap of knuckles on the front door . . .

'Halloooh! It is us!'

'It's IRMA!' say Archie and Billy in unison. All eyes are fixed on the kitchen door. A breathless Irma Armstrong and the tall figure of Bert behind her come bustling in, wreathed in smiles.

'Aw Irma, hen. Ah wiz hoping against hope ye would come tae see us off,' says Rhea.

'Ah thought they might,' says Ella.

'It's jist lovely tae see the pair of ye, today of all days!' says Drena.

The entire company surround their former neighbours. Tears are shed by the womenfolk as kisses are exchanged. Archie and Billy avoid looking at one another as their stiff upper lips grow weak. The two men wait until the initial welcomes are over – and they have their emotions under control – then . . . 'Irma, *liebchen. Kommst du mal hier*!' Archie Cameron spreads his arms wide. Billy McClaren stands beside him. Opens his arms. '*Liebe, Irmchen. Wieder in nummer achtzehn* Dalbeattie *Strasse*!'

'Fuck me!' says Ella. She looks at Drena. 'The El Alamein Reunion is early this year!'

'Help ma Boab!' says Irma.

Robert Stewart climbs to the top landing. Walks into the Camerons' house. Looks at the crowd in the kitchen. If they all had drinks in their hands, you'd swear blind there was a party going on. 'Rhea! Ma! The van's all locked up. It's gone *two* o'clock. Will you come on. We'll have to go!'

'Aye, Robert's right. We'll have tae face up tae it, girls.' Ella starts to shepherd everyone out of her kitchen. Drena lends a hand. 'C'mon, everybody doonstairs tae see them off. Let's go!'

As they troop down six flights of stairs, Bert Armstrong falls into step beside Robert. 'How did ye manage tae get a hold o' the van?'

'Kelvindale Laundry is one of Rossleigh's best customers. It was brought in to get two new tyres on. So I said I'd do them for nothing – if I could borrow the van for my Sunday flitting.'

'That was good thinking. It's just the right size.'

The party gather on the pavement. 'Rhea, you and my ma sit in the back of the Rover. Sammy's in the front with Louise. He's driving. I'm taking the van. Archie and Billy will be in with me, they're coming to give us a hand wi' the unloading.' He looks at Rhea and his mother. 'Best to make your goodbyes quick. Otherwise it'll be too much for you.'

Rhea hugs and kisses Teresa and Dennis. None of them are able to say more than the beginnings of a few words. Ella and Drena come over, stand either side of Rhea, link their arms through hers. Rhea swallows hard, nods towards the close mouth, then looks at her friends in turn. 'Ah'm really looking forward tae oor new hoose. Red-sandstone. Bay windows. Wally close. Ah know it'll be great . . .' Her voice fails her for a moment. 'But Robert and me were born in this close. We're baith forty-three and we've lived in it aw' oor lives. Oor parents have always been near at hand. It's sad tae leave it . . .' She breaks off as a figure emerges from the close. 'Agnes! Where huv ye been?'

Agnes Dalrymple hurries over, tears streaming down her face. 'Ah've been trying tae stay in the hoose oot the road, Rhea. Ah've known you and Robert maist o' your lives and Ah could'nae face the thought of saying cheerio tae ye.' She stops, dabs her eyes. 'Then Ah looked oot the windae a minute ago, and saw youse were ready tae leave,' she gives a shuddering sob, 'and Ah could'nae bear the thought of *no*' saying cheerio tae ye! So Ah've had tae come doon!'

'Aw, Agnes. That's lovely so it is.' Rhea kisses her on the cheek.

Agnes looks around her. 'Jist look at the state o' the place. Half the streets roon' aboot huv been knocked doon. Maist o' Dalbeattie Street's already gone. Ah've seen tidier bomb sites!' She dabs her eyes again. 'You'd think aw' the mess would make it easier tae leave, wouldn't ye? But it diz'nae.' She sighs.

All the womenfolk gather round Agnes and she is kissed and hugged as though *she* were leaving. Ella leans over to Drena's ear. 'Ah've telt ye afore. Agnes is a poet – and the poor soul diz'nae realise it.'

After all the fuss which has just been made of her, an embarrassed Agnes looks at her neighbours. 'Whit was all that fur? Are youse all flitting the day – and youse huv'nae telt me?'

Somehow, her arrival on the scene is the catalyst that's needed to get things moving. Minutes later, the Rover 90 and the laundry van start up and pull away from 18 Dalbeattie Street. Teresa O'Malley has decided that if 'herself' is going to make another appearance *this* will surely be the moment. While her neighbours wave and shout best wishes at the departing vehicles, she quickly spins her head the other way, looks up at what have always been Granny Thomson's windows. She is rewarded by the merest glimpse of a face topped with white hair, which instantly withdraws into the shadows. Teresa smiles. Murmurs, 'Gotcha, Bella! Oi knowed ye'd want tae see them off.'

CHAPTER TWENTY-ONE

Knowing Your Place

Archie Cameron junior stands at the close mouth. Another gust of icy wind blows in from the back court, cuts through him, and exits into the street. Jesus-johnny! That is straight from the buggering Arctic. He takes his watch hand out of his trouser pocket. Quarter tae eight. The hand is thrust back in, deeper than before. C'monnn, Lexie. Where the hell are ye?

At last there comes noise and movement from way up top. A door bangs shut. The faint jingle of keys is heard as she locks the front door. Her ma will already be at work doon the City Bakeries. Cleaners start early.

The cantata for heels gets louder as she clip-clops down the five flights of stairs, turns onto the last half-landing, and starts her descent to the close. Archie decides to put on the agony. As he comes into sight, Lexie finds he's doing a hunched-up, hands-in-pocket jig to show how chilled he is from waiting. He looks up. 'Where huv ye been fur God's sake?'

She stops in mid-step, her right hand resting on the banister. 'Whit dae ye mean "Where huv ye been?"?' She waits for his answer.

When he sees the change in her face, her manner, he fervently wishes he'd kept his big mouth shut. 'Eh, well, you're late. We'll huv tae hurry. We're usually away by noo, Lexie.' Oh, man! Ye know she never lets ye away wi' anything. Whit a stupid bugger you are.

'Nobody asked ye tae wait for me, sunshine. So don't you tell me "You're late"! And can I also point oot you live on the same landing. You can hear me coming out my door in the morning. Why didn't ye stay in your house until you heard me leave? There's no need tae freeze your arse off in the close!' She now proceeds to stride down the last few stairs like she's understudying Bette Davis in *All About Eve*.

As she approaches him, Archie feels his face flush. He didn't mean it like that. He's also annoyed at the confident way she has just faced him down. Are you ever gonny learn, Archie? You're forever trying tae impress her – but usually finish up looking like a fuckin' eegit. THINK before ye speak, yah dozey bugger!

Without another word she sets off at such a brisk pace across the street, he has to run a few steps to catch up with her. 'Ah did'nae mean that tae sound sort of snappy, Lexie. It wiz wan o' they things where you're trying tae be funny – and it comes oot all wrong. Ah wiz jist kidding on, with me being a bit cauld and –'

'Is that right. You could have fooled me.' She neither looks at him nor slows down as she speaks. After a while she becomes aware that he's rather subdued as he almost trots along beside her. Probably wishes he'd bitten his tongue.

A few minutes later he gives a humourless laugh. 'Well, my original idea was that I thought it would be nice if ye came doon the stairs and sort of, ye know, found your escort waiting. Anywye! You know whit Burns said aboot "the best laid plans".' She takes a quick glance at him as they stride down the Maryhill Road. God! You've not half cut the legs from him this morning, Lexie. Ah'll bet he thinks Ah'm a right bitch. Alwiz shooting him down. Anyway, leave it. Nae good letting him off the hook. Don't want tae give him the least encouragement. He'd have the cheek tae be asking me out again by the afternoon. Huh, he's had that! Hardly oot o' the jail ten minutes. No. That knock-back will dae him good. What a bloody check, trying tae tell me off!

It's later that same day. Agnes Dalrymple picks up some pieces of coal, carefully places them on the fire. As she hooks the tongs back onto the companion set, Granny Thomson comes into her mind. She looks up at the china dogs on the mantelpiece. Smiles. Makes herself comfortable in her fireside chair. Looks up again. Aye. That's your auld wally dugs, hen. Aw' them years they stood oan yer mantel-piece. She looks down. You never bothered wi' tongs, did ye? Picked the wee nuggets up wi' yer fingers tae put them oan the fire. 'Fingers were invented afore tongs!' ye used tae say. Ah cannae believe it'll be ten years, next year, since you've been gone, Bella. But you've nae idea how often ye get mentioned. '*Huh*!' You get *seen* noo and again – never mind mentioned! Her thoughts are interrupted by a squally shower of rain battering on her windows. She puts her feet up on a low stool. Looks at the bright fire. Feels suddenly cosy, contented. Ye picked a good week tae be off, Agnes. She reaches for last week's *People's Friend*, finds the story she wanted to read. Soon, the heat from the fire, the comfort of her chair, the sound of the rain being held at bay, all conspire together. The magazine begins to droop . . .

From the direction of a half-cleared Rothesay Street, with nothing in its way but the memory of recently demolished tenements, there comes a sudden WHUMPF! It rattles Agnes's kitchen windows. The crashing avalanche which follows makes her kitchen floor vibrate. Her heavy eyelids barely open. 'Harrumph!' She clears her throat. Murmurs, 'Jeez, that sounded like –' *Whumpf*! The second thump and crash are in a lower register. No vibration this time. She is still for a moment, begins to doze once more – then comes wide awake. 'They're demolishing again! Hah! No' before buggering time.' Agnes eases herself out of her chair, goes to the kitchen windows, lifts a curtain. The angular top of the long-idle mobile crane moves back and forth, increasing the momentum of the steel ball. She lets the yellow curtain drop. 'Aye! The praying mantis is back at work! Ah'll away doon tae Drena's.'

* * *

She knocks on the half-open door. 'Are ye in, hen?'

'Aye, in ye come, Agnes. Ah thocht you'd be doon when ye heard them starting up again.'

'They must huv got their money troubles sorted oot. So if they're demolishing here – they must be building again oan the Molendinar.' She pulls a kitchen chair out. 'Cause they cannae knock these doon, unless they've somewhere tae put us.'

Drena has started to mask a pot of tea. As the boiling water hushes over the teabags, she rythmically stirs. The sharp 'chink' of the spoon hitting the insides, gives the only clue that the blackened teapot was once aluminium. 'Will ye take a biscuit?' she says.

'Aye, go on. Ah alwiz waken up peckish. Ah wiz huving a grand wee doze in front o' the fire. Then crash, bang, wallop! Ah thocht the buggering Luftwaffe wiz back for a minute!'

'Ah've nae doot we can expect a letter fae the Hoosing Department in the next day or two. Might give us an idea when we'll be moving,' says Drena. She opens a biscuit tin, brings a couple of plates from the sideboard, sits herself at the table. 'Tae be honest, Ah huv'nae been aw' that fussed aboot flitting. But since Robert and Rhea and Mary went . . .' She pauses. 'The life is jist draining oot o' the close, in't it? It's no' the same any mair.'

'Aye. The game's a bogey, Drena. Even the Corporation diz'nae clean the street any mair. And the few of us that are left, only *sweep* the close and stairs nooadays. It's no' worth the bother washing them. Within two days the dust has blown in aff the street and they're mucky again.' Agnes sighs heavily. 'Every night, when Ah come hame fae ma work and Ah turn that corner, it's like walking intae a bomb site! Ah'm glad when Ah get intae the hoose. It's the only thing in Dalbeattie Street that's still familiar. My ain wee room and kitchen.'

'Well, at least,' Drena laughs, 'when Ella comes hame fae work the night and comes in for her cuppa – we'll huv something tae talk aboot. The men are back at work.' She pauses. 'Ah hope we're all gonny be close tae one another, when we flit tae the scheme. Ella and me huv already wrote in, and asked if we can take either side of a semi-detached . . .' She stops, listens.

'Hi-yah! Are ye in?' They recognise Irene Stuart's voice as she calls from Drena's lobby. She comes into the kitchen, still wearing her peenie, closes the door behind her. 'So, we might be on the move not long after the New Year, girls. Ah've been watching them oot the windae. They're not half knocking seven bells out of what's left o' Rothesay Street.'

'Ah must say to you, Irene. Ah wiz surprised when Ah heard you and Alec were gonny take a hoose in the Molendinar,' says Drena. 'Ah took it for granted you would dae the same as the Stewarts. Rent yerselves a nice red-sandstone in Kelvinside.'

'We did think aboot it. But we decided tae move tae the scheme first. Really, it's only because we want tae find oot what it will be like tae live in a brand new hoose. If it turns oot we don't take tae living in a housing scheme,' she shrugs, 'then that's what we *will* do. Move back tae the city and rent a nice self-contained flat. I would hope near the Stewarts and Marjorie and Jack.'

'Aye.' Drena begins to talk pan loaf. 'But if you do take up resi-daunce in a wally close in Kel-vain-side, do not forget tae pur-chase a briefcase – for the conveyance of your ashes doon to the midding in the mornings!'

'Oh! That reminds me,' says Agnes. 'Ah forgot tae tell youse. Ah wiz invited roon' tae Marjorie and Jack's a few weeks ago. And Ah must say. They might only be a stone's throw fae here, but, boy oh boy! Them flats in Wilton Street and Wilton Crescent are a hundred miles away in quality. Aren't they? They really were built in fine style. Ah'll tell ye – the Queen wid'nae say naw tae wan o' them!'

'Ah'll tell ye something else,' says Drena, 'it should'nae be long until we get oor invitations tae Robert and Rhea's hoose-warming.' Her face lights up. 'Ah'm fair looking forward tae it. Ah've never, ever been in a red-sandstone flat. And Ah'll bet you Rhea and Robert will huv theirs smashing, when they've finished doing it up.' She looks at Irene. 'How near are they tae Marjorie and Jack? They're all in Wilton Crescent aren't they?'

'Aye. Jist two closes apart,' says Irene. 'Mary Stewart was telling me, they've already been in and oot one another's houses a few times.' She glances to left and right, which is usually a sign she's about to impart some little titbit. 'Rhea was saying, that nowadays Marjorie *likes* tae have visitors who remember Jane. She enjoys hearing them talk about their memories of the bairn.'

'Aww! Noo isn't that a good sign.' Agnes thinks for a moment. 'Aye, it really is. Because as we all know, there wiz many a year when poor Marjorie could'nae bear tae be reminded aboot losing that wean.' She sighs. 'Oh! Wasn't she the bonniest wee thing. Granny absolutely doted on her.'

Irene sighs. 'Ah was fair pleased tae hear she can now talk aboot her.' She looks at her friends. 'Whit a loss that wee yin was. Ah've never seen such a turn-oot in the street, as there was on the day o' that wean's funeral.'

'Wasn't there jist!' Drena puts her cup onto its saucer. 'And of course, do ye realise that the next big funeral in Dalbeattie Street – will be the street itself!' She sits back in her kitchen chair. 'Aye! Ah don't suppose we'll get much of a turn-oot that day.'

As though on cue, there comes an extra-loud WHUMPF! Followed by the expected avalanche of blocks of sandstone, timbers and broken glass. All three look at one another as they feel the floor vibrate under their feet, listen to the empty teacups ringing in their saucers.

CHAPTER TWENTY-TWO

The Right Place at the Right Time

December 23rd 1971. The last Thursday before Christmas. It's been a busy day at Kinnaird's. Archie Cameron junior comes into the shop off the Maryhill Road. As usual he's parked the van round the corner in Wilton Street. He looks at his watch. Nearly half four. Ah hope there has'nae been any more orders came in. He gets that tingle in his stomach as he looks at the door to the back shop. Lexie will be in there. If Ah don't have tae go oot again, Ah can spend the next hour talking tae her. He's unable to stop that little voice chipping in – 'For all the good it'll do ye.'

The main street door lies wide open, there are no customers in. Mrs Kinnaird is behind the counter, busying herself with paperwork. That tingle of anticipation kicks in again as Lexie's voice floats out into the shop, followed by her and Jean Dalglish laughing. He steps over to the counter. The boss looks up. 'Get that yin done all right, Archie?'

'Aye. All done by kindness, as they say. Even gave me a two-bob tip . . .' he pauses, 'Ah can never get intae the habit of saying "ten pence"!'

'It's getting cauld. Push that door to, son.'

'Right y'are.' He does. 'Ah'm choking for a cup o' coffee, Mrs K. Will Ah make you one, tae?'

'Best idea Ah've heard the day.'

As he makes for the back shop, he asks that unnecessary question. 'Milk and half a sugar?'

'Aye. Same as always.'

The door to the rear is ajar. Lexie's in there! The tingle moves up to 'butterflies' status as he pushes it open. 'Nae need for youse tae pine any longer, girls. Ah'm back!'

Lexie is bending some wire into a circle. There has been a 'run' on Christmas wreaths. She knows she'll need more for tomorrow – Christmas Eve. She turns her head. 'Oh look, Jean! Santa's sent us an early present.'

Jean stops sweeping, straightens up. She tuts. 'But Santa's made a mistake. It wiz *Burt* Reynolds Ah asked fur – no' Debbie!' The two of them exaggerate their laughter.

Archie shakes his head. 'Ah'm so pleased tae get in the warm, Ah'm even prepared tae put up wi' your crap jokes. Ah'll tell ye, don't be surprised if we get a white Christmas this year.'

'Ah know. It's no' half turned cauld, huzn't it,' says Jean.

'But don't forget,' Lexie looks up, 'we often get snow before Christmas. Then somehow, it always seems tae vanish before the holiday. Ah cannae remember the last time we actually *had* a white Christmas.'

Jean leans on the brush. 'Aye. When Ah think aboot it. You're right.'

'Ah'm about tae make a coffee for Mrs K and me.' Archie reaches for the kettle. 'Will Ah make a cuppa for you two?'

As he waits for the full kettle to boil, he prepares the four mugs: coffee in three of them, a teabag in Jean's. He perches on the end of the table, seems to be paying attention to the girls conversation. In truth, he's barely listening, too busy with his own agenda. Mostly trying to work up his courage. Should Ah ask her? She'll jist bite your nose aff, Archie. You know what she's like. But it *is* Christmas. She might gie me a break. He looks at her. C'mon, it's worth the risk. 'Eh, Lexie. Ah'm gonny make a suggestion.' He turns his head for a moment. 'You're a witness, Jean. Ah'm gonny ask her to do something that is jist a one-off. Purely and simply for Christmas.' He feels himself blush, but determines to see it through.

Lexie gets in first. 'Ah don't know whit he's gonny ask.' She stops bending wire for a moment, also looks at Jean. 'But I can safely forecast – the answer is gonny be *naw*!'

'She alwiz lets me doon gently, dizn't she, Jean?' Archie shrugs. Turns once more to face his heart's desire. His throat begins to dry with nerves. 'Well, Ah'll tell you what it was, anyway. Did you know that the Hillhead Salon, ower in Byres Road, sometimes shows auld films on special occasions?' He doesn't give her time to answer, or interrupt. 'This week, because it's nearly Christmas, they're showing yon auld James Stewart picture from the forties – *It's A Wonderful Life*. Now, Ah was'nae gonny ask ye tae go oot on a date, Lexie. Okay? It was jist 'cause we work the 'gither. Sort of like a Christmas treat. Nae strings attached. That's all it was.' From the corner of his eye he sees Jean's head turn from him to Lexie.

She's bending wire again. Doesn't look up. 'Huh, sounds like a date tae me! And why ever would I want tae go and see that? Ah've seen it a hundred times. It's never off the telly.'

'But that's no' the point, Lexie. Don't you think it would be nice tae see it on a cinema screen? The way people seen it when it first came oot? Probably including oor mothers and faithers.'

'Well, it's nice of you tae ask. But no thanks.' She pointedly concentrates on her work.

'Och, well. It was jist a thought. Ah know you're no' seeing anybody at the minute. So Ah thought it would be a nice change for you.' His voice trails off, his cheeks burn red. Jean looks at him, gives a sympathetic smile. That hurts most of all. The kettle has boiled. In a silence that could be cut with a knife, Archie makes the drinks.

'Right, Jean. Here's your tea.' He tries hard to sound normal, as if everything is okay. 'Here's your coffee, Lexie.' He knows he's not fooling anybody.

'I'll take the boss's through.' Lexie holds her hand out. 'I want tae speak tae her about something. Better do it while it's in ma mind.'

Jean waits until Lexie goes through the front and they

hear her talking to Mrs K. 'She's gonny be a hard nut tae crack, Archie.'

'Aye, and then some.' He sips the hot coffee, puts the mug down, sits on the edge of the table used for making the drinks.

'And there's nae good beating aboot the bush, Archie. You know *why* she knocks ye back, dain't ye?'

He gives a wry smile. 'Aye. She makes it quite obvious. It's because Ah've done time.'

'That could be the main reason. But Ah think there's more tae it than that, son. Even if you had'nae done time, Ah still think she would say no. You're gonny have tae face it. You're no' her type, Archie. She diz'nae fancy ye that way. You'll always be wasting your time wi' Lexie.'

'Well, Ah don't agree. Ah jist think Ah'm gonny have ma work cut oot, Jean. It might take quite a while – but eventually she's gonny go oot with me!'

'Jeez-oh! Ah've got tae gie ye ten oot o' ten. You really are determined, aren't ye?'

'Jean, Ah've never felt as strongly aboot a lassie as Ah do –' He stops as raised voices, male voices, come from the front shop. Something's happening! The tone and aggressiveness of them immediately put him on alert. His adrenaline starts flowing. He has been involved in similar events too often to be mistaken. In street, in pub – in jail. This is trouble!

'Oh, my God! Whit's going –' He reaches out a hand, gently covers Jean's mouth. She falls silent. While Archie listens intently to what's happening out front, his eyes dart all over the workroom. Ah *must* find a weapon . . .

'Jist fuckin' hand ower the takings and naebody will get hurt. NOW!'

He hears the boss. Her voice high-pitched with fear. 'You're getting nae money here. So ye can get on yer bike! Go on, the pair of ye bugger off!'

Archie sets his jaw. So there's two o' them!'

'Huv Ah got tae use this, EH? HUV AH GOT TAE FUCKIN' USE THIS?' He hears Mrs Kinnaird half-gasp, half-squeal. The bastard's pulled a weapon. Jean is looking at him, eyes like saucers.

'Yesss!' The relief comes out of Archie as a sigh. Thank fuck! His eyes have alighted on the wooden pole used for pulling down the window blinds. Perfect! The five-foot pole, with its heavy metal hook and sleeve on one end, is ideal. He steps over to it on the tips of his rubber soles, tenderly lifts it, tiptoes towards the door. He peers into the shop through the few inches where it is ajar. From first hearing the voices, to standing with the reassuring heft of the pole in his hands, has taken less than thirty seconds. It feels like minutes.

Two young guys, maybe late teens, have their backs to him. The one nearest holds a camping-type knife. He speaks again. 'Hand it tae me or Ah'll be ower that counter. FUCKIN' HAND IT OVER RIGHT NOW! OR YOU'LL . . .'

As soon as Archie sees the knife he starts opening the door. When the guy begins to speak, it drowns out any noise he makes as he slips into the front shop. When the would-be robber starts shouting, there is no way he, or his mate, can hear the approach of their downfall.

Lexie feels relief wash over her when, from the corner of her eye, she sees Archie emerge from the back shop. Her confidence increases fourfold when she spots what he's carrying. She has the good sense not to look directly at him in case her eyes betray his coming. Since the robbers entered the shop, she has been rooted to the spot, her mug of coffee still in her hand.

Archie, both hands at one end of the pole, swings it in a downward arc as though it were a two-handed sword. It catches the knifeman a heavy blow on the right side of his head, gouges a furrow through his scalp and lays bare a small area of skull. Its momentum carries it down to where it tears the top two inches of ear away. It comes to a stop when it whacks him on his right shoulder. Badly dazed, he drops the knife as he falls forward, slumping onto the counter. His number two turns, shocked, wonders what has happened to him. His mouth falls open when he sees Archie. At this exact moment Lexie throws her mug of hot, black coffee into his face. As the youth lets out a screech, Archie turns, changes his grip on the pole and thrusts it forward as though it were a spear. The metal hook catches the assistant thief on his bottom lip, splits it wide open, and carries on into his mouth. As it does, it sends a jarring message along its shaft to tell Archie that two, maybe three, of the guy's teeth have been smashed.

The adrenaline now kicks in with this pair – but for flight, not fight. In the midst of their shock and pain, the thought uppermost in their minds is to get out of the shop and away, right now! Bleeding Mouth helps Hanging Ear to regain an upright position. They stand side by side for a moment, frightened, looking at Archie. He steps forward, holding his weapon of choice as though it were an axe, gently swings it back and forth. 'Right! Get tae fuck out of it or you're gonny get some more. NOW!' He smiles as they physically jump. 'Well, well! Where have the tough guys gone?' says Archie. 'Huv ye jist realised you've picked the wrong shop tae rob? Don't even THINK aboot coming past this shop in a month or two and putting a brick through a windae. Ah know whit youse look like – and Ah'll come lookin' fur ye. Be warned! Now get tae fuck out of it!' He steps forward, raising the pole as he does. It's enough. They somehow manage to get through the narrow street door at the same time and disappear into a darkening December evening.

Within ten minutes of the apprentice thieves departing, Archie has been sent a few doors along the Maryhill Road to acquire a bottle of brandy from a nearby licensed grocer's. While he's away, Lexie tops up the electric kettle, and it has already boiled as Jean unlocks the door to let him, and a brown paper bag, in. She locks the door, turns the plastic sign to 'Closed' and all four retire to the back. Mrs Kinnaird switches the lights off in the front shop.

'Dae ye all want a coffee wi' a shot o' brandy in it?'

As the boss pours a goodly measure into each mug, Archie poses the question. 'Are youse all okay?' The consensus is 'a bit shook up'.

Mrs K raises her mug, her shaking hand shows she

certainly hasn't recovered. 'Well girls, I think a "thank-you" is due tae Archie. Ah'm awfy glad he was here when they toerags came in. It diz'nae bear thinking aboot, whit might have happened if he had'nae been here.' She raises her mug higher. 'Well done, son!'

Jean and Lexie echo her sentiments.

Archie finds himself blushing as they look at him. 'Now listen, Ah'm no' trying tae be modest or anything like that. Ah just got really angry. Ah work here, and Ah'm no' gonny have two, well, shitbags come in here and threaten the lassies Ah work wi'. Especially wi' a knife.' He pauses. 'By the way, where is it?'

'Ah shoved it intae the drawer behind the counter,' says Mrs Kinnaird.

'It might be a good idea tae always keep it there,' suggests Archie. 'If somebody ever tries it on again, could be a good thing tae wave aboot under their nose. Might change their mind.'

Mrs Kinnaird broaches the subject. 'Dae ye think Ah should ring the polis?'

Jean looks surprised. 'Surely you've got tae send fur them? This was a serious thing.'

'Do you think Ah should, Archie?' Mrs K looks at him.

He takes a good mouthful of coffee. 'Ah'll tell ye what I think. But first of all, Ah'd like tae get something straight. You all know Ah've done time. So when Ah give ye my opinion, don't be saying, "Oh, Archie's not wanting tae be responsible for them two going tae jail." Because that's just not true.' He gulps another draught of coffee. 'It would'nae bother me in the least if the pair o' them got their collars felt. Oh, and another thing. Ah don't know them. They were probably still at school when Ah wiz last sent doon.' He looks at Jean. 'It might not be as good an idea as ye think tae report it tae –'

Mrs Kinnaird cuts in. 'Is that because ye think it might cause a lot of bother for me, Archie, if I involve the polis?'

He nods his head. 'Exactly! Ah wondered why you did'nae ring for them right away. Were you thinking along those lines yourself?'

'I was. I thought, I'll wait and see what Archie thinks about it before I give them a call.'

'Okay. This is how Ah see it. Yon two got a *lot* more than they expected. They will never try it on at these premises again.' He leans forward. 'And when the word gets around, neither will anybody else! It will definitely be a case of once bitten, twice shy. Now, we all know whit the two of them look like. The polis would find them nae bother. But if they were caught and charged, *that* would be the start of your troubles. Between then and the court case you would get nothing but harassment from their friends and family.'

'Aye, that's what was in ma mind, Archie. I've heard of other shopkeepers getting bother once they identified somebody and they were charged,' says Mrs Kinnaird.

'Okay, so do you think that what they got tonight, is enough punishment?' asks Lexie.

'*They* will consider it was. They would think tonight wiz gonny be dead easy. But it's finished up with one o' them wi' his heid split open and his ear hanging off. And his pal has got his lip badly split and a load o' painful dental work tae look forward tae.' He turns to Lexie. '*And* it looked like your coffee wiz still hot enough tae scald him. Ye must remember, Ah've mixed wi' people like these. Ah know how they think. They definitely backed a loser when they came in here the night. If you involve the law, believe it or not, they'll consider that you're really rubbing it in. All during the lead-up tae the trial we'd get nothing but threats, damage tae the shop, the van, and aw' the rest of it. If the polis are *not* involved, believe me, it'll be a case of "Well, that's fair enough. They did'nae half sort us oot that night – but it has'nae been reported. So we'll let it go as well."'

It's just gone six o'clock, a bit later than normal, when Archie and Lexie walk into the sombre, half-demolished Dalbeattie Street. As they enter their close, Archie smiles.

'What's funny?'

'Ah was just picturing yon guy's face when you threw that hot coffee ower him, then next second Ah gave him the end o' the pole tae chew on. Because the coffee wiz running intae his eyes, he never seen the pole coming so he could'nae dodge it. You did well.'

'I was really mad. There was'nae anything handy I could use as a weapon, so I thought, – "You can have ma coffee, ya bastard!"'

As they step onto the top landing, Lexie makes for her door. As he does every evening, Archie halts, about to say, 'Right, Ah'll see you the morra morning.'

Before he can speak, Lexie turns. 'What time are we meeting? When does the big picture start, at the Salon?'

His mouth opens, but nothing comes out.

'Oh, well. If you've changed your mind.' She shrugs, reaches for the door handle.

'Are ye gonny let me take you tae the pictures the night, Lexie?'

She lets go the handle. Turns. 'But let's get one thing straight, Archie Cameron. This is *not* a date, okay?' She carries on without pause. 'It's like you said. We work together. It happens tae be Christmas, so it's just company for one another seeing as neither of us are winching.' She looks him in the eye. 'And it's also a thank-you. Ah was very impressed with ye this afternoon. You did really well, Archie. So I will go tae the pictures with ye tonight' She leans forward. 'But don't forget – *it is'nae a date*!'

'Awww, hey! That's smashing. Right, Ah'll see ye oot here at half seven.' He shifts from foot to foot. 'Now ye don't have tae worry, Lexie. It is definitely jist two workmates going tae the pictures. But, eh, hey, it's still great so it . . .' His voice quavers and he chokes up.

She turns to look at him. Sees tears in his eyes. 'Right, half past seven on the landing.' She steps into her lobby.

Archie turns the handle of his door. Looks towards her. 'Jeez! Ah hope them two come back again next week!'

CHAPTER TWENTY-THREE

Goodwill To All Men!

It's late the next day. Christmas Eve 1971. Archie Cameron senior has had his dinner and now, at twenty minutes to eight on this Friday evening, is fighting to keep awake as he slumps in his armchair. Ella looks at him. 'You got any plans for the night, Captain Pugwash?'

'Ah'm no sure, hen. Ah'm a bit tired. Been working the day, ye know.'

'Oh! It's a pity for ye. You're no' the only wan. Whit dae ye think Ah was doing doon the Lux Tearooms the day? Huving a party?' Anywye, if you do happen tae revive, Ah take it any plans ye have are bound tae include the right honourable member for the close, William McClaren? And mibbe a late-night summit meeting in the Thistle Bar?'

'Ah! Well, Ah might surprise ye, Ella. Ah've had a hard week. We had tae get a big order finished, so Ah've been knocking ma pan in for the last ten days.'

'Did youse get it done?'

'Finished it jist efter three o' clock this efterninn.' She watches as he yawns and stretches.

'Right! So what dae ye mean "you might surprise me"?'

'Meeting Billy up the Thistle Bar is, def-in-ate-lee, *wan* of ma options. However. Believe it or not. Ah'm that bloody tired, if Ah don't liven up between noo and half eight, Ah might jist stay in and watch yon auld picture, *Scrooge*, wi' Alastair Sim. It's on later the night. It always puts me right in the mood fur Christmas so it diz.'

Ella sniffs. 'Huh, Ah thought only three pints of McEwan's pale ale had the power tae dae that!'

'No, Ah might jist stay in and keep ma wee wife company oan Christmas Eve, fur a change.'

As he finishes speaking, their door is knocked. 'Ah'll get it,' says Ella. He listens to her footsteps in the lobby, the front door being opened, then, 'Oh, hello! This is a surprise.' There now follow a few indistinct words before Ella finishes with, 'Right, Ah'll tell him. Cheerio, son!' She comes back into the kitchen. Smiles, then shakes her head as she looks at him. 'That was a funny conversation, Archie. It was the wee Thomson boy from the next close, wi' a message for you.' She looks at the ceiling. Concentrates. 'Let me get this right. "There's a man sitting in a car at the close. Says will ye tell Mister Cameron that Billy Webster would like tae see him. Tell him it's urgent!" Ella looks at her man. 'Aye, that wiz it. Diz that make any sense? Ah don't think Ah know that name. Webster?'

Archie sits up, now wide-awake. 'Ah know who it is. He runs Johnny May's snooker hall –'

She butts in. '*Huh*! That bloody place! Nearly the ruination of oor Erchie . . .'

'Never mind that, Ella. He would'nae come tae see me unless it wiz dead important.' He looks at her. 'And only if oor Erchie wiz in some sort o' bother.'

'Awww! My God! Aw, naw! Don't tell me he's gonny finish up back in the jail again.' She points dramatically. 'Ah'll throw maself oot that fucking windae if he goes back tae jail!'

Archie rises. 'Jist keep calm, Ella. Ah'll away doon and see him. Billy Webster and me have got quite friendly these last few years. If he's come here it's because he's trying tae help, trying tae warn us aboot something.' He takes both of her hands in his. 'Don't let your imagination run away wi' ye. Wait 'til Ah find oot whit's going on.'

Archie halts at the mouth of the close, looks both ways along the deserted, half-demolished Dalbeattie Street. To his left, three cars are parked by the pavement. One of them, a Vauxhall Victor saloon, he doesn't recognise. As he walks along the poorly-lit street towards it he sees movement inside. The front passenger door swings open, a hand beckons from the driver's seat. Archie opens the door wider, looks inside. 'This is a bit of a surprise, Billy.'

'Come in aff the street, Archie. Sorry for aw' this *Third Man* stuff. But it'll be better for me if Ah'm no' seen talkin' tae ye.' As he listens to Billy Webster's rasping voice, Archie yet again feels a pang of guilt, remembering that he caused all this damage to his throat.

Moments later the two of them sit, quite companionably, side-by-side on the front bench seat inside the warm car. Webster looks at him. 'Is your boy in?'

'Naw. Went oot aboot seven. He'll be in the Garscube –'

'*Fuck*! Ah was hoping he'd still be in the hoose. Well, if he's doon the Garscube Vaults he's gonny be in big trouble before the night's oot. Three shitbags are lookin' for him.'

'What for? Whit's he done?'

Webster looks at him. 'Has he no' telt ye what went on in the fruit shop, yesterday?'

'Never said anything tae me aboot something happening. Or to his mother, as far as Ah know. He huz'nae been stealing, has he?'

Webster tries to clear his throat. As usual he's unsuccessful. 'No,' he rasps, 'it's the exact opposite. Two young neds came intae the shop near closing time, tried tae rob Mrs Kinnaird.' He laughs. 'Your Archie knocked seven bells oot o' the two o' them.' He pauses, gasps a few breaths. 'Set aboot them wi' the pole used fur pulling the shop blinds doon. Did'nae half dae them some damage.' He looks knowingly at Archie. 'Must be a chip off the old block.'

'So who is looking for him?' He waits while Billy gets ready to speak.

'Well. The two toerags acted on their own. But unfortunately wan o' them is the son of Nathan Brodie's sister.' Billy shrugs. 'So all this Godfather shite has kicked in. Uncle

Nathan cannae let a family member get a doing and dae nuthing aboot it. That's why he's turning up in person the night.' Webster pauses. 'You know Brodie, don't ye?'

'Ah know *of* him. Never met him. Anywye, dae ye know whit they intend tae do?'

'Gonny smash baith kneecaps, Archie! They're gonny get him doon the Garscube Vaults.'

The silence which follows is heavy. Then, 'Mmmm. Zat right. Not if Ah get there afore the bastards.' Archie lays a hand on the door lock. 'Thanks for the warning, Billy. That wiz good of you.' He pulls the lever. Pauses a moment. 'Dae ye know how many will be coming?'

'As far as Ah know, three.'

'Three. Och well. That's no' too bad! Okay, nae time tae waste. Ah'll huv tae go up tae the hoose tae get some, eh, equipment. Then grab a taxi doon tae the –'

Webster cuts in. 'Ah'll gie ye a lift doon tae near the pub. Drop ye off in Firhill Street. Ah cannae take you tae the door in case Ah'm seen.'

'That'll be near enough. Ah jist hope tae fuck Ah'm no' too late. Right! Ah'm gonny dive up the stairs, get some things. Five minutes, Billy!'

'Ah'll have the engine running.'

As Archie Cameron makes for his close, Billy Webster watches him in his rear-view mirror. Once more he finds himself impressed at the way this ordinary man – No! This ex-para – can just switch it on. He smiles. Nathan and his heavies don't know it yet, but they're in trouble!

* * *

Archie comes running into the house and is met by a wide-eyed, Ella. 'Whit's going on? Is he in bother?'

'Come through the room. Ah'll tell ye while Ah'm gettin' ready. Just listen. Don't talk. There's nae time tae waste!'

He hurries along the lobby, Ella keeping pace behind him, and stops for a moment to shrug himself into his workaday gaberdine mac. Entering the bedroom, he makes for the double wardrobe, kneels down, pulls open the large bottom drawer, tries to block Ella's view with his back. She moves to the side.

'Ah know whit you keep in therr, Archie Cameron. Why are ye needing *them* things?'

'Ella! Ah huv'nae time tae piss aboot. Have ye heard the name, Nathan Brodie?'

'Of course! He's the big local gangster guy. Whit's he got tae –'

He speaks over her. 'Him and a couple of others are heading fur the Garscube Vaults. Gonny smash oor Archie's kneecaps.' He looks up. 'Ah'm gonny stop them! Oor Archie –'

She interrupts. 'Whit fur? Whit's he –'

'Ah wiz aboot tae tell ye. Will ye buggering jist listen! Archie stopped Kinnaird's gettin' robbed yesterday. Gave two guys a hiding. So they're efter him. Okay? Nae mair questions!'

Now silent, she watches him take articles out of the drawer. Things she has always known about, though they've not seen the light of day for years. He lays a three-foot-long, steel crowbar on the floor. Next are two German officers' daggers. Her heart leaps into her mouth as he reaches a hand into a far corner. As expected, it emerges holding a Luger pistol.

'For fuck sake, Archie! What are ye wanting with –'

'Shut up! Emergency use only. Not another fuckin' word!' He takes the safety catch off. She listens to the chilling metallic sound as he slides the top part back, then forward, to cock it. He clicks the safety catch back on, slips the gun into his inside pocket. She feels fear, yet at the same time her spine tingles as she looks at her man. At this moment he's not the 54-year-old man who comes hame from his work every night. How long is it since she last saw his 'Para face'? That look which probably made its first appearance as he hooked-up his 'chute's static line and got ready to jump out of a Dakota into Arnhem.

He rises to his feet. 'Walk wi' me tae the door.' As she does, he gives her final instructions.

'Don't be ringing the polis. They might stop Brodie the night – but he'll jist get him later. Don't worry aboot the gun. Ah'm jist gonny wave it aboot as a last resort. It's the Seventh Cavalry!'

Ella looks at him. Believes him. 'Okay. Ah know you'll only go as far as ye have tae.' She grabs the lapel of his shabby mac, pulls him towards her. Kisses him hard on the lips.

As the Vauxhall Victor drives onto the Maryhill Road, Archie turns his head. 'How did ye get wind of whit Brodie was intending tae do?'

'By good luck, Ah wiz in the Excelsior Bar for a sandwich and a pint at one o'clock. Who comes stoating in but Brodie, along wi' big Joe Devaney. That's his number wan heavy.' Billy laughs. 'Even though they don't know you, they know about you. That it wiz you did the damage tae me in the 419 Bar all them years ago. So,' he gives another croaking laugh, 'because they think you and me are deadly enemies, they were quite happy tae brag aboot how Archie junior is gonny get an early Christmas present – two smashed kneecaps. And how they're gonny get him the night, in the Garscube Vaults.'

'Whit's the story wi' this Devaney fella? Is he useful?'

'Ah don't think much of him, Archie. He's big. Well over six feet. But Ah think he relies oan his size tae intimidate people.'

'Whit aboot the main man, Brodie? Ah know nothing aboot him, either.'

'Nathan's intae his fifties. He's badly overweight. Spends maist of his time sitting on his fat arse behind a desk. Usually gets other people tae dae his dirty work. At heart he's a bully.'

'Okay. Ah'll huv tae deal wi' Devaney first. He's got tae be put oot o' the game right away.'

Webster nods in agreement. 'If you put Devaney doon, Nathan will shite himself.'

'There's a third wan, isn't there?'

'Oh, aye. Ah'm forgetting the boy. His nephew is coming tae. The one your Erchie did the damage too. He's only eighteen or nineteen. When Ah seen him in the pub the day, he had a dressing on his heid *and* his ear, where your Archie battered him. He's had stitches in both –' Billy stops speaking, peers through the windscreen. '*Fuck me*! That's Brodie's car!' He points. 'The Jag. Hey! We're jist on time. We don't need tae turn intae Firhill Street now. That's good. We know where *they* are – but they don't know aboot us. Ah'll hang back and we'll see how many get oot. When they go intae the pub, Ah'll move along a bit and drop you off.'

They watch Brodie's car bear left at Queen's Cross, drive forty yards into Garscube Road, then signal its intention to cross over to the Garscube Vaults. Billy slows as he passes Jaconelli's cafe, switches the Vauxhall's lights from beam, to sides, then off as he crawls the last few yards into Garscube Road. He comes to a stop outside the darkened Rennie Mackintosh church. Billy now sits back in his seat, keeps himself in the shadows. Archie leans forward, watches three figures climb out of the Jaguar. 'Good! They must think that'll be enough.' He looks at the biggest of them. That'll be Devaney. Yeah, you'll be the first tae go doon. The trio stand for a moment, talking. He watches Devaney step over to the pub's etched glass window, find a clear bit to look through. Archie's eyes narrow. Mmm. Be making sure my boy's in. The heavies stand for a moment longer then, as one, pull pickaxe handles up and out of their buttoned-up coats.

'Ah'm away, Billy. Thanks for your trouble.'

'Aw' the best!' rasps Webster.

* * *

Archie Cameron steps smartly across the Garscube Road, his eyes fixed firmly on the pub. The training from nearly thirty years ago kicks-in. Deep measured breaths to fill the lungs with oxygen, kick-start the adrenaline. As he approaches the pub he puts his left hand into his coat pocket. At the same time he lets the crowbar drop down inside his right sleeve, into his right hand, then slips it under his unbuttoned coat. Once there, he wraps his left hand – which is inside the pocket-lining – around it. Grips it firmly as he strides out.

He is just short of the pub's double-doors when they open, and a dozen or so customers exit onto the pavement. Some still hold their drinks. They are not best pleased.

'Mmm!' Them shitbags will huv ordered them oot, thinks Archie. Don't want any witnessess. He also finds a clear area in the etched glass, looks into the bar. The trio stand side-by-side, their backs to the entrance – and only exit. Archie junior stands at the bar. Isolated. His father reaches a hand out towards the doors.

'They'll no' let ye in, mister.' It's a voice from among the disgruntled customers.

'Aye, Ah know!' says Archie. He pushes a door open, steps inside, lets it swing shut behind him as he takes a few steps into the bar. He stops a yard or so behind the three heavies. The unexpected entry of his father into the pub immediately raises Archie junior's spirits. They are further lifted when his da has time to wink at him, just before big Joe Devaney turns to look at the nondescript, middle-aged man who has wandered in.

'Fuck off! The pub's shut at the minute.'

'Oh, sorry!' says Archie. He touches his cap, turns, obviously about to do what he's been told. Satisfied, Devaney turns back to attend to the work in hand. Archie reaches his right hand inside his coat and takes the crowbar from his left hand. He now removes this hand from the coat pocket and it joins the right at the end of the steel bar. Spinning round on his rubber-soled boots, he takes three paces back towards Devaney whilst raising the metal bar above his head. With all his considerable strength he brings it down onto the nape and left shoulder of the tall man. Without a sound, a pole-axed Devaney drops his pickaxe handle, falls onto his knees, then topples face-first onto the floor.

Nathan Brodie looks to his left to find out what's happened, and is perfectly on time to meet Archie's second swing. The claw-end of the crowbar strikes him on the chin just under his bottom lip. The front of his jawbone is fractured, his bottom lip and chin are split open to a length of three inches, and four teeth are knocked out. A few more are loosened. His wooden stave also falls from nerveless fingers as he sinks to his knees. Archie tuts. 'Butterfingers!'

About to turn his attention to Brodie's nephew, Archie notices Devaney is beginning to gather his senses and has raised himself to where he is kneeling on all fours. Archie turns, places the sole of his boot on the big man's side and pushes. Devaney topples to the side and rolls onto his back. He looks at Archie, raises a hand, points. 'Gonny fucking get you, yah wee bastard!'

His tormenter shakes his head. 'You are in *nae* position tae make threats, yah stupid cunt!'

He raises the crowbar and brings it down, full force, onto the big man's right knee. Devaney screams as his kneecap is shattered. He places both hands on top of it, turns onto his left side, and from this awkward position tries to rock back and forth to ease the pain.

Archie now has time to attend to the nephew. He walks past Brodie, who is lying on his back with both hands supporting his jaw. An occasional whimper comes out of him. The youth, who has been unable to move during the proceedings, throws his pickaxe handle onto the floor.

'Mister, Ah did'nae want tae come! Nathan made me. Ah got enough in the shop yesterday so Ah did. Honest!' His eyes are wide with fear.

'Whit's your name?'

'Jason, mister.'

Archie junior now speaks. 'He definitely did get plenty in the shop, Da.'

The youth's eyes open wider as he realises it's a father and son he's dealing with. For the last few minutes he has been wishing tae fuck he'd never gone near Kinnaird's.

'Okay. Go and sit ower in that far corner and don't say a word.' As Archie senior points, he is walking towards his son. He stops in front of him, his back to his two victims, leans in close. 'Take this crowbar and smash Brodie's knee-caps! Both o' them.' He looks into his son's startled eyes. 'Dae it!'

'Dae ye know think he's mibbe had enough, Da?'

His father shakes his head in disbelief. 'Why dae you think they came doon here the night?' He leans to the side, speaks into Archie junior's ear. 'Dae you know whit would be happening tae you at this minute, if Ah wiz'nae here? The guy who warned me they were coming tae get ye, told me they were looking forward tae doing *both* your kneecaps. That boy is Brodie's nephew! So you had tae be punished.' He presses the crowbar into his son's hands, withdraws his own. 'Ye huv tae be more ruthless than them, otherwise they'll be back! It has tae be done!' He stands to the side.

Archie junior walks over to Nathan Brodie, who still lies on his back. 'By the looks of the pickaxe handles, Ah guess ye were gonny do ma knees the night, Nathan.'

Brodie has both his, now bloodied, hands over his mouth. He watches Archie junior step to one side of him, change his grip on the crowbar.

Though he is having to speak through a mouthful of blood and damaged teeth, Brodie can still be understood. Even so, he spits out some more blood – and another tooth – to make sure.

'Aw, c'mon, Erchie. You've won. Ah've had enough. Let's call it quits, son.'

'The first lesson Ah learned aboot you, Nathan, wiz never tae believe a fuckin' word!' Archie junior swings the metal bar in an arc. Brodie just has time to scream an ignored 'ERCHIE!' as the first blow fractures his right kneecap. He faints before the second strike. Archie walks round to his other side and, in the welcome silence, deals as efficiently with his left kneecap. His father walks over, stands beside him. For a moment they look down at the two, supposed, toughest guys in Maryhill. Archie senior turns towards the bar. 'Have ye got an ice bucket?'

'Oh, aye. Certainly have, sir.' A somewhat overwhelmed bartender produces one from under the bar. As he hands it to him, he glances at the prostrate bodies, leans over in a confidential manner, speaks into the ear furthest away from the heavies.

'You huv done a fuckin' great job the night. Could'nae happen tae a more deserving pair!'

Archie walks over, stands between Brodie and Devaney and pours cold water, and the occasional ice cube, onto their faces. Just as happens in the movies, it's enough to revive them. Soon, they are gingerly touching their wounds, obviously unable to take in what has happened to them. Archie lobs the empty ice bucket over to his son. 'Put that on the bar, Erchie.' He takes up a position between Brodie's splayed legs, near to his feet. Looks hard at him while he reaches into his inside pocket. Brodie's mouth falls open when this hand emerges holding a Luger pistol. 'You'll probably huv guessed by now,' he points, 'Ah'm his faither!' He speaks mainly to Brodie. 'Don't get any ideas aboot coming after him or me.' He points the pistol at the floor and fires between Brodie's legs. The report is deafening in the bar room. The two heavies jump. 'If ye do, Ah will use this. If Ah was tae defend maself, and my family, by using this Luger against fuckpigs like you lot,' he smiles, 'there's not a jury in this city would convict me – Second

World War veteran, fought at Arnhem, hard-working family man – for defending himself wi' a war souvenir against known shitbags like you pair. In fact, Ah'd probably be awarded a fiver oot the poor box. Think aboot it!'

Devaney props himself up. 'It wiz you that done Billy Webster a few years back, wizn't it?'

'Aye. Every few years Ah huv tae come oot o' hiding and strike a blow fur freedom. Anywye.' Archie turns to his son. 'Hi-ho, Tonto! Oor work here is done.' He clicks the Luger over to 'safe', puts it away. 'C'mon, son. We'll huv tae hurry. *Scrooge* is oan at half-nine. Ah don't want tae miss it.'

CHAPTER TWENTY-FOUR

The Last Hogmanay

'Happy New Year, hen! And many o' them.' Billy and Drena McClaren slip their arms around each other's waist as Big Ben chimes midnight on the television. The Bells! They give one another a hard, lingering kiss. When they finally surface, they keep their arms where they are. Drena looks into her man's eyes.

'And the same tae you, Billy.' This is followed by a sigh. 'Well, here's hoping we'll be in oor new hoose for next Hogmanay.'

'Withoot a doubt!' He lets go her waist. 'C'mon, hen. We'll have a wee hauf tae bring the New Year in proper. Then straight up tae Archie and Ella's, eh?'

'And don't forget, make it a "wee" hauf. If ye gie me a big yin Ah'll jist leave most of it.'

'Okay, darlin'.'

Moments later they are toasting the New Year with a

measure of Glenfiddich. It's followed by a less lingering kiss. 'Oh! They malt whiskies are nice, in't they, Billy?'

He holds his shot glass up to the light, watches it turn to gold. 'They are that. If ye think back, Drena, it's no' that long ago since workingmen could hardly afford tae buy a blended whisky.'

'Ah know. My God! And some o' them were that fiery. Tae me, it wiz jist like taking medicine.' She screws her face up. 'No kidding. There wiz times Ah'd rather huv hud a dose o' cascara!'

He smiles. 'They wur'nae *that* bad! Anywye. Are ye for up tae the Camerons'?'

'Aye. Are ye taking the usual?'

'But of course.' He points to the table. 'A piece o' coal, a slice o' bread, and a wee twist o' salt. Got tae keep up the auld traditions, hen. Bring oor freens good luck for 1972.' He places the opened bottle of single malt beside the trio of gifts. '*Und naturlich, eine flasche* Glenfid—'

She cuts him short. 'And remember, Billy McClaren. It hud better no' finish up, that by two o'clock in the morning Ella and me urr sitting in wan corner, speaking Scots – and you and Erchie Cameron are sitting in the other slavering tae wan another in German!' She thrusts her head forward *and* carries out a minor bosom adjustment, to show she means business.

Three minutes later they close their front door. 'Jist come and look intae the street for a minute.' She takes his hand and they walk along the draughty, dingy close. She looks up and down their battered street. 'Aw, Billy. In't it depressing? There's hardly a sound tae be heard. Remember the days you would walk tae the close mooth, look alang the street, and nearly every windae wiz lit. Music coming oot of every hoose. Folk dashing oot their closes wi' message bags stuffed fu' wi' drink, shortbread and black bun. Off tae first-foot their neebours.' She falters, her voice trails off for a moment. 'Poor auld Dalbeattie Street! Look at the state o' it. If it wiz a dug, you'd huv took it tae the vet's long ago and got it put doon!'

'Och, it'll no' be long 'til we're away tae oor new hoose, Drena. Anywye! C'mon, let's go up tae Archie and Ella's. Once we get in there it'll be jist like auld times. *C'mon*!'

When they reach the top storey it's to find, as expected, that the Camerons' door is ajar. Their lobby light casts a golden sliver out onto the landing, as if trying to brighten-up the stairhead.

'The McClarens urr here! Happy New Year tae the Camerons!' Billy opens their door wide.

'C'mon! Get yerselves in here!' shouts Archie. 'Where huv youse been? It's gone five past twelve. We were thinking of phoning the polis tae report youse missing!'

Billy pushes the kitchen door wide open. Walks in with both arms up in the air. 'Happy New Year tae oor best pals!' As the McClarens enter the brightly lit kitchen, Ella and Archie stand either side of their heavily-laden table. The women kiss and exchange good wishes for the coming year. The men kiss each other's wives, then turn towards one another with one hand outstretched – the other holding a bottle of single malt.

'Archie! *Eine Glucklische Neues Jahr*!'

'*Danke sehr*, Wilhelm. *Und Du auch, meine alte Kamerad*!'

With lips that look as if they've just sucked on a shared lemon, Ella and Drena turn to face one another. Drena's eyes are already cast up to the ceiling. Archie winks at his '*Alte Kamerad*'. They await the onslaught.

'Whit did Ah say to you not ten minutes ago, Archie Cameron? Nae buggering German if ye don't mind!'

'Uh-huh! Uh-huh! Ah wiz saying the same tae him, Ella, at probably the same time. Like talkin' tae the bloody wall so it is!' The sentence ends with a magisterial sniff, instead of a full-stop.

'Don't worry, girls. That wiz a one-off. Jist tae bring the New Year in. Honest injun!' Archie turns to his pal. 'Now Billy, not another word in Deutsch. Don't forget.'

'Nae bother ma auld China. Scout's honour!'

Drena looks at her man. Frowns. 'You wiz never in the buggering scouts. You wiz in the BB!'

'Careful now,' says Billy, 'jist in case Lord Montague happens tae be oot oan that landing!'

At this same moment, over on Woodlands Road, Rhea and Robert Stewart are enjoying the last of a trio of quicksteps in the Bar Rendezvous. A few minutes later, reluctantly, they have to evacuate the dance floor as the combo hits the last notes of 'Crazy Rhythm'. 'Oh, wizn't that great, Robert?'

'Ab-so-lutely! The quickstep or the tango. Two of the best dances ever created. Bar none!' They saunter over and rejoin the select group which surrounds Madame Rendezvous herself, Ruth Lockerbie. They arrive there at the same time as Frank and Wilma Galloway.

Wilma leans over to her. 'Did ye enjoy that, Rhea?'

'No' half. They could play quicksteps the whole night, Wilma, and that wid suit me down tae the ground.'

Ruth smiles as she listens to them. Her right forearm stretches along the edge of the bar, her fingers holding what has long-since become her trademark. The tortoise-shell cigarette holder. She takes a languorous draw on a Black Sobranie, blows the smoke directly upwards. A movement from near the entrance catches her eye. She sits up straight, raises her left hand high in the air, waves only its fingers. 'Oh look, darlings! It's Ruby and Fred.' She gives a throaty laugh. 'Just watch! Ruby will have waited between the doors 'til the floor is clear. She'll now walk directly across it – while Fred, fearless bomber pilot, discreetly makes his way round the perimeter. She *so* loves a Grand Entrance does Ruby. Wonderful! You cannot knock her back – not even with a big stick.' The three women smile as they watch La Belle Ruby do exactly as forecast.

'Ruby, darling! I thought that was you I glimpsed *sneaking* in!' Ruth greets her.

'Sneaking? Mmm. There's a new word. Must look it up tonight!'

Rhea and Wilma smile and shake their heads as they

listen to them. Elaborate kisses and hugs are now bestowed on the newcomers.

'Where's George, darling?' Ruby gives a cursory glance at tonight's clientele.

'Working the room, dear. Visiting each table and banquette to wish our customers, old and new, a good New Year.'

'Is Vicky coming tonight?' enquires Wilma.

'I certainly hope so.' Ruth tilts a grey stalagmite on the end of the Sobranie into the ashtray. 'She rang me today to say she would – and that she'd be accompanied by her new escort!'

'Oh!' exclaims Ruby. 'Do tell.'

'Let's hope he's an improvement oan that weasel, Anderson!' says Rhea. 'He wiz nothing but a pig's leavings, that yin!' She gives it some more thought. Bristles. 'Ah wee rat so he wiz!'

Ruth keeps her face straight. 'Rhea, darling. Bad as he was, I don't think it's possible to combine, in one man, the worst attributes of – what was it? – a weasel, a pig and, oh yes – a rat!'

'Well, if anybody could dae it, it wid be yon wee snake!'

There's an outburst of laughter which Rhea isn't aware she has caused. Robert has to point out she has just added another denizen of the animal kingdom to the Steve Anderson file.

'Has Vicky had any further bother from him?' Frank Galloway looks at Ruth.

'No. I'm glad to say she has seen neither hide nor hair

of him from that night to this. He must have realised I meant business.'

Frank smiles. 'I'd love to know what hold you have over him, Ruth. It's certainly done the trick.'

'Aye, Ah'd like tae know as well,' says Rhea.

'I'll tell you what it might be, Rhea.' Robert looks at his wife. 'With all the animals you think he represents, maybe Ruth threatened to have him locked-up in Calderpark Zoo!'

Rhea looks at them all as they laugh. 'Actually, that's no' a bad idea. And while he's in, she could mibbe arrange tae huv him doctored!'

Twenty minutes later the heads of the group turn, as Vicky Shaw enters on the arm of her new beau. Everyone is delighted to see her. The womenfolk most of all. This is their chance to meet the new guy in her life . . .

'May I introduce . . . Jack Dale.' Vicky waits until everyone has greeted him, then makes her voice heard above the hubbub. 'And to save a lot of time, and a lot of questions, may I give you all a quick résumé on my lovely friend.' She doesn't wait for an answer. 'Jack, sadly, has been a widower for more than two years. He has two grown-up sons, both married. He works in the office at Bryant and May's factory. And we've been walking-out together for the last six weeks.' She pauses, links an arm through his. 'Mmmm, now let me see . . . Yes! He lives in Lambhill.' She pauses, looks at Jack. 'And I think that's all the nosey buggers need to know for the moment, darling.'

'Vicky, darling,' says Ruby, 'let's hope you've found your

perfect match!' When nobody laughs, Ruby puts her arms around the shoulders of Wilma and Rhea, pulls them in closer to Ruth and Fred. 'Pay attention, darlings. Jack works at the match factory – I'm hoping Vicky's found her perfect . . .'

'*Aw*! *Noo* Ah get it!' Rhea laughs. 'That's really clever, Ruby. Ah get whit ye mean, noo.'

'*Good*!' exclaims Robert Stewart. 'Because they've just struck up a tango. C'mon Vicky, you know you love doing the tango with me!' He holds his hand out.

As they watch them dance *onto* the floor, Fred Dickinson takes the newcomer by his elbow. 'C'mon along to this end of the bar, Jack. What would you like to drink? I already know what Vicky will want.'

As they lean on the counter, Fred turns to him. 'I think I can safely say, you're most certainly having a good effect on Vicky. Tonight is the first time I've seen her for a couple of months. She is looking *so* well.' He smiles. 'And presumably the credit for that should go to you, Jack. She looks to be very happy.'

'That's nice to hear, eh, Fred. As it happens, it's a two-way thing. We were both somewhat "down" when we met.' He smiles. 'We really have hit it off! Enjoy each other's company.'

'I've known Vicky for quite a few years, Jack. She's a genuine straight down the middle girl. Believe me. You've found a good 'un!'

It's just gone half-past one as Archie Cameron junior and Lexie Forsyth step out of the dance hall into Sauchiehall

Street. Archie turns, looks up at the swirling, neon-lit, *LOCARNO!* sign.

'Have you enjoyed yourself?'

'Ah have, Archie.' She raises an eyebrow. 'Considering all the time you've spent as a guest of Her Majesty these last few years, where did you find the time tae become no' a bad dancer. Did they run classes in Stirling Prison?'

He shakes his head. 'There were nae female partners available.' He looks both ways along an almost deserted Sauchiehall Street. Now and again a taxi speeds by, always occupied.

'Shall we set away, walking? If we spot an empty cab we'll take it. If no', it'll take us about forty-five minutes tae walk hame if we step-out.'

'Let's go!' She links her arm through his and they set off at a good pace.

Archie tosses an idea around for a moment. Decides to chance it. 'Ah'm Ah allowed tae tell you what a lovely feeling it gave me, when you took my arm there the now, Lexie.'

'Don't start! Just pals. Remember?'

'Ah know! Ah know! But it dis'nae alter the fact that it was nice. Just thought Ah'd tell ye.'

'Right. Thank you very much for the information. Appreciated.'

They hear the sound of a diesel engine. Archie turns. The cab's 'For Hire' light is on. He sticks his hand out. The engine's note changes, there's a slight squeal of brakes. He presses Lexie's arm to his side. 'We're on, kid!' The cab pulls in thirty yards ahead and they hurry towards it.

Conversation is flagging in the Cameron household. Drena looks up at Ella's mantelpiece.

'Twenty tae two, Ella. Ye know what. Ah'll bet ye they're huving a cheerier Hogmanay in Barlinnie!'

Billy McClaren looks up, focuses his bleary eyes. 'Ah'll tell ye something tae – we hud better New Years in Stalag VIIIB, so we did. Nae kidding!'

'You two urr'nae thinking of starting wi' the German, urr ye?'

'Naw, naw, hen,' says her spouse. 'It was jist, eh, a conversational . . . consternat . . . it wiz jist a wee remark, hen. Sort of jist threw it in.'

Drena is frightened to look at Ella. From the corner of her eye she can see her pal is gently vibrating as she tries to hold her laugh in.

'There's somebody on the sterrs!' Archie Cameron senior raises his hand, cups his ear. The foursome fall silent. Seconds later it's confirmed. They are all in agreement. There's more than one person climbing the stairs.

Drena looks around. 'If Granny Thomson wiz still alive, she could huv telt us who it wiz. She knew everybody's footsteps.'

'Well, no' quite everybody. She failed tae ID the Grim Reaper's tippy-toes the night he came for her,' says Billy. 'He definitely caught her on the hop!' As he and his pal go into stitches, the two women look at one another.

'That's no' funny! Poor auld sowel,' says Ella. Drena is about to join in, but just then they hear the footfalls change – they are now out on the landing! The front door is pushed open, a familiar voice comes from the lobby . . .

'Hallooo! It is Irma and Bert. Happy New Year everybody!'

Archie and Billy are immediately wide-awake. They look at one another, then the visitors. Their faces are wreathed in smiles as they rise, unsteadily, to their feet. They open their arms wide. '*Irmchen*! *Liebchen*! *Willkommen*!'

'Fuck me!' says Ella. 'A surprise attack! It's the Battle o' the Bulge all ower again!'

Drena nods over towards the kitchen windows. 'Dae ye think we could get intae that bunker?'

'Naw,' says Ella. 'Ah took delivery o' four bags o' coal oan Tuesday. There's nae room. We might as well surrender!'

By two a.m. the celebrations, at last, have begun to take-off. Next to appear are Archie junior and Lexie. Things improve even more when Lexie goes next door and returns with her Dansette record player and a dozen LPs. Singing and dancing are finally heard from 18 Dalbeattie Street.

There is a slight lull when Lexie takes off a record and flips through the others for her next selection. She is just about to call out a few titles, when movement is heard from the lobby. Those present fall silent as the kitchen door swings open . . .

'Can Ah come in? It's jist me.' All eyes focus on the door as it opens wide to reveal . . . Agnes Dalrymple! Resplendent in blue dressing gown, pyjamas, red and yellow check slippers – and a head full of curlers. Completely unabashed, she strolls in to join them, having just got out of her bed.

'Oh, my God! It's the Spirit of Christmas Past!' says Ella. 'Huv you jist fell oot your bed?'

'Aye. Well, ye see, with Lexie's mother being away at her sister's, and Teresa and Dennis O' Malley being ower in Ireland at his brother's . . .' She shrugs. 'And the fact that the close is half-empty, anywye. Och, Ah said tae maself, "It's gonny be a miserable Hogmanay, Agnes." So Ah jist took maself away tae ma bed before The Bells.'

'Ah hah! But the next thing, you waken up and find the place is jumping!' says Drena.

'No' half,' says Agnes. 'So Ah thought, Ah'll never get back tae sleep now, so Ah might as well go next door and annoy them buggers! Ah hope you don't mind me no' being dressed?'

'Nae bother at all!' says Archie senior. Everyone present now gathers round Agnes, and for the next couple of minutes she delights in being kissed, hugged and wished 'All the Best!' for the foreseeable future. There is so much hilarity going on, the arrival of *another* two guests goes unnoticed until . . .

'What *is* going on in this hoose? A sex orgy, wi' Agnes Dalrymple right in the middle of it! Ah hope somebody has sent fur the polis!'

'Robert and Rhea! In youse come this instant! We thought youse were over at your posh friends in Kelvin Court the night?'

Robert shakes his head. Points to his wife. 'Ask her!'

Rhea looks around at the faces of her long-time friends and neighbours. Folk she misses terribly since the move to Wilton Crescent.

'Well, we were aw' set tae leave the club and take a taxi tae Kelvin Court. Finish the night there like we always do . . .' They hear the tremor in her voice. She tries again. 'When it suddenly came tae me. Ah've got years and years tae bring the New Year in ower there. But tonight is ma last chance tae welcome a Ne'erday in Dalbeattie Street –' She bursts into tears.

Just as they did with Agnes a few minutes ago, everybody now gathers round Rhea and Robert and, amid laughter and tears, the last New Year celebration 18 Dalbeattie Street will see now gets into its stride. It will carry on valiantly until the first streaks of dawn begin to turn to daylight. Somewhere around five the last few stragglers disperse to their various landings, climb into recess beds, and sleep the sleep of the just for the next ten hours or more.

When some of them reluctantly awake, well into the afternoon of the first of January 1972, they will find they are unable to raise their heads from the pillows. Soon, entreaties are being made for the only tincture that can snatch them back from the brink of death. An ancient Caledonian remedy that some swear was known to be favoured by Robert the Bruce himself. Two Askit Powders washed down with copious amounts of Irn Bru. Neat!

CHAPTER TWENTY-FIVE

Postman's Knock

It's a cold, sunny morning in late February 1972. The Post Office van, a 30-cwt Ford, turns left off the Maryhill Road and pulls up in front of the last remaining tenement building in Dalbeattie Street. John Caldwell lights up a Woodbine and inhales deeply. 'Ahhh!' That first draw is always the best. He blows the smoke out, then places the cigarette between his lips as he uses both hands to lift his mailbag from the passenger seat.

'Right, lets see whit's for Dalbeattie,' he murmurs. 'Mmm. Bit more than there has been of late.' He slips the elastic band off the small bundle. His experienced eyes have already noted there are quite a few envelopes identical in size and thickness. He looks at the top one. 'Uh-huh!' It's cancelled by a familiar red meter-mark. As expected, the logo next to it bears the legend 'Glasgow Corporation Housing Department'. Oh, well. That'll be a few more folk getting the good news they'll soon be away tae the Molendinar housing scheme. He looks again at the bundle. No, there certainly are'ny enough here tae clear out the whole block. Seem tae be doing it in dribs and drabs.

As he puts the elastic band back round them, he glances again at Dalbeattie Street's last tenement. Next, he looks to his left through the passenger window, then straight ahead through the windscreen. In both these directions his view is unrestricted for a couple of hundred yards or more. Acres of half-cleared sites where once stood the tenements that made up Cheviot and Rothesay Streets. As with Dalbeattie Street, a lone survivor stands here and there. Isolated, still-occupied blocks. The surrounding wasteland bearing witness that four out of five buildings have been cleared of tenants, then demolished. Their former residents scattered to all airts and pairts. Until recently, he'd delivered to them all. Knew every one of them. Folk who'd lived next door to one another for decades. In some cases as long as fifty years. He takes a drag on the quickly burning Woodbine. And it's aw' for the best – so they tell us. The younger ones can handle it. But a lot o' the auld yins are taking it hard. Lived cheek by jowl wi' another two families on a landing for most o' their lives. It's whit they're used tae. As he takes another draw, there comes the rumble of a man-made avalanche. He watches a great gout of dust and soot rise into the air over where Rothesay Street – what's left of it – meets the Maryhill Road.

John Caldwell puts on his peaked cap, grips the mailbag

firmly with his left hand, reaches for the door handle. He pauses, looks through the windscreen again. Wants to take in, remember, this stark scene in front of him. He thinks back to his first days as the postman for this part of Maryhill. Late on in '46. Straight out o' the army. How old was I? He does his sums. Smiles. Twenty-four. Jeez! After four years in the Seaforths, it took a bit of getting used to, being back in civvie street. Living with Ma and Da again. Especially after that fifteen months with the army of occupation in the British Zone of Germany. Hah! Corporal Caldwell. The best time of my life. Definitely! Ah still don't know why I didn't sign on. The CO promised me I'd do at least another twelve months in Germany. He sighs as a kaleidoscope of sights and sounds flashes through his mind. Always the same ones. That first year after Jerry surrendered. Magic time! Twenty fags, a bar o' chocolate and a cake o' soap. He has to stop himself from laughing out loud. That was all you needed. Could drink and shag yourself to a standstill every weekend! What a time it was. He gives a juddering sigh. Thinks of his last girlfriend before demob. Ilsa. What a body! She'd take her bra off – and them beautiful tits would just stay where they were . . .

Someone walking out of 18 Dalbeattie Street breaks his train of thought. He shakes his head. Wonder what got me onto that? He looks through the windscreen again at the panorama of destruction, the half-cleared rubble, the occasional building still standing. Aye. That's what has sparked me off. It looks just like Munster did when we drove in to occupy it. The *entire* bloody city looked like this by the time the RAF had finished with it.

He's about to go off on another trip down memory lane when the pedestrian from Number 18 waves her hand in greeting. He looks at her. Oh, it's Mrs Stuart. Irene. Her man is Alec. He reaches into the bag, grabs the bundle of letters, winds down the driver's window.

'Ah see there's two or three letters for Number 18 from the Housing Department. Would ye like me tae see if your luck's in, Mrs Stuart?'

'*Oh*! Yes please, John.' She halts at the side of the van. Watches him riffle through them.

'Aye! You've won a prize, Mrs S.' With a flourish he reaches the long envelope out of the window towards her.

As she takes hold of it she looks at the other, similar envelopes, still held by the rubber band. 'Ah'm I allowed to ask who else up oor close has got one?'

He opens his mouth in mock horror. 'Heaven forfend, Irene Stuart! Me a servant of the crown, and you're asking me tae divulge information about which of your neighbours has got a letter fae the Hoosing De-part-ah-mont – before they even know thurself! You go too far Mistress Stuart!'

Irene bends lower, looks directly into his eyes. 'Tonight is my baking night, John. The Be-Ro book will be taken from its hiding place and will give up its secrets – shortly efter *Coronation Street*.' She clucks her tongue. 'You catch ma drift?'

'Pressuring me tae betray the trust placed in me by Her

Majesty. Dearie me! Ah think it will take more than . . . Eh, whit are ye thinking of making the night?'

She clears her throat. Looks both ways along the empty street. 'When ye come roon' in the morning, laid oot on oor kitchen table will be Victoria sponge, short pastry apple pie,' she pauses, 'treacle scones . . .'

'Devil wumman! The jail's too good fur you, Irene Stuart!' He pauses. 'Will half-past eight be too early?'

'Ah'll have the kettle bileing.'

'Ah'll jist huv a wee look and see how many there are for Number 18.'

'Ah don't want tae know aboot everybody. Jist two. Have Agnes Dalrymple and the O'Malleys got their letters?'

He flicks through the envelopes. 'There's one for Agnes . . .' There is further flicking. 'Naw. The O'Malleys huv missed oot this time.' He looks up at her. 'Now mind, Irene. Don't be letting on tae them that you knew before they did. Some folk are funny aboot things like that. Just let *them* tell you. Okay?'

She straightens up. 'I won't give the show away, John. Ah've more sense than that.'

He opens the van door, exits onto the pavement. 'Ah'll be chapping on your door in the morning at half eight on the dot. Eh, dae ye think it might be wise tae hide some o' that home baking – in case your Alec attempts tae snaffle maist of it before Ah can get here?'

'Don't worry.' Irene now looks at him in what can only be described as a coy manner. 'And Ah'll tell you something else, John. On Saturday just gone, Alec and I went into oor favourite delicatessen on the Byres Road.' She has his undivided attention.

'You did'nae!'

'We did! On the table tomorrow morning will be a pat of pure Normandy butter!'

'Oh, mammy-daddy! What a bad, wicked wumman you are, Irene Stuart! Eh, Ah think there's a possibility Ah might be even sharper in the morning. Mibbe twenty-past eight?'

Agnes Dalrymple is kneeling on her doormat, chopping sticks on the landing as John Caldwell climbs up the last flight to the top storey. 'Good morning! I have a letter here, from the Housing Department,' he holds it up, 'addressed to a Miss Agnes Dalrymple. Diz that happen tae be your good self?'

She straightens up, sits back on her heels. 'Ye know fine well it is, John Caldwell.'

'I'm afraid I'll have to insist on seeing some ID.'

'You'll be seeing stars – if Ah hit you a dunt on the back o' the heid wi' this chopper, so ye will.'

'Oh! Well, on second thoughts, Ah think Ah mibbe recognise ye after all, Miss D.' He hands her the letter.

'Did anybody else get wan, up this close?'

Yet again, he pretends to be shocked. 'It's more than ma job's worth tae divulge information like that, Miss Dalrymple.'

'It'll be mair than your *life*'s worth if ye don't!' She looks up at him. 'The kettle's on.'

* * *

It's some forty minutes later when Irene Stuart returns from the shops. She goes past her own landing and makes her way up to the top storey. 'Are ye in, Agnes?'

'Aye! In ye come.'

'Oh, hello, John. You have'ny got very far this morning.'

'Good morning, Mrs Stuart.' He watches as Irene takes 'the letter' out of her message bag.

'Ah've had a letter fae the Housing, Agnes. They'll be flitting Alec and me up tae Stobcross Avenue on the Molendinar, on Monday, March the 20th.'

Agnes manages to stop herself indulging in a bit of bosom adjusting. She lifts *her* letter up from the table. 'Me tae! Whit number is your new hoose, Irene?'

'Number 21.'

'Ah'm 23,' says Agnes. 'We'll have tae find oot if we're either side of one o' them semi-detached, or if we're separate hooses.'

'Ah already know,' replies Irene.

'You don't!'

'Ah dae. Ah got Irma tae let me know how the numbers run on the ones they've just finished building. We will be taking up either side of a semi-detached.'

'Oh, that's grand. That means we'll jist be through the wall from yin another, Irene. Ah was fair worried in case Ah got a complete stranger.' She sniffs. 'Be terrible if ye got a nosey bugger, alwiz wanting tae know your business!'

Both women turn to look as the postman suddenly chokes and goes into a fit of coughing. Irene comes to his rescue with a couple of well-placed thumps on his back.

'Eee, John. It's no' often people choke on a piece of City Bakeries Swiss roll,' says Agnes. 'They're noted for their softness.'

He gives a final cough then pats his chest a couple of times. 'No, it wiz'nae that, Agnes. Ah've nae idea *whit* could huv caused it.' He carefully avoids Irene Stuart's eyes.

CHAPTER TWENTY-SIX

Ah'll Never Forget Thingummy!

The Camerons are just finishing their dinner. Katherine looks at the clock on the mantelpiece.

'Are ye oot wi' Dermot the night, hen?' Ella reaches for her daughter's empty plate.

'Aye, we're meeting at the top of Buchanan Street.'

'Seeing as it's a Wednesday, Ah suppose it'll be the pictures, the night?' says her father.

'What are ye going tae see?' enquires Archie junior. 'Anything good?'

'It's called *Dirty Harry*. It got really good reviews in the papers and magazines when it came out. It's aboot this detective who is always breaking the rules.'

'Who's in it?' asks Archie junior.

'Clint Eastwood.'

Her father sits back in his chair. 'Clint Eastwood? Where dae Ah know that name from?'

'Do you remember yon series that wiz on the telly years ago? *Wagon Train*? It wiz in black and white,' says his son. 'Clint played "Rowdy" Yates. He helped the cook on the chuck wagon.'

'Oh aye, Ah know who ye mean. Yon wiz a good series. We used tae watch it every week. Auld whit's his name played the boss, eh, the wagonmaster. Oh, man! He wiz in stacks o' fillums wi John Wayne.' Archie senior stares up at the heavily-laden pulley for inspiration. 'Big fella he wiz. Jeez! Ah can *see* him . . .'

'Well ask him his name, then,' suggests Ella. Then adds, 'And tell him tae be carefy – in case he brings doon that pulley.'

This earns her a dirty look. 'You know whit Ah mean, Ella. And he wiz also in *The Quiet Man* wi' John Wayne . . .'

'Awww! Ye mean Victor McLaglen?'

'NAWWW, no' him! . . . Victor played Maureen O'Hara's brother. The guy Ah'm after. The wagonmaster. *He* played the priest in it.'

'Ah don't remember a priest in *Wagon Train*,' mutters Ella. She winks at Katherine, who seems to be in some pain as she holds her side, while making strange noises.

'Ah'll tell ye another picture he wiz in,' says Archie senior. 'He played the polis who stopped James Stewart jumping aff the bridge in *It's A Wonderful Life*! Remember? Stocky built guy.'

Katherine decides to come to her father's aid. 'Ah know who you mean, Dad. Ah cannae remember his first name, but his last name is Bond.'

'Awww!' says Ella. 'Ah know who ye mean. Brooke.' She seems unconcerned as her daughter lets out a wail and holds her side again.

'Brooke Bond's the buggering dividend tea!' says her husband. 'There wiz a wee, sort of postage stamp thing oan the side of every quarter. Ye stuck them inside a card and –'

Ella interrupts. 'You're right, Erchie. Ye hud tae save them up. And efter aboot twenty years they gave ye five shillings – if ye could remember where ye put the card.'

Archie lets out a large tut. 'It wiz'nae as bad as that!' He shakes his head in frustration. Suddenly. 'Ah've got him! Ward! It's Ward Bond! Ah knew Ah'd get him in spite of ye, yah bugger!' He sits silent for a moment. Then . . . 'Whit wiz the original question?'

'Nae good asking me,' says Ella. 'Ah loast the plot aboot five meenits ago.'

Moments later they hear somebody come up the stairs, step onto their landing. Their door is knocked, then opened. 'Is there anybody home?'

'Aye. In you come, Billy.' Archie junior has recognised the voice of Billy McClaren junior. All four watch as the kitchen door is opened and a smiling Police Sergeant McClaren enters. He has an unbuttoned gaberdine mac on, over his uniform. No hat. 'Evening all!'

'Bugger me! He's turning intae Dixon o' Dock Green!' says Ella.

Billy looks at father and son. 'It's mainly you two I've came up tae see. Has anybody told you the good news?'

'If they huv, Ah must huv forgot it,' says Archie senior.

'Me tae,' echoes his son. 'Whit is it?'

'Wait a minute,' says Ella. 'Ah'm that busy listening tae the three of you, Ah'm forgetting ma manners. You want a cup o' tea, son?'

'Naw. Thanks aw' the same, aunty Ella. I'm on my way home for my dinner.' He pauses. 'It's just that I was hoping I'd be the first to tell the boys the good news.'

Ella looks at him. 'Right! If you're no' wanting a cuppa – let's be hearing it.'

'Well, it'll probably be of more interst tae the two Archies.' He turns to them. 'Would you believe it! Nathan Brodie – the Big Boss – has retired! Sold up and moved to the Costa Del Sol. Already gone!'

'Never in the world! Jeez-oh! Noo that is'nae half a surprise!' says Archie junior.

Ella appears thoughtful as she looks at her husband, then her son. She turns to Billy. 'Ah take it you're telling these two, because it's them that's caused him tae pack it in?'

'That's right. Just like in the cowboy pictures, Ella. They've run the baddie out of town! He's had enough, so he's selling up and riding off into the sunset.' He looks at Archie junior, laughs out loud. 'Well, to be one hundred per cent accurate, Ah believe he actually went *limping* off into the sunset!' He looks knowingly at the two Archies.

'Mmm, imagine that!' says Archie senior.

Ella looks at her man. 'From leaving the hoose that night, tae coming back hame wi' the boy . . .' She tries to work it out. 'You were only away aboot forty minutes. Mibbe less.' She turns to Billy McClaren. Points to her husband. 'Dae ye know whit, Billy. Ah never get tae know the half of whit goes on when this fella gets his dander up and goes off somewhere. Because, when he diz come back hame, he never, ever tells us what he's been up tae. The *only* thing Ah know for a fact,' she glances at Archie again, 'is, that when he diz go oot tae get something sorted oot,' she is unable to hide the quiet pride in her voice, 'he's never away for long!'

McClaren laughs. 'Aye, so they tell me.' He nods his head in the direction of her son. 'And seemingly this one can also handle himself, when push comes tae shove!'

Katherine glances at her father and brother, then turns to her mother. 'Ah'm beginning tae think, Ma, that we're living here wi' Batman and Robin.' She nods in her brother's direction. 'Though mind, it has tae be said, it took Robin here quite a while before he got started!'

'Hah!' The father regards his son. 'Ah don't think he'll argue with ye aboot that, Katherine. But ye know the auld saying – better late than never!' He reaches a hand out and squeezes his son's forearm.

Mother and daughter look at one another. With their eyes full, they cannot trust themselves to speak at just this moment.

'Anyway, Ah'd better get away,' says the sergeant. 'Stella will have the dinner ready. I just couldn't resist making a wee detour. I wanted to see the boys' faces when I told them the good news. He takes a hold of the kitchen door handle. 'Whatever you did to Brodie and that toerag,

Devaney, down at the Garscube Vaults, I heard from a source of mine that Brodie quite simply lost heart. Decided he couldn't hack it any more.' He smiles. 'Oh! And Ah'll tell you a funny thing. The day after it happened, seemingly there was a surge in the sales of walking sticks in Maryhill!' Billy opens the door, turns back to look into the kitchen again. 'I can definitely vouch for that. I drove past Devaney on the Maryhill Road earlier today. He was hirpling along on a stick. And I also heard from my source, because he was there, that Brodie headed out to his plane at Prestwick on *two*!' The men laugh.

Ella looks at her daughter. 'They don't tell us anything these two, dae they?'

'Uh-huh! What it is, Ma. You and me, we are on whit they call A Need Tae Know Basis!'

Ella gives it a bit of thought. 'Mmmm. Well, in the long run that might be best, hen.'

CHAPTER TWENTY-SEVEN

To Seize the Chance

Wilma Galloway is first to notice the rain as she and Frank saunter along Argyle Street on a Thursday afternoon. 'Ah thought Ah felt a wee spit then, Frank.'

'Ah think you're right, hen.' He holds a hand out, palm upwards. Glances at the sky. 'There's a chance it might be jist a shower.' He looks at his wristwatch. 'Ah'll tell ye whit. We'll away intae Lewis's and have a coffee and a wee snaster in the cafeteria.'

'A good idea, SON!'

He looks askance at her. 'Who's that supposed tae be?'

'Excuse me! That was ma best Max Bygraves.'

'Aww! Is that who it wiz. And there wiz me thinking, that's a pretty good Valentine Dyall.'

Five minutes later finds them settled at a corner table with two cups of coffee, a German biscuit and a fern cake. Frank turns. 'Well, Ah guess there's nae good moaning,

Wilma. There's nae law says it's not tae rain on our day off.'

'Mmm. Anywye, we can always look forward tae getting oor feet up the night and watching the telly. *Mission:Impossible* is on. And *Father, Dear Father*.'

'Yeah. And if we have *Nationwide* with oor dinner, and *News at Ten* after the two programmes, that should nicely fill the –' Frank stops speaking as he becomes conscious a couple have walked over, and are standing to his right. He begins to raise his head . . .

'Frank Galloway!' That is all that is needed. He immediately recognises her voice. His first look confirms it. 'Rosemary, hen! Ah don't believe it. How marvellous!' He stands up, gives her a kiss on the cheek then continues to hug her, rocking slightly from side to side. He stops, holds her at arms-length, looks into her face. The catch in his voice only allows him to utter, 'Wonderful!' He turns to the man. They share a firm, two-handed handshake. Frank is able to manage, 'Grand tae see ye, son!'

As Wilma looks up at all three, it's obvious they are as pleased to see Frank, as he is them. He pulls out an empty chair, fetches another one from an adjoining table.

'Right, c'mon. Nae argument. Sit down. We'll have a cuppa and a blether. There's a lot o' catching up – Oh! I'm sorry! Wilma hen, this is –'

'Ah think Ah know who this is withoot needing an introduction,' says Wilma. 'It's Rosemary Fleming, isn't it?' She turns to the man. 'And you'll be Andy?'

The couple laugh. 'You must have a good memory,' says Rosemary.

'Och! Ah don't need a good memory. He talks about the two of you often,' she smiles at Rosemary, 'forever wondering how the pair of you are.'

'Well, I'm flattered.' She gives Frank an affectionate smile. 'We were such good pals back in the great days o' the trams. Driver and conductress. Aye, they were happy days, Frank.'

'And would you believe,' says Wilma, 'Ah'm the one that succeeded you. We did the last year of the trams together, then went onto the buses. And Ah'm his conductress tae the present day.'

Frank comes in. 'Aye, and ma wife.' He turns his head. 'So that's me well under control, Andy. Twenty-four hours a day. There's nae escape!'

'Mibbe so,' says Rosemary, 'but you're no' looking too bad on it. So don't you kid yourself, Frank Galloway.'

'Dae ye hear that, Andy? She's jist picking up from where she left off, eleven . . . no . . . 1960. It'll be twelve years ago.' They all become aware of Frank's voice faltering, trailing off. The momentary silence is heavy. Frank and Rosemary are suddenly reminded of *that* year. When their close working relationship came to an end. When she was told that, at last, she was pregnant. When, minutes after Rosemary told Frank the good news outside Dalmarnock depot, his wife Josie was fatally injured in a road accident a scant, few yards away.

Frank clears his throat. 'We just sort of lost touch, didn't we?' He doesn't wait for an answer, wants to get the conversation flowing again. 'It was a lassie you had, wasn't it? I remember the girls in the depot telling me.'

'Aye, a wee girl. Daisy.'

'Oh! That's a lovely, old-fashioned name,' says Wilma.

'Were you able to have any more?' asks Frank.

She smiles. 'Yeah, three years later I did the double. A wee laddie. Alexander.'

Frank pats the back of her hand. 'Oh, Ah'm *really* pleased for the pair of you. That's absolutely great. So, where are you living now. Still in Dalmarnock?'

As the conversation and the mood pick up, Wilma looks at the couple. An old idea has begun to resurrect itself. As she concentrates hard on her own thoughts, the voices at the table seem to drop in volume, merge into the background hum of the cafeteria. Should I ask them? You said you would if you ever got the chance, Wilma. Her mind begins to race . . . You have to! These are the only two who can help. They were there that day. Rosemary is blameless. Aye, but when she finds out the full story, will she be too upset tae help? Can Ah find the words to make them realise that only they can bring Frank and his son back together again? And if they say they'll help – how do I get his son, Daniel, to sit down and listen? He never gave his dad the chance to explain what *really* happened. He's convinced his dad was carrying-on with Rosemary, and the shock of seeing them kiss made Josie run blindly onto the road. What if Frank finds out what I'm up to behind his back? He'll blow his top! She lets out an involuntary sigh. And Ah don't even know where Daniel lives . . . Oh! My God! King Solomon could'nae sort this lot oot!

'Wilma! *Wilma*!' She becomes aware Frank is looking into her face. 'This bugger's gone intae a trance.'

'Oh! Sorry!' She looks around the table. 'Jeez! Ah was miles away. Eee, Ah'm sorry!'

Rosemary smiles. 'Ah think it would cost more than a penny for those thoughts, whatever they were!'

Frank laughs. 'A penny? It would be at *least* a fiver! Anyway, Ah'm just gonny pay a quick visit. Then before we go, we'll swop addresses.' He rises. 'Two minutes!'

Wilma clears her throat. Here goes! 'Listen.' She lays a hand on each of the couple's hands for a moment. 'You have no idea how often I've hoped I would get the chance to meet you. There's something I think you should know. But first of all, what Ah'm going tae tell you is just between the three of us. Frank mustn't get tae know until later.' She sees how serious the two of them now look. She squeezes their hands again. 'It's nothing tae worry aboot. I'll try tae explain it as best I can. It's something Frank never told you back then, Rosemary. With you having problems wi' your pregnancy, and leaving your job, he did'nae want tae risk upsetting you.' Wilma clears her throat. 'Ah don't imagine you'll know this, but since Josie died in that accident, Frank's son hasn't spoken to him from that day to this! He blames Frank for what happened to his mother!'

'But that's absolute nonsense! I was there. I was with

Frank . . .' Rosemary's voice drops as she thinks back to that dreadful day. 'Over the years, Wilma, you've no idea how often it comes into my mind. And I always think, what a horrible thing tae happen – on what should have been the best day of my life!' She pauses. 'Andy and I had been down tae see the consultant at the Royal. And I'd just been told that at long-last I was pregnant. So I get Andy to drive home via the depot. I'm bursting to tell Frank my good news.' She looks at Andy, smiles. 'The timing was perfect. Frank's jist coming oot the depot, going tae the cafe. I run across the road, "FRANK! FRANK!" We're kissing and hugging, jist aboot dancing along the pavement. Then there's a squeal o' brakes. And aboot two minutes later we find oot it's Josie! She'd been coming tae meet Frank. How awful! Ah'll never, ever forget it, Wilma.' She seems to shudder. 'So, why has Daniel fallen out with his father?'

Wilma takes one of Rosemary's hands in hers. 'Because Josie saw you run across the road into Frank's arms and put two and –'

'Oh, my God!' Rosemary's hand goes to her mouth. 'And she thought –' she breaks off.

'Uh-huh! That's the sad thing aboot it. Later that day, in the hospital, she telt Daniel she'd seen you and Frank kissing and hugging one –'

Andy interrupts. 'Ah was sitting in the van. It was totally innocent . . .' He raises his head. 'Here's Frank coming!' He squeezes Rosemary's forearm. 'C'mon, hen! Get yerself pulled the 'gether. We can talk aboot it later. It can be sorted oot.'

Rosemary leans nearer to Wilma. 'We'll have tae get Daniel put in the picture aboot that day. That's terrible that he thinks that aboot his father.' She stops. 'And about me as well!'

'Well, folks . . .' Frank sits down. 'All good things must come tae an end. But Ah have tae tell the two of you, it's been just wonderful bumping into you like this.' He reaches into his inside pocket, produces a pen. 'Right, let's swop addresses. We mustn't lose touch again.'

'Ah've got some paper in ma handbag,' says Wilma.

Frank looks at the Flemings. Nods in Wilma's direction. '*Huh*! And let me tell you. It would'nae have made any difference *what* you had been looking for.' He taps the handbag. 'Piece o' paper? Pneumatic drill? Sailor's hammock? You name it. She'll pull it oot o' that bag!'

Wilma gives a large 'tut'. 'That's jist stupid, so it is. Oh! And if ye have a phone number, write it doon, tae.' She winks at Rosemary while Frank isn't looking.

'Ah'm putting doon oor present address,' says Frank. 'But we'll no' be there for much longer. The street's nearly aw' doon. We'll be away tae the Molendinar, in a month at most. And Ah'll tell you something else. We've been going tae a smashing wee Italian restaurant for years. Stromboli. It's doon at the bottom o' the Byres Road. Shall we all go oot for a meal the 'gither, one night?'

'That's a great idea, Frank. We can spend a whole evening talking aboot auld times,' says Rosemary. She looks at Wilma. 'See if you agree wi' me. It might no' seem a lot. But do ye know what I look back on as some of my most enjoyable times when we worked on the caurs the 'gether?'

Wilma smiles. 'Easy! Sitting on a tram oot at the terminus, eating your piece and drinking oot o' your flask!'

'God! You tae, Wilma. What was so special aboot it? Frank and I just used tae sit and blether. Yet that's what always comes intae my mind when I think back tae them days. Piece-time!'

'Well, Ah still get tae enjoy them, Rosemary. Ah'm his conductress and he's ma driver right tae the present day. The only difference is, nooadays it's oan a bus instead o' a tram.'

'Yah lucky thing! Well, if ye cannae get a tram, Ah suppose a bus is the next best.'

As they exit Lewis's, onto Argyle Street, the foursome stand on the pavement for a few minutes to say their goodbyes. 'It's been lovely tae meet you, Rosemary.' Wilma gives her a kiss and a hug. Whispers, 'Ah'll give you a ring. We have tae get them two back together.'

Rosemary can only nod. As the couples go their separate ways, Wilma links her arm through Frank's. They saunter along Argyle Street in the direction of the Central Station bridge – the Hielanman's Umbrella. Frank seems lost in thought. Wilma, is soon busy with hers . . . That was great, at last getting to talk to Rosemary and Andy. Thank the Lord Ah found the words tae explain things tae them.

Frank comes out of his reverie, looks up at the sky. 'It

looks like it's starting tae clear up, Wilma. Might be set fair for tomorrow.'

She presses his arm tight to her side. Looks up at him. 'Aye, there's a good chance, Frank.'

CHAPTER TWENTY-EIGHT

Getting a Move On

Two Pickfords removal vans, parked back to back, stand outside Number 18. Both crews now have a short walk when they exit the close. It's the twentieth of March, 1972. Moving day for Agnes Dalrymple from the top storey, and Alec and Irene Stuart from two-up. Teresa O'Malley has returned from her office cleaning job and has gone up to help Agnes . . .

'Now there's no need t' be getting yerself excited, Agnes. The men do all the heavy lifting. Sure that's their job.'

'Ah know, Teresa. But it's no' that. You'll feel the same when it's your turn. It's the upheaval.' She looks around her kitchen. 'Last night, after we'd packed the delicate things, and you left,' she pauses, sighs, 'it wiz terrible. Ah'm sitting in the kitchen, surrounded by tea chests, nae curtains oan the windaes. Ah tried tae settle doon and watch the telly, distract maself . . . but, och! Ah wiz watching this play. It wiz a bit sad,' she tuts, 'so Ah finished up huving a wee greet noo and again.'

'Jayz! Ye should have picked sum'ting a bit cheerier, so ye should.'

'And when Ah went tae bed, Ah never slept a wink. Ah'm lying there wi' the light oot, and Ah'm thinking tae maself, this is the last time Ah'll ever sleep in ma recess bed.' She looks at her friend. 'Ah'm no' wanting a new hoose, Teresa. Ah jist want tae be left alone, so Ah do.' She starts to cry.

Teresa goes to her, gives her a cuddle. 'I know, me darlin'. It'll be the same for Dennis and meself in a few weeks. 'Specially about the recess bed. When Rhea and Siobhan left, me and himself could have took their bed through the room. But we didn't. There's nowhere finer on a winter's night, than tucked up in an auld recess bed wit' the curtains drawn. Sure there isn't.'

'It's just me, girls!' The kitchen door is pushed open and they watch Irene Stuart enter. 'How are you getting on?'

'Oh, Jayz! Don't be asking. Agnes has got the blues,' says Teresa. 'Gone a bit melancholy so she has.'

Irene looks at the ceiling. 'Ah hope you're taking that light bowl with you, Agnes?'

'Och, Ah cannae be bothered.'

'*Agnes*! You cannae leave that. That's a lovely thing.' She continues to look at the translucent bowl, with its pale, pastel-coloured flowers. 'That's from around 1930 or so. It'll look terrific in your new living room. Give it a bit of class.'

'It's too much bother.'

'Whit bother? You get up on a chair, then ontae the table. Unhook the three chains and lift it doon. Unscrew the three screws, and that's it. Ready for putting up in your new hoose.'

'Och!'

Irene looks at Teresa, shakes her head. 'I am *not* letting you go withoot it. You'll regret it, hen.' She pulls a chair out from under the table . . .

Five minutes later Irene is gently wrapping the Art Deco bowl in layers of newspaper. 'Ah've took the light bulb, tae. Make sure you take the bulbs from the lobby light *and* the bedroom as well. And Ah'll tell you something else. If you were tae leave that light bowl, later this afternoon wan o' the removal men would be stoating intae an antique shop on the Byers Road – and two minutes later walking oot wi' a fiver in his poaket!'

'Ah suppose you're right, Irene. Thanks.'

Irene now turns her attention to the mantelpiece. It has been cleared – except for two china dogs. She again turns to Agnes. 'Ah'm frightened tae ask, Agnes Dalrymple. You're no' gonny be leaving Granny Thomson's wally dugs, are ye?'

'Oh God, naw!' Agnes manages a laugh. She points over to the coal bunker. 'They're being left tae the last minute, then they'll be wrapped in them two *Evening Times*, placed in separate carrier bags, and they'll be travelling ower tae the Molendinar in style – sitting oan ma lap! They're my mementoes of Bella.'

* * *

Forty-five minutes later, Agnes Dalrymple is assisted up and into the cab of a removal van. Alec Stuart hands the carrier bags up to her. 'Remember, Agnes. If the driver has to brake for an emergency – throw yourself in front o' these wally dugs!'

It's the afternoon of the same day. Wilma Galloway makes her way upstairs to the tearoom at Hubbard's Bakery on Great Western Road. She's about to take a few steps into the large room, then stop while she looks for Rosemary Fleming. There is no need. The waving of an arm catches her eye. Both women smile.

'Where does Frank think you are, Wilma?'

'Ah said Ah was going over tae ma aunty Maggie's for a wee visit.'

'Good,' says Rosemary. 'So we'll be okay for time. Anyway, let's order whatever we're going to have, then we'll get down tae business.' She clears her throat. 'I don't mind telling you, Wilma, since we bumped into you in the cafeteria, I can't get it out of my head that Josie died believing Frank and me were carrying-on. And Daniel still thinks it's true!' She shakes her head. 'I hope tae God we can at least get him straightened out. All them years not talking to his father.' She smooths the white tablecloth. 'Have you gave any thought as to how we should go about it?'

'Well, first of all, let me put your mind at rest about one thing, Rosemary.' She gives a sad smile. 'Josie did'nae die believing Frank and you were having an affair. When we met in Lewis's, there wasn't enough time tae tell you the full story.'

'Oh! Ah thought she'd told Daniel she'd seen Frank and me kissing?'

Wilma looks heavenwards. 'It's so bloody complicated. When Josie arrived at the hospital on that day, she was unconscious and was immediately rushed intae the theatre because of her head injuries. Frank was told it would take some time, so he took the chance tae nip home and change out of his uniform. While Frank's away, Daniel arrives to see his mother. She had come round, and the first thing she tells him is that she'd seen you two kissing and hugging – and this is what made her run off and ontae the road!' Wilma breathes deeply. 'When Frank returns tae the hospital, Daniel dis'nae give him a chance. He raves and rants at his father, tells him that it's all his fault, and he doesn't want tae sit with him at his mother's bedside. Daniel goes off home, says he'll be back at nine o'clock – and diz'nae want tae see Frank still there!' Wilma pats Rosemary's hand. 'Now comes the part you'll be glad tae hear. Frank sits beside Josie, and tells her *why* you two were delighted to see one another – because, at long last, you were pregnant. He also tells her he'll get Andy and you to come and see her. She finally believes him. Says that when Daniel comes back at nine she'll tell him how stupid she's been.' Wilma looks at Rosemary. 'Frank leaves at quarter to nine to avoid another upset wi' Daniel. He knows it will all be sorted out later tonight. Whit happens? Sod's bloody law kicks-in, that's whit! Frank's not gone ten minutes when Josie takes a brain thingummy, eh, haemorrhage! When Daniel arrives back at the ward, his mother has been taken to the theatre. She never regains consciousness, and never gets the chance tae tell him she'd been wrong. From that day tae this he still believes what his ma told him, and won't have anything tae do with his father!'

'Oh, is that no' awful. Poor Frank.'

'Well, at least you now know, Josie did'nae die thinking Frank and you had cheated on her. That's a blessing!'

'Ah'm certainly glad to find that out, Wilma. But before we start working oot how to get Daniel told – let's order up another pot of tea, Ah'm choking!'

'Me tae. Ah'm spitting feathers!'

Five minutes later, a pot of Pekoe Tips is brought to the table and quickly poured.

Wilma places her cup back in its saucer. 'Right, Rosemary. First of all, we'll have tae find oot where Daniel lives. Do ye ever remember it being mentioned when you worked wi' Frank? Of course,' she pulls a face, 'that's more than ten years ago. He might have moved house a time or two since then.'

'Ah *know* where he lives!' Rosemary gives a big smile.

'You don't!'

'Ah dae!' She leans forward. 'He lives ower in Dennistoun.'

'Oh! That's great! That's us off tae a flying start,' says Wilma. 'How did you find that oot?'

'I didn't really "find it out". Ah've sort of . . . known for years.' Rosemary concentrates. 'It was when I worked with Frank. I remember him telling me about Daniel's wedding. It was quite a big do. Oh! And the lassie's name was Sheila.

And he said they'd already found a room and kitchen, ower in Dennistoun. Her parents knew a friend of a friend . . . you know, the usual story.'

'Mmm, that rings a bell wi' me,' says Wilma. 'Ah seem tae remember Frank, back in oor early days, mentioning the name Sheila. Even though the falling-out wi' Daniel had taken place a year or two before Ah met him, he'd still talk aboot him now and again. But that got less and less over time. Just a few years ago, ye know, they passed each other doon the toon. Frank stopped and said "Hello!"' Wilma's eyes moisten. 'Walked right past him. He never told me about it at the time. It was a long time after.' She stops. 'That really hurt him. Ah think that was when he finally gave up hope.'

Rosemary leans forward. 'Well, he's still in Dennistoun. And Ah should be able tae get his address. My cousin Mary is a great one for helping at the church. Has been for years. Especially things tae do wi' bairns.'

Wilma smiles. 'So you're Rose*mary* and yer cousin's *Mary*!'

Rosemary looks heavenward. 'Oh, yes. We're a good Catholic family, so we are. If I'd ever had a brother, Ah'm certain ma mammy would huv christened him Marytin or something not far off!' They both laugh. 'So, as Ah was saying. Oor Mary is involved in lots of things at the church. It's Saint Chad's, over in Dennistoun. Anywye, that first couple o' years after Ah fell pregnant and had to finish work, she was often over at my ma's for Sunday dinner, or just visiting. And she'd mention a Daniel and his wife Sheila now and again. And I used tae think, I wonder if that's

Frank's son? Then she said tae me one time, "Ah think Daniel's father works on the buses." Then another time, Sheila had told her Daniel and his father had fallen out years ago. Don't speak any more!'

'Mmm!' Wilma sits back. Looks at Rosemary. 'Ah'd say that's the clincher! Dae ye think so?'

'Yeah, seems a pretty safe bet!'

Wilma finishes the last of her tea. 'Let me tell you how Ah think we should go about getting in touch wi' Daniel.' She holds a hand up. 'But these are just ideas, Rosemary. If you come up with something better, Ah'll be *more* than happy tae go along with it.' She lifts her cup, realises it's empty, places it back in the saucer. 'Now, Frank is a stubborn bugger. And from what little Ah've heard of Daniel, Ah think he has inherited it!' She looks intently at Rosemary. 'Ah think we are only gonny get *one* chance tae persuade Daniel he is in the wrong.'

Rosemary nods. 'Yeah! And that's what worries me, Wilma. If we don't find the right words, we might only get halfway through telling him what we want tae tell him – and he'll not let us finish. Just get tae his feet and go storming oot!'

'Ah'm feart of that, too.'

'I agree with what you've said so far, Wilma. But what I don't want us to do, is come across as if we're begging Daniel to forgive his dad. There is nothing *to* forgive. We only want him to listen to us. Hear what really happened.'

'Oh! If we can jist get that over to him, Rosemary. Let him know that Andy was sitting in his van watching you and Frank, giving him the thumbs-up,' her voice catches, 'because it was such a happy day. And at the same time, just a few yards away – Josie thinks she's caught her man with another woman. Oh, God! Isn't it awful? You could'nae bloody make it up!'

'Could I make a suggestion, Wilma? Well, *two* suggestions. I think we should approach Daniel by way of his wife. If we can explain everything tae Sheila, we'll be halfway there. And I also think we should involve their parish priest. Mary is good friends with him. Fr McKenna. He's a lovely man. In fact, now that I think of it, maybe you, Andy and me should meet with him *first*. If he agrees to help, he can then arrange a meeting with Sheila. We can get over to her that Josie was mistaken. It was a terrible misunderstanding.' Rosemary folds her arms. 'Then afterwards, I hope, perhaps Fr McKenna will be willing to persuade Daniel to meet with *all* of us, Sheila included. But *not* Frank! Not yet. That will be last of all.'

Wilma nods. 'That sounds good tae me, Rosemary. Fr McKenna first, then Sheila. Aye, definitely.' She looks at her watch. 'Okay, so if you can see your cousin about fixing up a meeting with the Father, let's hope that will set the ball rolling.'

'Yeah. With a bit of luck, in a week or two we might be sitting down wi' Daniel.'

'Oh, wouldn't that be great, Rosemary. Now, how do we keep in touch? Ah think the best way is for me to give you a ring every week. Ah'll have to use a call box. We don't have a phone.'

* * *

It's just after five o'clock as Wilma Galloway sits on a bus taking her up Queen Margaret Drive towards the Maryhill Road. She's looking out a window, without really seeing. Every time she thinks back to her meeting with Rosemary, she gets a tingle. Jeez! It'll be smashing if this leads tae Frank and Daniel getting back the 'gither. He'll also get tae know his grandbairns. She frowns. But what if something goes wrong? We'll never get another chance, that's for certain. And Frank won't be ower pleased, either. She gives a heavy sigh. Well, if it diz fall apart, Ah'll jist remind him of one of his favourite sayings . . . 'Nothing ventured, nothing gained!'

CHAPTER TWENTY-NINE

Is Hinging Oot o' Windows Dying Oot? Discuss!

Agnes Dalrymple sits at the table in her living room, looking out onto Stobcross Avenue. The scattered pages of today's *Sunday Post* and *Sunday Mail* are spread out in front of her. She turns her head to look at the television. The test card is still on. A wee girl sits by her blackboard with a game of 'OXO' chalked on it, surrounded by multi-coloured balloons and toys. She stares back at Agnes. Huh, Ah bet ye she moves when Ah'm no' looking. Ah wonder how auld that photie is? She's probably aboot forty, noo. And merried wi' three weans. At least the music they play oan BBC2 is always good. A lush, full-string orchestra is playing a familiar tune. She narrows her eyes, concentrates . . . 'Time On My Hands'. Aye, that's it. Instantly, Agnes isn't looking into a street in a Glasgow housing scheme any more. Her eyes may appear to be, but that's not what she's seeing . . . It's warm in the crowded dance hall in Keswick. Nearly all the lads are in uniform. Mostly RAF. Every time the doors into the hall open, she stretches her neck, anticipating that first glimpse of Arnold. Sergeant Navigator Arnold Webb. She hopes he's not away on ops tonight. He often is. The images fade . . . Agnes turns her head, looks at the framed photo on the sideboard. There's a blue jewellery box tucked in behind it. Always is. Always will be. Their engagement ring . . .

The tune still plays, now far away in the background. 'Uh-huhhhh.' It ends in a sigh. October '44 they went doon. She works it out. Twenty-eight years nearly. Only two of them recovered. Both dead. Her thoughts always follow through. Right to the bitter end. A couple of hundred miles away, or whitever it is. Is he still lying there with his other six mates? Inside what's left o' that Lanc? Deep and dark and cold under the North Sea. And when I think of him, diz he know? Is there a wee swirl of water inside the fuselage? Jist the merest ripple. Be nice if there wiz. She glances again at the photo. His forage cap at a jaunty, gravity-defying angle. It always was. Always will be. She whispers, 'It's a good job ye cannae see me nooadays, Arnold. Get the fright o' your life so ye would. Coming up for sixty-four.' Her eyes flit back to his photo. 'You'll alwiz be thirty-five, son.' She can't make him out any more as tears brim. Agnes reaches for a tissue, realises the music has stopped. She turns towards the telly. The test card has gone, the BBC2 logo fills the screen. Oh! The wee yin must be away hame for her tea. The programmes will be on in a meenit.

Agnes returns to gazing out into the street. It's funny how folk, well, the women on these estates, even though they've come fae the tenements, they don't hang oot their windaes like they used tae. Folk jist sort of sit back a bit, look through the gap in their curtains. Makes it seem sneaky so it diz. Like they don't want tae be seen. We never did that in Dalbeattie Street. We alwiz . . . Somebody has stopped on the opposite pavement and is waving. '*Oh*! It's Irma!' Agnes, stiffly, slides onto the chair nearest the window, beckons energetically for her to come over. Her heart lifts as Irma starts crossing the street.

She extricates herself from the table and chairs, makes for the front door. By the time she gets there, Irma has already gone past and is walking up the side of the house, making for the back. Agnes swings the front door open. 'IRMA, hen! Ohhh! Where's she buggering gone?'

'HALLOOO! Agnes!' The voice comes, unmistakably, from the kitchen.

'Ah'm at the front!'

'Do you want me tae enter by the front –'

'Naw! Jist keep still 'til Ah find ye!' Agnes bangs the door shut. Seconds later they rendezvous in the kitchen. She laughs. 'Ah cannae get used tae huving two doors. Ah alwiz go tae the front. Keep forgetting aw' aboot the back yin.'

'Oh, crivvens! I still do it now and again – and I've been here for a year.'

'Now don't you tell me you hav'nae time for a cup o' tea, Irma. You're the first soul Ah've spoke tae since the van came roon' wi' the papers this morning.'

'Of course we will have a cuppa, Agnes. That is why I give you a wave – I know you will invite me.'

'Aw! That's grand, hen. Ah'll be demented soon if Ah don't find somebody tae talk tae.'

'Oh, *schade*! Just think what it is like for me, Agnes. I move here, and expect very quickly all my pals from Number 18 to follow. But what do they do? Stop building the new houses and I'm here on my own for *zoh* long.'

'At least, you've got Bert and young Arthur. Ah've got nae bugger!' Agnes busies herself brewing tea, laying out small plates, opening biscuit tins. 'How is young Arthur?'

'He has finished his trade since last year. Now he is a time-served moulder and brass finisher.'

'Oh! That sounds like a proper trade tae huv.'

'Yah,' Irma spreads her arms apart, as if in appeal, 'but michty me! You know what he then does?' She doesn't wait for a reply. 'He gets a job with Bert's firm, driving the long-distance lorries! Says he does not want to be stuck in a factory at the moment. He can get a job later at his trade. He wants to drive all over the country like his dad.'

'Och! You've nuthing tae worry aboot, Irma. Anywye, you should huv seen that coming. Remember in the school summer holidays, he used tae be forever pestering Bert tae take him for runs in the lorry?'

'You are right. I think those two have *Benzin* – eh, petrol, in the veins.'

Agnes finishes pouring the tea. Pushes the open biscuit tins towards her guest. 'Help yerself.'

Irma laughs.

'Whit are ye laughing at?'

'You! You are turning into Granny Thomson.'

'It's funny. Just before you waved over to me, Irma, Ah had been remembering. When folk in the tenements had nuthin' tae do, they used tae throw the windae up, put a cushion on the sill to lean on, and huv a look oot for a while. They don't seem tae do that on the hoosing schemes. Ah wonder why?'

'I have also noticed this. Is it because all the houses are low down? Not tall, like tenements?'

'Mmm, Ah would think that's part of it, Irma. But mibbe the main reason is because the scheme isnae busy. Hardly any folk go past. And if they do – you don't know who the buggers are, anyway!'

Irma gives it some thought. 'Yah, I would think there will be a bit of that. But if you try to imagine somebody leaning on their windowsill on the Molendinar –'

Agnes cuts in. 'Ah know. It wid'nae look right, wid it? Even Granny wid'nae get away wi' it! You can only lean on a cushion and hing oot the windae if ye live up a tenement! Therr ye are, Irma. Wan o' life's great mysteries solved!'

'*Bestimmt*!' laughs Irma. Agnes looks at her. 'Definitely!' she translates.

CHAPTER THIRTY

A Fine Romance

An April Thursday in 1972. Archie Cameron junior comes bustling into the shop.

'Hullo, Mrs Kinnaird. That's that well and truly delivered. Anything else came in?'

'Good lad. Naw, nothing at the minute, son. Away and get yersel' a cuppa.'

'You wanting one?'

She looks at her watch. 'Naw, it's nearly five. Ah'll survive. Enjoy one all the better when Ah get hame.'

He gives her a smile. Makes his way to the back shop. As he enters, Jean Dalglish looks up.

'Aw'right, Erchie?'

'Fine, Jean.' He tries to sound as if it's not a matter of great importance. 'Eh, where's Lexie?'

'A wee order came in. A bouquet for somebody in Henderson Street. She made it up and took a wee walk doon wi' it herself, seeing as it wiz a nice sunny day. Should be back any minute.'

'Good. Ah'm gonny make a brew – you wanting one?'

'A coffee would be grand.'

As Archie puts the kettle on, prepares the mugs, Jean busies herself with preparations to give her and Lexie a head start with tomorrow's orders as they come in. After a while, she glances at Archie. 'How's the big romance going? Making any headway?'

'No' really. If Ah start tae get whit she considers tae be too pushy,' he turns his head, looks at Jean, 'she immediately gives me The Gypsy's Warning! "Just workmates, Archie! You're forgetting again." So there's nae good arguing.'

'Oh, God! Naw. It'll huv tae be Lexie's way – or *no* way.' Jean stops for a moment, leans on her knuckles. 'But don't forget, Archie, there wiz a time when it looked like she wiz *never* gonny go oot with ye. Nooadays, you're oot at least once a week. Sometimes *twice*. So Ah suppose you should be thankful for small mercies.'

He grimaces. 'Och, aye. You're right, Jean.' He looks down at the mugs. 'And this last wee while,' he clears his throat, 'when we huv a night oot she, eh, quite often takes ma arm when we're walking hame.'

'Whit? Hey! Don't you complain, Erchie Cameron. That is definitely progress, kid. If Ah was you, there is no way Ah would rock the boat . . .' They look at one another as they hear the noise of the street door rattle, followed by Lexie talking to the boss. Jean goes into overdrive, starts moving like someone in a silent film. Picking up some discarded stalks and leaves she begins cutting madly at them, pieces flying from her shears like so much shrapnel. 'Jist act normal, Erchie. Throw her aff the scent. She'll never know we wiz talkin' aboot her!'

Archie goes helpless with laughter, has to sit on the edge of the tea table. Jean follows suit on the work table. The door to the back shop opens wide. Archie gets a tingle. Lexie stops on the threshold, looks at this helpless pair. 'Tell me the joke and Ah'll laugh too.'

Archie points. 'When she heard you coming,' he tries to control himself, 'she said, "Oh! Ah'd better look busy" and wiz lifting handfuls of offcuts and going berserk, like a human buzzsaw! Dauds fleeing everywhere. She looked like Tweety Pie – in the middle of a fit!' Archie and Lexie now regard the out-of-breath Jean.

'Ah've seen her dae that before,' says Lexie. 'The poor soul is badly needing treatment.'

Jean looks from one to the other. 'You should be sticking up fur me, Erchie Cameron, never mind cliping oan me.'

Archie turns to Lexie. 'You wanting a cuppa?'

'Naw thanks.'

Jean butts in. 'Ask her if she's wanting tae go tae the pictures the night, or the morra' night, Erchie.'

He blushes. Shakes his head. 'You're murder-polis so ye are, Jean Dalglish. If Ah was gonny ask her, Ah'd wait 'til we're walking hame.'

Lexie looks at her pal. 'Why dae you want tae know, Jean Dalglish?'

'Och, Ah like tae go hame fae ma work, knowing you two are going tae the pictures or the dancin' later that night.'

Lexie looks at her, then turns to Archie. 'She's stopped buying the *People's Friend*, you know. Says oor story is better than anything in the magazine!'

'You don't. Dae ye?' Archie blushes yet again.

'Ah keep telling her she should go back tae her magazine,' says Lexie. 'At least in there, she'll get a happy ending!' She instantly regrets saying that as the smile vanishes from Archie's face.

When Jean says, 'Awww!' then turns to look at her, she could bite her tongue.

'WHAT?' Lexie spreads her arms wide, shrugs. 'I'm no' saying anything I have'nae said before.'

'It's the *way* you said it,' says Jean. 'Watch ye don't leave the fella something tae hang ontae. Jeez! You can be such a hard bugger at times, Lexie Forsyth.'

'Oh, alllll right! Do ye want tae take me tae the pictures tonight, Archie?'

'Naw thanks.' He takes a mouthful of tea.

'Oh!' She feels her cheeks go red. Tries to recover. 'Okay, touché! Ah thought you said we might go and see Burt Reynolds in *Deliverance*, this week. So what happened?'

'Ah jist remembered Ah've still got some pride left!'

Jean giggles. 'Ohhh! Good for you, Erchie!' Lexie gives her a dirty look.

He looks at his watch, walks over to the shop door. 'Is it aboot time, Mrs K?'

'Aye! There'll be naebody in noo.'

'See youse the morra, girls.' He walks through the front shop. 'Goodnight, boss.'

'Ooooh! He's no' even walking with you up tae Dalbeattie Street, Lexie.' Jean watches her flush once more.

'Whit dae ye mean by that?' Lexie tries to stand her ground.

'You've just tried tae humiliate that boy, Lexie. That wiz'nae very nice. He's nuts aboot you. But he's no' gonny let ye walk all ower him – especially in front of other people. You're usually on the ball wi' things like that. Stringing a guy along. But Ah think you're losing your touch, hen. Ah don't *ever* remember you being, well, tae be honest – so nasty! If you don't want tae go oot wi' him, just tell him. There wiz nae need to treat him like that. Showing him up. *Huh*! You showed yerself up!'

Lexie Forsyth is still for a moment, then turns to face her pal. Jean's mouth opens in surprise when she sees tears. 'Ah do have feelings for him, Jean. But Ah don't know what tae do. He only came oot the jail last year. What if Ah get involved wi' him and he falls back intae his old ways? Ah hav'nae waited this long, tae finish up picking the wrong guy!' She bursts into racking sobs.

'Aww, Lexie!' Jean puts her arms round her, strokes her back. 'Well, ye definitely hud me fooled, hen. Ah thought he was jist somebody tae go oot wi'. Dead casual. Platonic and aw' the rest of it.' They both hear a slight noise, turn towards the door to the main shop. It swings open. Mrs Kinnaird, arms folded, leans on the jamb. She looks ceiling-ward, purses her lips. 'Problems in the heart department, is it?'

'Aye,' says Jean.

'Erchie?' enquires the boss.

'Uh-huh!' says Jean. Lexie reaches for a piece of the green tissue paper used for wrapping flowers, dabs her eyes.

'Ah've seen it coming fur at *least* the last two months!' Mrs K inspects her nails. 'Plain as the nose oan Jimmy Durante's face!'

'It wiz'nae!' Jean laughs. Lexie starts crying again. 'This last three weeks or so Ah've had an idea things might be warming up.' Jean gives Lexie's back another rub.

'Aye, well Ah'm aulder. Had mair experience,' says Mrs Kinnaird.

Twenty minutes later Lexie and Jean walk slowly up the Maryhill Road. 'Oh, Jean, do you think Ah've really huffed him?'

'Ye know fine well ye have. You were too hard on him. And there wiz nae need tae be. The lad had'nae done anything. You'd better face up tae it, Lexie, you've mibbe blown it! He's a strong character tae, ye know. He's no' gonny let ye treat him like dirt!'

Lexie stops on the pavement. Leans against the wall. 'Oh, Jean, Ah'll never sleep the night. And Ah cannae bear the thought of having tae face him in the morning. Ah'll jist die!' She gives a shuddering sigh. 'Ah do *not* know whit came ower me. It's the stupidest thing Ah've ever done in my life! Ah just got carried away. Thought Ah could mess him about, make myself look clever.'

Jean looks thoughtful. 'Dae ye want tae get it aw' settled the night? Then you'll no' be lying in bed torturing yerself. Dae ye?'

'There's nothing I'd like better – but how?'

'Jist trust your aunty Jean!'

Archie Cameron junior sits at the kitchen table plumbing depths of despair he never knew existed – not even in prison. His thoughts are miles away. Well, next door in the Forsyth household to be accurate.

Ella looks at her son, sniffs. 'You huv not touched that dinner. It's your favourite! Mince and tatties wi' dough-balls. Ye must be sickening fur something!' She shakes her head.

Katherine Cameron gazes at her big brother. 'Never seen him like this before. No' even when he wiz refused bail!' She gets no response.

His father looks at him. 'Ah'll bet you it's something tae dae wi' Lexie, next door!'

'Ah wish youse wid aw' leave me alane!'

His father nods sagely. 'Aye! The trouble's next door. Ah wish Ah could get a bet on it!'

They hear footsteps on the landing. Their door is knocked. 'Who can that be?' says Ella.

'We'll no' know unless ye open the buggering door!' says her husband. Ella tuts. She goes to the front door, closing the kitchen one as she does. There comes the murmur of voices. Ella returns. 'Archie! It's that lassie, Jean, that works wi' ye. She has tae speak tae ye. *Urgent*!'

He looks up. Thinks for a moment, then rises, goes to the door. Maddeningly, he also closes the kitchen door. He speaks in a low voice. 'Oh, hello, Jean. Whit is it?'

'She's doon on the half-landing on the second storey. Wants tae talk tae ye.' She takes hold of Archie's forearm. 'Now listen. She realises she got too big for her boots early on –'

'*Huh*! You can say that again!'

Jean grips his arm tighter. 'Now don't *you* bloody well blow it! When ye left, Ah gave her a right telling off!' Jean lets go his arm, draws herself upright. 'Started greeting like a wean she did. She wiz trying tae act tough – because she wanted tae hide the fact that *she* has been falling for *you*! Ye get ma drift, Erchie?'

He's silent for a moment. 'Why hide it?'

'Ah thought ye wid ask that. You'll jist huv tae trust me. Sometimes, when wimmen get involved wi' romance, well, it's like their heids are full o' broken bottles! Know whit Ah mean?'

'No' really.'

'Jist take ma word for it, son. Her main problem is, she's aw' worried that you and her will get the 'gether – and you might finish up in the jail again! Says she could'nae stand it if you did!'

Archie shakes his head. 'That is never, ever gonny happen again! You can believe that, Jean.'

'Ah take it you aren'y really finished wi' her. Are ye?'

He sighs. 'Ah'm crazy aboot her!'

'Oh! Well, that's good,' says Jean. 'Because Ah've got tae get the dinner oan. So wid you mind coming doon the stairs and Ah'll leave the pair of you tae get on wi' it. Youse can tell me how it went, when Ah see ye in the shop the morra morning.'

As they come down towards the chosen half-landing, Lexie stands with her back to the window.

'Ah'll see the two of you in the morning,' says Jean. 'Good night!'

'Well?' Archie stands in front of her. She raises a tear-stained face. 'Oh, Archie! Ah don't know what got intae me.' She looks straight into his eyes. 'Ah do love you. Ah just didn't want tae commit maself. Ah haven't blown it, have Ah?'

He looks at her. 'When Ah walked intae that shop for the first time. As soon as Ah laid eyes on you, that was it. Ah was thirty years of age, never had time tae fall in love before. The minute Ah looked at you, it was all over. That's why Ah'm always hanging about in the back shop. Can't get enough of you! But even so, Ah'll never let you walk all over me. Have you got that?' Her arms go round his neck and she gives him the most glorious kiss of his life! So far.

Ten minutes later they climb up to their landing. After another kiss he watches as she enters her lobby, smiles, then closes the door.

Archie Cameron, walking on air, enters his flat. As he goes into the kitchen, his mother, father and sister are waiting. 'What's happening?' Katherine looks up.

'I'm engaged!' says Archie.

'Fuck me!' says Ella, before dropping a dinner plate.

CHAPTER THIRTY-ONE

Who Said, 'The Truth Will Out'?

There is still light in the sky as Daniel and Sheila Galloway turn the corner into St Chad's Avenue. He looks at her. 'Well, I think your secret is as good as out now. We're obviously going to the chapel.'

She continues to look straight ahead. 'We're going to the presbytery as it happens.'

He frowns. 'Why ever are we going there? Especially on a Tuesday evening?'

'It won't be long until you find out. Content yourself, Daniel.'

As they pass the chapel, his eyes skim the familiar sign: St Chad's RC Church. Then the times of various services, phone numbers, and finally: Fr PJ McKenna. He smiles as he reads it. Patrick Joseph McKenna. Born to be a priest if you have a name like that. Seconds later they reach the gate to the presbytery. As he lays his hand on the catch, Sheila places a hand on top of his. 'Just a reminder, Daniel . . .'

He sighs. 'Ah promised you before we left the house, even though I did'nae know where we were going, that I'll stay to the end!'

'That's all I want to know, dear. But remember, the *very* end!'

'Jeez-oh! What's got intae you?'

'You'll soon find out, Daniel. If you stay the full course.'

He shakes his head. 'How many times do I have tae say it? If you ask me that one more time, I'm gonny finish up gettin' annoyed!'

Seconds after pressing the bell, they stand in the porch listening to steel-heeled shoes machine-gunning the length of a long passage. The image of Lee Marvin, striding at speed along that endless corridor in *The Killers*, comes into Sheila's mind. The staccato symphony changes key and increases in volume when it starts on the large, wooden-floored lobby. The front door is thrown open and there's a momentary disappointment for Sheila when the smiling face of Fr McKenna appears instead of Lee Marvin. 'Ah! 'Tis yourselves.' Greetings and handshakes are exchanged.

They have barely stepped away from the door, when the Father takes them both by the arm. He speaks to Daniel. 'How long have we known one another?'

After an initial look of surprise, he answers, 'Seven or eight years, Father.'

'Be ten years, would you believe, in a couple o' months.'

'Goodness!' Daniel smiles. 'As they say in the Latin – *tempus fugit*, Father.'

'Jayz, yes! Who ever was first to say that, certainly got it right. And believe me, son, the older you get – the quicker it fugits!' All three laugh. The Galloways sound nervous. The priest points towards one of the doors leading off the entrance hall. 'We're in here. There are some folk I want you t' meet.' He takes Daniel's hand in both of his. 'There might be a time, in this room tonight, when you'll t'ink everybody there is trying to, ohhh, make you accept something that seems t' be the *opposite* of what you think is true.' Fr McKenna looks earnestly at him. 'I'm going to ask you for only one favour, Daniel. Listen to the end. Don't interrupt, don't argue. Let these folk finish, *then*, if you want to cross-question, argue, that'll be fine. It'll be your turn. But first of all, hear them out.'

'Yeah, okay. Let's get started.' He glances at his wife. 'I'm beginning to think I *know* what this will be about. Anyway, c'mon. I've promised I'll listen. Let's get it over and done with!'

Sheila looks hard at him.

Fr McKenna puts a hand on his shoulder. 'You might be in for a surprise, son, if you listen.'

It's barely thirty minutes later. Daniel Galloway, with an occasional reminder from his wife and his priest, has grudgingly heard Rosemary and Andy Fleming describe what took place outside Dalmarnock Depot almost twelve years ago. The day his mother, Josie, met with her accident. He has also, grudgingly, listened to his father's wife, Wilma, relate what Frank has told her over the years – especially of his last conversation with Josie shortly before she died. Sadly, while Daniel was absent.

'Right, son.' Fr McKenna gestures towards Daniel. 'You've given these good folk a hearing. It's now your turn. I'm sure they'll be happy to answer any questions you have.' He looks at Rosemary, Andy and Wilma. They nod their heads in assent.

Daniel shifts in his seat. Makes himself look at Wilma. 'Why didn't my father go and see these two,' he nods towards Rosemary and Andy, 'a week or two after my ma died? That's when they should have come to try and persuade me my father had done nothing wrong. *Not* twelve years later!'

'Your father was devastated at losing your mother.' Wilma tries to control the quaver in her voice. 'It was weeks after her funeral before he began tae think about mibbe asking Rosemary and Andy if they would help him out. Tell them that you have had nothing to do with him since the day Josie died. But if he does, he's got tae tell them *why*! That Josie had seen him and Rosemary kiss, she'd thought they were carrying-on, and had ran off intae the road! He knows if things were normal, they'd help him out in a moment.' Wilma looks round the table. 'But things were'ny normal! Rosemary had started a difficult pregnancy.' She shrugs. 'There was *no way* your father wanted tae put them through that. Especially Rosemary. So he never told them. For all these years they've believed it was an ordinary accident – and you've believed your father had been cheating on your mother!'

Daniel clears his throat. 'How do you know that "not wanting to upset Mrs Fleming" wasn't just an excuse my father made up? Maybe he did ask her and she wouldn't lie for him. Couldn't bring herself to say the kiss was quite innocent! My mother didn't think it was!'

Sheila turns to her husband. 'You are totally out of order with that question, Daniel.'

Andy Fleming, red in the face, raps his knuckles on the table. 'Ah think it's maybe aboot time Ah said something?' They all turn to look at him, except for Daniel, who stares down at the table. Andy continues. 'Frank Galloway, Rosemary and me were great friends in the days when she was his conductress. If Ah was delivering in the area, and knew they we're gonny be in the depot, we'd regularly meet in the cafe at lunchtime. Rosemary lost her dad during the war, and Ah knew she very much looked on Frank as a sort of . . . adopted dad. As soon as we got the good news from the hospital that day, she couldn't wait to tell him. That was why we headed for the depot. I sat in the van and let her go across on her own, tell him her big news herself. He was delighted, gave her a kiss and a hug, then looked over at me and we were waving and smiling at one another. It was wonderful!'

Andy clears his throat, shifts in his chair. 'It's really quite insulting for you to say that you don't believe us. That maybe Frank really was having a fling with my wife!' Andy leans in Daniel's direction. 'Dae you know why I'm not getting angry about it?' He doesn't wait for an answer. 'It's because, not only is it ludicrous, but when Ah look round this table it's obvious naebody else believes it.' He looks at Daniel. 'And although it's you that's said it – you don't *really* believe it either! Do you?'

There is no reply.

'Could Ah say something else?' Wilma leans forward, looks at Daniel. 'Since the day your mother died you've never given Frank the chance tae explain his side of the story. You simply cut him dead, and you've never said one word tae him from that day tae this.'

Daniel looks up at her, shrugs. 'My ma told me what she'd seen on the day she died. I won't ever forget that!'

'We know that!' says Wilma. 'And naebody could blame you for believing it – *at the time*! At first, your mother also believed it. She'd seen them kissing. But after you stormed oot o' the hospital, Frank explained tae her why Rosemary had come to see him. She realised she'd jumped tae the wrong conclusion and told him she'd straighten it out wi' you later that night. Sadly, the poor soul never got the chance. But at least it's surely a comfort for you tae find oot – even after all these years – that she died knowing her man wasn't cheating on her?'

'*Huh*! Well once again, we only have my father's word for that!'

There's a collective '*Ohhh*!' from Rosemary and Wilma. Her face flushed, Rosemary turns in her chair. 'Your father is a lovely, decent man. I don't know who you take your nature from – but it's certainly not from your dad!'

'And what do you mean by that?' Daniel scowls at her.

'Right! You've asked, so I'll tell you. You've been saying things about me, about Andy, and about your father. I had no intention of bringing up what I'm about tae tell you. And it's going tae give me no pleasure to do it. But I think it must be said.' Rosemary looks at him. 'There was many a time, when your dad and me were sitting at a tram terminus having our break, and he'd say, "Oh, Josie's in one of her huffs again. I was talking to one of the neighbour's wives on the landing this morning and we were having a good laugh. Five minutes later I'm being accused of trying to chat her up!" He often used tae say to me, "Ah love my wee wife. But oh, my God! She just cannot help herself, she's compulsively jealous!"'

'Oh, aye! It's easy to run down the dead!' Daniel gets to his feet. 'Right! I've listened to all your arguments, and heard my mother get the blame for everything. You can tell my father his plan isn't going to work! I've no interest in him and me getting back together.'

Wilma stands up. 'Frank dis'nae know anything aboot this meeting. If he ever finds oot, he'll be furious. I organised it because, even though he never talks about you, Ah know he misses you. He would like nothing better than tae have a good relationship with you and be able tae see his grandbairns.'

Rosemary joins in. 'Andy and I only met Wilma, for the first time, a few weeks ago. We were horrified when she told us that you and Frank hadn't spoken for years because you believed he had been cheating on your mother, with me.' She looks hard at Daniel. 'Andy and I took the trouble to come here tonight, to tell you – at long last – that your father has done nothing wrong. We fully expected that within half an hour it would all be cleared up! Then you and Frank could get back together.'

Daniel tries to speak, but Rosemary holds up her hand. 'Let me finish! Sadly, I've found that you really don't want tae listen. You've accused me of kissing and cuddling with your dad outside the depot – while Andy lets us get on with it!' She watches Daniel blush. 'I've been sitting here listening to you, and seeing the look that comes over your face every time somebody says a good word about Frank.' She shakes her head. 'No! Ah think you've let this hatred for your father fester for such a long time, that you actually don't *want* tae hear what really happened. You don't *want* it cleared up, do you? You enjoy it!'

Daniel rises. 'Think whatever you like! C'mon, Sheila. It's hame time!'

Fr McKenna intervenes. 'Ah, now Daniel. I know it's been hard for you to listen to this. But I find meself having t' agree with Mrs Fleming, here. You've had your father for a hate figure for far too long! You've closed your mind t' reason – and now t' the truth!'

Daniel turns at the door, red in the face. 'I've never heard anything so stupid! I can tell you now – I'll never be inside this church again. EVER!' He looks at his wife. 'Let's go! Sheila. Unless, of course, you've also turned against me!'

As he storms out of the room, Sheila lingers a moment,

slowly putting her coat on. She waits until the door obligingly swings shut, then turns towards the others. 'Sorry, folks,' she whispers. 'There's going to be no' point in me trying to push him any –'

'Ohhh! Don't dae that,' says Wilma. 'It would jist cause all sorts of rows between you. Jist let him be.'

As they hear the outside door close, Fr McKenna speaks. 'Ah, now isn't that a shame? We've all tried our best, so we have. As the old saying has it, there's none so deaf as them who don't want t' hear!' He stands up. 'Anyways, I t'ink we could all be doing wit' a drop o' tay.' He makes for the room door. 'I'll give Mrs Finnerty a call. She always has the kettle simmering away, so she has.'

Rosemary turns to Wilma, lays a hand on top of hers. 'Are you going to tell Frank about tonight?'

'Oh, God! No way. He really would be angry if he wiz tae hear whit went on here, the night. Ah guess Ah'll jist have tae let it go.' Rosemary sees the tears in her eyes. 'Ah was so hopeful, that tonight Ah'd be going hame and telling him we'll be meeting Daniel, Sheila and the kids on Saturday for lunch. *Huh*! There's nae chance o' that!'

CHAPTER THIRTY-TWO

Days That Are Numbered

As Lexie Forsyth steps out onto the top-storey landing, it's to find Archie Cameron junior is waiting for her – one flight down on the half-landing. He turns his head, 'Hi-yah!' Then goes back to looking out the window, into what had been their back court. Lexie locks her front door, turns, and finds herself taken by this early morning scene. She stands still for a few seconds. Archie, hands in pockets, legs slightly apart, is silhouetted against the brightness of the landing window. To his right, the brown lavatory door is in shadow, it's worn brass handle trying vainly to brighten things up. It's the . . . oh, the Glasgowness of it that gets to her. And the melancholy.

'Hello! How are you this morning, Archie?'

'Fine.'

'What's taking your interest, out there?' She descends the dozen steps and joins him. They kiss on the lips.

'Ah was looking at what used tae be ma childhood playground. They've had tae leave oor middens standing, because the block's still occupied. But they've also had tae leave the wash-hooses as well,' he laughs, 'because the middens need them tae hold them up!'

Lexie glances at the brick lean-to middens. 'Aye, you're right. It's a mutual-support thing, in't it.'

He points straight ahead. 'You used tae be able tae look all the way along the back courts belonging tae this side of Cheviot Street. But once the tenements went,' he shrugs, 'the wash-hooses and middens could go the journey as well.'

'And we'd better go a journey, tae.' She takes his hand. 'Like, maybe doon tae Kinnaird's?'

He looks at his watch. 'You're right, hen. It's nearly twenty tae eight.'

As they descend the stairs, Archie looks at the steps. 'These seem tae be a wee bit cleaner, if ma eyes are'ny deceiving me.'

'They are cleaner. My ma got fed up wi' all the muck and stoor blowing about. So on Sunday, she swept the whole close from top tae bottom.'

'Good for Evie!'

'She filled two galvanised buckets mostly wi' paper and rubbish and dirt.'

As they walk along the close towards the brightness, Archie squeezes her hand. 'Ah hope when we're merried, Ah'll find you're every bit as hoose prood as your ma.'

'In your dreams, pal!'

He shakes his head. 'That does not augur well for our future, darling.' He avoids looking at her, keeps on walking.

She turns her head. Her eyebrows are raised so high, they're threatening to disappear under her widow's peak! 'AUGUR! Have ye swallowed a dictionary?'

He tuts. 'Because Ah speak in Glasgow dialect, diz'nae mean Ah have a poor vocabulary. It might interest you to know, that one used to read a lot – when one wiz doing porridge!'

As they walk the last few yards towards the shop, neither of them pays any attention to a Post Office van speeding north up the Maryhill Road. Less than five minutes later, John Caldwell turns left into the semi-derelict site that Dalbeattie Street has become. He parks in front of the solitary tenement, takes his peaked hat off and lays it on the dashboard, lights an obligatory Woodbine, then winds the driver's window down a touch. He reaches into his canvas bag and takes out the small bundle of mail. Smiles. Way over to his left, on the other side of the Scotia Bakery, he can hear the sound of the wrecker's ball getting stuck into the last remaining tenement in Blairatholl Street. Out of sight – but certainly not out of hearing. He looks at Dalbeattie Street's last block. I wonder why this was left to the end? I suppose there will be a reason. His eye is taken by movement as Drena McClaren, peenie tied tight, a knotted turban on her head, comes scliffing out of Number 18 wearing a pair of outsize check slippers.

He winds the window down further as she nears, keeps

his eyes fixed on her footwear. 'Do they belong tae Giant Haystacks?'

She gives a loud tut. 'Listen, Servant of the Crown. Ah saw ye fae the windae, so Ah thought Ah'd come oot and annoy – Ah mean, eh, *ask*, if there happens tae be, perchance, the odd missive fur the Hoose of McClaren?'

'You mean as well as the usual final demands?'

Drena puts on her best 'blase' – even though she's never heard of the word. She also manages to tap a foot whilst in the middle of a bosom adjustment. 'Listen, scunner-features, there's a good chance there *will* be a debt letter arriving fur me in a few days – when Ah get the bill fur your medical treatment efter Ah've gubbed ye wan!'

'Ah! Oh well, Mistress McClaren. In that case, I don't see any harm in huving a wee keek inside my bag,' he holds a finger up, 'even though it is strictly against regulations . . .'

'Your arse is against regulations!' Unable to keep the abuse going any longer they both burst out laughing.

John Caldwell is first to get himself under control. 'Oh! Drena. You're a case, so ye are.'

'Aye, and you're no' far ahint me.' She watches him take the small bundle of mail in his hands, riffle through it, now and then raising the corners of a number of long envelopes. Five in total, she notices. She feels a tingle on the nape of her neck. He turns the handful of mail round so she can see the selected ones face on.

'Do ye see what it says on that first envelope, Drena?' She leans forward.

'Oh! My God! It's fae the hoosing department.'

'Uh-huh!' He 'clucks' his tongue, then pushes his cheek out with it. 'And there are *five* of them!' He clucks again as he looks knowingly at her.

She looks quizzically at him. 'Are you in the process o' turning intae Donald fuckin' Duck?' This causes another burst of laughter. Drena has to move, hand over hand, along the side of the van and sit herself on its bonnet. Minutes later finds them dabbing their eyes, control having once more been regained.

'Aw, Drena. Ah don't know whit Ah'm gonny dae when you and yer pal, Ella, move tae the Molendinar. Ah'll be bereft.'

'Whit diz that mean when it's at hame?'

'It's a close second tae heartbroken!'

'Awww! That's the nicest thing anybody huz said tae me fur years. Anywye! Gonny gie me ma bloody letter, so's Ah can find oot when Ah'm moving?'

He looks stern. 'Sorry, Ah'm no' allowed tae hand letters oot the van windae, willy-nilly.'

'Zat right? Well If ye don't, Ah'll be dragging *you* oot the van windae – willy-first!'

This sets them off again.

He manages to find Drena's letter and passes it to her. 'Here, ya bad bitch that ye are!'

She stops laughing, tears open the envelope, extracts the letter. '*Hah*! We're moving next month! June the twenty-second. It's a Thursday.' She looks at him. 'Whit's the date the day, John?'

He consults his watch. 'This is Thursday, twenty-fifth o' May. So that's exactly four weeks.'

'Four weeks!' She turns round to look at the close. 'Ah would think the only person who is in at the minute is Dennis O' Malley. Ah'll wait 'til you've delivered his letter, then Ah'll get him tae open it –' She stops as she hears footsteps, turns, 'Oh, great! Ah'll no' have tae. Here's Teresa back from her offices.' Drena waves. 'Hurry up! Oor letters huv come.' She watches Teresa increase her pace, then turns to John. 'Get her letter oot, ready!'

He puts on his official face once more. 'You cannae tell me tae get somebody else's private –'

'Getterfuckin'letteroot!'

'Oh! Right. Certainly, Mrs McClaren!'

Moments later, the two women stand at the van midst the destruction and dereliction of almost everything they once knew. Teresa is given her letter. Drena and the postman watch her tear it open. Drena sways in her direction, trying to get a sneak preview. Teresa sways away from her, determined to be the first to read *her* letter.

She holds the missive to her breast. 'What date did yer say you'd got, Drena?'

'We're supposed tae be moving on Thursday, twenty-second o' June.'

Teresa takes another quick look. 'Sure, and we're the same. T'ursday as well.'

'Well, Ah'd think the five flats that are left, we'll aw' be flitting tae the Molendinar oan the same day. Eee! Ah cannae wait 'til Ella comes hame fae her work the night, so as Ah can tell her there's a letter waiting.' She looks at John. 'Us two, Ella and me I mean, we're moving intae either side of one of yon semi-attached hooses.'

'*Detached*!' say Teresa and John in unison.

'Anyway . . .' John puts his hat on, opens the van door and steps out into the street. He slings his bag over his shoulder, looks at Drena. 'Now Ah'm about tae deliver these last three letters. And Ah know that you hold keys for the rest o' the residents up the close. Ah just hope Ah don't come intae this street the morra morning, and find oot you've been intae their hooses and steamed open aw' their letters!'

Drena looks at Teresa, then back at the postman. Draws herself up. 'How dare you . . .' She pauses. 'Actually, that's no' a bad idea, John!'

As he starts up the stairs ahead of them, Drena and Teresa meander along the close. Teresa sniffs a couple of times. 'Jayz! Will ye just smell them cats. Oi've never known it as bad all the years Oi've lived at Number 18.'

'Ah think it's because all the other buildings huv been knocked doon. This is the only place left for the poor buggers tae congregate. Anywye, are ye coming in for a wee cuppa, Teresa?'

'Oi'll tell ye what. You come up t' my place for one. Dennis is always choking for a drink o' tay when Oi come back from me offices.' Side by side they approach the first flight of stairs. 'And at the same time, Oi can let himself know about the moving.' She pointedly doesn't look at Drena. 'The poor soul is always the last t' find out about t'ings. Sure, and didn't Oi' divorce him five years ago – haven't had the heart t' tell him yet!'

Drena stops, one foot on the first step. Soundlessly quivering, unable to get her laugh out, she crosses her legs, hangs onto the banister with one hand while reaching down to 'hold herself' with the other. 'Ma door's open. Will ye get ma lavvy key. Don't make me laugh – or there's gonny be an awfy accident!'

CHAPTER THIRTY-THREE

New Horizons

The site manager takes the three women out to the door of the wooden hut. 'Right, girls . . .'

Drena nudges Ella and Teresa. 'Dae youse hear that? Girls. If nuthing else, it's been worth getting a taxi aw' the way oot here jist tae get called "girls" in't it?'

The man continues. 'Mrs McClaren. You're Number 39.' He hands Drena the small bunch of keys. 'Mrs Cameron, Number 41.' Ella takes her keys. 'And Mrs O'Malley. You're on the opposite side to your friends. Number 52.'

'Oh, Jayz! The other side o' the street, is it.'

'That's wi' you being Catholic, Teresa. Aw' the proddies are on wan side, the Catholics on the other,' says Drena. The site manager smiles, shakes his head.

''Tis not!' says Teresa. 'Is it?'

'Pay nae attention tae her,' says Ella.

'Right, ladies.' The man looks at his watch. 'It's ten to

three. We finish at four on a Sunday. Don't forget to bring your keys back. There are still wee jobs to do in some of the houses, so Ah must have them back. Okay?' He points to the right. 'The odd numbers are along that side of Stobcross Avenue. You two are about a hundred yards along. You're a few yards further on, Mrs O'Malley. On the left, of course. You've been allocated one of the two-bedroom units. Your friends are three bedrooms.'

'Here we are! This is oors, Ella,' says Drena. She looks over to the other side. 'That's 44 and 46 across the street, Teresa. So you should be a couple of blocks along.'

Ella makes a suggestion. 'Why don't we go intae the hooses the 'gither? If we split up and go intae each hoose on oor own, we'll huv nae bugger tae talk tae, will we?'

'Eee, Ella. Don't know how we'd manage withoot you. Ah never thought o' that.' Drena takes her keys out. 'Right, 39 is first. Let's go, girls.'

Drena opens the front door, takes two steps into the lobby, then stops. Ella almost walks into her back. 'Go on! Don't be shy, it's your buggering hoose!'

'Ah know, Ella. But Ah sort of feel like Ah'm intruding intae somebody else's!'

The three of them stand for a moment in the lobby. Ella takes a deep breath. 'Jist smell aw' that newness.'

'It's the same smell loike when you've just distempered, isn't it?' says Teresa.

'Aye, but it's more than that.' Drena takes a deep breath. 'It's no' only fresh emulsion. There's the smell of new wood as well, in't there?' She inhales again. 'Mmm, new everything!'

''Tis lovely, so 'tis.' Teresa looks at the other two. 'Are we going any further than the lobby?' All three laugh.

'We're that bloody timid,' says Ella. 'Ah cannae get rid of the feeling we're trespassing.'

Ten minutes later, the living room, kitchen and dinette have been inspected and exclaimed over. The trio head upstairs. 'Ah cannae get ower how much light there is,' says Ella.

Drena nods. 'Ah know. There are that many windaes. When aw' the room doors are open the light jist floods in, dizn't it?'

'Oh, let's have a look at the auld lavvy,' suggests Teresa. She opens a door. 'Oh! Look, girls! Is that not wonderful? A bath and a wash-hand basin. Jayz! It used t' only be in the fillums ye saw facilities like this, so ye did.' She breaks off, looks into the corner behind the door. Her brow knits in puzzlement. 'Ah, eh, where's the auld cludgie?'

'The lavvy?' enquires Ella.

'Aye. It's nowhere t' be seen.' Teresa looks behind the bathroom door once more. As she does, Ella nudges Drena. 'We hud tae make a choice,' says Ella. 'A bathroom or a lavvy. Ye cannae huv both. We decided we'd rather huv the bathroom.' Ella tries not to look at Drena, who appears to be taking a keen interest in the window frames.

'But what do ye do, ye know, when nature calls?'

'There's a communal lavvy two streets away. It's a twenty-seater. And if you only need a wee-wee, well, you can jist dae whit we used tae dae in the middle o' the night in Dalbeattie Street – huv a pee in the sink!'

'Oh, Jayz! That's taken a bit o' the shine off t'ings,' mumbles Teresa.

'Naw it'll no'. The sinks are enamel. It'll no' dae them any harm. The site manager gave me his word oan that.' Ella looks round. Drena has her back to them, while turning the bath taps on and off, her shoulders shaking with the power of the water pressure.

'Right.' Drena clears her throat. 'Are we gonny huv a look at the bedrooms?' As she's about to open the bathroom door, there comes what sounds like a wail, followed by a door banging. All three hear it. They look at one another. 'What was that?' whispers Teresa.

'Where are yooooou?' The voice is female, plaintive.

'Fuck me!' says Ella. 'A brand new hoose and it's haunted already! Jist ma luck.'

'Anybodyyy theeeere?' drifts up the stairs.

Drena pushes the bathroom door closed. 'Huv you got a crucifix oan ye, Teresa?'

'Sure, Oi'm never without it.' The other two watch as Teresa reaches inside her blouse. Her fingers emerge holding a small crucifix.

'Right, you go first.' Drena opens the door. 'Haud the cross oot in front of ye. That should frighten it off!'

'Hellloooooo! Where the Devil are yoooou!'

'*Hah*! Holy Mary mother o' God! It's been sent by

Satan!' cries Teresa. She slams the door shut. 'We're trapped!'

'We definitely are, noo. Seeing as you've jist shut the buggering door!' says Ella. The three of them, hardly daring to breathe, press their ears against the wood. Listen. All seems quiet for a moment – until they hear footsteps climbing the uncarpeted stairs, the sound magnified by the boards as they approach the landing. Teresa continually blesses herself.

'Are ye in heeeere?' They watch in horror as the handle of the bathroom door turns slowly.

'AHHHHHH!' Drena and Teresa scream in unison. From outside the door comes an echoing screech and, 'Oh, my GOD! The place is haunted!' The footsteps make for the stairs.

Ella flings the door open, catches a glimpse of the spectre. 'AGNES! Is that you?' The fleeing feet halt. Agnes stands on the small half-landing. Looks up. 'My God, Ella. Ah nearly died. Ah thought evil spirits hud moved in afore the new tenants!'

Twenty minutes later, the door keys having been returned, they sit in Agnes's living room.

'Oh, bee-Jayzus! Have ye anyt'ing strong t' put in this tay? Oi' thought me time had come, so Oi did!'

'You're no' the only wan!' Drena reaches for her third piece of City Bakeries Swiss roll.

'What dae you think of your new hooses?' Agnes looks at the trio.

'Drena and me had a look inside mine. So we've a good idea whit we're moving intae. But Teresa is on the other side o' the street, Number 52. We never had time tae go intae it – efter oor nerves wiz shattered!'

'Och! It wiz'nae that bad,' says Agnes.

'How long have you been here, now?' asks Teresa.

'Roond aboot three months.' Agnes sips her tea.

'Have ye settled in aw'right?' Ella looks at her.

'Tae be honest, Ah hav'nae. The scheme is so big, Ah just feel isolated. Ah'm awfy glad Ah still work doon by St George's Cross. Ah'm fine at work – because Ah'm in Maryhill. But what Ah've started doing lately, two or three nights a week, when Ah finish work, Ah go and have something tae eat.' She looks at her friends. 'Then Ah go tae the pictures, or mibbe see a show. That way, Ah don't get hame 'til late and don't spend too much time in the hoose.'

'Jeez-oh! It cannae be that bad, surely?'

'You want a bet. It's so quiet. Ah really miss living up a close, so Ah dae.'

'Well, never mind, Agnes. Another couple of weeks and you'll have some more auld neebours from Dalbeattie Street moving in. That should be a help.'

Teresa looks at Agnes. 'Oi'm going t' have t' go a place. Have you got one with a lavvy? Or will Oi' have t' have a pee in the sink?'

'Eh?' Agnes looks bewildered.

Drena points at Ella. '*See*! That's your fault, Ella Cameron. You've got the poor soul aw' confused.'

Ella turns to Agnes. 'Tell Teresa where your lavvy is.' She turns back to Drena. 'When we were in ma new hoose, Ah was just about tae tell Teresa where the toilet was *and* tell her Ah'd been kidding her on – but Ah never got the chance. If you remember,' Ella inclines her head towards Agnes, 'The Ghost o' Christmas Past showed up!'

Drena frowns. 'Aye, you're right enough.'

Agnes looks mystified. 'Whit's it got tae dae wi' me?'

'Everything!' say Ella and Drena in unison.

Some time later, Ella looks at Drena and Teresa. 'Right, now fur the next big problem. How the hell dae we get back tae Maryhill?'

'How did you get here?' enquires Agnes.

'We clubbed the 'gither for a taxi, which was easy enough tae find on the Maryhill Road. But where's the nearest place tae here, where we might see a taxi going past?'

Agnes blows her cheeks out. 'If Ah had a phone, it would be nae problem. But Ah don't. The nearest phone box is aboot half a mile away. Trouble is, when ye get there you're liable tae find it's oot o' action. Either vandalised, or jist no' working.'

'Whit aboot getting a bus?' suggests Ella.

'Ah only know the time of ma bus in the mornings,' says Agnes. 'Ah huv'nae really learned whit times and services run through the scheme in the evenings.'

'Fuuuck me!' Ella shakes her head. 'Okay. Well, where is the nearest sort of auld-fashioned district wi' roads that huv buses running up and doon. You know. A bit like the

Maryhill Road? But mind, Ah mean somewhere within walking distance. Know whit Ah mean?'

Agnes looks ceiling-ward. 'Eh, probably London Road.'

'Now you're talking!' says Drena. 'That'll be handy fur Bridgeton. We'll easily get a bus or a taxi, there.'

Agnes bites her lip. 'Ah, well. Ah'm afraid it's no' the city end of London Road Ah'm talking aboot, Drena. This is the stretch of London Road that runs past the scheme. It's, eh, sort of left the city a bit behind and is running intae the countryside – heading fur Motherwell!'

'MOTHERWELL! Jesus Christ!' Drena slumps in her seat.

'Jayz! Dennis will have the polis out looking for me before the night's out,' says Teresa. She blesses herself.

'The polis? Huh! Be the buggerin' air-sea rescue, more like,' suggests Ella.

It's almost nine p.m. when Ella Cameron climbs to the top storey at 18 Dalbeattie Street. As she enters the house, Archie senior tears himself away from the television. 'Where huv ye been tae this time o' night, wumman? Ma stomach thought ma throat wiz cut! Ah hud tae finish up going oot fur a black pudden supper!'

Ella dramatically holds her bag out at arm's length, opens her fingers and lets it fall with a clatter onto the kitchen table. 'Where huv Ah been? Huv ye ever heard of Ooter Scabby Mongolia?' He doesn't reply, just looks at her. She starts unbuttoning her coat. Tries again. 'Well, huv ye?'

'Of course Ah huv.'

'Uh-huh! Good. Well, today Ah huv been oot tae the *far* side of *Ooter* Ooter Mongolia. And in a couple o' weeks' time we are aw' gonny be LIVING therr – because that's where the buggering Molendinar Scheme is!'

CHAPTER THIRTY-FOUR

Nostalgia Is'nae What It Used Tae Be

It's a Tuesday. Two days after the ill-fated expedition to Samarkand – or wherever it was. The Camerons have just dined, *en famille*, on the finest Bundoni's has to offer. Although it has gone seven o'clock they still sit at table. A feeling of indolence hangs heavy. Archie junior reaches for another chunk of fried fish.

'Ah thought you'd finished,' remarks his mother.

He crunches the crisp batter. 'As long as it's lying there, Ma, Ah'll no' be able tae resist reaching ower.'

'What is it that makes Bundoni's so good?' asks Katherine.

'They cook them in best beef dripping,' says her father.

'Just that?'

'And they only use top-class cod and haddock. If ye look at the price of a fish supper in other shops, most of them are a wee bit cheaper. But the Bundonis huv alwiz took a pride in their fish and chips. They're the best so they're a wee bit dearer.'

Ella joins in. 'But saying that, Archie. Ah think you'd have a job tae find a bad fish supper in Glesga, nooadays.'

'Aye, Ah'd say so. Any poor quality shops would eventually go oot o' business. Once they'd got a bad name, folk would just gie them a body-swerve, and head for the nearest good yin.'

'Do ye ever wonder how it came about that most of the cafes and fish and chip shops are run by Italians?' Katherine looks around the table. 'Is it just in Scotland? Or is it the same in England as well?'

'When Ah was in England during the war, Ah don't remember coming across many Tally-run cafes or chip shops. It was usually jist English folk.'

'I don't think they get called Tallys nowadays, Dad.'

'They've alwiz been Tallys. Naebody was running them doon or anything.' He shakes his head. 'Ye know whit Glesga folk are like. It's easier tae say Tally than It-tahl-ee-an. It's quicker, that's the only reason.' He snorts. 'Ah've jist said Glesga a minute ago. How come you're no' saying, "It should be Glasgow, Dad"? If there's a way tae shorten a word or a name – Glesga folk will find it. Poles instead o' Polish. Yanks rather than Americans. There's nothing nasty aboot it. If we can shorten it – we will.'

Archie junior is about to contribute, but before he gets the chance, their door is knocked. It's followed by a well-known voice. 'Hellooooh! It's only meeee!'

'Oh, my God!' says Ella. 'It must be the turn of The

Ghost o' Christmas Future!' She turns in her chair. 'Aye! In ye come, Agnes.'

The family watch their kitchen door open to reveal – Agnes Dalrymple.

'Hello, aunty Agnes.' Katherine rises. Gives her a kiss. Her mother follows suit.

'How are ye, aunty Agnes?' Archie junior remains at the table.

'Aw, no' sae bad.' Agnes sighs. 'Ah was jist looking at ma auld front door when Ah stepped ontae the landing. Dizn't it look sad when the nameplate and letterbox huv gone? Like a toothless auld biddy.' She manages a laugh. 'A bit like me, when Ah look intae the mirror in the morning.'

'To whit do we owe the honour of this visit, hen?' Archie senior smiles.

'Ah thought Ah'd drop in tae see how the girls got on, when they left ma hoose on Sunday.'

Archie looks at his watch. 'Ella and Drena made it back aboot an hour ago, but Teresa's been listed as "Missing in action"! There's an outburst of laughter.

'Don't pay any attention, Agnes. Sit yerself doon, hen. The kettle's on the boil.'

'Only a cuppa, Ella. Ah've already hud something tae eat at Jaconelli's.'

'Fine. You can stop and huv a wee blether for a while. Ah know you hate going hame too early tae your new hoose.'

Archie looks at his former neighbour. 'Aye, Ella was

saying you're finding it hard tae settle, Agnes. That's a shame. Dae ye no' like it, hen?'

'No' really, Archie. Ah wish Ah could afford tae rent a self-contained flat, back in Maryhill. You know, a nice red-sandstone.'

'Och, it'll no' be long until the rest of us come up tae join ye. Just aboot a fortnight or so.'

Eight o'clock finds the Camerons and Agnes Dalrymple still at the kitchen table. The television remains firmly off. Conversation is flowing and Agnes is obviously enjoying herself. Once more, footsteps are heard on the stairs, the Camerons' door is knocked . . .

'Hallooo! Is anyone at home?'

Archie senior's face lights up. '*Ist es Du, Irmchen*?'

'*Ja*! *Hier Irma, und naturlich Der Bert*!'

'*Kommst Du mal herein, Liebchen*!'

As the kitchen door opens and the smiling faces of Irma and Bert Armstrong are revealed, Ella pretends to be shocked, 'Fuck me! It's Eva Braun. So she did'nae die in the bunker!'

Irma giggles. 'Ella, *Du bist immer komisch*!'

'Is she swearing at me, Erchie?'

'Naw! Ah've got the exclusive rights tae that.'

Irma spots the other visitor. 'Agnes! You are here too. How nice!' Kisses and hugs are exchanged. As ever, Irma lights up the room when she appears.

Archie looks at Bert. 'How's life treating ye, son? And how's that team o' yours doing? It's Sunderland, in't it?'

Bert Armstrong screws his face up. 'Newcastle United if ye divn't mind. Ah've told yee before about using the "S" word, hinny.'

'Oh, aye. Anywye, how have they been playing?'

'They had their usual season, this year. Started badly – then faded!' He looks at Archie. 'A bit like The Jags!'

'Ah, now mind. That's a bit below the belt. Nae call for that.'

The hubbub of conversation dies down after a while. Ella turns to Bert. 'So whit's brought ye up tae Maryhill on a Tuesday night?'

He doesn't get the chance to answer. Irma takes over. 'We decide we are going to go up to the Rio, to see *Shaft's Big Score*. We saw the first one, last year.' She looks at Ella. 'But when we are coming in sight of Dalbeattie Street . . .' She sighs. 'I know the close will be empty soon and the building knocked down –'

Bert cuts in. 'So Irma says to me, "Just drive along to our old close for a moment . . ."'

Irma puts her hand on his arm. 'Let me tell it. So we finish up looking through the window of our old single-end.' She looks at Ella, then Agnes. 'And we can see our wallpaper, and the tiled grate,' she bites her lip, 'and I remember the first day when we come to the street. It is 1949. And *die alte* Granny comes to her window and . . .' They hear her voice tremble.

Ella jumps in. 'Urr ye gonny bloody shut up! You'll huv us aw' in floods o' tears in a minute!'

'Ah'll give ye the quick version,' says Bert. 'She says, "We can see the picture another time. This is maybe our last chance to be in Number 18."' He pauses, lifts a clinking, brown-paper carrier bag onto the table, 'so Ah went roond tiv the licensed grocers and spent the picture money – and then some – on a carry-oot!'

'Good man, yerself!' says Archie senior.

'Whit aboot Drena and Billy?' asks Ella. 'Have ye no' seen them?'

'Oh, yah. We go in there first. They say to come up to you – while Billy also goes to the licensed grocer. Oh! He says I have to tell you, Archie – he has gone for reinforcements!'

'YEEHAH!' Archie senior smacks his hands together.

'Jeez-oh!' says Ella. 'Ah'm supposed tae be early start in the morning. They've had that!'

Next there comes the sound of footsteps, and clinking bottles, from the lobby. The kitchen door is pushed open once more. 'Happy New Year! Everybody. All the best!'

Ella looks at Drena. 'Diz he no' know it's June?' Her pal shakes her head.

Billy McClaren points. 'ARCHIE! *Unsere* Irma *ist wieder zuruck*! Zat no' great?'

'*Jawohl*! *Die susse* Irma.' Archie stands up, opens the press door next to the fireplace. 'Wilhelm. *Ich habe hier, eine flasche* single malt. How dae ye say "single malt" in German?'

'Fucked if Ah know!' The two of them start to giggle.

Drena looks at Ella. 'Ah wid'nae mind so much,' she nods in Billy's direction, 'but he's no' even hud a drink, yet!'

Ella looks at Archie. 'Neether has he!' She gestures towards Irma. 'It's her that causes it. It's the Irma Effect! It's time somebody investigated the power this wumman huz.'

'*Ja, bestimmt*!' says Drena. She keeps her face straight.

'Huv you gone ower tae the other side?' asks Ella.

'Only kidding,' says Drena.

'*Gott sei dank*!' says Ella. The two of them are pleased to see their men, and Irma, are staring at them open-mouthed. Ella spreads her arms wide. '*Was is los*?'

'Where did ye get the German?' asks Archie.

The two wives look disdainfully at their husbands, then turn to the company. 'We've been listening tae these two blethering tae wan another in German jist aboot every Setterday night since 1945!' says Ella. 'And they want tae know – where did ye get the German?' She shakes her head. '*Dumkopfs*!' She turns to her pal. '*Denken Sie so*, Drena?'

Drena has been inspecting her fingernails. She looks up, shrugs. '*Ich weiss nicht*!'

'Michty me!' says Irma.

Slowly but surely a spontaneous party has developed in the Cameron residence. As the evening has gone on, the attendance has risen. Archie junior slipped next door sometime after eight, and returned with Lexie and her mother, Evie. Before nine o'clock struck, Drena made her way to the first-storey landing and had no difficulty in recruiting Teresa and Dennis O'Malley to the cause. The guest list is finally completed some time after ten, with the late arrival of Frank and Wilma Galloway, still in their Corporation Transport uniforms, having just finished their shift. 'Och! We'll stop for ten minutes or so, then slip away,' Frank said. He even made it sound as if he meant it.

And all the while, Agnes Dalrymple sits at the Camerons' table, an almost permanent smile on her face . . .

'Are ye enjoying yersel', hen?' Ella puts a hand on her shoulder.

'Oh, Ella. It's jist like auld times, in't it?' Her glistening eyes say it all.

'Noo are ye sure you're no' wanting anything stronger than Tizer, Agnes?' Archie comes into their conversation. Ella gives him a 'look'.

Agnes smiles. 'Now Archie, have you forgotten my, eh, little contretemps with the sherry bottle a few years ago?'

Archie holds up both hands, palms forward in supplication. 'Sorry! Sorry! Ah have, Agnes. Ah clean forgot aw' aboot that. So are ye still off it?'

'Never bothers me, Erchie.' She leans forward, confidentially. 'Ah jist get high on people nooadays!'

'Good fur you, hen.' He looks at her. Smiles. 'Mmmm! "High oan people." Ah like that, Agnes.'

By half-past eleven, the party is beginning to show signs of winding down, then Billy McClaren comes up with a suggestion that acts like a pick-me-up on all present . . .

'ORDER! ORDER! Best of order puh-lease!' Billy looks around, makes sure he has everybody's attention. 'Ah'm gonny suggest something here. Just a wee bit of fun. Now quite a few of you were in the company last year, when we went tae the Blythsie tae see its last fillum.' He is gratified to see they are all listening. 'After we came oot, we aw' went ower tae the Shakey for a wee refreshment if ye . . .'

'A *wee* refreshment?' says Drena, *sotto voce*. 'Nearly drunk the place dry!'

'Best of order, now!' says Archie, rallying to his friend's support. 'Billy huz the floor.'

'Aye, he'll need it. Probably be lying oan it by the end o' the night!' This appears to come from the same source. Billy ignores the prediction. 'Ah don't think anybody will argue wi' me,' he pauses, looks at his beloved, 'when Ah say that the session in the Shakey was great fun.'

'Hear, hear!' says Archie.

'Where? Where?' enquires Ella. She tries not to look when Drena, shoulders shaking, withdraws to the rear and has to lean on the coal bunker for a minute.

Billy carries on. 'It's a simple wee game. We went roon' the table that night and everybody had tae choose one – jist one – best fillum that they ever seen in the Blythsie. This is the same idea. But this time – it's television. So get your thinking caps on. Whit would ye choose as your best-ever TV series or programme or drama?' He holds up a hand. 'And incidentally, just before we start . . .' He points at Agnes. 'A word to the wise! If you ever have the chance, get Agnes tae tell youse aboot aw' the stars she has seen at the Glasgow Empire. From 1945, until it closed in the sixties, Agnes and her pal seen all the big stars that appeared.' He nods his head. 'And mind, I am not talking aboot the Beatles and aw' these other long-haired buggers, battering their banjos! Ah'm talking aboot your actual *stars*! She hud us enthralled!' He looks at those who had been present in the Shakespeare Bar on the night. 'Am Ah right?' They all enthusiastically endorse his comments. Agnes blushes, but is obviously delighted with this accolade.

'Okay, let's go!' Billy points at Frank Galloway. 'Right, Frank. All-time favourite thing ye ever seen on TV. But you're limited tae only *one*!'

'Well, then . . .' They watch as Frank strokes his chin, obviously giving it a lot of thought. 'Right. There are lots of entertainment shows, plays and dramas that Ah've really enjoyed, and I'd be hard-put tae choose just one. So what I'm going tae do is pick something that made a big impression on me.' He looks up. 'That documentary series that was on BBC2 a couple of years ago – Kenneth Clark's *Civilisation*.' He smiles. 'Might seem a bit highbrow. But I didn't find it so. In fact, I thought it was riveting!'

'Yeah, I watched that too, Frank,' says Lexie. 'Thought it was brilliant!'

Billy looks around. 'Any volunteers?'

'It will have tae be *The Forsyte Saga* for me,' says Ella. 'Ah loved every minute of it.'

'Well, Oi can give ye mine no bother,' says Teresa, '*Dr Kildare*'s the one for me. Wild horses couldn't have dragged me away from that telly the nights it was on.'

Agnes Dalrymple deliberately waits until everyone has

made their choice. She watches Billy McClaren look around, his eyes go past her – then come back. 'You haven'y gave us your selection, Agnes, huv ye?'

'No!' says Archie. 'You haven'y. Ah hope you're no' trying tae dodge the column, Agnes?'

She laughs. 'No. I've been enjoying listening tae all the choices. There has'nae been a bad one amongst them.' She shifts in her chair. 'I'm going tae choose a series that finished last year. And Ah have absolutely loved every minute of it. *Dr Finlay's Casebook*.'

There are murmurs of agreement . . . 'Oh, me too,' says Teresa. 'In fact, Oi seem t' go for all o' these medical, doctor t'ings. Oi must be a bit of a hypodermiac!' She's pleased as they all laugh.

'Ah've read quite a few of his books,' says Wilma.

'Ah did'nae know Dr Finlay wrote,' says Drena.

'No, Ah mean AJ Cronin, the author. He was a doctor as a young man, and wrote the book that the Dr Finlay series wiz based on.'

'Awww!' says Drena.

Agnes continues. 'Anyway, what I want to do, is tell you my favourite scene out of *all* the episodes there has been. Some of you might remember it.' She appears to be having difficulty composing herself. 'In case one or two of you did'nae watch the series, Old Dr Cameron is the head of the practice. He can sometimes be a bit grumpy. Young, idealistic Dr Finlay is the junior partner. They both live at Arden House, somewhere in Scotland, and are looked after by Janet, their spinster housekeeper. She's about sixty, and speaks with a lilting, Highland accent. Anyway, my favourite episode opens early one morning with young Dr Finlay already out on his calls. Janet is pottering about doing a bit of dusting, and Dr Cameron is in his study. Suddenly, we hear Dr Cameron's voice . . .

'"Janet! JANET! Come in here a minute. Ah want ye." It's said in his usual gruff manner.

'"But, Doctor! It's very busy I am at the moment."

'"Never mind busy, Janet. Get in here this minute. And remember – no knickers!"

'"Oh! Doctor," she says in her lilting brogue. "Ah ken what ye mean – but my hole's too wee!"'

There's a momentary silence from her audience then, as could have been forecast, Ella and Drena are the first to succumb – quickly followed by the rest. Only when she sees they are all in various stages of helplessness, does Agnes join in.

Later, a thoughtful Teresa turns to her. 'Jayz! Oi must have missed that episode!'

CHAPTER THIRTY-FIVE

A Distant Bugle

Wednesday the fourteenth of June 1972.

'Where are you and Lexie off tae the night, son?'

Archie junior swallows the forkful of dinner he's been chewing. Washes it down with a sip of tea. 'Going doon the toon for a wee drink somewhere nice, Ma.' He has another drink. 'Then, more than likely away tae the jigging.'

'Whit aboot you, Katherine? Are ye meeting Jessie?'

'Excuse me!' Archie senior comes in. 'If you're referring to her fellow assistant at West End Modes – the enchanting Chantelle . . .' He pauses to rub his upper left arm, grimacing as he does, 'Ah think a bit of respect would be in order.'

Ella narrows her eyes. 'Whit's the matter wi' your arm? That's two or three times you've done that since ye came in fae your work.'

'Ah think Ah've mibbe pulled something. It started this afternoon.'

'Mmm, gie it a rub wi' embrocation later on.'

'Aye.'

She continues to look at him. 'Ah don't suppose it'll stop ye going up tae the Thistle Bar?'

'Some folk huv a rendezvous wi' fate, Ella. Ah huv mine wi' Billy McClaren – usually at eight on a Friday!' He rubs his arm while he talks.

'Take a couple of aspirins, Erchie.'

'Good idea. Ah'll take them just before Ah go oot.' He turns to Archie junior and Katherine. 'Who's getting ready first, between you two?'

'Me,' says his daughter.

'Right! Ah'll sit by the fireside wi' ma back tae the sink . . .'

Archie junior takes his cue. 'And Ah'll away through the room for a read.'

His father slides back on his chair. 'Never mind. Less than two weeks and Aw' this will jist be a memory. You'll have a proper bathroom tae get ready in.' He pushes himself up from the table.

'OHHH! Yah bugger!' His wife and children look at him. He stands between table and chair, bent slightly, his left arm held across his chest, its hand under his armpit. He grips his upper left arm with his right hand, as though trying to force the pain out of it. Not rubbing as before. His pallor is a deathly white. 'OHHH! Fuckin' hell!' he says as he hunches himself inward.

Ella bangs the kettle down onto the cooker; hot water spits from the spout. She steps towards him. 'Archie! Will Ah send for the –'

He groans, squeezes his chest with folded arms, looks up towards the ceiling, then drops to the floor in front of them. His chin makes a clacking noise as it hits the edge of the kitchen table. He lies frighteningly still. No movement, no sound.

'Oh, Archie! Ma Archie!' Ella steps towards him.

Her son comes between. 'Let me see tae him, Ma.'

Katherine comes to her mother and they stand close together, arms around each other's waists, instinctively knowing their husband and father is dead, yet wanting to let Archie attempt to revive him.

Some minutes later he rises, looks down at his father for a moment longer, steps over to his mother and sister. 'Ah'll go and phone for an ambulance.' He reaches out to his mother, takes her hand – she snatches it away . . .

'Don't you tell me anything bad! Don't you dare! Ah don't want tae hear it!'

Katherine starts to wail. Ella clasps her closer, then leans to the side to look for her man. He lies midst the legs of table and chairs, dead on his kitchen floor.

Ella and Katherine continue to stand at the other end of the table, unable to move. Katherine howls and sobs in turn. If she tries to speak she is incoherent. Tears stream down Ella's cheeks as she comforts her daughter. It gives her something to do. She regularly says, 'Wheeesh, hen, wheesh.' As though Katherine was a child again. It keeps her from giving vent to her own grief – for the moment. They listen to Archie's footsteps echoing back up the stairway as he descends three at a time. When he reaches the close he halts outside Drena's, knows he'll have to go in . . .

He rattles the letterbox, steps into the dark lobby. The kitchen door is ajar, a bright column of light propping up the lintel. There is the smell of cooking. 'It's me, Archie!'

'In ye come, son!'

He pushes the door open. The McClarens look up with smiling faces which vanish when they see him. Drena looks hard at him. 'Whit's the matter?' She starts to rise. He can't look at them, doesn't want to see the hurt which he's about to cause. He clears his throat, finds no other way to say it. 'My da has just fallen on the floor. Ah'm sure he's deid!'

Drena's clenched hands go to her mouth. Just as Katherine did she starts to wail, then howl. Billy McClaren slumps back onto his fireside chair. 'Ma pal. Ma best pal!' He bursts into tears, reaches for a hand towel which hangs from a kitchen chair and buries his face in it. He sobs as though he will never stop. The sadness of the last few minutes gets to Archie. Since childhood days his Da and Billy are the strongest men he knows. Tougher than John Wayne or Gary Cooper or a hundred Hollywood heroes. It begins to weigh him down. My da's lying deid on the kitchen floor and Billy's greeting like a bairn!

'Ah'm jist going ower tae the bakery tae use their phone. Could you go up tae . . .'

Drena has got herself under control. 'Of course, son. Whit else would Ah dae?' She puts her arms round him, kisses him on the cheek. 'God! Ah'm needing comfort maself, Erchie. But Ella needs me.'

'Okay! Ah'll be back in a minute.' Archie runs out into the close, makes for the Scotia Bakery.

Drena turns to her man. 'Ah'll go up first. Gie me ten minutes or so.' She goes over to him. Pulls the towel away from his face. Kisses him. 'Ah know it's terrible for you, Billy. There is'nae two better pals.' She leaves her house, starts climbing the stairs. As she ascends she sees everything with such clarity. The stairs, half-landings, windows, lavvy doors. How many times have Ah climbed these tae go up tae Ella's? Usually for good things, happy things. But no' the night, Drena. Archie has died. Archie! Oh, my God! The sorrow tries to drown her. *C'mon*! You'll huv tae keep yerself the 'gether. Ella and Katherine are up there. She quickens her pace.

As she steps onto the landing both the Camerons' doors are wide open, light spilling out. She sighs. It'll have tae be done. She steps into the lobby, looks through into the kitchen, can see Archie lying dead on the floor. Poor Archie! That's no' fucking right! A good man like Archie Cameron. As she enters the kitchen Ella and her daughter still stand by the table. Their eyes meet. Now Ella can start to grieve. Drena opens her arms as she walks towards her. Katherine lets her mother go . . .

'Drena, Ah cannae believe it. How can ma Erchie be away?' Those are the last words she'll say for a few minutes.

Nor can she get her grief out. It's too painful. Won't come. They stand with their arms round one another. Drena sobbing, Ella grief-stricken, unbelieving.

The next couple of hours drift by for the Camerons. Everything is unreal. A doctor appears, police, undertakers, a mortuary van down in the street. Ella and Katherine go away through the room while Archie is recovered from the floor and removed, then they return. The undertaker comes to see Ella.

'Where would you like Mr Cameron to be? We have a nice chapel of rest not too far –'

'Oh, no. No. My man will lie in this house. Through the room, there. Nane o' this modern stuff. He'll lie in there for the three days. Jist like he should.'

'That's fine, Mrs Cameron. I have to ask you, it's just a formality.'

A few minutes later Drena takes the undertaker to one side. 'There's always a post-mortem wi' a sudden death, in't there?'

The man keeps his voice low. 'There is. I don't want to mention it just yet to Mrs Cameron. It can be very upsetting when you tell folks so soon after the death.'

'Yes, you're right,' says Drena. 'The reason I'm bringing it up is because we're all being flitted, the five families that are left up this close. We're away tae the Molendinar on Thursday the twenty-second. Ah take it that gives ye plenty of time for whitever needs tae be done?'

'Mmm. This is the fourteenth.' The undertaker does his sums. 'Oh, yes. It'll be fine.'

Ella has managed to focus long enough to catch the gist of this conversation. 'Is there a problem, Drena?'

'Naw, hen.' Drena puts an arm round her. 'Jist a wee formal matter. Ah'll tell ye about it the morra'. You've enough on your plate at the minute. Archie junior and me will see to it.'

Ella sighs. Nods. 'Aye, Ah'll leave it tae you.' They turn as they hear footsteps enter the lobby.

Billy McClaren stands just inside the front door. Stays in the lobby. Drena realises this is his first appearance since she left him almost three hours ago. She walks over to him. 'Is this you jist coming up?'

'Drena, Ah cannae face seeing Ella and the kids for the first time. Ah've had tae have a couple of wee haufs. And the thought that Ah'm never gonny see Archie . . .'

Ella hears his voice, walks over to the doorway. Billy turns, bursts into tears at the sight of her. 'Ella! Whit Ah'm Ah gonny dae withoot ma pal? Ah could'nae face the thought of seeing you and . . .' He can't speak for sobbing. Ella puts her arms round him, kisses him on the lips.

'Don't say any more, Billy. We know it's as bad for you as it is for us. Nae need for excuses. Ah know your heart is broken tae.'

By midnight all the remaining residents have gathered in the Camerons' flat. Word has gone out and they've been joined by most of the former residents: Robert and Rhea Stewart, Marjorie and Jack Marshall, Agnes Dalrymple, Alec and Irene Stuart. Then, in floods of tears from the moment she enters the close, comes Irma, with Bert Armstrong close behind. Irma goes to Ella.

'Oh, Ella! We are here just days ago. How can my lovely Archie be gone?' She has to stop. Ella tries to comfort her. 'Ah know, hen. Ah know. Him and Billy tormenting the life oot of you. Ah know how much you'll miss him, Irma. You don't have tae try and tell me, hen. We could always see your face light up whenever you'd visit us – especially if him and Billy were already here.' Ella pauses. 'And mind, so did his and Billy's. When you came through that door the two of them knew they were in for some good fun!' They have to stop, embrace, and cry for a while.

'I know people say such things at sad times, Ella. But I never will forget him. All my life I will remember my good friend Archie.'

'Ah know ye will, Irma. Ah know ye will, hen.'

Most of the visitors have gone and it's approaching one a.m. before Ella has time to go to her son. He has been sitting quietly, Lexie holding his hand, over by the bunker. She turns a fireside chair round, pulls it close, sits facing him.

'How are you doing, son?' She lays both her hands over his and Lexie's clasped ones. Leans forward to kiss them both.

'Ah still cannae believe it, Ma. My da was'nae meant tae die at fifty-five. It's a mistake. He's too strong tae go at that age.' His voice trembles, becomes a whisper. 'But it's happened.'

Ella looks at Lexie. Tears are coursing down her cheeks. 'Ah'd imagine you'd feel the same when your dad died, Lexie?'

She nods. 'We were talking about it earlier.' She clears her throat. 'He was *my* daddy, so he could'nae possibly die. But he did!'

Archie speaks. 'One of the things that's really getting tae me, Ma, is that him and I were getting on so well. Better than we have done for years. Going oot for a pint now and again.' He has to stop for a moment. 'And now it's aw' spoiled.'

Ella squeezes both their hands, leans forward. 'Aye, but if ye think aboot it, Archie, you've nothing tae get bitter aboot. Just think if he'd died while you were in the jail? At least you were getting tae be pals again. And Ah can tell you now, what he used tae say tae me. Jist a couple of weeks ago he wiz saying, "Oor Archie really means business this time, dizn't he?"' She looks at Lexie. 'And you'd better get ready tae blush, hen! He thought you were great! The best thing that could huv happened tae numpty-heid, here! That's his exact words.' They manage to laugh. The first today. She looks her son straight in the eye. 'The best thing for you tae dae, Archie, is jist carry on the way you're doing. You promised your faither you were gonny go straight.' Ella leans her head to the side. 'Because he's died, that's nae excuse tae let him doon. Or me either.'

Archie Cameron junior leans forward, kisses his ma on the forehead. He turns to look at Lexie. 'Don't worry aboot a thing!'

CHAPTER THIRTY-SIX

Through Time and Space

It's business as usual at Le Bar Rendezvous. Saturday-night business. The place is jumping as Robert and Rhea Stewart arrive. They wait just inside the doors for a minute until the combo finishes a swinging rendition of 'Too Marvellous For Words', then, before they strike up their next number, make haste to join the Lockerbies at the bar.

'Darlings!' Ruth balances her cigarette holder with its lit Sobranie across an ashtray, steps down from her stool, and welcomes her friends with kisses and hugs.

'Any of the gang already in?' enquires Robert.

'Vicky and Jack Dale are in, somewhere,' says George. He stretches his neck . . . 'Ah! They're over talking to someone sitting at the tables.'

'The two of them really seem tae be a couple nowadays, don't they?' says Rhea.

'Yes, thank goodness.' Ruth smiles. 'It's time Vicky had some luck with a fella.'

'Not half.' Rhea sighs. 'That's the trouble when you lose somebody like Johnny McKinnon. You have tae be really lucky tae meet another one.'

'The same thing applies when he was a close friend.' Ruth looks wistful. 'It's three years since Johnny's been gone. He was the best friend I ever had. I adored him. Always there with good advice or a helping hand.' Rhea can tell she's really talking to herself. 'You don't get many Johnny McKinnons in half a dozen!'

'Ah know what ye mean,' says Rhea. 'Ah wish Ah'd known him for longer than Ah did.' She looks over to where Vicky Shaw and Jack Dale still sit with their friends. 'Ah must say, Ah like Jack.' She bristles slightly. 'Though mind, anybody wid be an improvement after that toerag, Anderson. Getting rid of him for her was one of the best day's work you ever did, Ruth.'

'Yesss.' Ruth exhales after drawing on her Black Sobranie. 'Rumour has it that you weren't too enamoured of him.' She looks sideways at Rhea. Then, 'Ah! Here they come, Vicky and Jack.'

At this same moment, Ruby Dickinson makes her usual dramatic entrance: straight across the dance floor – with Fred bringing up the rear. Warm welcomes are again exchanged as they all gather round 'Madame Art Deco' as Rhea has started calling Ruth.

It's only twenty minutes later when the last of the 'usual suspects' turn up. Frank and Wilma Galloway make their entrance, having come via the Stromboli Restaurant.

It's sometime after midnight, when the announcement, 'Take your partners for the last dance,' causes everyone to doubt their watch, and believe that time really does fly. Robert and Rhea 'two-step' another wonderful evening to its close. As they return to the bar, Rhea is now hoping she'll hear those magical words from Ruth . . . 'Would any of you darlings like to come back to our place?' An invite to finish the night at the Lockerbies' is, as Rhea has told her friends, 'The Piece of the Resistance!'

It begins for her, the moment they leave the club. Everybody standing on the pavement while George locks-up, then all piling into the waiting taxis for the short ride to Kelvin Court. Once there, as Ruth opens her front door, Rhea will stand on tiptoe to catch her first glimpse of the illuminated, de Lempika 'Autoportrait' as it looks down at her from the facing wall. Rhea is 'gone'. A tingle runs down her spine as she steps over the threshold and the Art Deco splendour of Ruth's Time Machine surrounds her. She quickly squishes herself into the stylish leather armchair she always occupies. George will place a 5-star cognac, accompanied by a cup of the finest Alta Rica coffee, near at hand. She will take a sip from both, sit back with a sigh, and let herself be taken over. For the rest of her visit there will be a minimum of conversation between her and the other guests. Ruth's record collection will not be found wanting, as it supplies the soundtrack – the last ingredient needed – to transport Rhea four decades into the past . . . Fred Astaire singing with the Ray Noble orchestra; 'Hutch' with 'Begin the Beguine' and others from the Cole Porter songbook; the orchestras of Duke Ellington and Carroll Gibbons will make regular appearances, as will early Crosby accompanied by Paul Whiteman. And, of course, Al Bowlly. As she listens to the music, looks at the decor, sips her cognac, Rhea, yet again, floats off to where she wants to be. An era she has no memory of – yet remembers well. And once a month, courtesy of Ruth and George Lockerbie at Kelvin Court, it is all possible.

It is some time after half-past one. The menfolk have congregated in the kitchen. 'Are you for another drop of the cratur, Robert?' George holds a badly wounded bottle of Glenmorangie.

'Thanks aw' the same, George. Ah'd rather have another mug o' coffee if there's any left.'

Fred Dickinson excuses himself a moment to rush a Campari and lemonade, with ice, out to Ruby. She is deep in conversation with Ruth and Vicky. As he passes Rhea, she dreamily looks up. 'Zat you, Fred?'

He interrupts his mercy mission. 'It is indeed, sweetheart.'

'Wi' all this beautiful music tae keep people happy, you wid'nae think there's gonny be a war soon, would ye?'

'A war, darling?'

Rhea sips her cognac. 'Uh-huh! That bugger Hitler. He'll be the cause. If he hud went tae the dancing mair often, he'd huv been all the better for it! Far too serious, yon yin!'

'I think you might have something there, Rhea.' He looks slightly bewildered. 'Just a trifle too late, darling.'

'Awww! Dae ye think?' She tuts. 'That's a shame.' She gives the matter some more thought. 'A couple o' nights a week at the F&F Ballroom ower in Partick, would huv done him the world o' good.' She raises her glass, pauses. 'Though mind, he'd huv tae lose the moustache!'

He watches her half-close her eyes, drift back to where she's been. Having given Ruby her drink, and taken further orders from Ruth and Vicky, he returns to the kitchen, nudges Robert. 'I've just had the most surreal conversation with your wife.'

'Well don't remind her of it. She dis'nae know whit surreal means. If you mention it, she'll only finish up making a doctor's appointment on Monday morning!'

It's ten minutes later. Robert Stewart tries to snap finger and thumb together. He misses. 'Ah knew Ah had something tae tell you, George. You'll surely remember Archie Cameron, lived up on the top landing? Married tae Ella.'

George tries to get the memory banks to open. He looks up at the ceiling. Turns to Robert. 'Aye, of course! Ex-para, captured at Arnhem.'

'You've got him. He dropped dead while having his dinner, last week!'

George blows his cheeks out. 'Oh, my God! He would'nae be a great age?'

'Fifty-five.'

'Jeez! No age at all. It's funny, but I got tae know him better *after* I left the close. Yon times when Ruth and I came up to you for Hogmanay. We'd always finish up getting together with him and Ella – and *their* pals, Billy and Drena. If you remember, it was those two who got my flat in the close, when I left to move in with Ruth.'

Robert continues. 'Rhea and I went up to Dalbeattie Street tae see them, last week. Ah'll tell you, they are absolutely broken-hearted. And not just his family. Drena and Billy are every bit as bad. They've been the best of best friends over the years. More like family.' He sighs deeply. 'And Billy McClaren. Ah'm not kidding. You'd think he'd lost a brother.'

George gives it some more thought. 'Aye, it's all coming back to me. The four of them were great fun. Always together.' He sips his whisky. Shakes his head. 'Fifty-five. Jeez-oh!'

'And it could'nt have happened at a worse time, George. His funeral is this coming Tuesday. And two days later the last of the tenants at Number 18 are being flitted oot tae the Molendinar. So poor Ella is having tae move two days after she buries her man. She was telling us, Archie never even got the chance tae see the inside of his new house.'

George shakes his head. 'Who was it said, "Life's a bitch – and then you die!" He rubs his chin. 'Was it Woody Allen?'

Robert shrugs his shoulders. 'If it wiz'nae – it should have been!'

CHAPTER THIRTY-SEVEN

Among My Souvenirs

Ella Cameron sits at the top table in Hubbard's Tearooms. She looks at the plate of food in front of her, then pushes it away. Doesn't want to smell it, see it, or taste it. God! It's no' yet an hour since Ah saw Archie laid tae . . . BURIED! He wiz *buried,* Ella. The strength has just drained oot o' me. Once they lowered Archie intae his grave, that was it. Ah'm finished. Ah've hung on for a week – that bloody, buggering post-mortem dragging things oot. Then climbing intae the funeral car efter the service. Ah thought that wiz it at last. Wishing it would jist *go*! She sighs. Ah should'nae have looked back tae the graveside. But Ah could'nae help it. Christ! You wid think they'd wait a few minutes tae let the cars move off. Not a bloody bit of it! The two o' them shovelling the dirt and clay back intae that hole as fast as they could. Nae respect.

She manages to get rid of that picture, glances round the large tearoom at the mourners. All getting stuck in. Och! Ye cannae blame them for that, Ella. Ah've done it maself many a time. Never mind, ye had a good turnoot, Erchie. That wiz a comfort.

'Are ye no' gonny eat, Ma?' Her son looks at her.

She leans to her right, nearer to him. 'Ah jist want tae go hame tae the hoose, Archie. Ah've had enough. Right this minute, Ah want tae be sitting at ma ain fireplace wi' a cup o' tea. Talk aboot your da. Then have a wee lie doon for an hour or two. Ah'm as weak as a kitten.'

'Will Ah go doon tae the door, hail the next taxi that goes by? There's always plenty up and doon the Great Western Road. Ah'll get one nae bother.'

She nods. 'Aye, that wid be good, son. Away you go.' She leans forward, looks past him at Lexie. 'Tell Lexie Ah want her tae come hame wi' us, tae.' Ella turns to her left. 'Ah'm sending Archie doon tae get us a taxi, Katherine. Ah just want tae go hame.'

'Me tae, Ma. Ah want some peace and quiet. Just us.'

Ella now catches Billy McClaren's eye. Beckons to him. He immediately rises, comes to her.

'Aye, Ella?' He places a hand gently on her shoulder.

'Ah've had enough. All of a sudden Ah'm exhausted, Billy. We're jist gonny slip oot. Archie's away for a taxi. As soon as we've gone, would ye mind standing up and making an announcement. Tell them the truth . . . Ah'm tired. Thank them aw' for coming, it was a lovely tribute . . .' She feels her lip tremble. Ah'd better get off the subject.

'Tell them it's aw' paid for, and Archie's family insist they get stuck in.' She raises her hand, places it on top of his on her shoulder. 'If you and Drena want tae come up, make it about eight o'clock or so . . .' She pauses as Archie junior comes back into the room. He nods. Ella has to put both hands on the table to push herself up. 'Ah need a wee rest. Ah'll see the two of you about eight, Billy.'

He puts his arms around her. 'You've done well, hen.' She can hear his voice going.

'Don't say any more, Billy.' She looks him in the eye. 'If Ah start – Ah'll never stop. Not another word!'

He kisses her on the cheek, holds her at arm's length for a moment. Their eyes are full to brimming. He nods, turns, goes back to his chair.

Ella gives a grateful sigh as the tearoom door swings shut behind them and they start down the stairs. Thank God that's over. From halfway down she can see the welcome sight of a taxi at the pavement, getting bigger and nearer as they descend. Archie and Katherine are either side of her, Lexie close behind. Ella half turns, 'Are you all right, hen?'

'Aye, fine, Mrs Cameron. Ah think this is a good idea. You've had enough.'

As they reach the bottom of the stairs, Archie stretches a hand out, pushes the street door. Ella steps closer to Lexie. 'Ah wanted you tae come tae the hoose with us.' She takes her hand for a moment. 'This last ten days or so, you've been part o' the family, hen. Archie . . . Archie senior, he thought you were the best thing that's ever happened tae the boy. The first time he met ye, he said tae me you were special.' She takes a steadying breath. 'He wiz right!'

Less than ten minutes later, they decant themselves onto the pavement outside Number 18. As Archie pays the driver, they stand close together, marooned amongst the debris and destruction. Their tenement is now the only one for hundreds of yards. The driver engages gear and moves off. For a moment they all have a feeling, though unspoken, of being isolated.

'Let's get up them stairs!' says Ella. 'When Ah'm in ma ain bit, Ah can forget aboot this mess.'

It has just turned six o'clock when Ella comes through from the room. Archie, Katherine and Lexie all look up as she enters the kitchen, her eyes red-rimmed. They had all listened to her breaking her heart, minutes after she'd first gone through – until she cried herself to sleep.

'Have you had a good wee sleep, Ma?' asks Katherine.

'Aye, thank the Lord. Ah did'nae half need it.'

'What was that banging noise from the room a minute ago, Ma?'

Ella shakes her head. Tuts. 'Trust me! When Ah got up, Ah never bothered tae put the light on. And Ah'd forgot all aboot the tea chests the Pickford's fellas left us. Ah nearly went arse ower tit in the dark!' They all laugh.

'Will I make ye a drink o' tea, Ma?'

'Ah'd love wan. In fact, dae ye know whit Ah really fancy,

right this minute?' She looks at their faces. 'A dirty big fish supper oot o' Bundoni's! Ah did'nae have anything tae eat at Hubbard's, so Ah'm starving.'

'Good for you, Ma.' Archie looks at his sister, then Lexie. 'Will Ah get four?'

The table is covered with scrunched up newspapers, greasy plates and bits of batter scattered about. 'A feed fit for a king!' says Archie. He manages to stifle a hiccup.

'For the rest o' the night, if anybody comes intae this house they'll no' need two guesses tae find out what we had for our dinners,' says Lexie.

Ella lights a cigarette. She looks at her son. 'Do ye know what Ah think we should do, now?'

He gives it some thought, then, 'Nope!'

'We are gonny be run off our feet the morra, filling them tea chests. We flit, the day after tomorrow, remember.' She draws on the Capstan. 'While it's quiet, this would be a good time tae sort oot your faither's drawer in the wardrobe.'

'Aye. Ah suppose it would.' Archie looks sad. 'It's strange . . .' He clears his throat. 'Now and again over the years, Ah've sometimes thought that the day will eventually come when what's in that drawer will be left tae me. Well, most of it Ah would imagine. But it was alwiz a long way off in the future. Years from now.' He looks at his ma. 'But now that it's here, Ah don't really want tae . . .' His voice trails off. He turns to Lexie. 'It's the big drawer at the bottom of the wardrobe. My da kept aw' his army stuff in it.' He looks at his ma, smiles. 'As a kid, Ah used tae have sneaky looks in it when you two were at the pictures. Ah hav'nae looked in it for years.'

Katherine laughs. 'I used to do the same when I was about five or six.'

Ella turns to her daughter. 'Ah take it you'll have nae objection to Archie getting your da's medals and stuff like that?'

'Oh, for goodness sake, of course not!'

It's shortly before eight o'clock. All four of them have enjoyed a look through Archie senior's keepsakes. Especially the photos: Archie with his comrades in North Africa, Italy, then France and Germany; his transfer from the infantry to the Parachute Regiment.

'Ah can see why you fell for him, Mrs Cameron.' Lexie holds a photo of Archie with his sergeant's stripes, the paratrooper's wings on his shoulder.

'Aye . . .' It ends as a sigh. 'He was Jack the Lad in them days.'

'Hey!' says Archie. 'He could still be Jack the Lad when he felt like it.' His voice catches. 'If ye don't believe me – jist ask Nathan Brodie!'

Ella looks at her son, her eyes full. 'Aye, he could, couldn't he!' She reaches into the drawer. Brings out something that's wrapped in two yellow dusters. Balancing it on one hand, she folds back the top duster. Six highly-polished medals are revealed. Four of them bronze-coloured stars, the other two are round silver medals. They are mounted on a bar, ready to be worn.

'Oh! Don't they look smashing!' says Lexie.

'Aye!' Is all Katherine can manage.

'Just keep holding them, Ma, while Ah read what it says on them.' Archie is kneeling on the floor, he slides nearer to his mother, starts with the first on the left . . . '1939–45 Star, Africa Star, Italy Star, and France and Germany Star.' He turns the silver medals round. 'War Medal, Defence Medal.'

Ella lays them gently on the floor. 'There are these as well, son.' She brings out the red beret with its metal paratrooper's cap badge. Next it's the embroidered, blue cloth wings that show a man is a trained paratrooper. Finally, the cloth shoulder flash with the winged horse, Pegasus, on it – the sign of the Parachute Regiment. 'These all go tae you, son. He'd want you tae have them.'

'And Ah'll tell you something now, when Lexie and me get our own place, Ah'll have these mounted behind glass – the medals, his cap badge, the wings and Pegasus – and that good photo of him. All hung on the chimney breast. Pride of place, Ma!'

'That'll be a nice thing tae dae, son.' Ella reaches deep into the drawer, comes out with the Luger pistol. 'Whit are you gonny dae wi' this? And these German daggers?'

'Don't worry, Ma. These are war souvenirs. Ah'll stash them away somewhere safe.'

'Aye, you'd better.' She bends low, sweeps her hand far into the back of the large drawer. 'Ah think that's all . . . Oh! Whit's this?' Her hand emerges with a small, brown box with a 'Post Paid' mark on it. 'It's addressed tae Mr A. Cameron,

18 Dalbeattie Street. So it's your da's. That's jist like the box his medals came in. Only it wiz bigger, so as tae hold the six o' them.' She moves her open palm up and down, weighing it. 'It's heavy. Must be something in it.'

Archie laughs. 'Take the lid off, Ma. It must be my da's – so it'll be aw'right.'

They watch as she opens it, folds back the dried-out wax paper the object is wrapped in. 'It's another medal! She looks at Archie and Katherine, then lifts it out by the ribbon with its alternating pattern of thin bands of red, white and blue. King George the Sixth is on the front. She turns it over, narrows her eyes to read it. 'Distinguished Conduct Medal. Whit is this?'

Archie blows his cheeks out. 'As far as Ah know that's a bravery medal. Whit they call a decoration. It's usually jist known by its initials – the DCM! But why is it no' on the bar wi' the rest o' them? It might no' be his. It could have belonged tae one of his pals that wiz killed. Ah know there wiz a lot o' decorations won at Arnhem.'

'Will Billy McClaren know?' says Lexie. 'Will I go and get him?'

'Good thinking, hen,' says Ella. 'Away and ask him tae come up.'

Minutes later, Billy and Drena come into the bedroom accompanied by Lexie.

'We've found this DCM in my da's drawer, Billy. The War Office box is addressed tae him, but we don't know if it is his.'

'Gie me a look at it,' says Billy. 'If it is his, he never let on tae me aboot it. Anywye, it'll be easy tae tell whether or no' it belonged tae him.' They watch as he turns the medal on its side, looks at its rim. His mouth opens in surprise. 'It *is* his! It's got his name, rank and number engraved on the rim.' He points. 'If you look at the two silver medals mounted on the bar, they'll also have his name and number engraved on them – same as mine have.' He looks at Ella. 'When he came hame efter the war, did he never mention this wan?'

'Naw. Not a word. So has he won this for daeing something special?'

'Oh, aye. You don't find these inside cornflake packets!' Billy shakes his head as he tries to work it out. 'He never told you or me. He did'nae mount it wi' the rest of his campaign medals. When you mount one of these, it's placed as the very first one on the left. Bravery medals – decorations tae give them their proper name – they alwiz take precedence over your campaign gongs.' He smiles, shakes his head again. 'Mind, you know whit he wiz like, Ella, he either did'nae want tae put it up wi' the others, in case folk thought he wiz showing off, *or* – maybe by the time they sent it tae him, he'd already got his medals mounted, and did'nae want all the bother of getting them done again.' He smiles at Ella. 'You know whit a bolshie bugger he could be when he felt like it.'

'Aye,' Drena decides to contribute,' but don't ye think it would be nice tae know whit he got it for?'

Ella looks at her. 'It would, Drena, wouldn't it?'

'It's fairly easy tae find oot,' says Billy. 'Jist write tae the

War Office . . .' he pauses. 'Ah think it's called the Department of Defence nooadays. Anywye, when somebody gets a bravery medal, it comes wi' whit they call a citation. That describes the action, and why they got it. Write tae them – the address is Whitehall, London. And tell them you'd like tae know all about it.'

Archie looks at his father's best pal. 'The most important thing for us, Billy. This is *definitely* my da's DCM?'

'No doubt about it, son. His name's on it.' He pauses. 'Ah still cannae believe it. Think of all them years your da and me huv been pals. Up the pub on a Friday or Saturday night. All the times we've hud a really good drink up here, or doon in oor hoose, at Hogmanay or whitever. And nae matter how drunk he got – he never let slip that he'd won the DCM.' He laughs. 'Ah've never known anybody like him! Ah could'nae huv done that. When Ah came back in '45, Ah'd have wanted *every* bugger tae know Ah'd won the DCM! Ah'd probably huv got Drena tae sew the medal ribbon on ma pyjamas!' He shakes his head in wonderment. 'He wiz some man, your da!'

CHAPTER THIRTY-EIGHT

When You Gotta Go . . .

Drena McClaren is the first to see them. She's busy wrapping the last few articles in newspaper then finding space for them in the tea chests, when there comes the sound of diesel engines. Moving shadows successively darken her room as large lorries drift by her windows, and she reads the legend *Pickfords* four times. The fourth leaves her permanently in the gloom when it draws up directly outside. As Drena loves to be first with the news, she hurries out into the close, cups a hand either side of her mouth and bawls, 'THEY'RE HERE!'

The four other households, all upstairs, have their front doors open and instantly receive this latest intelligence.

In the last occupied single-end, on the top landing, Evie Forsyth looks at her daughter. 'That must be them, Lexie.'

'Ah hope so, or maybe Drena's hallucinating!'

Evie throws up one of her windows, looks sixty feet down

into the street. 'Aye, it's them. There's four big vans and a wee yin. The wee yin will be for us.'

Lexie noisily draws a breath in through her teeth. 'Sherlock Holmes could'nae haud a candle tae you, Ma!'

'You're getting tae be a cheeky bizzum so ye are, Alexandra Forsyth!'

'Ooooh! Sunday name is it?'

'Ah'll away next door, see how Ella's getting oan.' Evie takes the dozen steps needed to leave her flat, cross the landing and enter Ella's lobby. She looks round the kitchen door. 'Did you hear Drena shout that they've arrived?'

Ella is sitting on a fireside chair. 'Did Ah hear? The Hunchback of Nottrie Dam wid huv heard – and he's corned beef!'

Evie shakes her head, smiles. 'Ah! That sounds like mibbe the auld Ella is starting tae come back tae us. Good for you, hen.'

'There's nae option, Evie, is there?'

'Exactly! Don't forget, Ah've been the same road as yerself. Ah lost ma man back in '64. At the time, you think you'll never get ower it. But ye dae. Anywye, Ah jist thought Ah'd come ower in case ye hud'nae heard Drena say Pickfords wiz ootside.'

Ella looks up. 'Ye could'nae miss her! There's folk roon' the Maryhill Road heard her, started packing – and they're no' even flitting!'

Ella listens as Evie laughs all the way back to her flat. It becomes quiet again. A stillness. She looks around her kitchen. The alcove where the recess bed had been has two pieces of linoleum covering its floor. Until this morning they have lain out of sight for years in what is known as 'under the bed'. There has been no reason to replace them. The valance hung to the floor so they were never seen. She takes time to look at them, at their busy, complicated pattern of brown, yellow and green. *So* 1940s. Ah don't suppose they've ever been walked on. The galvanised bath that holds the dirty washing has been slid in and out over one of them a thousand times. It's worn a trail. And yon two, seldom used, cheap suitcases were kept under there as well. She looks again at the pattern on the linoleum. Gives a heavy sigh. Ah remember the day Archie and me bought that roll of lino. He'd hardly been oot o' the paras a year. Be '46. Bought enough tae dae the kitchen from a cut-price shop doon the Cowcaddens. We had tae walk aw' the way hame wi' Erchie carrying it on his shooder – it wiz too big tae go on the tram. Her eyes begin to fill with tears. You'd be aboot twenty-nine, Erchie. Ah'd be two years younger. Started laying it as soon as we got hame, aw' excited, dying tae see it doon. The image comes to her, so sharp and clear . . . Archie getting to his feet late that evening, 'Therr ye are, hen. Aw' done!' The two of them standing looking at it. The electric light beating down on Archie and their new purchase. The kitchen looking different. The weans long ago through the room, sound asleep. She smiles. And the next thing we're on top o' the recess bed having the hottest sex. That used tae happen jist aboot every time we bought something new for the hoose, or finished decorating. Ah wonder why? These precious images drift away from her. She looks at the waiting tea chests, the two pieces of lino, the table, chairs, sideboard. My kitchen's in an uproar. She turns her head. Takes in the clean patches on the walls where prints, photos, and successive calendars have hung for years. There now come loud voices as the removal men enter the close, some start climbing the stairs.

This is Thursday, 22nd o' June. Ah'm flitting oot o' Number 18 for good. Her eyes dart around her almost unrecognisable kitchen. Ah'll never be in here again. This is the last time! Oh, Erchie. Jist over a week ago, at this time o' the morning you were still alive, at your work. Not a thing wrong with ye. Noo you're deid and buried! How can that be, Erchie? How am Ah gonny manage withoot ye? It's no' right!

Two landings below. Teresa O'Malley wipes her brow. 'Roight! We're as ready as we'll ever be, Dennis.'

'We don't have t' do everyt'ing ourselves, Teresa. Let these fellows earn their money. Sure, and they're doing this every day that God sends, so they are.'

'Now never mind trying t' find excuses t' be slacking! Yer always trying t' find ways of dodging the column so ye are, Dennis O'Malley!'

His mouth falls open, he looks up at the pulley, hoping for divine intervention. When there is none forthcoming, he takes up his own defence. 'Will ye listen t' this woman?' He looks up once more. 'We've got everyt'ing packed that can be packed, there's just heavy stuff left for the bhoys t' manhandle. Oi'm seventy years of age and this woman's wantin' me t' kill meself!' He drops his voice. 'Are ye wanting me t' be the last man t' have a heart attack in Dalbeattie Street? Is poor Archie up the stairs, not enough for ye?'

Teresa thinks for a moment. 'Jayz! Now that *is* sumt'ing t' t'ink about.' She blesses herself. 'Archie was fifteen years younger than you and fit as a whip – yet he still went the journey!' She runs a judicious eye over her husband. 'Yer right. Look at the state yer in. No good tempting fate. We'll let them spalpeens from Pickfords earn their money so we will!' She points to a kitchen chair. 'Sit yerself down there, darlin'. Take yer ease.' She leans forward. 'Would ye loike me t' dig the tay things out – wherever they are – and make ye a dish o' tay?'

Dennis sits back on the kitchen chair with a sigh. 'No, Oi'll be fine. Never got the chance t' finish last night's *Evening Times*. Oi'll just have a read at me paper.'

By eleven o'clock in the morning the five vans are loaded. Ella, the O'Malleys, Evie and Lexie Forsyth, Frank and Wilma Galloway, and Drena and Billy McClaren stand on the pavement. Some carry suitcases containing personal items and delicate pieces such as china. A single-decker bus has been hired to take the tenants, in convoy with the removal vans, to the Molendinar housing scheme. The sun beats down, little dust whirls blow here and there, sometimes on the road, other times where a tenement block once stood. The site foreman and an assistant stand with the former residents of Number 18. From either end of the street comes the growl of heavy diesel engines, which is at once drowned out by the clatter of tracks as two cranes, wrecker's balls swinging menacingly, take up position, waiting for the vans and coach to depart.

'By the look of it, as soon as we leave you'll be making a start,' says Frank Galloway.

The foreman laughs. 'Ah'll have to. Ah've got a few Southern Irish lads in the squad. Very superstitious. Believe in banshees and aw' the rest of it.' He points to the cleared site opposite 18 Dalbeattie Street. When we were knocking doon the block that was here, they said they kept catching a glimpse of somebody – well, they say a banshee – looking at them from a window up your close. They were terrified she'd start crying and wailing – that would be a sign someone is going to die . . .' He breaks off as Teresa pushes herself in between Frank and Wilma Galloway.

'What window was it, can ye remember?'

The foreman gives her a patronising smile as he's about to answer. This causes Teresa to change her mind. 'Oi'll tell ye what – let me tell *you*!' She points to the double-window above the close entrance. 'It would be from there. The single-end, one-up?'

His smile fades. 'Yeah, it was.'

Teresa looks at her friends in triumph. 'Tell the man who they were seeing.'

Drena and Ella answer in unison. 'Granny Thomson!'

Teresa turns back to the foreman. 'She died ten years ago. Had lived up there for over fifty years so she had. Every time that single-end fell vacant she'd move back in – her spirit, that is. Then, when we'd get a new tenant, she'd move out again. Wouldn't bother them. Sure, and Oi've seen her regular over the years. We was great friends, her and me.'

'Just a minute!' says the foreman. One of his crew is walking past. 'DANNY! Come hear a minute.' As the man approaches, the foreman drops his voice. 'Danny says he's seen her many a time this last few months. Have a word with him. I won't say anything.'

The now former residents of 18 Dalbeattie Street move in closer as the young man joins them.

'Yes, gaffer?'

'This lady wants to speak to you.'

'Yer gaffer's been telling me, you've been seeing me old friend now and again.' Teresa points. 'At the window just above the closemouth.'

'Indaid I have. Manys a time.'

'Can I be asking ye – what colour hair has she?'

Danny leans forward. 'White as the driven snow so 'tis! It's the hair of her that catches me eye. I never get a clear look at her face.' He smiles at Teresa. 'The bhoys think she's a banshee. But over toime, I've got the feeling there's no harm in her. I t'ink she just likes t' watch us.'

Teresa nods, lays a gentle finger on his chest. 'I think you're like meself, son. Got a little bit of "the gift" in ye.' She points again at Granny's windows. 'But herself. Ah! Now there was a one who *was* fey. Never seen one better!'

Five minutes later they board the coach that will take them out of Dalbeattie Street for good. Teresa makes sure she is first on, walks the length of the bus and sits at the back. She half-turns on the broad bench seat to look up at Granny's double-windows for the last time. She is confident Bella will not let her down. Not today. As the bus begins to pull away, Teresa sees the crane at the far end of their building cough out a great gout of blue smoke as the driver moves forward, starts the steel ball swinging. She turns away, raises her head once more to look at Granny's windows – feels a tingle from head to toe. Her old friend is already there. Looking on as the last of her neighbours leave the street. As Teresa expected, there is no withdrawing into the shadows on this last day. She can see her face under the shock of white hair. They look at each other for two or three seconds until the departing coach narrows the angle and she is lost to view.

'Did ye see her?' says Drena.

'Clear as a bell!' confirms Ella.

They turn to look at Teresa. She has a beatific smile on her face. 'That's the only time she's let me see her proper. I knew she wouldn't move away, today.'

Drena looks thoughtful. 'But where will she go, wance the building's doon, Teresa?'

'To her rest. She was happy t' be in her old house as long as the building was standing. Tonight will be her last night in there. By tomorrow, she'll be in company with Donald McNeil, Samuel Stewart, and wee Jane and yon kaleidoscope.' She looks at Ella. 'And your Archie,' she says softly, 'she'll be a comfort to him 'til he's settled.'

* * *

As the coach accelerates down the Maryhill Road, the dust from the long unswept Dalbeattie Street, whirls out of its tyre treads like a vapour trail. Ella, her eyes moist, leans back in her seat. Drena sits quietly beside her, glances out of the corner of her eye, then lays a hand on top of hers. Ella looks out the window at the so familiar shops going by. Thinks of Teresa's words. Tries to picture Archie and Bella Thomson meeting tomorrow, having a grand blether. It's a comfort – even if it's probably no' true. Her thoughts go onto the last week or so; Archie, the funeral, aw' the work tae get ready for the move. Ah have not got one ounce of energy left. As the coach sways her through St George's Cross her eyes begin to close. God! Ah've never felt so tired. It'll be at least half an hour afore we get there. She moves in her seat, gets comfortable. 'Mmmm.' Mind, it wid be lovely if Archie and Granny really could be in company, the morra. Familiar faces roond him tae make him feel at hame. Especially auld Donald McNeil. Archie liked Donald. Doubts begin to bother her . . . Ah'm sure it'll no' be like they used tae show it in the fillums. Like yon picture wi' Don Ameche, when he dies. Technicolor and aw' the rest of it. Ochhh! If Ah want tae believe it's like that – Ah can. And nae bugger's gonny stop me! By the time the coach passes the Normal School, Ella is sound asleep.

It's barely an hour later when Robert Stewart, on his lunch break, drives out of Rossleigh's garage behind the wheel of his old Rover 90. Minutes later he parks on the Maryhill Road as near as possible to the blocked-off Dalbeattie Street.

Since the last of the tenants left a minor amount of preparatory work has been done on the large slates of the sixty-feet high roof. The cranes with their wrecker's balls stand silent, the street deserted. It's piece-time.

Robert walks the hundred or so yards to the wooden bothy, knocks, then opens its door. There are less than ten workmen in situ – the majority preferring to head for the local pubs. Sandwich boxes, old army 'small-packs' and a combination of flasks and half-pint mugs litter the table. Their heads turn as one to see who's disturbing their break. Robert easily homes in on the foreman; older, better dressed – sporting a tie. He looks at the gaffer, but speaks to them all.

'Sorry tae interrupt your break, lads. But could –'

The site foreman interrupts him. 'Come away in. Put the wood in the hole, there's a lot of dust flying around this morning. What can I do for you?'

Robert does as requested. Takes a few steps into the hut. 'Hi! My name's Robert Stewart. I work at Rossleigh's, further down the road.' He nods in the general direction of the soon-to-be-demolished tenement. 'I was born and brought up across the street, at Number 18. Would you allow me tae bung one of your lads to unscrew the close number, and nip up a ladder and unscrew one of the street nameplates?'

The foreman smiles. 'Mind, your timing's perfect. After we've had our piece we'll be starting with a steel ball at either end of the building.' He looks round the bothy. 'Any volunteers?' Four hands go up. 'You might as well have the job, Mick.' There are one or two disappointed faces.

'C'mon, now,' says the foreman, 'the lad's only just started. He's on a week's lying-time. Money will come in handy.'

Just over five minutes later, a slightly breathless Mick returns to the hut, places a square white-enamel plate with the number '18' embossed in black on it, on the Formica-covered table. Beside it he lays the long, rectangular nameplate with 'Dalbeattie Street' embossed in two shades of blue enamel. 'There y'are, sur.'

Robert reaches into his back pocket for his wallet, extracts a fiver. 'That's grand, son.'

'Oi have'ny any change, sur.'

'I don't need any change.'

'Jayz-oh!' The lad looks at his gaffer. 'Oi was going t' ask ye for a sub, boss.' He beams. 'Sure, and Oi don't need it now.'

The foreman looks at Robert. 'Yah bugger! If Ah'd known it was a fiver – Ah'd have gone and got them myself!'

Robert does a 'U-turn' on the Maryhill Road, heads back to Rossleigh's. He's already decided where the two mementoes should go – above the kitchen door. He can 'see' them in his mind's eye. The '18' in the centre, over the wooden door frame – the nameplate, just above that. He has a feeling there will be no objections from Rhea. He's right.

CHAPTER THIRTY-NINE

Just Dropping In

A Sunday afternoon. Ella Cameron is sound asleep in her new 'wing' armchair. She had earlier rested a cushion on her shoulder, nestled it into the nook where the back of the chair meets the start of the wing then – with head and neck comfortably supported, Cannon gas fire sending out enough heat to smelt iron – she had settled down to watch an old black and white movie on BBC2; *Hobson's Choice*. Together, the above three ingredients have proved more efficient than a dose of morphine. With the television's volume turned down so low that Charles Laughton can't hear himself bawling-out John Mills, it isn't long until Ella's eyelids feel as though weighted with lead. Within ten minutes of the film starting she has succumbed to all these enticements, slipped into a lovely sleep, and the TV plays on to an audience of none.

She doesn't hear the knock on her front door. The

letterbox being rattled loudly barely causes her to stir. It takes a series of raps on the living room window and her name being called, to finally drag her, unwillingly, from the half-nelson of Morpheus. Opening her eyes, it takes a full two seconds for her to realise somebody's chapping the window. She turns, and at first glance doesn't recognise Jack Marshall. Fortunately, Marjorie steps into view. 'Oh! My God!' Ella waves an arm, semaphores a message that is deciphered as 'Ah'm coming' and, stiff as an old board at first, gets out of her chair and makes for the front door.

'Eeeh! Marjorie! Jack! How long huv you been trying tae rouse me?'

Jack looks at his watch. 'Forty minutes!'

'Ye huv'nae, yah lying big bugger!'

'That's exactly whit the Queen said tae de Gaulle, last time he came tae the palace fur his tea!'

Marjorie shakes her head. 'Pay no attention, Ella.'

'Anywye, in youse come. Eeeh! This is a lovely surprise!' Big Jack Marshall gives her a hug then a kiss on the cheek. Marjorie kisses her on both cheeks. Ella winks at Jack. 'Baith cheeks, if ye don't mind! It's well seen she works doon the City Chambers, in't it?'

As they enter the lobby and Ella takes their coats, Marjorie speaks. 'Jack was fancying a wee run out in the car. Suggested Helensburgh.' She pauses. 'But I said no, I'd prefer to take a run over to the Molendinar and see how you're doing, Ella.' She smiles. 'So here we are.'

'That's awfy nice of the two of you. Ah'm glad you did,

hen. And on a Sunday efterninn. That'll give us plenty of time for a good auld fashioned blether.'

'Exactly!' says Jack. 'How long huv ye been here now, Ella?'

'This is the middle of July . . .' She works it out. 'Almost exactly three weeks.'

'You settling in okay, hen?'

'Aye. Better than Ah thought.' She walks towards the kitchen. 'C'mon through here with me while Ah make a cuppa, so as we can keep on talking.'

Marjorie says, 'Och, you don't have to go tae all that trouble . . .'

Ella looks at her. 'Ah do! Ah'm choking for a drink o' tea. Ah've jist woke up, if ye remember?'

Ten minutes later, Jack carrying a wooden tray laden with tea things, they troop back into the living room. At just this moment all three see a figure flit past the window.

Ella looks heavenward. 'Oh-oh! That's the game a bogey. Here's Desiree fae next door!'

Marjorie looks at her. 'Oh, Ah thought Drena was your neighbour?'

'She is!'

'It's only me!' Drena comes in via the back door.

'Aye! That's whit we're aw' worried aboot!'

Drena enters with a 'Tut!' Looks at Ella's visitors. 'Youse two did'nae think you could get ontae the Scheme withoot being spotted, did ye?'

'Away and get another cup oot the kitchen, Drena. There's plenty of tea made. Oh, and bring a plate, tae.'

'So you feel you're settling, Ella?' Marjorie looks at her former neighbour.

'So far, so good. Ah have been thinking, that if Ah'd still been in ma auld hoose, there would huv been too many memories of Erchie.' She looks at them. 'He never even got tae see this place, the poor soul.' Another movement takes their eyes as someone just goes out of sight behind the house.

'I think you're about to get another visitor,' says Marjorie.

'Aye, Ah seen her.'

'Who is it?' enquires Drena.

'Magda!'

'Magda? Who's Magda?'

They hear the back door being opened. Ella looks at them, cups a hand to her ear, points towards the kitchen.

'Halloooh! It is only me. Have I seen Marjorie and Jack enter your house?'

'Magda Goebbels!' says Ella. 'Ah telt ye.'

'Fuck me!' says Drena.

Ella fixes her with a stern eye. 'Ah've told you before, Drena. Ah wish you'd wait until my visitors huv fucked off before you start swearing!' Even the sainted Marjorie joins in the laughter.

Jack smiles. 'It definitely is good, Ella, tae see you're getting your life back together.'

'Oh, aye,' says Drena. 'She's beginning tae see light at the end of the funnel!'

Ella shakes her head, looks heavenwards. 'As you can see, my task here is not yet done!'

* * *

At this exact moment Frank and Wilma Galloway are also having a cup of tea. They, too, are watching *Hobson's Choice*. Frank lays his cup on its saucer. 'Ah'll tell you what, Wilma. Ah did'nae realise what a bloody good film this is.'

'In't it! Ah seen it when it first came oot. But somehow, Ah'm enjoying it even more this time. Ah seem tae be seeing a lot more in it –' She stops speaking as a car draws up at the pavement.

Frank turns his head. 'Is this us getting a visitor?' They both look on as the car's front doors open at the same time. A man and woman climb out – Wilma feels her heart leap!

Frank rises to his feet, turns to her. 'That's my son Daniel! And his wife Sheila. Ah don't believe it! Whit could they be wanting?'

Wilma says nothing. She is not supposed to know them. Or to ever have met them. She sits upright in her chair, watches them lock the car, then walk up the path. Oh, God! Could it be? Please, *please* do it for Frank!

Frank goes to the door, opens it before they reach it. Hopes his estranged son hasn't come to cause bother about something – real or imagined. He looks at his boy. I've only seen him once in the last twelve years. Okay, here goes. 'Hello, Daniel. Hello, Sheila.' He wonders if he should offer his hand. Risk a possible rebuff.

Sheila smiles. 'Hello, Frank.' All at once he gets a good feeling.

Daniel stretches out his arm, offers his father his hand.

'Hello, Dad. Could we come in?' Clears his throat. He'll be a bit nervous, too. 'I'd like to talk to you.'

Frank looks at him, takes his hand, finds he is unable to stop the tears coming. He doesn't care.

Sheila comes closer, kisses him on the cheek. She looks into his face, almost whispers, 'It's going to be all right. He now knows the full story.'

'C'mon, come inside.' Frank can't control the emotion in his voice.

As they walk into the living room Wilma rises from her chair. Frank gestures towards her. 'This is my wife, Wilma.' He looks at his son and daughter-in-law, 'And this is Daniel and –'

Daniel interrupts him. 'Sheila and I have already met Wilma.'

Frank shakes his head. Can't figure that out. 'When did you –'

Sheila comes in. 'Daniel and I are here because of Wilma. It's her you've got tae thank for this visit.'

They can see the last few minutes have overwhelmed Frank. Too much for him to take in. He looks at Wilma. 'How have you managed tae bring all this aboot, hen?'

All three look at her. She continues to stand by her chair, tears coursing down her cheeks. Sheila walks over, stands beside her, puts an arm round her waist. 'We'll tell you all about it later, Frank.'

'Phew! Ah don't normally drink during the week,' he says, 'but Ah'm gonny have to have a wee half right now!' He looks at Wilma then his visitors. 'Anybody else?'

Daniel speaks. 'I think I'd prefer a *big* half, rather than a wee yin.'

Sheila looks at the tearful Wilma, then says, 'I think a wee half will be fine for Wilma and me – as soon as possible!' She turns back to her. 'You've got a lot to tell him, haven't you?' Wilma can only nod.

CHAPTER FORTY

Conversation Pieces

The Ford van with the legend *Kinnaird's: For Your Fruit, Veg & Flowers* on its side, turns into the top end of Stobcross Avenue on the Molendinar housing scheme. Archie Cameron crosses over to the right and stops a few doors short of Lexie's house. He glances down to the left, to his own. As he could have forecast, he can see the TV flickering in the living room. Knows his ma will be in the kitchen getting the dinner ready. She always leaves the telly on. Says she read somewhere it's not good for them tae be continually switched on and off. He turns to Lexie. 'You want tae go oot the night, pal?'

'No thanks. Tuesday nights are dullsville. Everywhere!'

'Yeah, aren't they. Ah don't think there's any good movies on doon the toon, either. Ach! Ah'll just stay in as well.' He half turns in his seat, looks at her. 'The trouble is, Lexie Forsyth, Ah don't like going out on ma own, any more. It's no' fun unless my girl's with me.' He gives a sigh. 'Ah hope tae hell there is something worth watching oan the telly, the night. If there is'nae, Ah'll mibbe jist slash ma wrists!'

'Isn't *Van Der Valk* on? I'm sure it's Tuesday nights for it,' she says.

'Ah think you're right. Ah like that.' He leans over towards her, she gives him a kiss.

'You'll have all the neighbours keeking at us from behind their curtains, Archie Cameron.'

He laughs. 'Who cares? The folk up this end of the Avenue are nearly all fae Dalbeattie Street. So they know aboot us anyway.'

'Mmmm. I suppose so.' They sit in companionable silence for a while. She has her hands folded on her lap. Her engagement ring catches his eye, sets off a train of thought . . . The day Ah came out of jail, getting back tae Maryhill, walking intae Kinnaird's to introduce maself, and setting eyes on Lexie for the first time. He hides a smile. Jeez! She would'nae have given me a nod in the desert back then . . . Lexie is snapping her fingers in front of his eyes; his 'fast forward' memory stream melts away . . .

'Hello! Hello! Whatever are you thinking of? You were miles away then. Practically in a trance.'

Archie is now back in the van. Looking sheepish. Then he looks at her. Love for her wells up in him. 'Would you like me tae tell you whit Ah was thinking about?'

She senses he wants her to say yes. 'Yeah, I would like to know.'

'Ah'll tell you, then. But you have tae promise me one

thing. If Ah'm gonny let you know just how much I love you, don't use it to try and be smart, or feel you can take liberties because you've got me dangling on a string. Okay?'

'Those days are gone, Archie. I tried it once. Never again.' She lays a hand on top of his. 'I know you wouldn't put up with it. And I'd be frightened in case I lost you for good!'

He leans over, kisses her on the lips. Sits back. 'What Ah was thinking about was the very first day I set eyes on you, and how you totally overwhelmed me. Then I looked at our engagement ring – this is where you might get a bit big-headed – and Ah was thinking, how the hell did you ever get *her*, Archie Cameron?'

She laughs. 'I sometimes think about that, Archie. That first day you walked into Kinnaird's.' She shakes her head from side to side. '*Not* impressed! And you did'nae help your case either, because you were so full of yerself. And then, when we finished for the day, to my horror I found you not only lived up *my* close, but on *my* landing! Yeuch! I thought, what have I done to deserve this?'

'Don't haud yerself back, hen. Jist tell it like it is, will ye!' He manages to keep his face straight, taps her on the forearm. 'And, eh, excuse me, missis. Dae ye mind if Ah point oot it's *my* close! Ah wiz born up there.'

'Yes! But may I point out, you were spending most of your time in the clink!'

'Oh, aye! Go on. Put the boot in, why don't ye. You're no' averse tae hitting below the belt, urr ye, Lexie Forsyth. Whit a bad wee bizzum you are when ye start!' The two of them now dissolve into laughter. He prods her on the shoulder. 'It was my intention to finish up by telling you just how much Ah love you, scabby drawers!' She starts to giggle. 'However, Ah'm not gonny tell you now.' He leans back against the van door.

'Well that is too bad – because you just have!'

'Oh, Jeez! Ah have, haven't Ah?' He emits a mega-tut.

'Right, let's get back tae real life,' says Lexie. 'After you've watched *Van Der Valk*, that's if it's on, you can come over for an hour or two. My ma likes having you about the house.'

'Aye. Just as if Ah was next door's cat! Anyway, Ah'll probably dae that. Might even suggest a wee hand or two at pontoon to Evie, if there's nothing worth watching on the telly.'

Lexie laughs. 'She'll definitely be up for that. Loves tae play cards for a few coppers.'

'And don't I know it. Took aboot thirty bob off me, last time Ah fell intae her trap!'

'One pound fifty, if you don't mind. We're decimal now.'

'Call it whit ye like. It wiz still one pound, and half a pound. And that comes tae thirty bob as far as Ah'm concerned.'

She glances round the interior of the small, nearly-new van. 'It's great, isn't it, Mrs K letting us use the shop van to go back and forward to work? Otherwise, it would be two buses morning and evening.'

'Not half. Saves us time *and* money. But really, the van is safer sitting in front of my house, here on the Molendinar.

When we used tae park it roon' the corner in Wilton Street, it regularly got interfered wi'. Scratched, tyres let doon, stuff like that.'

She squeezes his hand. 'And I think she's pleased the way you take care of it. It's always immaculate.'

'Well, it's only fair.' He looks at his watch. Gives her another kiss. 'And of course, we have'ny mentioned the main benefit. When the winter comes, it'll be handy for daeing a bit of winching inside it. Definitely beat a draughty back close in Dalbeattie Street oan a snawy night. In fact, Ah think Ah'll ask Mrs K if we can huv reclining seats fitted before the winter.'

She gives him a 'big lassie's slap' on the shoulder. 'You will not, Archie Cameron!' She reaches down to the foot-well for her bag. 'I'd better go, beloved.'

He looks at her. 'Tell me something, engaged lady. When wiz the last time Ah telt you – you're the light of ma life?'

She smiles. 'Must be days ago.'

'Right! Ah must try and remember tae tell ye the morra!'

'*What*!'

'Only kidding, sweetheart.' He moves his face to within kissing distance. 'Lexie Forsyth, Ah love you tae bits. You're the best thing that's ever happened tae me. Honest injun!'

'Aww, Archie! That's the nicest thing anybody's said tae me for yonks.'

He tuts. 'Yonks? Your English is'nae half going doon the Swanee, hen.'

'It's keeping company wi' you that diz it. See ye later!' The final kiss is quite passionate.

Archie opens the kitchen door. 'Hi-yah, Ma!'

Three pans are gently steaming on the cooker. Ella has a turban on, from which the obligatory damp strand of hair has escaped and fallen onto her forehead. Every sixty-eight seconds or so she brushes it upwards with the back of her hand. Soon after she takes the hand away it flops back to where it wants to be. He goes over to her, kisses her on the cheek. Something he started to do days after the death of his father.

'Why don't ye tuck that strand of hair up *under* the turban, Ma?'

'Mind yer ain beeswax!'

'Ye cannae help some people.'

'Away an' bile your heid!' She stirs a couple of pans, then. '*Oh*! At last Ah've remembered while you're in.' She points. 'Sit doon at that table, right this minute. Ah have been gonny ask you something for weeks. But every time it comes intae ma heid, you're either at work or oot wi' Lexie. Then when ye do come hame, Ah'm watching telly and Ah've forgot all aboot it.'

She points imperiously at the kitchen table. '*Sitz machen*!'

He laughs out loud. 'Eh, God! My faither would be proud of ye, Ma.'

She also laughs, but it ends in a sigh. 'Aye, he would,' she says softly.

He takes his usual chair. She sits on hers. 'It happened

on the day of your da's funeral, when we all arrived at Hubbard's. Ah had climbed the stairs and was heading for the restaurant. As Ah came through the door, there was this very tall man standing tae the left, waiting. As soon as he seen me, he said, "Mrs Cameron, could Ah have a wee word with you?" He took me by the arm and led me tae one side.' She looks at Archie. 'And Ah've never in ma life heard anybody wi' such a raspy, croaky voice as –' She breaks off as Archie smiles. 'Ah! You know who it is, do ye? That's good, son. Ah've been wanting tae know who wiz talking to me –'

Archie interrupts. 'And *Ah'll* be wanting tae hear what he had tae say. Be aboot my da Ah'd imagine.'

'It was. And how come your faither knew him and Ah did'nae? What wiz the connection? Ah'd never seen him before in ma life – yet he had such good things tae say aboot your faither.' She blows her cheeks out. 'He had something about him, Archie. Ah'm no' quite sure whit it was. Sort of different, not like your faither's other pals. He definitely wiz'nae run o' the mill.' She sighs. 'Then, efter he'd said whit he wanted tae say, he wiz gone! He never stayed for the meal. Ah never saw him again in the room. He must huv came tae the funeral, then went tae Hubbard's because he wanted tae speak tae me.' She looks at Archie. 'So whit's his name?'

Archie leans his elbows on the table. 'His name's Billy Webster. He runs Johnny May's snooker hall oan the Maryhill Road. Has done for years.'

'Oh, that bloody dive! *Huh*! Ah remember that place

right enough. That's where you used tae mix wi' aw' that bad company, then go and get yersel intae trouble.'

'Ah know, Ma. But Billy jist manages the place. He never got me intae trouble. It was other guys.' He pauses. 'And mainly maself. Naebody twisted ma arm, ye know.'

'*Humph*!'

'Do ye want me tae tell you aboot this guy, or not?'

'Ah dae. Keep talking.'

He's silent for a moment. 'Ah'm trying tae figure oot where's the best place tae start.'

'Whit aboot the beginning!'

He laughs. 'Okay. You mentioned that croaky voice he has. My da gave him that!' Ella's about to speak. He holds a hand up to stop her. 'About twenty years ago, Billy had the reputation of being the hardest man in Maryhill. A real violent bugger. Would shiv somebody as soon as look at them.' Once more he stops his ma from making a comment. 'Then wan day Billy got it wrong. He picked on ma da in the 419 Bar. Ah've been told it lasted less than sixty seconds!'

'Aye! Well he made a bad mistake, that day.' There's a look of pride on his mother's face.

'Now, Ah don't know all the ins and outs of it. But as far as Ah can gather, when he found oot ma faither was an ex-para, dropped intae Arnhem and aw' the rest of it, he seems tae have developed this great respect for him . . . *Oh*! And Ah'll tell you another thing. My da telt him never tae come back intae the 419. Barred him! And he never showed face again!'

Ella shakes her head in admiration for her man. 'Jeez! Whit a tough bugger your da was.'

'The next time they came across one another, as far as Ah know, was aboot ten years later. That was the night Ah took money from your purse. And ma da came storming doon tae Johnny May's tae drag me oot! Ah remember listening tae the two of them. My da had been in the hall a wee while before Billy realised who he was – and vice versa! The two of them finished up talking as if they were auld pals! And the last time Billy came intae things was last year. He came up tae oor street in his car, and got the wee Thomson laddie from the next close tae run up the stairs and tell ma da he wanted tae see him –'

Ella cuts in. 'Awww! That wiz Christmas Eve last year. Ah! So that's who wanted tae see your da that night. It wiz this Billy Webster.' She points at Archie. 'Aye, he'd got wind that yon big gangster fella wiz looking for you, so he came up tae warn ye.' She thinks it over. 'Jeez! He really did finish up a good friend tae yer da, didn't he?'

'Not half! *And* tae me! If they'd got me on my own that night, Ma, at the very least Ah'd have finished up in a wheelchair!' He sits back. 'Ah think that's pretty much all Ah know about my da and Billy.' Archie leans forward again. 'You have'nae yet told me what he had tae say tae you about ma da, when he spoke to you at Hubbard's?'

'Well, first of all son, after listening tae you telling me about him and your da, whit this Billy Webster had tae say tae me in Hubbard's now makes more sense. When he took me by the arm and walked me tae the side,' she swallows hard, he sees her eyes glisten with tears, 'he had tae bend doon a bit, with him being sae tall. And he says, "Mrs Cameron, I wanted tae come here the day, tae have a wee word with you. Ah've known your husband for quite a few years. And Ah wanted tae tell you I considered him to be one of the finest men I've ever known. And I'm very sad to think I won't be seeing him again." Then he took my hand in both of his, and he said, "What impressed me the most about your husband was that most folk would pass him in the street and not give him a second look. He was just an ordinary Glasgow man going hame from his work – he was anything but!" Then he squeezed ma hand and gave me a wee kiss on the cheek. And that was jist about it as far as Ah can remember, son.'

Archie has to clear his throat. 'Yeah, that, eh, was really good of him. Ah guess he jist wanted you to know how highly he regarded my dad.'

It's the next day. Archie parks the van and walks across the Maryhill Road to the snooker hall. He opens the so familiar sound-proofed door, manages to take two steps inside before the smell of cigarette smoke, stale air and unwashed bodies drapes itself over him like a blanket. As he heads for the wooden office he looks at the guys playing on a couple of tables. Doesn't recognise any of them. The tall figure of Billy Webster sits in the dimly-lit office.

'Hello, Billy!'

'Did'nae think Ah'd see you in here again, young fella!' He offers his hand and they shake. He rises from his chair, turns, sits on the corner of the desk so that they face one another. 'How's your ma?'

'Not too bad. We're living up the Molendinar, now.'

'Aye, Dalbeattie Street's completely gone. They've already started on new maisonettes doon the far end. Look quite good.' He smiles. 'So, whit have you come in tae see me aboot?'

'My ma just got roon' tae telling me last night, what you'd been saying aboot my da, when ye spoke tae her at Hubbard's. She was quite touched – and impressed by you! So Ah had tae tell her a wee bit about ye.' He holds a finger up. 'Don't worry! Only the good bits. About how you and my da got tae know one another ower the years.'

'Ah thought your father was an exceptional man, Archie. Ah really did.'

'That's why Ah've called in, Billy. Ah've got another wee story tae tell you aboot him. We were sorting oot his stuff a few days after he died. You'll never guess what we found. A DCM – still in its box! He'd never telt anybody about it. Not my ma, not even his best pal. He could have added it ontae the clasp with the rest of his medals. But he didn't. Jist kept it tae himself. We don't even know what he did tae get it. A good chance it would be at Arnhem.'

Billy Webster shakes his head. '*Huh*! That seems tae be just typical of the man, doesn't it?'

'Anywye, Ah've got a stack of deliveries tae do, Billy, but Ah thought Ah'd drop in and tell you about the medal.'

'Yeah, as they say – it just adds tae the legend. Oh! And

what's this Ah've been hearing, Archie? You've been getting yourself engaged.'

Archie blushes. 'Yeah, I have.'

'And they tell me she's a bit of a looker!' Billy laughs. 'Though mind – I did hear somebody say, "Ah don't know whit she sees in him!"'

'Ah'll be the first one tae agree wi' them, Billy!'

The two of them walk towards the door. 'So you're on the straight and narrow now, Archie?'

'Oh God, aye! Ah've too much tae lose. And it would definitely be the end of my ma if I got intae trouble again and wiz sent doon. After losing my faither, she jist could'nae handle it. She'd fall tae bits.'

'Aye, you're just like myself, Archie. The older you get, the wiser you get – and thank God for it!' They both laugh.

Archie opens one of the street doors. The sun has come out and now seizes a rare chance to slip into the dark hall from the busy Maryhill Road. 'Right, Ah'll see ye when Ah see ye, Billy.'

'Aye, we might have a pint or two one night.' He lays a hand on Archie's shoulder. Smiles. 'Ah'm just thinking. Wouldn't it have been appropriate if we could have met for a drink in the 419 Bar? That's where this all started. It's a pity it's gone. *Hah*! That would have amused your father.'

Archie steps outside, continues to hold the door open. Billy Webster stays inside, the deep gloom of the hall behind him. 'All the best.' Archie lets the door go. Webster takes the weight, holds it open with the flat of his palm.

Archie pauses, turns. 'Has there been any news aboot Nathan Brodie since he went tae Spain?'

'Last thing Ah heard, he can now get around wi' jist one stick!' He closes the door quietly.

As Archie, eyes narrowed against the glare, makes his way to the van, Billy Webster wends his way in the low light, through the maze of tables towards his wooden office. Aye, young Archie's father was some man. You don't get many Archie Cameron's in a pound.

CHAPTER FORTY-ONE

Planning and Strategy

'Zat you jist in fae your work, Ella?' Cigarette hanging from her lips, flowered peenie tied round her ever-expanding waist, Drena McClaren busies herself blanching some pommes frites for later.

'Huv you any idea how often Ah've considered taking early retirement, so's Ah'll no' huv you asking me that buggering question every night?' Ella lays her bag against the nearest leg of the kitchen table. Flops down into a chair. 'Ah'm banjaxed!'

Drena pushes over an open cigarette pack and box of matches. 'You wanting an Embassy?'

'Thanks.'

'They seem tae be working you tae death doon the Lux Tearooms at the minute, Ella. Is there a Christmas rush on?'

'Aye. There's a shed-load of orders in for bespoke

decorated cakes. Ah'm the only confectioner, so Ah'm run aff ma feet so Ah am.'

'Whit's "bespoke"?'

'It's when . . .' Ella pauses, finds she can't resist it . . . 'folk want ye tae decorate a cake for somebody who's getting a bike fur Christmas.' She avoids eye contact. 'You've nae idea how long it takes tae make a bike oot of icing.' She draws on her cigarette. 'And Ah'll tell ye another thing – sales o' tandems must be going through the ceiling this year!'

'Ah thought your boss wiz gonny take on another confectioner?'

'Says he cannae get wan.' Ella watches as Drena completes the blanching. 'Looks like there's a bit of the auld haute cuisine going on in here. Whit's Billy getting fur his dinner the night?' Unfortunately, Ella is raising her cup to her mouth as she makes this enquiry.

'Egg an' chips.'

Drena turns as she hears her friend splutter. 'Something go doon the wrong wye, hen?'

It's a short time later. They sit together at the kitchen table. 'Did you know it's six months tae the day, since we flitted oot of Dalbeattie Street, Ella?'

Ella is quiet for a moment. 'Aye, right enough. June the 22nd. This is December 22nd.' She sits quietly for another few seconds. 'Archie died, six months past on the fourteenth.'

'Aye, Ah remembered, hen.'

Ella lays a hand on top of Drena's, squeezes it. 'Ah knew ye wid.' They don't look at one another. Ella draws on her cigarette. Thoughts far away. 'It's still awfy sore.'

'Ah'll bet it is.'

Ella clears her throat. 'Whit are we gonny dae at Hogmanay?' She looks at her pal.

Drena turns to look at her. 'Enjoy oor fuckin' selves!' They simultaneously lean forward onto the the table, burst out laughing – in spite of the tears in their eyes.

Minutes later Billy McClaren pulls up outside in his van – *W. McClaren. Painter & Decorator* proudly emblazoned on its side. He enters via the back door.

'Ella, me darling!' She receives her usual kiss and hug.

'Whit aboot me?' Drena looks at him.

'Gie us time! You're on the other side o' the table. Huv'nae got roon' there yet.'

'Well you'd better be quick aboot it!'

He turns to Ella. 'Zat no' terrible? Alwiz ready tae find fault nooadays, this yin.'

'Aye, you've got a hard life.' She stubs out the cigarette. 'Ah was just thinking, when Ah heard ye pull up in the van. Remember aw' them years when you used tae push a handcart wi' your ladders and pots o' paint, to your jobs. Changed days, eh?'

'Not half. Ah done that for the best part o' twenty years. Never dreamed Ah'd ever have a van.'

'We've been making plans for Hogmanay,' announces Drena.

'Good!' says Billy. 'You looking for any ideas?'

'Naw. It's aw' done and dusted. No' needing any!' she replies. As Ella looks at his face she can't help laughing. Drena starts giggling.

'*See*! Since Ah lost ma pal youse two are taking over. Ah've got naebody tae back me up!'

'Ye never hud! We always finish up getting oor ain way,' says Ella.

Drena looks at him. 'And now you're in a *minority* of wan. *Huh*! You've nae chance, pal. Get used tae it!' She turns to a laughing Ella. Tries to keep control of herself. 'Are we needing any ideas? Women dae aw' the work at Hogmanay – clean the hoose, dae the baking and the cooking and anything else that's needing done. All he diz is get in the way – then get drunk!'

As he has a feeling he's redundant, Billy hangs his jacket up in the hall, empties his piece-bag and pours cold water into his flask. Leaves it to steep in the sink. He decides to chance a question. 'Wid it be considered pushy tae ask what you've come up with for Hogmanay? Or am Ah just supposed tae go along wi' it?'

'Ohhhhh!' says Drena, turning to look at Ella. 'Ah think he wull huv tae alter his tone before he gets tae know the plans.' She carries out an exaggerated bosom adjustment. 'That sounded a tad oan the aggressive side, if Ah'm no' mistaken!'

Ella looks at Billy's face, tries to keep control. 'Will you stoap it, Drena! Ye know Ah've got a weak bladder. If Ah wee this chair it'll be your ain fault!'

'Aw'right,' says Drena. Serious now. She looks at her

dearly beloved. 'We are gonny have a *joint* party. We split the cost of the eats and drinks doon the middle. The *main* party is gonny be held in Ella's. When ye think of it, it's quite a good idea. We live either side of a semi-detached. Everything will be laid oot in Ella's, and aw' the guests will be in there. All the spare drink and eats will be lying ready in oor hoose, Billy. When we run oot of something in Ella's, we just come through tae oor hoose and get some more! And the beauty of it is, Billy, on New Year's morning oor hoose will still be spotless – and Ella's will be a midden! Isn't that great, eh?'

Barely an hour later, some three miles across the city as a sparrow with emphysema flies, a full complement of Stewarts sits round the table in the kitchen of their Edwardian, red-sandstone flat in Wilton Crescent. As he has done for months, Robert Stewart occasionally glances at his two souvenirs above the kitchen door when they catch his eye. The enamel nameplate with Dalbeattie Street, and the small, square one with '18' on it.

'You can't take your eyes off them, Dad, can you.' His son, Sammy, laughs.

'I love them. That's my roots, and your mother's.' He leans forward. 'And, may I remind you, it's yours and Louise's as well. You were both born and brought up there too.'

Rhea looks at her son and daughter. 'Aye, and don't you forget it, either! Jist because you're at Glasgow Uni, Sammy . . .' she then turns to her daughter, 'and you're talking pan loaf every day ower at West End Modes oan the Byres Road, diz'nae mean ye should forget your roots, or try and deny them!'

They all turn to look at Robert's mother, Mary Stewart, as she laughs heartily. 'Aye. It's no' where you were born that counts. It's where you finish up – and how you conduct yourself on the way.' She nods her head. 'Your father and mother have done well, and all through hard work. When Ah was a young married woman in Dalbeattie Street, Ah thought of people who lived in these buildings, wally closes, as toffs. Well, your ma and da have joined them.' She points up to the Dalbeattie Street plates over the kitchen door. 'And they make no secret of where they started off. We all had a good life up Number 18. And you could'nae find better neighbours. Hard-working, honest folk who would'nae see you go hungry. So there!'

'Gran! Ah wasn't criticising my dad – or my mum,' says Sammy. 'I was just commenting on how much pleasure my dad gets from having his two souvenirs of Dalbeattie Street. That was all. And for the record, I also think I had a smashing childhood running about the streets and back courts up there. I loved it!' He turns to his sister. 'What about you, Louise?'

They all watch as she raises an eyebrow. '*Moi*! Dalbeattie Street? Not me, darlings. I was wafted down to Earth on a feathery cloud, landed in a flower bed somewhere out the far end of the Great Western Road – and was found by the *kindest* people, who raised me as their very own.'

She looks imperiously around the table. 'Well, at least that's whit Ah put oan ma joab application!'

Rhea pauses, with her second cup of tea halfway to her mouth. 'Oh! Ah've just remembered, Robert. Ruth rang me at the office this afternoon. Hogmanay is a Sunday, so the club will'nae be open. Her and George would like us tae come tae them and bring the New Year in at Kelvin Court. Ah said we almost certainly will. Is that okay?'

'If Le Bar Rendezvous is closed, I could'nae think of anywhere better to bring it in. You can ring her and confirm, if you want.'

Sammy looks at his parents in turn. 'You don't half keep that Club Rendezvous to yourselves, you two.'

'You're no' auld enough, son! You have tae be ower thirty,' says Rhea.

'It's a sophisticated night club for mature people,' says Robert. 'They wouldn't let a young poseur like you through the door.'

'That means it's no' fur a skitter like you!' says his mother.

'I take it you've got plans for New Year's Eve, Sammy?' His father looks at him.

'Been invited to a party up in Bearsden. One of the guys in my year.'

Robert turns to Louise. 'What about you, darling?'

'Chantelle and I have tickets for a New Year do at the Emerald Club. Excloozeeve!'

'Awww!' says Rhea. 'Are ye no' going oot wi yer pal Jessie this year? Shame!'

Robert leans towards his wife. 'May I remind you, darling. Jessie *is* Chantelle!'

Rhea dramatically covers her mouth with a hand. 'Oh, sorry! Ah alwiz forget so Ah dae.'

Louise gives her mother a withering look. 'Chantelle will be coming up for me on the night. If *anybody* calls her Jessie, I will NEVER speak to them again!'

'*Oh*!' says her brother. 'I might find that *too* good an opportunity to miss!'

CHAPTER FORTY-TWO

Dalbeattie Street Blues

Hogmanay 1972. A Sunday.

'It's just me, Ella!' The back door being opened and the call come together. As Drena steps into the kitchen, Ella reaches for the kettle. Five minutes later finds them sitting at the kitchen table. Ella draws on her cigarette. 'Ah brought a lot of stuff hame from oor bakery, yesterday. Ah think folks are gonny be surprised by the spread tonight, Drena. A mix o' the traditional, along with a selection of oor Continental finger-food. They're things that are selling well in oor bakery department at the minute – and going like a bomb, upstairs in the Lux Teaooms.'

'Continental?' says Drena. 'Ah hope it's no' gonny be too way-oot for oor neebours, Ella?'

'It'll no' be. It'll be fine. And Billy picked up the stuff we ordered?'

'Aye. Craig's the butcher's has had tae open the day. A

lot of his aulder customers don't huv fridges, and they'll no' take delivery the day before. So when Hogmanay falls on a Sunday he has nae option but tae open. Billy picked it up in the van this efterninn . . . three big ashet pies, smoked ham, sausage rolls, bridies and, of course, Ah've made a big pan of ma Scotch broth.'

'Well Ah'll tell ye, hen. If we did'nae huv another thing the night, as long as they get a plate o' your Scotch broth, there wid'nae be a word oot o' them! Thick broth wi' big cubes of lean ham.' Ella dabs her lips with a Kleenex. 'Jeez! Ah'm slaverin' at the mooth jist thinking aboot it!'

Drena basks in this praise. 'Aye, eh, even if Ah say it maself, Ella,' she carries out a reflex bosom adjustment, 'it's a meal in itself.'

'It is'nae half, hen.'

'Ah collected the other things yesterday. Black bun, Dundee cake, clootie dumpling, oatcakes, various cheeses, shortbread – oh, and Ah got some o' them Ritz Crackers. They are'nae half catching oan. Billy and me could eat them tae a band playing! Ah'll wait until nearer The Bells before Ah bring the broth through. We'll heat it up on your cooker.'

'Sounds good tae me, Drena. And when they see aw' that stuff laid oot beside the Continental specialities. Hey! We wull be the talk o' the Molendinar! Tastes are changing, ye know. And wi' me working in a bakery . . .' she nudges Drena, 'Ah've got ma finger oan the pulse. More and more folk are going abroad fur their holidays nooadays. They're experiencing new tastes. The days when Skegness wiz thought of as daring, huv gone!'

They hear footsteps, the back door is opened. 'It's just me, Mum! Oh hello, aunty Drena!' Kathleen Cameron makes her entrance. Ella looks at the clock. Five past five.

'Hello, hen!' Drena smiles. 'You're aw' dressed up. Where huv you been?'

'Been out with the girls from the office. We met for lunch at the Kelvingrove Art Gallery.'

'Nice. And whit are the plans for the night?' asks Drena.

'Ah'm bringing the New Year in over at Dermot's folks'. In Shettleston,' she adds.

'Aye, you're an engaged person noo. Got tae share yersel' oot between the families.'

'Exactly, aunty Drena.' She turns to her mother. 'Ah'm a wee bit peckish, Mum. Got anything handy?'

'Take a slice of quiche oot o' the fridge.'

Drena chokes on the smoke she's just inhaled . . . 'KEECH! Whit the buggerin' hell's that? Ah hope it's no' whit it sounds like?'

Katherine looks at her mother, they both laugh. 'It's *lovely*, aunty Drena.'

'Is it. Well Ah think they should consider a name change. Something called "keech" is never gonny catch oan in Glesga!' She sniffs. 'Whit else huv ye goat in that fridge?'

'Vol-au-vents.' Ella and daughter look at her. Stifle a giggle.

'Volley-vaunts? Ah'm feart tae ask. Whit urr they when they're at hame?'

'Little cases of puff pastry, filled wi' things like creamed mushrooms or, ohhh, salmon. You'll love them, Drena. Honest.'

During the next hour, Ella and Drena continue to sit at Ella's kitchen table, taking pleasure from the growing excitement of the younger members of their families as a New Year looms. It's almost seven when Katherine Cameron, bathed, hair done, in full makeup, perfumed, and wearing a brand new frock, comes downstairs to present herself . . .

'What do you think, ladies?' She does a few twirls.

Drena shakes her head, turns to Ella. 'That yin could be a movie star if she wanted, Ella. Ah'm no' kidding!'

Ella stares at her daughter. 'You look beautiful, Katherine. If only your faither was here to –' She breaks off.

'Oh, Mum, don't!' Katherine walks in a circle, waving her open hands in front of her eyes. 'If you start me off my mascara will run!'

'Okay! Okay! Ah won't. Eh, how are you getting intae the toon?'

'I've got my usual taxi guy, Andy, coming for me at seven. My overnight bag is lying by the door.' There is the sound of a car's horn . . .

Thirty minutes later Irma's son, Arthur Armstrong, presents himself. 'Hello aunty Ella, aunty Drena. I've been next door. Charles is just finishing getting ready, so I thought I'd come in and say hello!'

'Whit's your uncle Billy daeing?'

'Ah, he was sleeping in the chair when I arrived.'

Drena looks at Ella. 'Humph! Par for the course. Though, if Ah'm honest, he did go and pick up the grub – and he huz read *two* Sunday papers the day. He's bound tae be exhausted!'

Drena's youngest son, Charles, comes through to join them. His mother looks at him. 'Whit's oan the agenda for you two the night?'

Charles answers. 'We're no' too sure where we'll be early on, Ma. Wherever we can get in, probably. The first thing will be tae get something tae eat.'

'Ye can have something here afore youse go. Oor two hooses are overflowing wi' food!' says Ella.

'Naw, it's aw'right, aunty Ella, honest. We'll enjoy finding somewhere. The only place where we definitely intend to finish up is doon in George Square for The Bells. We've never heard that carillon thing that they have. Ah'm told they play tunes when it's getting near midnight.'

Drena smiles. 'We did that one New Year, didn't we, Ella? Your da and me and aunty Ella and uncle Archie. We brought the New Year in at George Square. It's good. It used tae be a woman who played the bells. Don't know whether she still diz.'

After the boys leave, there's a quiet spell of almost twenty minutes. Ella looks at the clock once more. Gone ten past eight. She turns to her pal. 'Ma bum's getting sore sitting!'

'Me tae.'

'We'll put up with it fur another half hour,' says Ella. 'Jist long enough tae huv another cuppa and a gasper.

Then we'll swing intae action.' She pauses. 'Well, lurch will be more like it!'

'Lead on, McDuff!' Drena reaches for another Embassy tipped. She lights it. Then, 'Who wiz it said that? "Lead on, McDuff!"'

'Something tells me it wiz Shakespeare,' says Ella.

'Him that owned the pub doon in Raeberry Street?'

Ella shakes her head. 'You are well oan the way tae turning ignorance intae a fine art, Drena.'

'Whit a nice thing tae say.'

'Don't mention it.'

'Right, c'mon, hen. Twenty minutes tae nine.' Ella rises, stiffly, to her feet. 'It's time we were making a move. We'll get the eatables laid oot. Bring the broth through – but no' light the gas yet. Get aw' the drink lined up oan the work tops. Lay oot plates and cutlery. Then, most important of all, make oorselves desirable!'

They both turn in the direction of the kitchen door as there comes the sound of more footsteps. Archie and Lexie enter.

'Hello, Ma. Aunty Drena.' He looks at the unadorned table, the two women in their peenies, Drena still wearing her turban. 'Huz this place had a New Year by-pass? Are youse giving it a miss this year?'

Lexie turns to him. 'Don't be fooled, pal. These are two professionals. They've organised more Hogmanay parties than you've had Penny Dainties! I'll take a bet this place will be transformed in an hour.'

Ella winks at her. 'Takes a pro' tae recognise a pro', Lexie.'

'Where are you two going the night?' Drena looks at them.

'Right here!' says Archie. 'Gonny keep my wee mammy company. Aren't we, Lexie?'

'It's the only place to be!'

Drena beams. Looks at Ella. 'Noo isn't that nice. When these two get merried, ah can see them moving in wi' you, Ella, and never getting roon' tae moving oot!'

'Fuuuck sake, Drena! Don't be putting ideas intae their heids.'

With the help of Archie and Lexie all the comestibles are soon on display. A wide selection of drinks – from soft to hard – are neatly lined up on the work tops. The kitchen table plus a smaller one have been placed together and a large tablecloth spread over them. Once the dishes, plates and bowls of foodstuffs have been laid out, scarcely an inch of cloth can be seen.

Ella and Drena stand side by side, hands on hips, as though about to take a bow.

'What aboot that then?' says Ella. Lexie turns to Archie. 'Told you it would'nt take them long.'

'Oh! Ah've just remembered,' says Ella. She turns to her son. 'Did you get booked up for you and Lexie at Stirling?'

'Yeah, we did. Just for two nights. We go up on Tuesday and come back on Thursday.'

'Huv'nae been booking yerself intae the jail again, huv ye?' asks Drena.

Archie laughs. 'None the fear of it. You'll no' find me in Craigmill Prison again. No, we're at the Golden Lion in Stirling. Two nights, dinner, bed and breakfast. Fifteen pounds a night.'

'That for a double room?' enquires Drena.

'Aye.'

'Dirty devils!' she says. 'Should'nae be allowed.'

'How are ye travelling?' asks his mother.

'Train. Doesn't take long.'

'And because it's just after Christmas and New Year, Mrs Kinnaird can spare us. She says the shop's always dead the first week in January.' Lexie smiles. 'This will be our first time away, together.'

'Oooooh! Be a bit of practice fur when you eventually go oan honeymoon!' says Drena. 'Ye cannae beat having the auld jig-a-jig in a hotel!' She laughs out loud at the embarrassment on the faces of the couple.

Ella shakes her head. 'Ye cannae take her anywhere . . . well, mibbe doon tae the midden!'

'Not long now!' Ella and Archie, Lexie and her mother, Evie, stand watching the television. There is less than a minute to go before 1973 marches in through doors and windows. Archie has an arm around Lexie's waist. He leans towards her ear.

'Would ye mind if my ma was the first one I wished a happy New Year. With it being . . .'

'I'd been going to suggest you should. This is her first year without . . .' She breaks off as rising voices and increasing excitement from the TV give notice 1973 is imminent. She nudges him. 'Go on. I'll do my mum.'

'C'mon, Ma.' He puts his arm on her shoulder. She turns towards him, smiles. Her eyes are already brimming with tears from thoughts of his da. The television at last allows the New Year to come in. He kisses her, puts his arms around her. 'Happy New Year, Ma! This is oor first wan withoot him.'

'Happy New Year tae you, son!' He can tell she is *just* holding herself together. 'Ah cannae believe he's no' here. It wiz his favourite time o' the year. Ne'erday. He loved it. Him and Billy and Irma with aw' their German carry-oan,' she pauses, 'and Drena and me tormenting the life oot o' them.' She gives a juddering sigh. 'Ye think it'll go on for ever, year efter year . . . but it diz'nae.' He pulls her close, she weeps quietly, her face buried in his shoulder. His own eyes are full, about to spill down his cheeks. He's not bothered who sees. They're for his da. Ella clears her throat, swallows hard, moves her head back. 'Right, that'll huv tae do, Erchie. Folk will be coming through that door soon, we'll have tae be ready for them. Ah've telt them this is a Dalbeattie Street reunion the night.' She raises a hand, brushes away tears from underneath his eyes. There's noise, then voices from the kitchen . . .

Archie moves quickly to Lexie. 'Here's Billy and Drena coming. Better take our chance while the going's good.' They put their arms around each other. Look into one another's eyes. 'Here's a Happy New Year to the girl Ah thought Ah'd never find,' he puts a finger on her lips as she's about to speak, 'and when Ah *did*, Ah had'nae got the first clue how Ah could make you see I'm the guy for you!'

'And a Good New Year to you, Archie! And I'll let you into a secret. The longer we're together, the more I see in you. And I . . .' he hears the emotion in her voice, 'I love you very much!' They kiss . . .

He glances towards the kitchen door. 'But I'll have to be honest with you, Lexie.' He shrugs. 'Ah can't say, I love you!' He sees her face fall. 'Well, it would'nae be true – because I ADORE you, Lexie Forsyth!'

'You're an absolute beast!' She punches him on the shoulder. Hard! Tears have sprung into her eyes. 'That was *not* funny, Archie Cameron! I could have died just then!' He makes time to kiss her again.

'Happy New Year, everybody!' Billy and Drena McClaren enter the living room. Billy's eyes search for Ella. He goes straight to her. 'Ella, hen!'

'Don't mention him, Billy! If ye dae, that'll be the two of us loast!'

He nods his head. 'You're right. Happy New Year, Ella. And many o' them!'

'Aw' the best, Billy!' They kiss and hug. Billy turns away immediately afterwards.

'Ah know where Ah'm going next. Lexie Forsyth!' He addresses the assembled company. 'You've nae idea how much Ah've been looking forward tae the New Year. Jist so as Ah can get tae kiss the best-looking lassie on the Molendinar!'

Drena looks heavenwards. 'Ah weesh he'd change the

record. Thirty-five years ago he wiz telling me *Ah* wiz the best looking lassie in Govan! The only thing he changes is the district!'

'Is that her casting aspidistras at me?' He turns to Archie. 'You don't mind yer auld uncle Billy stealing a kiss, dae ye, son?'

Archie laughs. 'It's Ne'erday. You're entitled. But mind, if it lasts longer than five minutes there's gonny be a bucket o' watter thrown ower the pair of ye!' Archie now looks around. 'Right! Where's ma future mother-in-law? C'mon, Evie Forsyth. Pucker up!' He taps Drena on the shoulder. 'And you jist stay there. You're next.'

'Right, c'mon everybody . . . 1973 has'nae been toasted, yet. Get intae that kitchen and get a glass of whatever your poison is.' Ella shepherds them out of the living room. 'There's everything you can think of here. Get tore in!'

Just then, the back door is opened. 'Halloooh! Everybody. Happy New Year!' A beaming Irma and Bert stand on the threshold.

Drena turns. 'Ohhh, they must huv got an early finish doon the bunker, the night!'

'*Irmchen! Eine gluckliche Neues Jahr*!' Billy goes to her, gives her a kiss and a hug. She looks at him. 'Oh, Billy. How can there be no more Archie?'

'*Ich kenne nicht*. It's too soon tae talk aboot him, hen. We'll get upset, and that will upset Ella. So! *Heute morgen wir mussen nicht uber Der Archie sprechen. Denkst du so*?'

Irma looks sadly at him. Nods. '*Ja. Du hat recht*.'

Drena nudges Ella. Says, *sotto voce*, 'Ah think Wilhelm

and Fraulein Braun urr planning World War Three ower therr. Ah could swear blind Ah heard Blitzkrieg mentioned.'

'Anybody home?' Another voice from the back door.

'My God!' exclaims Drena. 'Ah think you should get a revolving door fitted fur next year, Ella!'

'That's Big Frank!' says Bert Armstrong.

Frank and Wilma Galloway come smiling into the living room. Just before greetings and kisses are exchanged, Frank holds up his hand. 'Now if you just wait for about sixty seconds, you can do the double. Irene and Alec Stuart are right behind us.'

He's barely finished his forecast when they come through the kitchen door. 'Hello! Happy New Year everybody!'

'In you come!' calls Archie. 'Join the gang!'

Irene looks around the guests. She moves over to Drena. 'Ah expected to see Teresa and Dennis already here. Their lights are out.'

'Aw' they're ower in Ireland. Teresa's sister is'nae very well.'

Irene tuts. 'That's a shame. Ah always like it when Teresa's in the company at the New Year.' She shakes her head. 'She's a scream when she gets a wee half ower her neck.'

'Och, we'll no' miss oot. When they come back, we'll huv them in for a drink. She'll soon get warmed up!'

Twenty minutes later, her voice not heard above the hullabaloo, Agnes Dalrymple opens the door to the living room. It's a few seconds before she's spotted . . .

'Look who's here. It's Agnes!' Frank takes her by the hand and she joins him and Wilma.

'Agnes, hen! A guid New Year to ye! And many o' them!' Inside a minute, to her great pleasure, she is surrounded by friends and former neighbours. Five minutes after that, having been almost kissed to death, Agnes is escorted through to the kitchen and ordered to fill two plates, one savoury, one sweet. She returns to the living room and sits herself on a chair next to Irene and Alec. She will, quite happily, remain there for the rest of the party.

As the old-fashioned civilities of New Year are being aired and celebrated on the Molendinar, three miles away, five male students are walking up the Maryhill Road, hoping Bearsden is still where it used to be. They have a long-standing invitation to a party. One of their number is Sammy Stewart. With the exuberance of youth – fortified by drink – and unable to find a taxi for hire, they have decided they will walk there. It's only a few miles. Mercifully, it's a dry, if cool, night.

Sammy halts the intrepid party at the opening to what was once Dalbeattie Street. 'Stop a moment, boys.' He looks at the vast, cleared site. Not only has Dalbeattie Street gone, but also Blairatholl, Cheviot, and Rothesay Streets. At the far end, a few hundred yards distant, stands a long stretch of one-storey, red-brick maisonettes. Lights burn in most windows. It is, after all, New Year. In Glasgow.

'Why have you stopped us, Samuel?'

'Because, Henry, until recently this was an ordinary street of tenements. Dalbeattie Street by name.' He points. 'And about forty yards from here, on the right, is where I was born and raised. At Number 18. Now I know that you are somewhere to the left of Karl Marx, and I'm sorry to disappoint, but I had a smashing childhood. Never felt in the least deprived.'

'Good for you, Stewart. Can we get on? I'm rather lightly clad.'

Alistair Beecham chips in. 'It will be of no interest to us unless you had a dreadful childhood, Sammy. If you can't match up to the stereotype it'll be too, too dull!' He lays an arm along Sammy's shoulder. 'However, would you believe me, I've known for quite some time that you hail from Maryhill.'

'Oh, who told you?' asks Sammy.

'Nobody. I discovered it by means of a deduction that the Great Detective himself would have applauded!'

'What's Columbo got to do with it?' enquires someone.

'Fool!' says Beecham. 'I'm referring to the one who has rooms at 221B Baker Street.'

'Ohhh! Sexton Blake. Sorry, Beecham.' He receives a withering look.

'You gave me directions one day, Sammy. During which you mentioned Bilsland Drive.'

'Uh-huh. So what's special about Bizzland Drive?' asks Sammy.

Alistair Beecham turns to another member of the group. 'You say it.'

'Bilsland Drive.'

'Ah!' says Henry. 'I've *got* it! Bizzland versus Bilsland.'

'Elementary, my dear Watson,' says Beecham. 'Maryhill

folk always say *Bizz*-land. The rest of the world says *Bils*-land.'

'I say, Beecham. Well done! The Great Detective would certainly have appreciated that.'

'Wonderful! Can we get on?' says someone. They resume their trek.

They have only gone a few yards. 'Got him!' says Henry.

'Got who?'

'Alistair's Great Detective.' He keeps his face straight. 'Dixon of Dock Green!' Then, just a few yards later. 'HUZZAH! A cab. It's stopping!'

Perhaps a mile and a half away from the footsore students, another group of former Dalbeattie Street luminaries – including Sammy's parents – are enjoying themselves. They sit round the Lockerbies' dining table at Kelvin Court. This is not the usual late-night visit after an evening spent at Le Bar Rendezvous. Ruth and George have laid on a meal as a New Year's Eve celebration. Though the repast is long-since finished, the conversation is good so they continue to sit at table. Fred Dickinson looks at Rhea Stewart. He turns to Robert. 'Alas, Robert. Poor Rhea is not getting her trip in the time machine, tonight.' He turns to her. 'You prefer to have been at the club first, don't you, Rhea? Then come back here and let Ruth's Art Deco masterpiece whisk you back in time.'

'Ah do, Fred. But Ah must say, I'm enjoying the conversation, even though most of it is over my head.' She smiles. 'But it's the *way* you've all been saying it. Easy on the ear.'

She looks at her friends. 'So, Ah will refrain from opening ma gub! And youse will aw' think: "Ah'll tell ye, she's deep, that Rhea Stewart. Soaks it aw' up – but never commits herself!" Thank you!' She inclines her head. 'Jist carry on.'

They all laugh. Ruth kisses her on the cheek. 'Rhea, darling. How would we manage without you?'

'Badly!'

Ruby Baxter raises her fourth flute of champagne. 'I'll drink to that, darlings. And anything else you can think of!'

Vicky Shaw nudges her partner, Jack Dale. 'Now?'

He clears his throat. Taps his coffeespoon on his saucer. 'Could I, eh, have your attention, please.'

The table falls silent – but Rhea can't resist. 'Oh, Oh. Ah bet you Ah know whit this is gonny be.'

She looks at Vicky. 'Am Ah right?'

Vicky nods. 'Uh-huh!'

'Oh, goody!' says Rhea. 'We're aw' going tae a wedding!'

Back on the Molendinar, things have slowed at Ella's. Everybody has gravitated to the living room and there are now two, sometimes three, separate conversations going on. Irene Stuart leans nearer to Agnes. 'Alec and I have decided we're gonny go back tae the city.'

'Have ye? Do ye no' like it here?'

'We like the house, Agnes,' says Alec, 'but we feel so isolated. We really do miss the Maryhill Road. And we're fed-up with having to take buses everywhere.'

'Where are ye gonny go?'

'We've asked Robert and Rhea, and Marjorie and Jack, to keep an eye open for flats to rent where they are. Wilton Street, Wilton Crescent, Belmont Street. You know where we mean. Red-sandstone buildings, but handy for the Maryhill Road. We've also left our name and requirements with estate agents.'

'Ah'm the same as you. Ah'm not happy oot here at all. Ah'd love tae find one of the older, self-contained flats. Not red-sandstone, Ah could'nae afford them. But maybe doon Henderson Street, Napiershall Street way. That would do me. It'll be a wee bit extra rent –'

Alec interrupts her. 'Not as dear as you think, Agnes. You work on the Maryhill Road. If you get back into that area, think of what you'll save on bus fares!'

'Eeeh, Alec. Ah never gave a thought about saving fares. Ah'm awful woolly-heided ye know.'

'Have you left your name with any estate agents?'

'Ah, well, no. Ah hav'nae. Ah've just been looking in their windows.'

'Dearie me! Leave your name with them. Tell them what you're looking for. They don't have everything in the window you know, Agnes. And, put your name down with *more* than one shop.'

Agnes sits back. 'Ah'm awfy glad Ah've spoken to ye. Ah'll be right down tae see two or three estate agents when Ah start back on Tuesday. Put ma name doon with them all.'

Alec squeezes her hand. 'Ah'll take a bet with you. Within about three months, we'll come into your branch of the

City Bakeries – and you'll be telling us that you're living down on Napiershall Street or North Woodside Road. They found you a lovely, self-contained flat.' He sits back. 'Three months, Agnes.'

Agnes feels the excitement building in her. New hope. 'This is the trouble wi' living on your own. Ah never know how tae go aboot things like this.'

'It's easy, hen. You're the customer. They do the looking for you.'

'Aye.' Agnes's eyes sparkle. 'Eeeh, Ah wish it wiz Tuesday!'

CHAPTER FORTY-THREE

Dream a Little Dream

As the train slows on its approach to the platform, Archie waits until the first sign with Stirling on it appears. He leans closer to Lexie. 'It's not yet eighteen months since Ah was leaving this station, heading in the other direction. Boy! Was I worried aboot going back tae Glasgow. Living with my ma and da, having tae share a room again with oor Katherine, starting at Kinnaird's, keeping oot of Nathan Brodie's way.' He gives her a sad smile. 'And just think how perfect things would be right now, Lexie, if my da had'nae died.'

'I know.'

'Ah cannae get it out of my mind. Things were going great. You and I had got together, Da and me were getting on smashing.' He looks at her. 'Then, from out of nowhere . . .'

She lays a hand on his. 'We're only here for two nights, Archie. And I want us to –'

He comes back in. 'Sorry, hen. Don't worry. Ah had nae intention of bringing it up. But when the train rolled intae the station and Ah saw the sign, Stirling, one memory triggered off another. We *are* gonny enjoy oorselves – until the money runs out!'

'We won't run out of money. As long as you don't mind having fish and chips two afternoons on the trot!'

'Hey, there's nuthing wrong wi' that.' He looks at her as he reaches for their case. 'As long as it's sit doon fish and chips . . .' he pauses, 'wi' a pot of tea and bread and butter!'

'Of course. We're on oor holibags, Archie. In fact, you can even have mushy peas with them. No expense to be spared on this trip.'

They stop for a moment outside the Golden Lion Hotel. He looks at her. 'There you are, kid. This is gonny be our first time together at a hotel.'

'The first of many, Archie.'

'Yeah.' He looks up at the stone-built frontage. 'I hope it's as grand as it looks.'

'Mmm, me too.' She puts a foot on the first of the steps, assuming he's about to climb them. He doesn't. She laughs. 'Will we be going in eventually?'

'Oh, aye. Of course.' He makes no move, gives a nervous laugh. 'Believe it or no', Lexie. Ah've never been tae a hotel before. Do I, eh, book us in as man and wife?'

She giggles. 'It would be best. Otherwise, it'll have to be Archie Cameron and fancy-bit!'

'Whit would happen if they were tae find oot we're no' married? Would they, eh, ask us tae leave?'

Lexie's giggling is becoming uncontrollable.

He looks at her. 'Stop it! If they see you, they'll wonder what's going on.'

'Just remember how many times you've seen it done in the movies, Archie. We are going to walk intae reception as if we are an old married couple. That's it. Let's do it . . .'

The girl behind the desk, smiles. 'Good afternoon. Can I help?'

'Yes. Hello. We have a double room booked for two nights. The name's Cameron.'

The porter lays their suitcase across the strong straps of the luggage stand. 'There you are, sir. Enjoy your stay.'

'Thank you. Oh, eh, just hang on.' Archie delves into his pocket, brings out a handful of change. Selects two twenty-pence pieces. 'Thank you.'

'Thank *you*! Sir.'

Three or four coins drop onto the floor as Archie returns the change to his pocket. 'No! It's all right. Ah'll get them,' he says. As the man leaves, Lexie turns away quickly. He knows she's got the giggles again. He waits until the door is closed before he starts scrabbling for the coins.

He straightens up. '*Whit*? That's what they dae in the pictures, in't it? Tip the porter.'

She falls onto the bed, helpless. At last she manages . . . 'Ah thought he was going to hug you. You do realise, if it's fish and chips for lunch, tomorrow, it'll just be a single-fish for you.' She begins to lose control. 'You've just given away your chips *and* mushy peas!'

He falls onto the bed beside her. 'Ah thought that wiz dead cool. Ah based it on Cary Grant.'

'It was pretty good, except for one thing. Cary would only have given him twenty pence!'

Being in a hotel room, on their own, begins to work its sexual spell. He raises his head, looks into her eyes. 'It's only just gone three. *Plenty* of time. Do you fancy trying oot this bed?'

'Mmm, we're supposed to be married, so it should be okay. Obligatory really.'

They kiss, then quickly undress.

They lie together.

'I'll have to take you to hotels more often, Archie.'

He cuddles her in closer. 'Ah think that's one of the best things about being away. We know neither my ma or Evie are going to walk in on us. Means we can relax.'

'Yeah.'

'Fancy a wee snooze?'

'Not half!'

'Turn round, then.' She does. He coories into her; his chest, stomach and thighs mould themselves into her back. 'Aye. Jist a wee half hour tae freshen up.'

'Yeah . . .'

'Lexie!' She stirs. 'LEXIE! It's twenty to six!'

Her eyes are wide-open as she turns to face him. '*Never*!'

After a moment, she relaxes. 'Who cares? That was lovely, wasn't it?'

'Not half!' He kisses her shoulder.

'Okay. Let's take time to get ready, Archie. Then, we'll saunter down to the dining room in our best bib and tucker, have a leisurely meal, a half-bottle of wine, and really enjoy our first trip away from home.' She stretches like a cat . . . 'And later tonight, you can have me all over again!'

He fondles her breasts. She feels him getting hard. '*Right*!' She throws the covers back, slips out of bed, makes for the bathroom. 'Let's keep it for tonight, darling.'

It has just turned eight-thirty when they leave the dining room. They amble into the lobby then stop. 'What do you want to do, Archie?'

'Ah'd like tae go for a walk – there's something Ah want tae show ye.'

'Is it not too cold, Archie? It's January, remember.'

'It's just about perfect for what I have in mind.' He looks at her. 'Something I've wanted to do since we started going out together.'

'Let's go up to the room and get our coats. Just in case.'

They are walking away from the town centre. 'You won't get chilled, sweetheart. It's uphill all the way, the exercise will keep us warm. It's not far. But as they say in Stirling, it's up the brae.'

Their conversation is light as they step out midst the stone buildings that line either side of Upper Bridge Street. Archie points. 'We're gonny take the right fork, along Union Street. Then not far, right, onto Causewayhead Road. And we'll just about be there.' Five minutes later, they are.

He points again. 'See the gap in the buildings. That's where the road runs over the River Forth and that's where we want tae be. We'll get a clear view up the hill from there. They halt just on the road bridge. He squeezes her arm to his side. 'It's funny. I know this area well, yet Ah've never set foot in it. Never seen it from *this* viewpoint.' He gestures to the right. Off in the distance, illuminated from below, stands a tall, Gothic-style tower. 'That's the monument to Sir William Wallace. It's no' as old as it seems. It was built in Victoria's time. Made to look ancient.' He laughs. 'I think it was Walter Scott who called it "that great rotting-tooth of a monument"!'

'Huh! He got that right,' says Lexie.

'That bridge, further on. That's Stirling Old Bridge.' He looks at her. 'And there is'nae any prizes for guessing *why* Ah've brought you tae this spot, darling.' They look up the hill that rises from the edge of town. In the distance, a mile or more from where they stand, Craigmill Prison dominates the crest of the bleak, treeless hill.

Lexie narrows her eyes. Makes out the long stretch of prison wall that looks down on them. All of four hundred yards. Behind it, two large cell blocks stand end to end. Their top two rows of barred windows look over the wall. Lights burn in every cell.

Archie sighs. 'The right-hand block. Look at the top row of windows. Second one in from the right, B4-27, that was mine, Lexie. For nearly three years, if it was a clear night, Ah'd stand up on my chair after "lights out", slide open the ventilation pane in my window, and look down into the town. Winter nights were the best, when the sky wiz heavy wi' stars. More than we ever get tae see in Glasgow.' He looks at her. 'Ah'd watch the cars go by. But best of all was when a couple would walk along the road, this one we're standing on, and Ah'd wish the guy was me.' He looks at her again. She presses his arm against her side. 'Ah promised myself that one day it would be.'

He looks up at the prison. Clears his throat. 'That was the beginning of me deciding Ah was'nae going tae jail any more. You've no idea how much Ah wanted tae be the guy wi' the girl and the nice settled life.' He turns his head, kisses her on the side of her mouth. She barely hears him as he manages to say, 'And here I am.'

She rests her head on his shoulder a moment, then looks up. 'Yeah. You've fulfilled the first part of your dream, Archie.' She stands on tiptoe, kisses him on the cheek. 'Did you know there's a second part? *Our* dream. We're a couple now. With the rest of our lives to live. So we'd better get to planning.' She holds her head to one side. 'What are Archie and Lexie Cameron going to do?'

He's relaxed now. Told her what he wanted her to know. 'Okay, Lexie Forsyth. Ah'll tell you what Ah've been thinking about lately. But first of all . . .' He lifts his coat collar up, stamps his feet a few times. 'That breeze is turning cold. What about heading back tae the hotel for a cup o' coffee – and a wee snifter!'

'Well, if that's your first idea for the future, I like it.'

'It'll no' take us too long tae get back. It's doonhill all the way. Ah'll start telling ye my ideas as we go.' He smiles. 'And Ah'd think you'll know if they might work.'

'C'mon then, Archie. I'm dying to hear what you've been thinking.'

'When Ah first took the job at Kinnaird's, well, it was jist gonny be a stopgap. Keep ma probation officer happy. And then – Ah got my first look at you. So Ah thought, och, Ah'll stick it a wee bit longer. But now, after about a year and a half, Ah'm actually getting tae like the fruit and veg business. And Ah'm *really* impressed by the flower side of things. You and Jean don't half know your stuff.'

'Oh! Thank you, kind sir.'

He stops for a moment. 'Ah've began tae get ideas about you and me opening oor own shop.' He turns to face her. 'What dae ye think, Lexie?'

'I'd love to have my own shop. It's been my dream.' She shivers. 'Let's get back to the hotel for that night-cap, Archie. We can talk as we go.' Stepping-out with a will, through the near deserted streets of Stirling, heels clip-clopping and echoing off darkened buildings, they make their excited way towards the Golden Lion, bouncing ideas off one another as they go . . .

'We'll have to save a bit of money, first, Archie. Show the bank that we're serious before we approach them for a business loan.'

'Aye, Ah can see that. Where would ye like the shop tae be. Further doon the Maryhill Road?'

She shakes her head. 'No! We want an upmarket area, Archie. Think big.'

'Great Western Road?'

'You're getting warm.' She tilts her head up, looks him straight in the eye. 'The Byres Road!'

'*Huh*! The West End. Don't haud yerself back! Surely Malcolm Campbells dominate that?'

'Yes, they've got the top end. But the Byres Road is long. The bottom half, near the University Cafe, there's plenty of opportunity round there. The same type of customer. And also, Dumbarton Road is just around the corner. A really busy area with a big population. Between the two of them, a great mix!'

'Jeez! To listen to you, anyone would think you've already done your homework!'

'I have! I was on my day off. Be a few months ago. I'm having a nice wee stroll down the Byres Road, and at the same time keeping an eye open for a shop like ours. I like to compare notes – maybe pinch some ideas. There isn't one!'

'Hey, Lexie! That sounds great. Ah! But maybe somebody's opened one by now. We'd better do a recce when we get hame . . .'

'Calm yourself. I had a wander along there a few weeks ago. Still nothing!'

'Great! We'd better start getting some money put by . . .'

As they almost dance down the street, an elderly woman comes painstakingly towards them, slowed by the sloping pavement. She stops at the door to her flat, begins the nightly search for her key. Oblivious to her presence, Lexie and Archie are still bouncing ideas off one another. She gets the gist of their conversation as they go by, pauses, her hand in her bag, and turns to look at their receding backs. In the stillness of the night she listens for as long as she can to their echoing, excited chatter. And they hurry off into their future.